Pharaoh

ALSO BY WILBUR SMITH

The Egyptian Series

River God

The Seventh Scroll

Warlock

The Quest

Desert God

The Ballantyne Series

A Falcon Flies

Men of Men

The Angels Weep

The Leopard Hunts in Darkness

The Courtney Series

When the Lion Feeds

The Sound of Thunder

A Sparrow Falls

The Burning Shore

Power of the Sword

Rage

A Time to Die

Golden Fox

Birds of Prey

Monsoon

Blue Horizon

The Triumph of the Sun

Assegai

Golden Lion

Thrillers

The Dark of the Sun

Shout at the Devil

Gold Mine

The Diamond Hunters

The Sunbird

Eagle in the Sky

The Eye of the Tiger

Cry Wolf

Hungry as the Sea

Wild Justice (UK);
The Delta Decision (US)

The Elephant Song

Those in Peril

Vicious Circle

Predator

Pharaoh

Wilbur Smith

HARPER LUXE

An Imprint of HarperCollins*Publishers*

PHARAOH. Copyright © 2016 by Wilbur Smith. All rights reserved. Printed in the United States of America. No part of this book may be used or reproduced in any manner whatsoever without written permission except in the case of brief quotations embodied in critical articles and reviews. For information address HarperCollins Publishers, 195 Broadway, New York, NY 10007.

HarperCollins books may be purchased for educational, business, or sales promotional use. For information please e-mail the Special Markets Department at SPsales@harpercollins.com.

FIRST HARPERLUXE EDITION

ISBN: 978-0-06-249667-6

HarperLuxe™ is a trademark of HarperCollins Publishers.

Library of Congress Cataloging-in-Publication Data is available upon request.

16 17 18 19 20   ID/RRD   10 9 8 7 6 5 4 3 2 1

I dedicate this book, *Pharaoh,* to my wife, Mokhiniso.
From the very first day I met you, you have been the
lodestone of my life. You make every day brighter and
every hour more precious.
I am yours forever and I shall love you forever, Wilbur.

Pharaoh

Although I would rather have swallowed my own sword than openly admit it, deep in my heart I knew that finally it was over.

Fifty years ago the Hyksos multitudes had appeared without warning within the borders of our very Egypt out of the eastern wilderness. They were a savage and cruel people with no redeeming features. They had one asset that made them invincible in battle. This was the horse and chariot, which we Egyptians had never seen or heard of previously, and which we looked upon as something vile and abhorrent.

We attempted to meet the Hyksos onslaught on foot, but they swept us before them, circling us effortlessly in their chariots and showering us with their arrows.

We had no alternative but to take to our boats and fly before them southward up the mighty Nile River, dragging our craft over the cataracts and into the wilderness. There we lingered for over ten years, pining for our homeland.

Fortuitously I had managed to capture a large number of the enemy horses and spirit them away with us. I soon discovered that the horse, far from being abhorrent, is the most intelligent and tractable of all animals. I developed my own version of the chariot, which was lighter, faster and more maneuverable than the Hyksos version. I taught the lad who was later to become Tamose, the Pharaoh of Egypt, to be an expert charioteer.

At the appropriate time we Egyptians swept down the Nile in our fleet of riverboats, landed our chariots on the shores of our very Egypt and fell upon our enemies, driving them into the northern delta. Over the decades that followed we had been locked in the struggle with our Hyksos enemies.

But now the wheel had turned full circle. Pharaoh Tamose was an old man, lying in his tent mortally wounded by a Hyksos arrow. The Egyptian army was melting away, and tomorrow I would be faced by the inevitable.

Even my intrepid spirit, which had been vital in

carrying Egypt forward over the past half century of struggle, was no longer sufficient. In the last year we had been beaten in two successive great battles, both bitter and bloody but in vain. The Hyksos invaders who had seized the greater part of our fatherland from us were on the threshold of their final triumph. The whole of Egypt was almost within their grasp. Our legions were broken and beaten. No matter how desperately I attempted to rally them and urge them onward, it seemed that they had resigned themselves to defeat and ignominy. More than half our horses were down while those still standing were barely able to bear the weight of a man or chariot. As for the men, almost half of them bore fresh and open wounds that they had bound up with rags. Their numbers had been reduced by almost three thousand during those two battles that we had fought and lost since the beginning of the year. Most of the survivors staggered or limped into the fray with a sword in one hand and a crutch in the other.

It is true that this shortfall in our roster was caused more by desertion than by death or wounding in the field. The once proud legions of Pharaoh had finally lost heart, and they fled before the enemy in their multitudes. Tears of shame ran down my cheeks as I pleaded with them and threatened them with flogging, death and dishonor as they streamed past me on their way to the rear. They took no heed of me, would not even glance in my direction as they threw down their weapons and hurried or limped away. The Hyksos multitudes were gathered before the very gates of Luxor. And on the morrow I would lead what would almost certainly be our last feeble chance to avert bloody annihilation.

As night fell over the field of battle I had my manservants clean the fresh bloodstains from my shield and my armor and beat out the dent in my helmet that earlier in the day had deflected a Hyksos blade. The plume was missing, sheared off by the same enemy blow. Then by the flickering flame of a torch and the reflection in my polished bronzed hand mirror, I contemplated my own image. As always it gave my sorry spirits a lift. Once again I was reminded how readily men will follow an image or a reputation when common sense warned of imminent annihilation. I forced a smile into the mirror, trying to ignore the melancholy shadows in the depths of my eyes; then I stooped out under the flap of my tent and went to pay my respects to my well-beloved Pharaoh.

Pharaoh Tamose lay on his litter attended by three of his surgeons and six of his numerous sons. In a wider circle around him were gathered his generals and high councillors, and five of his favorite wives. All of them wore solemn expressions and his consorts were weeping, for Pharaoh was dying. Earlier in the day he had received a grievous wound on the field of battle. The shaft of the Hyksos arrow still protruded from between his ribs. None of his physicians present, including even me, the most skilled of them all, had had the temerity to attempt to withdraw the barbed arrowhead from so near to his heart. We had merely snapped off the shaft close to the lip of the wound and now we awaited the inevitable outcome. Before noon on the morrow Pharaoh would almost certainly have vacated the golden throne in favor of Utteric Turo, his eldest son, who was sitting by his side trying not to make it too obvious that he was relishing the moment when the sovereignty of this very Egypt would pass to him. Utteric was a vapid and ineffectual youth who could not even imagine that by the setting of tomorrow's sun his empire might no longer exist; or rather that was what I believed of him at that time. I was soon to learn how sadly I had erred in judging him.

By now Tamose was an old man. I knew his age almost to the hour, for it was I who had delivered him as an infant into this harsh world. It was popular legend that his first act on arriving had been to piss copiously upon me. I suppressed a smile as I thought how over the ensuing sixty-odd years he had never hesitated to make even his mildest disapproval of me manifest in the same manner.

Now I went to him where he lay and knelt to kiss his hands. Pharaoh appeared even older than his actual years. Although he had recently taken to dyeing his hair and beard, I knew that beneath the bright ginger pigmentation he favored it was actually white as sun-bleached seaweed. The skin of his face was deeply wrinkled and speckled with dark sun spots. There were bags of puckered skin beneath his eyes: eyes wherein the signs of approaching death were all too obvious.

I have not the faintest idea of my own age. However, I am considerably older than Pharaoh, but in my appearance I seem much less than half his age. This is because I am a long liver and blessed by the gods—most particularly by the goddess Inana. This is the secret name of the goddess Ishtar.

Pharaoh looked up at me and he spoke with pain and difficulty, his voice husky and his breathing wheezing and labored. "Tata!" He greeted me with the pet name he had given me when he was but a child. "I knew that you would come. You always know when I need you most. Tell me, my dear old friend, what of the morrow?"

"Tomorrow belongs to you and Egypt, my Lord King." I know not why I chose these words to reply to him, when it was a certainty that all our tomorrows now belonged to Anubis, the god of the cemeteries and the underworld. However, I loved my Pharaoh, and I wanted him to die as peacefully as was possible.

He smiled and said no more but reached out with a hand that shook and fingers that trembled and took my own hand and held it to his chest until he fell asleep. The surgeons and his sons left his pavilion, and I swear I saw a faint smile cross Utteric's lips as he sauntered out. I sat with Tamose until well after midnight, the same way I had sat with his mother at her parting, but finally the numbing fatigue of the day's battle overwhelmed me. I freed my hand from his, and, leaving him still smiling, I staggered to my own mattress and fell upon it in a deathlike sleep.

My servants woke me before the first light had touched the dawn skies with gold. I dressed for battle with all haste and belted on my sword, then I hurried back to the royal pavilion. When I knelt once more at Pharaoh's bedside, he was smiling still, but his hands were cool to my touch and he was dead.

"I will mourn for you later, my Mem," I promised him as I rose again to my feet, "but now I must go out and try once more to make good my oath to you and to our very Egypt."

It is the curse of being a long liver: to survive all those whom you love the best.

The remainder of our shattered legions was assembled in the neck of the pass before the golden city of

Luxor where we had been holding the ravening hordes of the Hyksos at bay for the past thirty-five desperate days. In review I drove my war chariot along their decimated ranks and, as they recognized me, those who were still able to do so staggered to their feet. They stooped to drag their wounded comrades upright and to stand with them in their battle formations. Then all of them, men who were still hale and strong together with those who were more than halfway to their deaths, raised their weapons to the dawn sky and cheered me as I passed.

A rhythmic chant went up: "Taita! Taita! Taita!"

I choked back my tears to see these brave sons of Egypt in such desperate straits. I forced a smile to my lips and laughed and shouted encouragements back at them, calling to those stalwarts in the throng whom I knew so well, "Hey there, Osmen! I knew I would find you still in the front rank."

"Never more than a sword's length behind you, my lord!" he shouted back at me.

"Lothan, you greedy old lion. Have you not already hacked down more than your fair share of the Hyksos dogs?"

"Aye, but only half as many as you have, Lord Tata." Lothan was one of my special favorites so I allowed him the use of my pet name. When I had passed, the cheering dropped into a dreadful silence once more, and they sank to their knees again and looked down the pass to where they knew the Hyksos legions were waiting only for the full light of dawn to renew their assault. The battleground around us was strewn thickly with the dead of the many long days of slaughter. The faint predawn breeze bore the stench of death to where we waited. With each breath I drew, it clung as thick as oil to my tongue and the back of my throat. I hawked and spat it over the side of my chariot, but with every subsequent breath it seemed to grow stronger and more repellent.

The carrion eaters were already feasting on the piles of corpses that were scattered around us. The vultures and the crows hovered over the field on wide pinions and then dropped to the ground to compete with the jackals and hyenas in the shrieking and struggling mass, ripping at the rotting human flesh, tearing off lumps and tatters of it and swallowing them whole. I felt my own skin crawl with horror as I imagined the same end awaiting me when finally I succumbed to the Hyksos blades.

I shuddered and tried to put these thoughts aside as I shouted to my captains to send their archers forward to retrieve as many of the spent arrows from the corpses as they could find to refill their depleted quivers.

Then above the cacophony of squabbling birds and animals I heard the beat of a single drum echoing up the pass. My men heard it also. The sergeants bellowed orders, and the archers hurried back from the field with the arrows they had salvaged. The men in the waiting ranks came to their feet and formed up shoulder to shoulder with their shields overlapping. The blades of their swords and the heads of their spears were chipped and blunted with hard use, but still they presented them toward the enemy. The limbs of their bows had been bound up with twine where the wood had cracked, and many of the arrows they had retrieved from the battlefield were missing their fletchings, but they would still fly true enough to do the business at point-blank range. My men were veterans, and they knew all the tricks for getting the very best out of damaged weapons and equipment.

In the distant mouth of the pass the enemy masses began to appear out of the predawn gloom. At first their formations seemed shrunken and diminished by distance and the early light, but they swelled rapidly in size as they marched forward to engage us. The vultures shrieked and squawked and then rose into the air; the jackals and other scavengers scurried away before the advance of the enemy. The floor of the pass was filled from side to side by the Hyksos multitudes, and not for the first time I felt my spirits quail. It seemed that we were outnumbered by at least three or even four to our one.

However, as they drew closer I saw that we had mauled them as savagely in return for how they had treated us. Most of them had been wounded, and their injuries were bound up with bloodstained rags, as were ours. Some of them limped along on crutches, and others lurched and staggered as they were harried along by their sergeants, most of whom were wielding rawhide whips. I exulted to see them obliged to use such extreme measures to induce their men to hold their formations. I drove my chariot along the front rank of my own men shouting encouragement to them and pointing out the Hyksos captains' use of their whips.

"Men like you never need the whip to convince you of your duty." My voice carried clearly to them above the beat of the Hyksos drums and the tramp of their armored feet. My men cheered me and shouted insults and derision at the approaching enemy ranks. All the time I was judging the dwindling distance that separated the leading ranks of our opposing armies. I had only 52 chariots remaining out of the 320 with which I had begun this campaign. The attrition of our horses had been bitterly hard to bear. But our only advantage was that we were in a strong position here at the head of the steep and rugged pass. I had chosen it with all the care and cunning learned in countless battles over my long lifetime.

The Hyksos relied heavily on their chariots to bring their archers within easy range of our ranks. Despite our example, they had never developed the recurved bow but had clung stubbornly to the straight-limbed bow, which was incapable of loosing an arrow as fast and therefore as far as our superior weapons. By forcing them to abandon their chariots at the bottom of the rocky pass, I had denied them the opportunity of getting their archers swiftly to within easy range of our infantry.

Now the critical moment arrived when I must deploy my remaining chariots. I led this squadron in person as we raced out in line ahead and swept down the front of the Hyksos advance. Loosing our arrows into their massed ranks from a range of sixty or seventy paces we were able to kill or maim almost thirty of the enemy before they were able to come at us.

When this happened I leaped down from the platform of my vehicle, and while my driver whisked it away I squeezed myself into the center of the front rank and locked my shield in between two of my companions and presented it toward the enemy.

Almost immediately followed the tumultuous

moment when the battle was joined in earnest. The enemy phalanx crashed into our front with a mighty clangor of bronze on bronze. With shields interlocked, the opposing armies shoved and heaved against each other, straining to force a breakthrough of the opposing line. It was a gargantuan struggle that wrapped us all in a state of intimacy more obscene than any sexually perverse act. Belly-to-belly and face-to-face we struggled so that when we grunted and screamed like animals in rut, the spittle flew from our twisted mouths into the faces of the enemy that confronted us from mere inches away.

We were packed too closely to be able to use our long weapons. We were crushed between banks of bronze shields. To lose one's footing was to go down and be grievously trampled if not killed by the bronze sandals of allies as well as those of our enemies.

I have fought so often in the shield wall as to have designed a particular weapon especially for the purpose. The long blade of the cavalry sword must stay firmly in its sheath and be replaced by a thin dagger with a blade no longer than a hand's span. When both your arms are trapped in the press of armored bodies and the face of your enemy is only inches from your own, then you will still be able to make use of this tiny weapon and place the point of the blade in a chink in your enemy's frontal armor and thrust home.

This day before the gates of Luxor I killed at least ten of the swarthy bearded Hyksos brutes on the same spot, and without moving my right hand more than a few inches. It gave me an inordinate sense of satisfaction to look into the eyes of my enemy, to watch his features contort in agony as he felt my blade pierce his vitals, and finally to feel his last breath blow hot into my face as he expelled it from his lungs before he collapsed. I am not by nature a cruel or vindictive person, but the good god Horus knows that my people and I have suffered enough at the hands of this barbarous tribe to revel in whatever retaliation becomes available to us.

I do not know just how long we were locked in the shield wall. It seemed to me at the time to be many hours of brutal struggle, but I knew by the changing angle of the pitiless sun above us that it was less than an hour before the Hyksos hordes disengaged from our ranks and fell back a short distance. Both sides were exhausted by the ferocity of the struggle. We confronted each other across the narrow strip of ground, panting like wild animals, sodden with our own blood and sweat and reeling on our feet. However, I knew from hard experience that this respite would be short-lived, and then we would fly at each other again like rabid dogs. I also knew that this was our last battle. I looked at the men around me and saw that they were close to the end. They numbered no more than twelve hundred. Perhaps they could survive another hour in the shield wall, but little more than that. Then it would be over. My despair came close to overwhelming me.

Then suddenly there was somebody behind me, tugging at my arm and shouting words at me that at first made little sense. "My Lord Taita, there is another large detachment of the enemy coming up in our rear. They have us completely surrounded. Unless you can think of a way to save the day, then we are done for."

I spun around to confront the bearer of such terrible tidings. If this were true, then we were damned and double damned. And yet the man who stood before me was someone that I knew I could trust. He was one of the most promising young officers in the army of Pharaoh. He commanded the 101st Squadron of heavy chariots. "Take me and show me, Merab!" I ordered him.

"This way, my lord! I have a fresh horse for you." He must have seen how near I was to complete exhaustion for he seized my arm and helped me back over the piles of dead and dying men and abandoned weapons and other warlike accoutrements that littered the field. We reached the small detachment of our own legionnaires in the rear who held a pair of fresh horses for us. By then I had recovered sufficiently to shake off Merab's helping hand. I hate to show even the slightest sign of weakness before my men.

I mounted one of the horses and led this small group back at a gallop over the ridge of high ground that lay between us and the lower reaches of the River Nile. On the crest I reined in my steed so abruptly that it arched its neck and pranced around in a tight circle. I found myself at a loss to express my despair.

From what Merab had told me earlier I expected to find perhaps three or four hundred fresh Hyksos troops marching up behind us to engage us. That would have been sufficient numbers to seal our fate. Instead I was confronted by a mighty army of literally thousands of infantry and at least five hundred chariots and as many again of mounted cavalry, which thronged the nearest bank of the Nile. They were in the process of disembarking from a flotilla of foreign warships that was now moored along the bank of the river below our golden city of Luxor.

The leading formation of enemy cavalry had already disembarked, and as soon as they spotted our pathetic little troop of a dozen or so men they came galloping up the slope to engage us. I found myself caught up in a hopeless quandary. Our horses were all but used up. If we turned tail and tried to outrun those magnificent and obviously fresh animals, they would catch us before we had covered a hundred paces. If we stood at bay and tried to make a fight of it, they would cut us down without working up a sweat.

Then I forced back my despair and looked again at these strangers with fresh vision. I felt a faint tugging of relief, enough to bolster my spirits. Those were not Hyksos war helmets that they were wearing. Those were not typical Hyksos galleys from which they were disembarking.

"Hold your ground, Captain Merab!" I snapped at him. "I am going forward to parley with these newcomers." Before he had a chance to argue with me I had unhooked my sword sheath from my belt and, without drawing the naked blade, I reversed it and held it aloft in the universal sign of peace. Then I trotted slowly down the slope to meet this troop of foreign horsemen.

I vividly recall the sense of doom that overshadowed me as we closed. I knew that this time I had pushed Tyche, the goddess of Providence, too far. Then to my astonishment the leader of the band of horsemen barked an order and his men obediently sheathed their swords in a sign of truce and halted in a tight formation behind him.

I followed their example and reined my own steed down to a halt, facing them but with a few dozen strides separating myself and the leader of the group. We studied each other in silence for the time it takes to draw a deep breath, and then I lifted the visor of my battered helmet to show my face.

The leader of this foreign band of horsemen laughed. It was a most unexpected sound in these fraught circumstances, but at the same time it was hauntingly familiar. I knew that laugh. However, I stared at him for fully half a minute before I recognized him. He was a graybeard now, but big and muscled and sure of himself. He was no longer the young buck with the fresh and eager face searching to find his place in this hard, unforgiving world. Clearly he had found that place. Now he had the air of high command about his person and a mighty army at his back.

"Zaras?" I said his name dubiously. "It cannot possibly be you, can it?"

"Only the name is somewhat different, but everything else about me is the same, Taita. Except possibly I am a trifle older and I trust a little wiser."

"You remember me still, after all these years. How long has it been?" I demanded of him wonderingly.

"It has been a mere thirty years, and yes, I remember you still. I will never forget you, not if I live for ten times longer than I have already."

Now it was my turn to laugh. "You say your name is changed. What name are you known by now, good Zaras?"

"I have taken the name Hurotas. My former name had certain unfortunate connotations to it," he replied. I smiled at this blatant understatement.

"So now you have the same name as the king of Lacedaemon?" I asked. I had heard that name before, and it was always uttered with the deepest awe and respect.

"The exact same," he agreed, "for the young Zaras you once knew has become that king of whom you now speak."

"Surely you jest?" I exclaimed in astonishment, for it seemed that my old subordinate of yesteryear had risen high in the world—in fact, to the very pinnacle. "But if you speak the truth tell me what has happened to the sister of Pharaoh Tamose, the Royal Princess Tehuti, whom you abducted out of my charge and care."

"The word you are groping for is wooed and not abducted. And she is no longer a princess." He shook his head firmly. "She is now a queen, because she showed the good sense to marry me."

"Is she still the most beautiful woman in the world?" I asked more than a trifle wistfully.

"In the vernacular of my kingdom, Sparta means 'the loveliest one.' I named the city in her honor. So now the Princess Tehuti has become Queen Sparta of Lacedaemon."

"And what of the others who are also dear to my heart and memory that you took north with you, all those years ago—?"

"Of course, you are speaking of Princess Bekatha and Hui." King Hurotas cut my questions short. "They are also now husband and wife. However, Hui is no longer a lowly captain. He is the lord high admiral and the commander of the Lacedaemon fleet, the same fleet that you see down there on the river." He pointed behind him at the tremendous array of ships anchored against the bank of the Nile. "Right now he is supervising the landing of the remainder of my expeditionary force."

"And so, King Hurotas, why have you returned to Egypt now after all these years?" I demanded.

His expression became fierce as he replied: "I came because at heart I am still an Egyptian. I heard from my spies that you in Egypt were hard pressed and on the verge of defeat at the hands of the Hyksos. These animals have despoiled our once lovely homeland.

They have raped and murdered our women and children; among their victims were my own mother and my two young sisters. After they had violated them, they threw them still alive onto the blazing ruins of our home and laughed as they watched them burn. I have returned to Egypt to avenge their deaths and to save more of our Egyptian people from a similar fate. If I succeed, I hope to forge a lasting alliance between our two countries: Egypt and Lacedaemon."

"Why have you waited twenty-three years before you returned?"

"As I am sure you will recall, Taita, when we last parted we were a mere handful of young runaways on three small galleys. We were flying from the tyranny of a Pharaoh who wanted to separate us from the women we loved."

I acknowledged the truth of this with a nod. It was safe to do so now, for the Pharaoh in question was Tamose and, as of yesterday, he was dead.

King Hurotas, who had once been the young Zaras, went on, "We were seeking a new homeland. It took all this time for us to find one and build it up into a formidable power with an army of more than five thousand of the finest fighting men."

"How did you achieve that, Your Majesty?" I asked.

"By a little polite diplomacy," he replied guilelessly,

but when I looked skeptical, he chuckled and admitted, "Together with more than a little blatant force of arms and outright conquest." With a wave of his hand he indicated the mighty army that he was disembarking onto the east bank of the Nile below us. "When one has a warlike array such as that you see before you, strangers are seldom disposed to argument."

"That sounds more like your style," I agreed, but Hurotas dismissed my retort with a nod and a smile and went on with his explanation.

"I knew it was my patriotic duty to give you all the succor and assistance in my power. I would have come a year earlier, but my naval squadrons were not sufficient to carry my army. I had to build more ships."

"Then you are more than welcome, Your Majesty. You have arrived at precisely the critical moment. Another hour and you would have been too late." I swung down from the back of my horse, but he anticipated me and he jumped down from his own mount, as sprightly as a man half his age, and strode to meet me. We embraced like brothers, which was what we were at heart. However, I felt more than mere brotherly love for him, for not only had he brought me the means to save my very Egypt from this marauding pack of vicious predators, but it seemed also that he had brought back to me my darling Tehuti, the daughter of Queen Lostris.

Mother and daughter, those two women are still the ones I have loved best in all my long life.

Our embrace was warm but fleeting. I drew back and punched Hurotas lightly on his shoulder. "There will be more time for these reminiscences anon. However, at this moment there are several thousand Hyksos waiting at the head of the pass for our attention: mine and yours." I pointed back up the ridge, and Hurotas looked startled. But he recovered almost immediately and grinned with genuine pleasure.

"Forgive me, old friend. I should have known that you would provide me with generous entertainment immediately on my arrival. Let us go up there at once and deal with a few of these nasty Hyksos, shall we?"

I shook my head in mock disapproval. "You have always been impetuous. Do you remember what the old bull replied when the young bull suggested that they rush down upon the herd of cows and cover a few of them?"

"Tell me what old bull said," he demanded with anticipation. He has always enjoyed my little jokes. I did not want to disappoint him now.

"The old bull answered, *Let us rather saunter down at our leisure and cover the lot of them.*"

Hurotas let out a delighted guffaw. "Tell me your plan, Taita, for I know you have one. You always do."

I set it out for him quickly because it was a simple plan, and then I turned away and vaulted back into the saddle of my mount. Without a backward glance I led Merab and my small band of horsemen back up the hill. I knew that I could rely on Hurotas who had once been Zaras to carry out my instructions to the letter; even if he was now a king, he was sufficiently astute to know that my counsel was always the best available.

As I crested the hill again I saw that I had not arrived ahead of time, for the Hyksos horde was advancing once more upon the battered and depleted ranks of Egypt, who stood to meet them. I urged my horse into a gallop and reached the shield wall only seconds before the enemy fell upon us again. I turned my mount free and seized the bronze shield that somebody thrust into my hands as I squeezed into my station in the center of the front rank. Then with a sound like summer thunder, the Hyksos front rank crashed, bronze on bronze, into our enfeebled line once again.

Almost at once I was swallowed up in the nightmare of battle wherein time loses all meaning and every second seems to last an eternity. Death pressed in upon us in a dark miasma of terror. Finally, after what seemed like an hour or a hundred years, I felt the unbearable pressure of Hyksos bronze upon our fragile front line ease abruptly, and then we were moving rapidly forward rather than stumbling backward.

The discordant bellowing of triumphant enemy war cries was replaced by terrified screams of pain and despair in the barbaric Hyksos tongue. Then the enemy ranks seemed to shrivel and collapse upon themselves so that my forward vision was no longer totally obscured.

I saw that Hurotas had followed my orders exactly, as I knew he would. He had moved his men in two wings around both our flanks simultaneously, catching the Hyksos aggressors in a perfect encircling movement, like a shoal of sardines in the fisherman's net.

The Hyksos fought with the recklessness born of despair, but my shield wall held firm and Hurotas' Lacedaemons were fresh and eager for the fray. They drove the hated foe against our line, like slabs of raw meat thrown down upon the butcher's block. Swiftly the conflict changed from battle to slaughter, and finally the surviving Hyksos threw down their weapons and fell to their knees on the ground that had become a muddy quagmire of blood. They pleaded for mercy, but King Hurotas laughed at their pleas for quarter.

He shouted at them, "My mother and my infant sisters made the same entreaty to your fathers as you make to me now. I give you the answer that your heartless fathers gave my dear ones. Die, you bastards, die!"

And when the echoes of their last death cry had sunk into silence, King Hurotas led his men back across that sanguine field and they cut the throats of any of the enemy who still showed the faintest flicker of life. I admit that in the heat of battle I was able to set aside my usual noble and compassionate instincts and join in celebrating our victory by sending more than a few of the wounded Hyksos into the waiting arms of their foul god Seth. Every throat I cut I dedicated to the memory of one of my brave men who had died earlier that same day on this field.

N ight had fallen and the full moon stood high in the sky before King Hurotas and I were able to leave the battlefield. He had learned from me much earlier in our friendship that all our wounded must be brought to safety and cared for, and then the perimeter of the camp had to be secured and sentries posted before the commanders could see to their own requirements. Thus it was well after midnight before we had fulfilled our responsibilities and the two of us were able to ride down the hill to the bank of the Nile where his flagship was moored.

When we went on board Admiral Hui was on the deck to meet us. After Hurotas he was one of my favorites, and we greeted each other like the old and dear friends that we truly were. He had lost most of the once dense bush of hair on his head and his naked scalp peeped shyly through the gaps in the gray strands, but his eyes were still bright and alert and his ubiquitous good humor warmed my heart. He led us to the captain's cabin and with his own hands poured both the king and I large bowls of red wine mulled with honey. I have seldom tasted anything as delicious as that draft. I allowed Hui to replenish my bowl more than once before exhaustion interrupted our joyous and raucous reunion.

We slept until the sun was almost clear of the horizon the following morning, and then we bathed in the river, washing off the grime and bloodstains of the previous day's exertions. Then when the combined armies of Egypt and Lacedaemon were assembled on the riverbank, we mounted up on fresh horses and with both Hurotas' legions and my own surviving fellows marching proudly ahead of us, pennants flying, drums beating and lutes playing, we rode up from the river to the Heroes Gate of the city of Luxor to report our glorious victory to the new Pharaoh of Egypt, Utteric Turo, eldest son of Tamose.

When we reached the gates of the golden city, we found them closed and bolted. I rode forward and hailed the keepers of the gate. I was forced to repeat my demands for entry more than once before the guards appeared on top of the wall.

"Pharaoh wants to know who you are and what is your business," the captain of the watch demanded of me. I knew him well. His name was Weneg. He was a handsome young officer who wore the Gold of Valor, Egypt's highest military honor. I was shocked that he didn't recognize me.

"Your memory serves you poorly, Captain Weneg," I called back. "I am Lord Taita, chairman of the Royal Council, and commanding general of Pharaoh's army. I come to report our glorious victory over the Hyksos."

"Wait here!" Captain Weneg ordered and his head disappeared below the battlements. We waited an hour and then another.

"It seems that you may have given offense to the new Pharaoh." King Hurotas gave me a wry smile. "Who is he, and do I know him?"

I shrugged. "His name is Utteric Turo, and you have missed nothing."

"Why was he not on the field of battle with you over these last days, as was his royal duty?"

"He is a gentle child of thirty-five years of age, not given to low company and rough behavior," I explained, and Hurotas snorted with laughter.

"You have not lost your way with words, good Taita!"

Finally Captain Weneg reappeared on the ramparts of the city wall. "Pharaoh Utteric Turo the Great has graciously granted you the right to enter the city. However, he orders you to leave your horses outside the walls. The person standing with you may accompany you, but no others."

I gasped to hear the sheer arrogance of the reply. A retort rose to my lips, but I bit down hard upon it. The entire army of Egypt together with that of Lacedaemon were listening with full attention. Almost three thousand men. I was not disposed to follow that line of discussion.

"Pharaoh is most gracious," I replied. The Heroes Gate swung ponderously open.

"Come along with me, you unnamed person standing with me," I told Hurotas grimly. Shoulder to shoulder, hands gripping the pommels of our swords but with visors raised, we marched into the city of Luxor. However, I did not feel like a conquering hero.

Captain Weneg and a troop of his men marched ahead of us. The city streets were hauntingly silent and empty. It must have taken the full two hours waiting that Pharaoh had enforced upon us to clear the streets of the customary swarming crowds. When we reached the palace the gates swung open seemingly of their own accord, without fanfare or cheering multitudes gathered to welcome us.

We climbed the wide staircase to the entrance of the royal audience hall, but the cavernous building was empty and silent except for the echoes of our bronze-shod sandals. We marched down the aisle of empty stone seats and approached the throne on its high dais at the far end of the hall.

We halted before the empty throne. Captain Weneg turned to me and his voice was harsh, his manner brusque. "Wait here!" he snapped, and then without lightening his expression he silently mouthed the words that I had no difficulty lip-reading: *Forgive me, my Lord Taita. This form of welcome is not of my choosing. I, personally, hold you in the highest esteem.*

"Thank you, Captain," I replied. "You have performed your duty admirably." Weneg acknowledged me with a clenched fist held to his chest. He led his men away. Hurotas and I were left standing at attention before the empty throne.

I did not need to warn him that we were certainly under observation from some hidden peephole in the stone walls. Nevertheless, I felt my own patience under strain from the strange and unnatural antics of this new Pharaoh.

Finally I heard the sound of voices and distant laughter, which became closer and louder until the curtains covering the entrance to the hall behind the throne were jerked aside and Pharaoh Utteric Turo, self-styled the Great, strolled into the audience hall. His hair was dressed in ringlets that hung to his shoulders. There were garlands of flowers around his neck. He was eating a pomegranate and spitting the pips on the stone floor. He ignored Hurotas and me as he ascended the throne and made himself comfortable on the pile of cushions.

Utteric Turo was followed by a half-dozen young boys in various stages of dress and undress. All of them were decked with flowers, and most of them had painted their faces with blood-crimson lips and blue or green shades around their eyes. Some of them were munching fruit or sweetmeats as Pharaoh was doing, but two or three of them carried cups of wine, which they sipped from as they chatted and giggled together.

Pharaoh hurled one of his cushions at the leading boy and there were squeals of laughter as it knocked the wine cup from his hands and the contents spilled down his tunic.

"Oh, you naughty Pharaoh!" the boy protested. "Now, just look what you have done to my pretty garment!"

"Please forgive me, my dear Anent." Pharaoh rolled his eyes in penitence. "Come and sit beside me. This will not take too long, I promise you, but I have to speak to these two fine fellows first." Pharaoh looked directly at Hurotas and me for the first time since he had entered the hall. "Greetings, good Taita. I hope you are in excellent health as always?" Then he switched his gaze toward my companion. "And who is this you have with you? I don't think I know him, do I?"

"May I present King Hurotas, monarch of the Kingdom of Lacedaemon. Without his assistance we could never have overcome the forces of the Hyksos who were slavering at the very gates of your mighty city of Luxor." I spread my arms to indicate the man at my side. "We owe him a deep debt of gratitude for the continued survival of our nation . . ."

Pharaoh held up his right hand, effectively cutting short my impassioned speech, and he stared at Hurotas thoughtfully for what seemed to me an unnecessary length of time. "King Hurotas, you say? But he reminds me of somebody else."

I was taken off balance and could think of nothing to say to contradict him, which was uncharacteristic of me. But before my eyes this feeble and apathetic sprig of the House of Tamose was being transformed into an angry and formidable monster. His countenance darkened and his eyes blazed. His shoulders began to tremble with fury as he pointed to my companion.

"Does he not resemble someone named Captain Zaras, a common soldier in the army of my glorious father, Pharaoh Tamose? Surely you remember that rogue, do you not, Taita? Even though I was a very young child at the time, I certainly remember this Zaras person. I remember his evil leering countenance and his insolent manner." Pharaoh Utteric's voice rose to a shriek; spittle flew from his lips. "My father, the Great and Glorious Pharaoh Tamose, sent this Zaras creature on a mission to Knossos, the capital city of the Supreme Minos on the island of Crete. He was charged with the safe conduct of my two aunts, Princess Tehuti and Princess Bekatha, to Crete. They were to be married to the Supreme Minos in order to consolidate the treaty of friendship between our two great empires. In the event this Zaras creature abducted my royal relatives and spirited them away to some barbaric and desolate place at the very edge of the world. They have never been heard of again since then. I loved both my aunties, they were so beautiful . . ."

Pharaoh was forced to break off his string of accusations. He panted wildly in an effort to calm his breathing and regain his composure, but he continued to point his shaking forefinger at Hurotas.

"Your Majesty . . ." I stepped forward and spread both my hands in an attempt to divert his wild and irrational anger, but he rounded on me just as furiously.

"You, you treacherous scoundrel! You may have duped my father and all his court, but I never trusted you. I always saw through your wiles and machinations. I have always known you for what you are. You are a forked-tongued liar, a scheming black-hearted villain . . ." Pharaoh shrieked wildly and looked around for his guards. "Arrest these men. I will have them executed for treachery . . ."

Pharaoh's voice sank and dried up. A profound silence filled the royal audience chamber.

"Where are my bodyguards?" Pharaoh inquired querulously. His young companions huddled behind him, pale-faced and terrified. Finally the one he called Anent spoke up.

"You dismissed your guards, darling. And I am not going to arrest anyone, especially not those two thugs. They look like blatant killers to me." He turned and trotted back through the curtained doorway, followed immediately by the rest of Pharaoh's pretty boys.

"Where are my royal guards? Where is everybody?" Pharaoh's voice sank to an uncertain, almost apologetic pitch. "I ordered them to wait in readiness to make the arrests. Where are they now?" But silence answered him. He looked back at the two of us suited in our armor, gauntleted hands gripping the pommels of our swords and our faces scowling. He backed away toward the curtained exit in the rear wall. I strode after him, and now his expression became one of unmitigated terror. He sank to his knees facing me, arms outstretched toward me as though to fend off the blows of my sword.

"Taita, my dear Taita. It was just a little joke. It was all in good-natured fun. I meant no harm. You are my friend, and the dear protector of my family. Don't hurt me. I'll do anything . . ." And then an extraordinary thing happened. Pharaoh shat himself. He did it so loudly and malodorously that for a stunned moment he stopped me like a statue, with my one foot in the air, suspended in midstride.

Behind me Hurotas exploded in a burst of delighted laughter. "The royal salute, Taita! The ruler of mighty Egypt greets you with the highest honor in the land."

I don't know how I stopped myself from laughing along with Hurotas, but I managed to keep my expression serious and, stepping forward, I reached down and took a firm grip of Pharaoh's hands with which he was trying to fend off my putative attack. I lifted him to his feet and told him gently, "My poor Utteric Turo; I have upset you. The great god Horus knows I never meant to do so. Go up to your royal suite now and bathe yourself. Put on fresh robes. However, before you do so please give me and King Hurotas your permission to take your glorious armies north into the delta and fall upon that rogue Khamudi, the self-styled king of the Hyksos. It is our sworn duty to wipe clean forever the curse and the bloody stains of the Hyksos occupation of our homeland."

Utteric pulled his hands free of mine and backed away from me, his expression still terrified. He nodded his head frantically, and between his sobs he blurted out, "Yes! Yes! Go at once! You have my permission. Take everything and everybody that you need and go! Just go!" Then he turned and fled from the royal audience chamber, with his sandals squelching at each stride.

King Hurotas and I left the great hall of audience alone and went back through the empty streets of the city. Although I was anxious to begin the next phase of our campaign, I did not want Pharaoh to receive reports of our hasty departure from Luxor from his spies and agents. Of course there would be many of them hiding in the buildings and alleyways, keeping us under surveillance. When we finally emerged through the Heroes Gate of the city, our combined armies were still awaiting our return.

I heard later that their ranks had been tormented by rumors that had grown more alarming the longer we remained locked away behind the gates of the city. There were even suggestions we two generals had been arrested on trumped-up charges and hustled away to the dungeons and thence to the torture chambers. The reaction of our battle-hardened men to our return was moving and deeply touched the hearts of both King Hurotas and me. Old veterans and young recruits wept, and they cheered us until their voices cracked. The front ranks surged forward and some of them went down on their knees to kiss our mailed feet.

Then they hoisted us on to their shoulders and carried us down to the banks of the Nile where the Lacedaemon armada was anchored, singing the songs of glory at the top of their voices until both Hurotas and I were well nigh deafened by the cacophony. I must admit I thought little more of the childish antics of the new Pharaoh—there was too much of real import to occupy my mind. I thought that Hurotas and I had put him firmly in his place, and that we would not hear much more from him.

We went aboard the Lacedaemon flagship, where we were greeted by Admiral Hui. Although by then the tumultuous day had fled, and it was almost dark, we went immediately into planning the final chapter of our campaign against Khamudi, the leader of what remained of the Hyksos rabble in the northern delta of Mother Nile.

Khamudi had made his capital at Memphis, downriver from where we were now. My information on the state of Khamudi's forces was extensive and up to date. My agents were well established in the Hyksos-occupied and -dominated territories of our very Egypt.

According to these agents, Khamudi had stripped his territory in northern Egypt almost bare of warriors and chariots and sent them all south to participate in what he had hoped would be the final drive to shatter the remnants of our Egyptian forces there. But, as I have already related, the timely arrival of King Hurotas had put an end to Khamudi's grandiose aspirations. The great majority of the Hyksos forces now lay dead at the head of the pass below Luxor, a feast for the scavengers. There would never be another equally fortuitous opportunity to put an end to the Hyksos presence in our very Egypt than was ours for the taking right now.

What remained of Khamudi's Hyksos army, foot and cavalry, in the north numbered not more than three thousand men in total, whereas Hurotas and I could field a total force of almost twice that number, including several hundred chariots. Nearly all these were Lacedaemons, so despite the fact that I was indubitably the most experienced and skilled commander in Egypt and probably in the civilized world, I felt I should as a matter of courtesy concede command of our combined forces to King Hurotas. I made my concession apparent by inviting Hurotas to express his views as to how the second phase of our offensive should be conducted, which was as good as offering him supreme command.

Hurotas gave me that boyish grin I remembered from long ago and replied, "When it comes to command, I bow to only one man, and he just happens to be seated at this very table opposite me. Please proceed, Taita. Let us hear your battle plan. Where you lead we will follow."

I nodded my approval of his wise decision. Not only is Hurotas a mighty warrior, but he never lets his pride override his good sense. So I aimed my next questions at him: "Now I want to know how you suddenly appeared at Luxor without any of us, including the Hyksos, knowing of your arrival. How did you bring your flotilla of twenty large war galleys hundreds of leagues upriver, passing the Hyksos forts and walled cities to reach us here?"

Hurotas dismissed my question with a casual shrug. "On my ships I have some of the very best pilots that there are on this earth, not counting you of course, Taita. Once we entered the mouth of the Nile River we traveled only at night and tied up to the bank and hid under a camouflage of cut branches during the day. Fortunately the sky goddess Nut granted us a dark moon to cover our nightly progress. We passed the main enemy strongholds on the banks of the river after midnight, and we kept to midriver. Perhaps a few fishermen saw us, but in the dark they would have taken us for Hyksos. We moved fast, very fast. We made the journey from the mouth of the River Nile to where we met you here in only six nights' hard rowing."

"So then we still have the element of surprise on our side," I mused. "Even if a few of the enemy survived the battle at the pass, which seems unlikely, on foot they would take many weeks to find their way back to Memphis and spread the alarm." I jumped to my feet and paced the deck, thinking quickly. "Now what is absolutely vital when we attack Khamudi's capital city is that none of the enemy manage to escape and somehow make their way eastward to the border of Suez and the Sinai, and from there reach their ancestral homeland farther east where they might be able to regroup and come against us again a few years hence—to repeat the same sorry cycle of war and conquest and enslavement."

"You are right, Taita," Hurotas agreed with me. "We have to finish this. Future generations of our people must be able to exist in peace and flourish as the most civilized nation in existence, without fear of the barbaric Hyksos hordes. But how might we best reach such a happy conclusion?"

"I plan to use the bulk of the chariots as a blocking force along the eastern border to prevent any the surviving Hyksos making a run for safety to reach their ancient homeland," I told them.

Hurotas considered my proposal for just a few seconds before he smiled. "We are fortunate to have you, Taita. You are without doubt the most experienced and skillful charioteer that I know of. With you guarding the border I would not give any Hyksos a dog's chance of making it back to his kennel."

Sometimes I suspect my old friend Hurotas of ribbing me with his extravagant praise, but as on this occasion I usually let it pass.

By this time it was almost midnight; however, the darkness barely slowed our preparations for departure. We lit brush torches, and by the light they afforded us we reloaded all the chariots aboard the Lacedaemon galleys. When this was done, we boarded our men, including the remnants of my own native Egyptian regiments.

With this additional cargo the ships were so crowded that there was no room for the horses on board. I gave orders to the grooms to drive the loose horses northward along the east bank of the Nile. Then, still in darkness, we pushed off from our moorings and headed downriver to enter Hyksos-held territory, with the leadsmen chanting the soundings in the bows and the pilots calling every twist and turn of the river. The trotting herds of horses almost kept pace with the speed of the flotilla, even though our ships had the favorable current to carry them onward.

We covered almost thirty leagues of the voyage downstream before sunrise. Then we went ashore to rest through the heat of the day. Within a few hours the herds of horses had caught up with us and were grazing on the pastures and the crops growing on the riverbank.

These crops had been planted by Hyksos farmers, for we were now in enemy-held territory. We thanked them for their generosity. And then we sent them to their places on the rowing benches of Admiral Hui's galleys where the slave chains were buckled snugly onto their ankles. Their womenfolk were hustled away by Hurotas' men; however, I made no inquiry as to what became of them. War is a brutal business, and they had come into our land without invitation and seized the fields from our peasants and treated them worse than slaves. They could not expect to be treated any better by us.

When all was secure, the three of us sat under the sycamore trees on the riverbank, while the cooks served us a breakfast of roasted sausage and crisp brown bread hot from the clay ovens, which we washed down with jugs of freshly brewed beer; and which I for one would not have exchanged for a banquet at Pharaoh's board.

We went on board again as soon as the sun had passed its zenith and continued our northward voyage toward Memphis. But there was still almost two days of sailing ahead of us, and this was the first time since Hurotas and Hui had returned so unexpectedly that I had been given the opportunity to speak to them about the life we had known together so many years ago. In particular, I was anxious to learn about what had become of the two young princesses they had taken into exile with them when they fled from the wrath of the princesses' brother, Pharaoh Tamose.

The three of us were seated on the poop deck of the flagship, and we were alone and well beyond earshot of any members of the crew. I addressed myself to both of them.

"I have questions for both of you that I am sure you would rather avoid. You will remember that I had a special affection for the two beautiful young virgins that you coarse ruffians had the gall to steal away from me, their protector, and Pharaoh Tamose, their loving brother."

"Let me put your mind at rest, for I know just how it works, that lascivious Taita mind." Hurotas cut me off before I was able to put to him my first question. "They are no longer either young or virgin."

Hui chuckled his agreement. "However, we love them more with every year that passes for they have proven themselves incomparably loyal, true and prolific. My Bekatha has given me four fine sons."

"And Tehuti has borne me a single daughter who is lovely beyond the telling of it," Hurotas boasted, but I was skeptical of such claims because I am well aware that all parents have an inflated opinion of their own offspring. It was not until much later, when I laid eyes for the first time on Hurotas and Tehuti's only daughter, that I realized that he had done her a serious injustice.

"I do not expect that either Tehuti or Bekatha gave you messages to pass on to me." I tried not to sound wistful. "The chances of us meeting again were remote, and surely their memory of me has faded over the years . . ." They would not let me complete my modest disclaimer before both of them burst out laughing.

"Forget you?" Hurotas demanded through his laughter. "It was only with the greatest difficulty that I convinced my wife to remain in Lacedaemon rather than return to Egypt with us to find her darling Tata." It made my heart lurch to hear him mimic her exact rendition of my pet name. "She did not even trust me to memorize her messages to you, so she insisted on writing them down on a papyrus scroll for me to deliver to you in person."

"A papyrus!" I exclaimed with delight. "Where is it? Give it to me at once."

"Please forgive me, Taita." Hurotas looked abashed. "But it was really too bulky to carry with me. I had to consider leaving it in Lacedaemon." I stared at him in dismay, trying to find the words to castigate him as severely as he deserved. He let me suffer only a little longer, and then he could contain himself no longer and he grinned. "I knew what you would think of that idea, Taita! So I have it in my saddlebags, which are in my cabin below."

I punched his shoulder harder than was truly necessary. "Fetch it at once, you rogue, or else I shall never forgive you." Hurotas went below and returned almost immediately carrying a bulky scroll of papyrus. I snatched it out of his hands and carried it to the foredeck where I could be alone and uninterrupted. Gently and almost reverently I broke the seal and unrolled the first leaf so I could read the salutation.

Nobody that I know of can paint a hieroglyph as artistically as my beloved Tehuti. She had rendered "The Falcon with a Broken Wing," which is my hieroglyph, so that it seemed to be endowed with a life of its own and flew from the painted sheet of papyrus through the mist of tears that filled my eyes and went straight to my heart.

The words she wrote touched me so intimately that I cannot bring myself to repeat them to another living soul.

On the third morning after leaving our moorings below the city of Luxor, our flotilla had reached a point only twenty leagues upstream of the Hyksos stronghold of Memphis, which stood on both banks of the Nile. There we beached our galleys, and we unloaded the chariots. The grooms drove up the horses and sorted them into their teams, and the charioteers buckled them into the traces.

The three of us held a final war council aboard the flagship of the Lacedaemon fleet, during which we once again ran over our plans in minute detail, covering every possible contingency that we might encounter during the assault on Memphis, then I embraced both Hui and Hurotas quickly but fervently and called down the blessing and favors of all the gods upon each of them before we parted company. I set off with my team of chariots for the head of the Red Sea to block the Hyksos escape route from Egypt, while the others continued their voyage northward until they were in a position to launch their final assault on the stronghold of the Hyksos chieftain, Khamudi.

When Hurotas and Hui reached the harbor below the city of Memphis, they found that Khamudi had already abandoned it and set fire to the shipping moored within its stone jetties. The pall of black smoke from the burning vessels was visible even to me and my charioteers waiting on the border of Egypt at Suez many leagues distant. However, Hurotas and Hui arrived in time to save nearly thirty of the Hyksos galleys from the flames, but of course we had not enough crews to man these valuable ships.

This is where my squadron of chariots came into play. Within only hours of taking up our stations along the border of Egypt with Suez and the Sinai, we were hard at work rounding up the hundreds of refugees who were fleeing from the doomed city of Memphis. Of course each one of them was laden down with their valuables.

These captives were sorted carefully. The elderly and infirm were first relieved of all their possessions and then allowed to wander away into the Sinai Desert, after being charged never again to return to Egypt. The young and strong were roped together in gangs of ten, and then I started them, still carrying their possessions and those of their compatriots who had been allowed to proceed, back toward Memphis and the Nile. In the case of the men, these captives, no matter how illustrious their rank, were destined to a short life chained on the rowing benches of our galleys or laboring like beasts of burden in the fields on the banks of the Nile; the younger women—those who were not too grotesquely ugly—would be sent to do service in the public brothels, and the rest of them would find employment in the kitchens or the dungeons of the great mansions of our very Egypt. The roles had been completely reversed, and they would receive the same treatment as they had dealt out to us Egyptians when they had us in their power.

When we reached the city of Memphis with these doleful lines of captives marching ahead of our chariots, we found it under siege by Hurotas' legions. However, chariots are not the most effective means of siege breaking, so my dashing charioteers were dismounted and set to tunneling beneath the walls to excavate a series of breaches to enable us to winkle out Khamudi and his rogues from their sullen lurking within the city.

Like all sieges this was a dreary and time-consuming exercise. Our army was forced to encamp outside the walls of Memphis for almost six months before, with a rumble and a roar, and a column of dust that was visible for many leagues around, the entire ramparts of the eastern section of the city collapsed upon themselves and our men could pour through the breaches.

The sack of the city went on for many more days, for it was spread on both banks of the river. However, our victorious troops were at last able to apprehend Khamudi, where he and his family were found cowering in their hiding place deep in the dungeons beneath his palace. It was most fortuitous that they were sitting on a vast treasure of silver and gold bars, as well as innumerable large chests of jewelry that had taken him and his predecessors almost a century to collect from the enslaved Egyptian populace. This brood of royal rogues and rascals was escorted down to the harbor on the Nile by Hurotas' troops, where to the accompaniment of music and laughter they were drowned one after another, beginning with the youngest members of the family.

These were a pair of twin girls of about two or three

years of age. Contrary to what I had come to expect of the tribe, they were not really repulsive to look at; in fact, they were pretty little mites. Their father, Khamudi, wept as they were plunged into the Nile and held beneath the surface of the river. I was not prepared for that either. Somehow I had come to believe that, like all the brute animals, the Hyksos were incapable of loving and grieving.

The dreaded Khamudi himself was reserved for last on the execution roster. When his turn came, he was accorded a more elaborate departure from this world than the others of his family. This began with skinning him alive using knives that were heated to a glowing red in charcoal braziers; followed by drawing and quartering, which evoked further merriment from the spectators. It seemed that Hurotas' men have a particularly robust sense of humor.

I managed to maintain a neutral countenance during these proceedings. I would have much preferred to have taken no part in them, but had I absented myself it would have been seen as a display of weakness by my men. Appearances are vital, and reputations ephemeral.

Hurotas, Hui and I were subdued on our return to the Memphis palace. However, we soon became our usual cheerful and lively selves when we began counting and cataloging the contents of the cellars beneath the palace of Khamudi. I find it truly remarkable how when all else in life has lost its flavor, gold alone retains its full fascination and appeal.

Even though we had fifty of Hurotas' most trusted men to assist us, it took us several days to lay out all this treasure. When at last we turned our lanterns upon this mass of precious metal and colored stones, the reflected light was strong enough to dazzle us. We stared at it in awe and astonishment.

"Do you recall the Cretan treasure we captured at the fortress of Tamiat?" Hurotas asked me in hushed tones.

"When you were still a young captain of legionnaires, and your name was Zaras? I will never forget it. I thought that there was not that much silver and gold in the whole wide world."

"That was not even one-tenth part of what we have here and now," Hurotas pointed out.

"This is just as well," I replied.

Both Hurotas and Hui looked at me askance. "How is that, Taita?"

"That is because we have to share it at least four ways," I explained, and when they were still uncomprehending I went on: "You and Hui; me and Utteric Turo."

"You don't mean Utteric, that utter prick, do you?" Hurotas looked aghast.

"Exactly!" I confirmed. "Utteric the Great, the Pharaoh of Egypt. This treasure was originally stolen from his ancestors."

They considered what I had said in silence for a while and then Hurotas asked tactfully, "So then it seems that you intend to remain in Utteric Turo's realm?"

"Naturally!" I was taken aback by the question. "I am an Egyptian nobleman. I possess vast estates in this country. Where else would I go?"

"Do you trust him?"

"Who?"

"Utteric the Utter Prick; who else?" Hurotas demanded of me.

"He is my Pharaoh. Of course I trust him."

"Where was your Pharaoh at the battle of Luxor?" Hurotas asked remorselessly. "Where was he when we stormed these battlements of Memphis?"

"Poor Utteric is not a warrior. He is a gentle soul." I tried to make excuses for him. "However, his father, Tamose, was a fine and furious warrior."

"We are discussing the son, not the father," Hurotas pointed out.

I was silent again while I contemplated the implication of his words; finally I asked, "May I take it, then, that you will not return with me to Luxor when I go to make my report to Pharaoh Utteric Turo?"

He shook his head. "My heart lies in Lacedaemon with the lovely woman who is my queen, and with our daughter. My business in Luxor is finished. Besides which, there are people in that city who still remember me as young Zaras. I have only met your Pharaoh Utteric Turo once, and he gave me no good reason to like or trust him. I think I would rather return to my own citadel where I have control of the situation." He came to me and clapped me on my shoulder. "My old friend, if you are as wise as we all believe you to be, you will give your share of this splendid treasure to me, to keep it safely for you until you call upon me to return it to you. In that case, no harm will have been done. However, if I am correct in my suspicions, you will have good reason to be thankful to me."

"I will think on it," I muttered unhappily.

Hurotas and Hui lingered another ten days while they loaded their ships with the slaves and other booty they had captured in Memphis, including my share of the Hyksos treasure, which I had reluctantly agreed to place in Hurotas' care. Then they sent their chariots and horses on board and we said our farewells standing on the stone jetty on the west bank of the Nile.

Four of Hui's sons by Princess Bekatha were with us at Memphis. Each of them commanded a squadron of chariots. There had been little opportunity for me to become acquainted with them; however, it seemed they took after their father and their royal mother, and that meant to me that they were fine young men, and brave and skillful charioteers. The eldest was named Huisson for obvious reasons; and the other three were Sostratus, Palmys and Leo. Barbaric Greek names, to be sure, but they embraced me and called me "Revered and illustrious uncle," which endorsed my high opinion of them. They promised to convey my loving duty to their mother and their aunt immediately on their return to Lacedaemon.

Hurotas had written out the sailing orders for a voyage from the Nile Delta to the island of Lacedaemon; and this, together with a receipt for my share of the treasure of Memphis, he pressed into my hands. "Now you will have no excuse for failing to visit us at the very first opportunity that presents itself to you," he told me, his voice gruff as he tried to mask his distress at this our second significant parting.

On the other hand, I had written a papyrus scroll for each of my two beloved princesses, Tehuti and Bekatha, for their husbands to deliver to them as soon as they reached their homes. I could not trust those two amiable ruffians to deliver verbatim my precious words to their spouses. These were expressions of such poetic beauty that, even after all these years, repeating them silently to myself can reduce me to tears.

Then all of them went aboard their galleys and pushed off from the pier. The drums beat the cadence for the rowers; the long oars dipped and swung and dipped again. In line ahead they unwound like some mighty sea dragon awakening, and with the Nile current urging them onward they disappeared around the first bend in the river, heading for the delta where the river debouched into the great Middle Sea.

I was left alone and pining.

Three days later I went aboard my own galley and we headed southward, homeward bound for the golden city of Luxor. But my heart was still heavy and my thoughts were traveling in the opposite direction to that in which the wind and the banks of oars were carrying me.

When we reached the port of Luxor below the city, it seemed that the news of our magnificent victory at Memphis had been carried ahead of us by carrier pigeon to Pharaoh Utteric's palace. Three of his senior ministers were waiting on the river wharf at the head of what appeared to be the entire population of Upper Egypt. In the background of this multitude there stood at least twenty wagons, each of them drawn by a team of twelve

oxen. I presumed these were to carry the Hyksos treasure up to the city of Luxor where Pharaoh's treasury,
no doubt, stood ready and eager to receive it. A massed
band of harps, flutes, lyres, trumpets, tambourines and
drums were roaring out a spirited rendition of the new
anthem to the glory of Pharaoh Utteric Turo, which it
was rumored he had composed himself. The Egyptian
populace seemed to have stripped every palm tree in
the land of its fronds, which they waved enthusiasti-
cally as they chanted along with the bands.

When my flagship docked at the main wharf, I was
prepared to acknowledge the praise and grateful thanks
of Pharaoh Utteric Turo and all the people of Egypt
for ridding them of the menace of Khamudi and his
ghastly tribe for all time and of returning to them such
a fabulous treasure from the enemy coffers.

Utteric's chief minister was a beautiful young man
who had made a great fortune in the slave trade. His
name was Lord Mennakt. He was a bosom companion of Pharaoh, and possibly much closer to him in the
other more intimate parts of the flesh than merely the
bosom, for I had heard it rumored that they shared the
same prurient predilections. A scribe must have written out his speech on a papyrus scroll, for he read it in
a dreary monotone, stumbling over words of more than
one syllable. I could have forgiven this lack of stage-

craft, but what irked me at once was that he made no mention of my part in the final brilliant campaign that I had led against the Hyksos. In fact, he did not mention my name at all. He spoke only of his patron, Pharaoh Utteric Turo, and of the loyal and brave legions he was supposed to have commanded in battle. He extolled the leadership and courage of Pharaoh and his wisdom and sheer genius in liberating our very Egypt from a century of slavery and foreign domination. He pointed out that the five Pharaohs who had immediately preceded him, including his own father, Tamose, had been dolefully unsuccessful in their attempts to achieve the same conclusive results. He ended his tribute by pointing out that this magnificent victory had surely earned Pharaoh Utteric Turo a prominent place alongside Horus, Isis, Osiris and Hathor in the pantheon of our fatherland. For this reason, Mennakt explained, the main part of the treasure that Pharaoh Utteric had won from the Hyksos at Memphis would be used to build a temple to celebrate his rise above the mere human state to that of the celestial and immortal.

While Lord Mennakt was regaling and enlightening us with this speech my crew was unloading the treasure that we had carried with us and piling it on the wharf. It made a magnificent display, which completely diverted the attention of the assembled multitudes away from Mennakt's wit and mastery of the spoken word.

When Mennakt finally stumbled into silence, the order was given and the wagons rolled forward and the sweating slaves loaded the treasure chests into them. Then the drivers cracked their long whips and an escort of heavily armed palace guards immediately surrounded them and they started up the causeway toward the main gates of the city of Luxor.

All this took me completely by surprise. I had presumed that it would be my honor to lead this procession and to make the formal offering of the treasure to Pharaoh. When he accepted my gift Pharaoh would be obliged to accord me his full recognition and approval. I started forward to make my protest to Lord Mennakt and demand my rightful place at the head of the treasure train.

What I had not been aware of in the press of bodies all around me and the exigencies of the moment was that six more high-ranking officers of the palace guards had come aboard my flagship from the crowd on the wharf. Without any fuss or outcry they had managed to surround me with a cocoon of armor and drawn weapons.

"My Lord Taita, in accordance with Pharaoh's express command I place you under arrest for high treason. Please come with me." The leader of this contingent spoke quietly but firmly in my ear. I turned and stared at him in astonishment. It took me a moment to realize that he was Captain Weneg for whom I had such a high regard.

"What nonsense is this, Captain Weneg? I am probably Pharaoh's most loyal subject," I protested indignantly. He ignored my outburst and nodded to his henchmen. Immediately they crowded me so closely that I could not struggle. I felt one of the men behind me slip my sword from its scabbard, and then I was being hustled to the gangplank. At the same time Lord Mennakt gestured to the band that was gathered behind him and they burst into yet another lively and spirited hymn of praise and worship to the divine Pharaoh, so that my protests were rendered inaudible. By the time my guards and I had reached the stone wharf, the dense crowds of spectators had turned away to follow the band and the procession of treasure wagons up the road to the main gates of the city.

As soon as we were alone Captain Weneg gave orders to his men and they bound my wrists together at the small of my back with rawhide ropes, while others of their party brought up four war chariots. When they had me trussed up securely they pushed me up on to the footplate of the leading chariot. The whips cracked and we set off at a canter, not following the bands and the treasure train up the hill toward the main city gates, but taking one of the subsidiary tracks that bypassed the city and then branched off toward the rocky hills beyond. The track was little used; in fact, it was assiduously avoided by most of the citizenry. This was not extraordinary when its final destination was taken into consideration. Less than five leagues beyond the royal palace and the main city walls rose a low line of hills; and sitting astride their summit was a somber edifice of chiseled native rock, a sullen shade of blue in color and unambiguous in design. This was the royal prison, which also housed the gallows yard and the state torture chambers.

We had to cross a small stream of water to reach the slopes of the hills. The bridge was narrow and the hooves of the horses hammered loudly on it; to my heated imagination they sounded almost like the drumbeat of the Death March. My escort and I were not accosted until we reached the appropriately named Gates of Torment and Sorrow, which gave access through the massive masonry wall into the bowels of the prison. Captain Weneg jumped down from the footplate of our vehicle and hammered on the doors with the hilt of his sword. Almost immediately a black-clad warder appeared on the bridge of the portcullis high above us. His head was enclosed in a hood of the same color, and it hid his features entirely except for his eyes and mouth.

"Who seeks entry here?" he bellowed down at us.

"Prisoner and escort!" Weneg replied.

"Enter at your peril," the warder warned us. "But know ye, all enemies of Pharaoh and Egypt are eternally doomed once they are within these walls!" Then the portcullis was raised ponderously and we drove through. We were the only vehicle to enter. The other three of our escort remained outside the walls when the portcullis rumbled closed once again.

The interior walls of the first courtyard were decorated by rows of niches that rose tier upon tier to such a height that I had to throw my head right back to see the tiny square of blue sky high above.

In each niche grinned a human skull: hundreds upon hundreds of them. It was not the first time I had passed this way. On occasion I had visited other unfortunates who had been incarcerated within these walls, to offer them what little help and comfort was in my gift. However, my spirit never failed to quail and my skin to crawl at the presence of death in such dire abundance, more so now that the threat was so personal and particular to me.

"This is as far as I can take you, Lord Taita," Weneg

said quietly. "Please understand that I am merely following my orders. There is nothing personal in what I have to do, and I take no pleasure in it."

"I understand your predicament, Captain," I replied. "I hope that our next meeting will be more pleasurable for both of us."

Weneg helped me down from the footplate of the chariot and then severed the bonds at my wrists with a sweep of his dagger. Swiftly he went through the formality of handing me over to the prison warders and delivering to them my scroll of impeachment. I recognized Pharaoh Utteric's hieroglyph at the foot of this document. Then Weneg saluted me and turned away. I watched him jump back onto his vehicle, seize the reins, and wheel his team to face the gateway. As soon as the portcullis was raised high enough he ducked under it and without a backward glance drove out into the daylight.

There were four prison warders to receive me. As soon as Weneg had left the courtyard one of these lifted off his black headdress and confronted me with a derisive grin. He was a grossly obese creature, with garlands of fat drooping down from his jowls onto his chest.

"We are honored by your presence, my lord. It is not often that we get the opportunity to play host to such an illustrious personage, a man of the highest reputation and most fabulous wealth—after Pharaoh himself, of course. I am determined not to give you short measure. First let me introduce myself. My name is Doog." He bowed his great bald head, which was covered with obscene tattoos of stick figures doing repulsive things to each other, but he went on speaking: "A man of your erudition and learning will realize at once that *Doog* is *Good* spelled backward, and he will know then what to expect of me. Those who know me well often refer to me as Doog the Terrible." Doog had a nervous twitch, which caused him to blink his right eye rapidly at the end of each sentence he uttered. I could not resist the temptation, so I winked back at him.

He stopped grinning. "I see that you like your little jokes, my lord? In due course I will give you jokes that will cause you to die laughing," he promised. "But we must defer that pleasure for a short while longer. Pharaoh has arrested you for high treason, but not yet tried you nor found you guilty. However, that time will come, and I shall be ready for it, I assure you."

He started to circle me, but I turned at the same speed to keep facing him. "Hold him still!" he snarled at his henchmen, and they seized both my arms and twisted them to bring me down to my knees.

"You have beautiful clothes, my lord," Doog commended me. "I have seldom seen such splendid garments." This was true, for I had been expecting to address Pharaoh and his state council when I delivered to him the Hyksos treasure. I was wearing the golden helmet I had captured from a Hyksos general on another battlefield a long time ago; it was a masterpiece in gold and silver. Around my shoulders hung the Gold of Valor and the Gold of Praise, equally magnificent chains that had been awarded to me by the hand of Pharaoh Tamose himself for the service and sacrifice I had given to him. I knew that, adorned thus, I was a wondrous sight to behold.

"We must not let such lovely garments become dirtied or damaged. You must remove them at once. I will take them into my safekeeping," Doog explained. "But I assure you that I will return them to you as soon as you are found innocent of the charges against you and are released from custody." I regarded him silently, not giving him the pleasure of hearing my protests or entreaties. "My men will help you to undress." Doog ended his little speech, which I was certain that he had also addressed to all the men who were now but skulls in the niches of the walls above me.

He nodded at his henchmen and they ripped the helmet from my head and the gold chains from around my neck; then they tore away the lovely garments that covered my body, leaving me naked except for a brief loincloth. Finally they dragged me back onto my feet and forced me to walk to the doors in the back wall of the courtyard.

Doog lumbered along beside me. "All of us who work here within the prison walls are so excited and happy about the ascension of Pharaoh Utteric Turo to the throne." He winked four or five times to express his excitement, his head bobbing in time to the blinking of his eyes. "Pharaoh has changed our lives and made us some of the most important citizens in this very Egypt. During Pharaoh Tamose's reign, we hardly ever drew blood from one week to the next. But now his eldest son keeps us busy from morning until night. If we aren't chopping off heads, we are drawing the entrails out of men and women; or twisting off their arms; or hanging them by their necks or their testicles; or peeling off their skins with the hot irons." He chuckled merrily. "My brothers and my five sons were all out of work only a year ago, but now they are full-time executioners and tormentors, as I am. We are invited by Pharaoh Utteric Turo nearly every few weeks to the royal palace in Luxor. He likes to watch us carrying out our duties. Of course he never comes visit us here. He is convinced that there is a curse on these walls. The only persons who ever come here do so to die; and we are the chosen few who help them to do it. But Pharaoh particularly loves to see me work on the young girls, especially if they are pregnant. So we take them down to the palace to do so. One of my little foibles is to hang them from the scaffold on bronze hooks through their tits, and then I use other hooks to rip the living fetus out of their wombs." Doog salivated like a hungry animal at his own description. I felt my gorge rise to have to listen to such obscenities.

"I will let you watch while you are waiting for your own turn. I usually charge a fee, but you have let me have your helmet and gold chains for which I am so grateful . . ." He was one of the most repulsive persons I have ever encountered. The black hood and cloak he wore were obviously meant to disguise the blood of his victims, but this close to him I could see that some of the stains were still damp, and the ones that had dried had begun to rot the fabric, so the stink of putrefaction and death hung over him like a dank miasma over a swamp.

His assistants dragged me on through this human abattoir where their colleagues were going about their grisly business. The screams of their victims echoed against the bare stone walls and blended with the cracking of the whips and the jovial laughter of these professional tormentors. The smell of fresh blood and human excrement was so overpowering that I found myself choking and gasping for breath.

Eventually we descended a narrow flight of stone steps to reach a tiny, windowless underground cell. It was lit by a single candle, but otherwise it was bare. There was just enough room for me to sit on the floor, if I kept my knees up under my chin. My captors shoved me into it.

"Your trial by Pharaoh is set for three days from today. We will come to fetch you for it. Otherwise we will not bother you again," Doog assured me.

"But I need food and fresh water to drink and wash myself," I protested. "And I will also need clean clothes to wear for my trial."

"Prisoners make their own arrangements for such luxuries. We are busy men. You cannot expect us to be bothered by such trifles." Doog sniggered as he blew out the candle flame and thrust the stump into a pocket of his cloak. Then he slammed the door to my cell, and I heard his keys rattle in the outside of the lock. Three more days without water in this airless and sultry stone cell would be bitterly hard to bear, and I was not certain that I could survive it.

"I will pay you." I heard my own voice rising with desperation as I shouted.

"You have nothing with which to pay me," Doog's voice carried back to me, even through the thick door, but then the footfalls of my captors receded into silence and my cell into utter darkness.

In particular circumstances I am able to weave a spell of protection over myself that serves me in the same fashion as does the cocoon of certain insects. I am able to retreat to a secure place deep within my own self. This is what I did now.

Early on the morning of the third day of my incarceration, Doog and his henchmen had great difficulty summoning me back from the distant place in my mind to which I had retreated. I could hear their voices faint and faraway, and gradually I became aware of their hands pummeling and shaking me, and their boots kicking me. But it was only when I felt the splash of a bucket of water thrown into my face that I recovered my full consciousness. I seized the bucket in both hands and poured what remained of the water down my throat and swallowed it, despite the efforts of three of the tormentors to rescue it from my clutches. That draft of filthy lukewarm water was my salvation; I could feel the power and energy flowing back into my parched body and the bastions of my soul being replenished. I was hardly aware of the lash of Doog's whip across my naked back as they hustled me up the staircase into the light and the sweet airs of day. Indeed, the noxious odors of that prison were like the nectar of roses compared to the cell from which I was being dragged.

They hauled me back to the Courtyard of Skulls where I found Captain Weneg waiting beside his chariot. After a single glance Weneg averted his shocked gaze from my battered face and my desiccated frame, and he busied himself in making his hieroglyph at the foot of the scroll that Doog demanded he sign for my release. Then his charioteers helped me aboard the vehicle. Although I tried not to show it, I was still weak and reeling on my feet.

As Weneg took up the reins and wheeled the chariot around to face the open gateway, Doog looked up at me with a grin and called out, "I look forward to your return to us, my lord. I have worked out a few new procedures especially for your execution. I am sure that you are going to find them diverting."

When we reached the stream at the bottom of the hills, Weneg reined in his horses and offered me his hand to help me alight from the chariot and he led me down the bank of the stream.

"I am sure you will want to refresh yourself, my lord." Unlike good Doog, Weneg used my title without even a touch of irony. "I have no idea what has become of your splendid uniform, but I have brought a fresh tunic for you. You cannot go into the presence of Pharaoh dressed as you are."

The water of the stream was sweet and cool. I purged myself of the dried blood and prison grime that coated me, and then I combed out my long dense hair of which I am so justly proud.

Of course Weneg must have been fully aware from previous experience what had happened to my helmet and gold chains once Doog laid eyes upon them, and so he had brought with him a plain blue charioteer's tunic to cover my nakedness. Strangely, this enhanced rather than detracted from my appearance, for it showed off my lean muscled torso to perfection. I did not have a bronze mirror with me, but my reflection in the waters of the stream gave me heart. Naturally I was not nearly at my best, but even with the facial bruising that Doog's men had inflicted on me, I could lift my chin high in the certain knowledge that very few could equal me for looks, even before the high court of Pharaoh.

Weneg had also brought food and drink for me: bread and cold fillets of river catfish from the Nile with a jug of small beer to wash it down. It was delicious and nourishing. I felt renewed strength coursing through my entire body. Then we mounted up and drove on to the palace of Pharaoh, which was situated in the innermost courtyard of the walled city of Luxor. My trial was scheduled by Pharaoh to start at midday, but we entered the great hall of the palace a good hour in advance of that time. We waited until the middle of the afternoon before Pharaoh and his train entered. It was at once apparent that they had all been drinking strong liquor, most especially Pharaoh. His face was flushed, his laughter was raucous and his gait was ungainly.

All of us who had been awaiting his arrival these past many hours now prostrated ourselves before him and pressed our foreheads to the marble floor. Pharaoh settled himself on the throne facing us, while his band of sycophants sprawled on each side of him, giggling and making arcane jokes that were amusing only to themselves.

While this was happening the ministers of state and the members of the royal family entered the great hall and took their seats on the line of lesser stone benches that had been arranged behind Pharaoh but facing me, the accused.

The most senior and important of these witnesses was the second-oldest son of Pharaoh Tamose, the next in line to the throne after his half brother Utteric Turo.

His name was Rameses. His mother was Pharaoh's first and favorite wife. Her name was Queen Masara, but she had borne him six daughters before she gave birth to a son. In the meanwhile another of Tamose's later and less beloved wives, a harridan named Saamorti, had deprived her by a mere matter of months of the honor of bearing the firstborn son, and the heir to the throne. This was Utteric Turo.

This audience maintained a dignified silence, which was in contrast to Utteric Turo and his minions, who went on chattering and hooting with laughter for some time longer. They completely ignored me and my escort, forcing us to suffer at Pharaoh's whim and pleasure.

Suddenly Pharaoh looked up at me for the first time and his voice cracked like a whip, sharply and viciously, "Why is this dangerous prisoner not manacled in my presence?"

Captain Weneg replied without raising his head and looking directly at Pharaoh, "Your Mighty Majesty . . ." I had never heard this obsequious term of address before, but I learned later that it was required terminology when addressing Utteric Turo, on pain of the royal wrath. ". . . I did not think to chain the prisoner as he has not yet been tried nor has he been found guilty of any crime."

"You did not *think*, fellow? Is that what I heard you to say? Of course you did not think. Thought presupposes a brain to think with." The toadies gathered at his feet giggled and clapped their hands at this royal sally, while two of Weneg's men hauled me into a sitting position and locked Doog's manacles back on my wrists. Weneg could not look me in the eyes for shame as they carried out Pharaoh's commands. When I was secured they pushed me facedown on the floor once more.

Suddenly Pharaoh Utteric Turo started up from his throne and paced up and down in front of me. I dared not raise my head, so I could not see him, but I could hear his sandals clacking on the marble. I could judge from their increasing tempo that he was lashing himself into a fury.

Abruptly he bellowed at me, "Look at me, you treacherous pig-swine!"

Immediately one of Weneg's men behind me grabbed a handful of my hair and hauled me backward into a sitting position and pointed my face toward Pharaoh.

"Look at that ugly, simpering and self-satisfied face! Tell me, if you dare, that is not guilt also written in gigantic hieroglyphs from ear to ear across it," he challenged everybody in the great hall. "I shall now relate to you the list of crimes against me and my family that this lump of excrement has committed. You will learn how richly he deserves the traitor's death that I have prepared for him." He was starting to tremble with the force of his anger as he pointed the forefinger of his right hand into my face. "His first victim that I know of for certain, although there were probably scores before her, was my paternal grandmother Queen Lostris."

"No! No! I loved Queen Lostris," I burst out in anguish, unable to contain myself at the mention of her name. "I loved her more than life itself."

"That is the probably the reason you murdered her. You could not have her so you killed her. You killed her and boasted of your foul deed in the scrolls you left in her royal tomb. Your actual written words, which I have seen with my own eyes, are: *I killed the evil thing of Seth that was growing in her womb.*"

I moaned at the memory of the growth that the foul god Seth had placed inside her body. In my medical tracts I have given it the name of "carcinoma." Yes, I plucked that monstrosity from her dead body, mourning the fact that all my skills as a physician were inadequate to save her from its onslaught. I cast it into the flames and burned it to ashes, before I began the mummification of her still beautiful remains.

However, I did not have the words to explain all this to her grandson. I am a poet who rejoices in words, but still I could not find the words to defend myself. I sobbed brokenly, but Pharaoh Utteric Turo continued remorselessly with his list of accusations against me. He smiled with his lips, but his eyes were like those of a standing cobra: filled with cold and bitter hatred. The venom he spat at me was every bit as noxious as that of the snake itself.

He related to the assembled noblemen and scions of royalty how I had stolen a vast fortune in gold and silver from the royal treasury that his father, Pharaoh Tamose, had placed in my trust. As proof of my treachery he cited the fabulous fortune in landed estates and treasure that I had accumulated over the years. He flourished a scroll and then read aloud from it. This purported to record all my embezzlements from the treasury. These amounted to well over a hundred million lakhs of silver; more silver than exists on all our earth.

The charges were so preposterous that I did not know where to begin my rebuttal. All I could think of in my defense was to deny the accusations and repeat over and over: "No! That's not the way it happened. Pharaoh Tamose was like a son to me, the only son I ever had. He gave all that to me to reward me for the services I carried out on his behalf over the fifty years of his life. I never stole anything from him, not gold or silver, not even a loaf of bread."

I might not have spoken, for Pharaoh went on listing the charges against me: "This assassin Taita used his knowledge of drugs and poisons to murder another precious royal woman. This time his victim was my own beautiful, gentle and dearly beloved mother, Queen Saamorti."

I gasped to hear that monstrous trollop so described. I had treated many of her slaves that she had personally emasculated or beaten half to death. She had delighted in mocking me cruelly over my damaged and mutilated manhood, bemoaning the fact that others had been ahead of her with the gelding knife. Her handmaidens had been gainfully employed in smuggling a seemingly endless train of male slaves into her elaborate sleeping quarters. The obscenities she practiced with these sorry creatures had probably resulted in the birth of the very person who stood before me now reading out my death warrant: His Mighty Majesty Pharaoh Utteric Turo.

One thing I knew with the utmost certainty was that the potions and medicines that I administered desperately to Queen Saamorti had not been sufficiently therapeutic to cure the filthy diseases that one or more of her myriad paramours had squirted into her lower bodily orifices. I wish her peace, although I am certain that the gods in their wisdom will deny it to her.

However, this was not the end of the horrific accusations that Pharaoh Utteric had to bring against me. The next was as far-fetched as all the previous charges lumped together.

"Then there was his flagrant treatment of two of my royal aunts, the Princesses Bekatha and Tehuti. It is true that my father managed to arrange a marriage for both of them with the most powerful and fabulously wealthy monarch in the world, the mighty Minos of Crete. Pharaoh, my father, sent these royal virgins in a caravan to their wedding with the Minos. Their retinue reflected our own wealth as a nation. It was several hundred persons strong. The treasure that was the dowry of my sisters was almost two hundred lakhs of fine silver bars. My father, Pharaoh Tamose, once again placed his trust in this sordid criminal and reprobate you see before you: Taita. He gave him command of the caravan. His assistants were two military officers named Captain Zaras and Colonel Hui. My information is that this creature, Taita, succeeded in reaching Crete and marrying my sisters to the Minos. However, in the eruption of Mount Cronus caused by the rage of the eponymous god Cronus, he who is the father of the god Zeus and has been chained for all eternity by his son in the depths of the mountain . . ."

Here Pharaoh paused briefly to catch his breath and then hurried on with his wild accusations: "The Minos was killed by the fall of rocks when the island of Crete was devastated by the eruption. In the ensuing chaos those two pirates, Zaras and Hui, abducted both my aunts. They then hijacked two of the vessels that belonged to my father's fleet and fled northward into the unexplored and savage archipelagos at the far end of the world. All this was against the will of my aunts, but with the connivance and encouragement of the accused scoundrel, Taita. When he returned to our very Egypt, Taita told Pharaoh that his sisters had been killed in the volcanic eruption, and Pharaoh called off the search for them. Taita must bear the full guilt for their abduction and the hardships they must certainly have suffered. That dastardly deed alone warrants the death sentence for its perpetrator."

Once again the only verdict I could truthfully plead was guilty: guilty of allowing the two young women I love more even than they love me the opportunity to find true fulfillment and happiness after they had done their duty to the utmost. But once again I could only gape at my accuser and maintain the silence that I had promised to Bekatha and Tehuti when I sent them to find happiness with the men they truly love.

Pharaoh turned away from me, drew himself to his full height and gazed upon the ranks of noblemen and princes, who were stunned into stillness and silence by his revelations and accusations. He regarded them one at a time, drawing out the suspense. Then at last he began to speak again. I expected no mercy from him, and he did not disappoint my expectations.

"I find the prisoner guilty of all the charges brought against him. He is to be deprived of all his assets, be they large or small, fixed or movable, situated any-where in the world. They are all forfeited to my trea-sury, nothing excepted."

A buzz ran through the ranks of his audience, and they exchanged envious glances, for they all knew what riches this short recital entailed. It was common knowl-edge that I was the richest man in Egypt after only Pharaoh. He let them discuss it between themselves for a short while before he held up one hand for silence, and they immediately froze. Even in my dreadful pre-dicament I was amazed at how terrified they all were of their new Pharaoh, but I was learning the wisdom of their fear.

Then Pharaoh giggled. This was the moment when

first I realized that Utteric Turo was raving mad, and that he placed neither restraint nor control on his own madness. That high-pitched giggle was a sound that could only be uttered by a lunatic. Then I remembered that his mother had also been mad—only her madness merely took the form of sexual incontinence. In Utteric Turo it took the form of total megalomania. He was unable to restrain any of his baser instincts or fantasies. He wished to be a god, so he declared himself one and believed that was all that was required for him to become one.

On this realization my heart went out to my fellow citizens of this, the greatest nation in the history of the world. They were only just beginning to realize what fate awaited them. I did not care about my own destiny for I knew that it was already fixed in the garbled mind of this madman. But I cared deeply for what was about to happen to my beloved Egypt.

Then Pharaoh began to speak again: "I am only mortified that death will come too quickly to this felon after all the suffering he has inflicted on my family. I would prefer to see him suffer to the limits of his evil soul for the airs and graces he has always affected, and for his pretense of wisdom and learning."

Here I managed to smile at how Utteric could not disguise his envy of my superior intellect. I saw the quick flush of anger that my smile evinced, but he went ranting on.

"I am aware that it is not adequate punishment; however, I decree that you shall be taken in your rags and chains from hence to the place of Torment and Sorrow. There you shall be given over to the tormentors who will . . ." Here he recited a list of atrocities so frightful that it left some of the gentler females in his audience pale with nausea and weeping with horror.

Finally Pharaoh turned back to me. "I am now prepared to listen to your expression of remorse and regret before I send you to face your destiny."

I rose to my feet, still manacled and half naked, and I spoke out clearly, for I had nothing more to lose. "Thank you, Your Mighty Majesty Pharaoh Utteric Turo. Now I understand why all your subjects, not excluding me, feel as they do toward you." I made no effort to disguise the sardonic tone of my voice.

The coward Utteric shot me a disgusted glance and waved me away. I was the only person in the great hall of Luxor still smiling. That smile of derision was the only rebuke that was in my power to inflict on the monster who now ruled Egypt.

As Pharaoh had decreed, Weneg and his platoon marched me out of the great hall of Luxor Palace, wearing only my loincloth and my chains. At the head of the great staircase I paused with astonishment and gazed down on the multitude that filled the open square at the foot of the steps. It seemed that every single citizen of our great city was assembled there, filling the square to overflowing. They stood in complete silence.

I could sense their hatred and enmity. Yet most of them had been my people. They or their fathers and grandfathers had fought with me in fifty battles. Those who had been crippled in the fighting I had taken in and succored on my estates, giving them shelter from the elements and at least one substantial meal a day.

Their widows also were certain of my bounty. I had given them useful employment and had schooled their offspring, equipping them for a place in this hard world. I realized that they had resented my charity and had come today to give free rein to their feelings.

"Why are they here?" I asked Weneg softly, barely moving my lips.

His reply was a whisper even softer than my question had been. "It is Pharaoh's command. They are here to revile you as a traitor and splatter you with ordure."

"That is why he ordered my clothing to be taken from me." I had wondered why Pharaoh had so insisted on that. "He wants me to feel the filth against my skin. You had best not follow me too closely."

"I will be one pace behind you. What is good enough for you, Taita, is good enough for me."

"You give me too much respect, good Weneg," I protested. Then I braced myself and started down the stairs toward the sea of angry humanity. I could hear the footsteps of my guards pressing close behind me, willing to share my ordeal. I did not hurry or slink, but walked calmly with my shoulders back and my head held high. I searched the faces of that mighty crowd awaiting me, looking for their expressions of hatred, waiting for the storm of their abuse to break over me.

Then, as the faces of the front rank of the dense

throng came into clearer focus, I felt suddenly confused. Many of the women were weeping. That I had not expected. The men looked grim and—dare I even think it?—as sorrowful as the mourners at a funeral.

Suddenly a woman broke through the line of armed guards, ostentatiously placed there to keep the crowds under control. The woman stopped a few paces from me and threw something at me. It fell at my feet, and I stooped and picked it up from the stone slabs between my manacled hands.

It was not a ball of excrement as Pharaoh had decreed, but a lovely blue water lily from the Nile waters. This was the traditional offering to the god Horus, a token of love and deep respect.

Two of the guards broke from the ranks behind the woman and took her by the arms to restrain her, but they were not angry; their manner was gentle and their expressions sorrowful.

"Taita!" the woman called to me. "We love you."

Then a second voice shouted from the mass of humanity behind her, "Taita!," and then another called, "Taita!" And suddenly a thousand and then two thousand voices were crying my name.

"We must hurry to get you beyond the city walls," Weneg shouted in my ear, "before Pharaoh realizes what is happening and descends upon us in his wrath."

"But even I don't understand what is happening," I yelled back at him. He gave me no answer, but instead grabbed my upper arm. One of his men got a firm grip on my other arm. They almost lifted me off my feet as they ran with me down the open pathway, which was shrinking as the crowds surged forward to try to touch or embrace me; I was uncertain which it would be.

At the end of the alley four of Weneg's men were holding the chariots. We reached them just before the crowds overwhelmed us. The horses were panicked by the uproar, but as soon as we were aboard the charioteers gave them their heads. They galloped in single file down the cobbled streets, headed for the main gates of the city. Soon we had left the massed humanity behind us. The gates were already closing when we came in sight of them, but Weneg cracked his whip over the backs of his team and urged them through the narrow gap and out into the open countryside.

"Where are we heading?" I blurted, but Weneg ignored my question and handed the key of my manacles to his archer who stood close behind me, steadying me in the lurching cockpit of the chariot.

"Get those things off his wrists, and then cover the magus's nudity." The captain did not reply to my question but looked smug and mysterious.

"What do you intend to use to cover me?" I demanded, glancing down at my naked body. Again he ignored my question, but his archer handed me a sparse bundle of clothing from the bin in the coachwork of the chariot.

"I never knew you were so famous," the archer said as I pulled a green tunic over my head. Annoyingly, it was the only one in the bag I had to choose from. Green is my least favored color; it clashes appallingly with the color of my eyes. "Did you hear them shouting for you?" the archer enthused. "I thought they were going to spurn you; but they loved you. All of Egypt loves you, Taita." He was beginning to embarrass me, so I turned back to Weneg.

"This is not the shortest road back to Doog at the Gates of Torment and Sorrow," I pointed out to him, and Weneg grinned at me.

"I am sorry to disappoint you, my lord. But it has been arranged for you to meet somebody other than the honorable Doog." Weneg whipped up the horses and turned them onto the paved road that led down to the harbor on the Nile. However, before we reached it, he again turned the heads of the horses, but this time onto a northerly track that ran parallel to the great river. We drove in silence for several leagues at a fast trot. I would not give Weneg the satisfaction and importance of questioning him further. I was not sulking—that is something that I never do—but I must confess that I was slightly irritated by his mysterious reticence.

I had glimpses of the river through the thick forest that grew along the bank, but I feigned indifference and looked away to the far hills on the eastern horizon. Then suddenly I heard Weneg grunt and exclaim, "Ah! There he is, right where he promised to be."

I turned, but in a leisurely and uninterested manner. But suddenly I sat bolt upright on the transom of the chariot, for there, only a hundred paces off the near bank of the Nile, was the flagship of our battle fleet, indubitably the finest and fastest trireme in existence. She could run down any other ship afloat and board her with a hundred fighting crew.

I was not able to remain sitting calmly. I scrambled to my feet, and before I could restrain myself I had blurted out, "By the brimming breasts and the unctuous slit of the great goddess Hathor! That ship is the *Memnon*!"

"By the prime prick and turbulent testicles of the great god Poseidon! I believe that you are right; for once at least, Taita," Weneg mimicked me.

I bridled for an instant and then, before I could prevent myself, I laughed and pounded him between the shoulder blades. "You should never have shown me such a beautiful ship. It will only serve to put a host of naughty ideas into my head."

"Which was fully my intention, I must confess." Weneg called to his team of grays, "Whoa now!" The magnificent animals nodded their heads and arched their necks to the drag of the reins, and the chariot came to a halt on the bank, looking out across the Nile toward the great warship.

The instant they recognized us on the bank, the crew of the *Memnon* sprang to the windlass on the foredeck and winched up the heavy copper cross-shaped anchor. Then under staysails and a flying jib, the warship sauntered in on the light westerly breeze toward the bank where we waited ecstatically to greet her.

My enthusiasm in particular was overwhelming, because I sensed that my salvation was at hand, and I was being spared another assignation with the dreaded Doog at the Gates of Torment and Sorrow.

"Memnon" was the baby name of my beloved Pharaoh Tamose, he who had so recently been laid low by the Hyksos arrow that his corpse had not yet completed the embalming process that would enable him to be laid to rest in his tomb, which stood ready to receive him in the Valley of the Kings on the westerly bank of the Nile. There he would lie with his ancestors through all eternity.

The *Memnon* was an enormous vessel. I know her specifications intimately because, after all, I was mainly responsible for her design. It is true that Pharaoh Tamose claimed full honors for that feat, but he is gone now and I am not so mean as to take the credit away from a dead man.

In length the hull of the *Memnon* exceeded a hundred cubits. She drew three cubits of water fully loaded. Her crew numbered 230. She shipped a total of fifty-six oars in three banks a side, as her designation of trireme suggests. The staggered lower rowing benches and the outriggers on the top tier of oars prevented the strokes of the oars interfering with one another. Her width was less than thirteen cubits, so she was lightning fast through the water and easy to beach. Her single mast could be lowered, but when raised it spread a massive square sail. She was quite simply the most beautifully designed fighting ship afloat.

As she came in to moor on the riverbank I noticed a tall mysterious figure in the stern. He was dressed in a long red robe and a hood of the same color that covered his face, except for the eye slits. It was apparent that he did not wish to be recognized, and as the crew made the ship fast, he went below without revealing his features or giving any other suggestion of his identity.

"Who is that?" I demanded of Weneg. "Is this who we have come to meet?"

He shook his head. "I cannot say. I will wait for you here ashore."

I did not hesitate but clambered up onto the *Memnon*'s bows and strode down the length of the upper deck until I reached the hatch down which the red-robed figure had disappeared. I stamped my foot on the deck, and immediately a deep but cultured voice replied. I did not recognize it.

"The hatch is open. Come down and close it behind you."

I followed these instructions and stooped into the cabin below. The headroom was minimal, for she was a fighting ship and not a pleasure cruiser. My red-robed host was already seated. He made no attempt to rise, but he indicated the narrow bench facing him.

"Please excuse my attire, but for reasons that will be immediately clear to you I need to keep my identity hidden from the common flock, at least for the immediate future. I knew you well when I was a child, but circumstances have kept us apart since then. On the other hand you were well acquainted with my father, who held you in the highest regard, and more recently my elder brother who is less enthusiastic . . ."

Before he finished speaking I knew beyond any doubt who it was that sat before me. I scrambled to my feet to accord him the respect that he so richly deserved, but in the process I cracked my head resoundingly on the beams of the upper deck above me. These were hewn from the finest Lebanese cedar, and my skull was no match for them. I collapsed again on my bench with both hands cradling my head and a thin trickle of blood running into my left eye.

My host leaped to his feet, but he had the good sense to remain crouching. He whipped the red hood off his own head and rolled it into a ball. Then he clapped it over my wound, pressing down hard to stem the flow of my life's blood.

"You are not the first to sustain the same injury," he assured me. "Painful but not fatal, I assure you, my Lord Taita." Now that his hood was adorning my scalp, rather than covering his features, I was able to confirm that this was indeed the Crown Prince Rameses who was tending my injury.

"Please, Your Royal Highness, it is merely a scratch, which I richly deserve for my clumsiness." I was embarrassed by his solicitude, but grateful for the opportunity to gather my wits again and reassess the prince at such close quarters.

His formal title was Lord High Admiral of the Fleet, and he was so assiduous in his duties that he very seldom made himself available for light socializing and mingling with any other than his own naval officers or, naturally enough, his father. Of course I had romped with him as a child and had told him fairy tales of noble princes saving lovely maidens from dragons and other monsters, but as he approached puberty we had drifted apart and Rameses had come totally under his own father's influence. Since then I had never again been familiar with him. So now I was surprised at how closely he resembled his father, Pharaoh Tamose. Of course, this resemblance reaffirmed the high regard in which I had always held him. If anything, he was even more handsome than his father. It gave me a twinge of conscience to even think this; however, it was the truth.

His jawline was stronger, and his teeth more even and white. He was a little taller than his father had been, but his waist was leaner, and his limbs more supple. His skin was a most remarkable shade of deep gold, reflecting his mother Queen Masara's Abyssinian ancestry. His eyes were a brighter and more lustrous shade of the same hue, and their gaze was piercing, but at the same time intelligent and kindly.

My heart went out to him once again, as though the intervening years had never existed. His next words confirmed my instincts: "We have many things in common, Taita. But at the moment the most pressing of them is my elder brother's baleful and implacable enmity. Pharaoh Utteric Turo will never rest until he sees both of us dead. Of course, you are already under sentence of death. But so am I, although not as openly but with equal or even greater relish and anticipation."

"Why?" I asked. "Why does your brother hate you?" The question came easily to my lips. I felt that with this man I was perfectly in accord. I had nothing to hide from him, nor had he anything to hide from me.

"It is simply because Pharaoh Tamose loved me and you more than he loved Utteric, his eldest son." He paused for a heartbeat, and then went on, "And also because my brother is mad. He is haunted by the ghosts and phantoms of his own twisted mind. He wishes to dispose of any person wiser and nobler than he is."

"You know of this for a certainty?" I asked, and he nodded.

"For a certainty, yes! I have my sources, Taita, as I know you do also. In secret and only to his sycophants, Utteric has boasted of his hostile intentions toward me."

"What are you going to do about it?" I asked, and his reply rang in my ears like my own voice speaking.

"I cannot bring myself to strike him down. My father loved him: that is enough to stay my hand. But neither am I going to let him murder me. I am leaving Egypt this very day." His tone was calm and reasonable. "Will you come with me, Taita?"

"I served your father with joy," I answered him. "I can do no less for you, my prince who should be Pharaoh." He came to me and clasped my right hand in a gesture of friendship and accord, and I went on speaking. "However, there are others who have put themselves at risk for my sake."

"Yes, I know who you mean," Rameses agreed. "Captain Weneg and his legionnaires are fine and loyal men. I have spoken with them already. They will throw in their lot with us."

I nodded. "Then I have no further quibble. Wherever you lead I will follow, my Lord Rameses." I knew very well where that was, better indeed than the prince himself. However, now was not yet the time to broach that subject.

The two of us went up on deck again, and I saw that on the bank Weneg and his men had already dismantled the chariots; as we watched, his men carried the parts over the gangplank and sent them down into the ship's hold. Then they swayed the horses aboard and sent them down below also. In under an hour the *Memnon* was ready to sail. We cast off from the bank and turned the bows into the north. With the wind in our sails, the river current pushing us and the treble banks of oars beating the Nile waters to foam, we headed northward toward the open sea and freedom from Pharaoh's malignant and pernicious thrall.

One of the few benefits of being a long liver is to be gifted with remarkable powers of healing and recuperation from injury. Almost within the hour the self-inflicted wound to my scalp stopped oozing blood and began to dry up and shrivel away, and before we reached the estuarine mouth of the Nile where it debouched into the great Middle Sea, the whip welts, bruises and other injuries inflicted upon me by the dreadful Doog and his minions had healed completely, leaving my skin smooth and glowing with health, like that of a young man again.

During the ensuing long days as we rowed northward down the river toward the sea, the prince and I had plenty of time to renew our acquaintance.

The next pressing decision we had to make was to decide our ultimate destination once we had left Egypt. It seemed that Rameses had conceived the horrifying notion of sailing out through the rocky Gates of Hathor at the end of the world—just to see what lay beyond them. I knew very well what lay beyond. The great nothingness lay beyond. If we were so ill-advised as to take that course, we would simply drop off the end of the world and fall in darkness through all eternity.

"How do you know that is what will happen to us?" Rameses demanded of me.

"Because nobody has ever returned from beyond the Gates," I explained quite reasonably.

"How do you know that?" he wanted to know.

"Name me one who has," I challenged him.

"Senebsen of Hispan."

"I have never heard of him. Who was he?"

"He was a great explorer. My great-grandfather met him."

"But did you ever meet him?"

"Of course not! He died long before I was born."

"So your great-grandfather told you about him?"

"Well, not really. You see, he also died before I was born. My own father told me the story of Senebsen."

"You know how much I respect the memory of your father; however, I never had the opportunity to discuss this Senebsen's travels with him. Moreover, I doubt I would have been sufficiently convinced by thirdhand accounts of what lies beyond the Gates to take the risk of traveling there myself."

Most fortuitously, I had a dream two nights later. I dreamed that the Princesses Bekatha and Tehuti together with all their multitudinous children had been captured by Farsian pirates and chained to a rock at the edge of the sea as an offering to appease the terrible sea monster that was known as the Tarquist. This creature has wings with which it is able to fly through the air like a great bird or swim through the sea like a mighty fish. It also has fifty mouths, which are insatiable for human flesh and with which it is able to destroy even the greatest ships ever built by men.

Naturally I was extremely reluctant to tell Rameses of my dream, but in the end I had to consider the solemn duty I had sworn to the royal house of Egypt. Of course, Rameses was fully aware of my reputation as a soothsayer and a reader of dreams. He listened quietly but seriously to my own interpretation of the dream, then without giving his own opinion he went to the bows of the ship where he sequestered himself for the remainder of the afternoon. He came back to me in the poop as the sun was setting and wasted no words.

"I charge you most strictly to tell me the truth about

what happened to my two aunts when they were sent by my father, Pharaoh Tamose, to the Empire of Crete to become the wives of the Great Minos, the King of Crete. I understood that they carried out their duty as my father decreed and they became the wives of the Minos, but then they were killed in the violent eruption of Mount Cronus. This is what my father told me. But then I was present when my brother Utteric accused you of treachery and false pretenses. He says that my aunts survived the volcanic eruptions that killed their husband, the Minos, but then they neglected their duty and rather than returning to Egypt, they eloped with those two rogues Zaras and Hui and disappeared. I discounted Utteric's accusations as the ravings of a lunatic, but now this dream of yours seems to endorse the notion that they are still alive." He broke off and regarded me with that piercing gaze of his. "Tell me the truth, Taita," he challenged me. "What really happened to my aunts?"

"There were circumstances," I said, hedging at the direct question.

"That is no answer," he chided me. "What do you mean by *There were circumstances.*"

"Please let me give you another example, Rameses."

He nodded. "I am listening."

"Suppose a prince of the royal house of Egypt becomes aware that his elder brother who is Pharaoh was intent on murdering him for no good reason, and he decided to flee his country rather than stay and be killed. Would you consider that to be dereliction of his duty?" I asked, and Rameses rocked back on his heels and stared at me in astonishment.

At last he shook his head as if to clear it, and then said softly, "You mean, would I count that as extenuating circumstances?"

"Would you?"

"I suppose I would," he admitted, and then he grinned. "I suppose I already have."

I seized upon his admission. "Very well. I will tell you about your two aunts. They were lovely girls, loyal and true as well as clever and very beautiful. Your father sent them to Crete as brides of the Minos. I was appointed their chaperone. They did their duty to your father and to Egypt. They married the Minos despite the fact they were in love with men of their own choice. Then the Minos was killed in the eruption of Mount Cronus and suddenly they were free. They eloped with the men they truly loved, and rather than discouraging them, I assisted them."

He stared at me in fascination as I went on, "You were correct in your suspicions. Both your aunts are still alive."

"How do you know that?" he demanded of me.

"Because, not more than a month ago, I discussed the subject with their husbands. I want you to come with me to visit them. You can travel incognito, as the captain of the *Memnon,* not as a prince of the royal house of Tamose. Then you will be in a position to judge them and compare their decision to disappear to your own decision to do exactly the same thing."

"What if I still think that my aunts reneged on their royal duty?"

"Then I will sail with you through the Gates of Hathor and jump with you over the edge of the world into eternity."

Rameses let out a shout of laughter, and when he regained his composure, he wiped the tears of merriment from his cheeks and asked, "Do you know where to find these two elusive ladies?"

"I do."

"Then show us the way," he invited me.

Two days later we reached the mouth of the Nile without further serious delays. The Hyksos fleet was destroyed, and there was no other ship afloat that dared challenge our right of way, for the *Memnon* ruled the river just as her namesake had ruled the land. The Middle Sea lay ahead of us. We passed out through the Phatnic mouth, the largest of the seven mouths of the River Nile, and my heart rejoiced within me to ride once more the waves of the greatest of all oceans.

I knew that on the northerly course we had to take we would be out of sight of the land for days and possibly even as long as a week at a time. At this season of the year the clouds would probably blot out the sun for days on end. Navigation was always a problem in these circumstances, so it was time to show Rameses my magic fish. This had been given to me many years ago by an African medicine man. I had saved his eldest son from death by snakebite and his gratitude had been fulsome.

This magic fish is carved out of a rare and weighty type of black stone found only in Ethiopia above the last Nile cataract. It is known to the tribesmen as the "going-home stone," for with it they are able to find their way home. There are many that disparage the wisdom of the black tribesmen, but I am not one of those.

My magic fish is about as long as my little finger but merely a sliver thick. When needed I glue it to a piece of wood carved to the shape of the hull of a boat. This miniature boat with the fish on board is floated in a round bowl of water. The bowl must also be made of wood and decorated with esoteric African designs in vivid colors. Now comes the magical part. The carved stone fish swims slowly but doggedly toward the northernmost point on the bowl's circumference, no matter in which direction the bows of the ship are pointed. On this leg of our voyage we had only to point the bows of the *Memnon* slightly to the left of the direction in which the nose of the fish was aiming. Night or day the magical fish is infallible. On our return journey we would simply point the *Memnon*'s nose in the reciprocal direction; that is always supposing that we would ever have call to return to Egypt.

Rameses scoffed at my little fish. "Can it also sing an ode to the gods, or fetch me a jug of good wine, or point the way to a pretty girl with a cunny that tastes sweet as honey?" he wanted to know. I was deaf to such unbecoming levity.

Our first night on the open sea the sky was obscured completely by cloud. There was no sun, moon or stars to guide us. We sailed all night in Stygian darkness with only the going-home stone to show us the way. Long before dawn the two of us went up on deck and sat over the wooden bowl, watching it in the feeble light of a sputtering oil lamp. Rameses passed the time by making more of his little jokes at my expense. He was mortified when the day broke and the clouds cleared to reveal that the *Memnon* and my little fish were holding the precise course slightly west of north.

"It really is magic," I heard him mutter to himself when this happened the third morning in succession. Then on the fourth morning, as the sun pushed its fiery head above the horizon, the blighted island of Crete lay not more than five leagues dead ahead of our bows.

Many years previously, when I first laid eyes on them, the mountains of Crete had been green and heavily forested. Great cities and ports had marked the island's shores as the most prosperous in the world. The waters around its coast had teemed with shipping: both men-of-war and cargo ships.

Now both forests and cities had gone, scorched to blackened ashes by the fiery breath of the great god Cronus, who in a fit of pique had destroyed the mountain wherein his own son Zeus had enchained him, blowing it apart in a fiery volcanic eruption. The remains of his singular mountain had sunk beneath the waters, leaving not a trace of its previous existence. We altered course and sailed in as close to the land as seemed safe, but I could recognize no features that had previously existed. Even after all these years, the air still reeked of sulfur and the odor of dead things, both animals and fishes. Or perhaps that was really only my vivid imagination and my keen sense of smell. In any event, the waters under our keel were devoid of life; the coral reefs had been killed off by the boiling sea. Even Rameses and his crew, who had never known this world, were subdued and appalled by such total destruction.

"This bears abundant testimony to the fact that all the strivings of man are trivial and insignificant in the face of the gods." Rameses spoke in a hushed voice. "Let us hurry away from this place and leave it to the apocalyptic anger of the god Cronus."

So I ordered the helmsman to put the rudder over and increase the beat. We bore away northward into the Grecian Sea, still sailing a few points west of true north.

For me these were unexplored waters into which we were sailing. Crete was as far north as I had ever ventured. Within a day we had passed out of the area laid waste by the volcano, and the sea resumed its friendly and welcoming aspect. Rameses had a quick and inquiring mind. He was eager to learn and I was pleased to accommodate him. He wanted particularly to know all I could tell him about his family history and origins, about which I knew a great deal. I had lived with four generations of Pharaohs at firsthand. I was pleased to be able to share my knowledge with him.

But we were not so involved with the history of Egypt that we neglected our duties as commanders of the finest warship afloat. The time that we spent in examining the past was as nothing compared to that we spent preparing for future contingencies. As befitted a ship of its class, the crew had all been handpicked by Rameses and were as fine a bunch of men as I had ever seen in action, but I have always believed in improving upon perfection if it is even remotely possible. Rameses drilled his men pitilessly, and I assisted him in keeping them up to the highest levels of training.

The very best military commanders have an instinct for danger and the presence of an enemy. By noon of the third morning after we had left the island of Crete behind us, I began to experience the familiar nameless unease. I spent much of my afternoon surreptitiously searching the horizon not only ahead of the ship but behind us as well. I knew from experience that it was dangerous to ignore these premonitions of mine. Then I saw that I was not alone in my unease. Rameses was becoming restless also, but he could not hide his concern as well as I was able to do so. He was of course much less experienced than I was. In the late afternoon, when the sun was only a hand's span above the western horizon, he laid his sword and helmet aside and clambered to the top of the mainmast. I watched him staring back over our wake for a while, and then I could contain myself no longer. I also divested myself of my weapons and half-armor and went to the foot of the mast. By this time the crew and especially those taking their turn at the long oars were watching me with interest. I climbed from the main deck to the crow's nest at the peak without pausing and Rameses made room for me, although it was a tight squeeze for the two of us in the bucket of the crow's nest. He said nothing but regarded me curiously for a while.

"Have you spotted him yet?" I broke the silence and he looked startled.

"Have I spotted whom?" he asked carefully.

"Whoever it is that is shadowing us," I replied, and he chuckled softly.

"So you have sensed them also. You are a sly old dog, Taita."

"I didn't get to be an old dog by being stupid, young man." I am sensitive to references to my age.

Rameses stopped laughing. "Who do you think it is?" he asked more soberly.

"This northern sea is the hunting ground of every pirate who ever cut a throat. How could even I pick out one of them?"

We watched the sun sink ponderously into the sea. However, the horizon behind us remained devoid of life, until suddenly we shouted together, "There he is!"

Just the instant before the sun was sucked under the waters, it shot a golden shaft of light over the darkling waves. We both knew that this was a reflection off the skysail of the ship that was stalking us.

"I think he's after our blood, otherwise why is he being so stealthy? He is expecting us to shorten sail or even heave to entirely at the setting of the sun, so he is conforming in order not to overrun us. He wants to creep up on us in the darkness without causing a collision," I conjectured. "So now we should plan a little surprise for him."

"What do you suggest, Taita? I am more accustomed to fighting other ships in the confines of the Nile, not out here in the open ocean. So I yield to your superior knowledge."

"I saw that you have a change of sail in the after-hold."

"Oh, you mean the black sail. It comes in handy for night work, when we don't want to be discovered by the enemy."

"That's exactly what we need right now," I told him.

We waited until the last glimmer of daylight faded into darkness. Then we altered course ninety degrees to port and sailed for what I judged to be roughly a mile. There we hove to and brought down our white sail and replaced it with the black one. This maneuver was complicated by the darkness, and it occupied us for longer than I had hoped. At last, under our midnight-black mainsail, we circled back onto our original course, which maneuver was made possible by my magic fish and an occasional flash of sheet lightning that lit the clouds briefly.

I was hoping that the other ship was following our original course and in the delay while we changed sail it had passed us and was now sailing along ahead of us, with every member of its crew staring fixedly over the bows. Obviously the captain of the pirate vessel would be piling on all his sail in order to overhaul us; so I ordered Rameses to do the same thing. The *Memnon* tore along through the darkness with spray coming in over the bows and pelting us like a hailstorm. Every member of our crew was fully armed and ready for a fight, but as time slipped by, I began to doubt even my own calculations of the relative positions of the two ships.

Then suddenly the pirate ship seemed to spring at us out of the night. I hardly had time to shout a warning to the helm and there she was dead ahead and broadside to us, lit up by another fleeting flash of lightning. It seemed that the pirate skipper had given up all hope of coming up astern of us. He had convinced himself that he sailed past us in the darkness, so now he was trying to come onto the opposite tack and beat back to seek us out. He was full in the path of the *Memnon* and lying like a log in the water. We were charging in on him at attack speed and our ax-sharp bows would have cleaved him through and through, but would themselves have been staved in by the ferocity of the impact.

It was a tribute to Rameses' maritime skill and the training of his crew that he was able to prevent a head-on collision that would have demolished both vessels and sent them and all of us to the bottom of the ocean. He managed to alter course just enough to present our broadside to that of the stationary ship. Nevertheless, the impact was sufficient to throw every member of the pirate crew to the deck, including the captain and the helmsman. They lay there in heaps, most of them hurt or stunned, and even the few of those who were able to regain their feet had lost their weapons and were in no condition to defend themselves.

Most of the crew of the *Memnon* had been given sufficient warning to be able to brace themselves and seize onto a handhold. The others were catapulted from the deck of the *Memnon* onto the deck of the pirate ship. I was one of these. I was unable to decelerate by my own endeavors, so I chose the softest obstacle in my path and steered myself into it. This happened to be the pirate captain in person. The two of us crashed to the deck in a heap, but with me on top, sitting astride the other man's torso. I had lost my sword in this abrupt change of ships so I was unable to kill him immediately, which was probably just as well, for he groaned pitifully and pushed the visor of his bronze helmet to the back of his head, and stared up at me. Just then another lightning flash lit the face of the man beneath me.

"In the name of Seth's reeking fundament, Admiral Hui, what are you doing here?" I demanded of him.

"I suspect it's exactly the same as what you are doing here, good Taita. Garnering a little spare silver to help feed the baby," he answered me hoarsely, trying to regain his breath and to struggle up into a sitting position. "Now, if only you would get off me I will give you a hug and offer you a bowl of good red Lacedaemon wine to celebrate our timely reunion."

It took some time to get both crews on their feet, to care for the more seriously wounded and then to get the pumps on the pirate ship manned and working to prevent her from sinking, for the damage she had sustained in the collision was much worse than ours.

Only then did I have an opportunity to introduce Rameses to Hui. I did not do so as the next in line to the throne of Egypt, but simply as a plain ship's captain. Then in turn I introduced Hui to Rameses, not as his uncle-in-law but as admiral of the Lacedaemon fleet and part-time buccaneer.

Despite the discrepancy in their ages, they took to each other almost immediately, and by the time we started on the second jug of red wine they were chatting like old shipmates.

It took the rest of that night and most of the following day to repair the damage to both ships, and for me to stitch up the gashes and splint the broken limbs of the casualties that both sides had suffered. When eventually we set sail for the port of Githion on the south coast of Lacedaemon, Hui led the *Memnon* in his flagship, which he had named, after his own wife, the *Bekatha*.

I left Rameses in command of the *Memnon* and I went aboard the *Bekatha* so I was able to explain to Hui in private the complicated circumstances of our sudden arrival. Hui listened to my explanation in silence, and only when I had finished did he chuckle with amusement.

"What do you find so funny?" I demanded.

"It could have been much worse."

"In what way, pray tell me? I am an outcast, denied entry to my homeland on pain of death, deprived of my estates and titles." It was the first time since being forced to fly from my very Egypt that I had the opportunity to bemoan my circumstances. I felt utterly wretched.

"At least you are a rich outcast, and still very much alive," Hui pointed out. "All thanks to King Hurotas."

It took me a moment to remember who that was. Sometimes I still thought of him as plain Zaras. However, Hui was right. Not only was I still a wealthy man, thanks to the treasure that Hurotas had in safekeeping for me, but I was also about to be reunited with my darling princesses after being parted from them for almost three decades.

Suddenly I felt rather jolly again.

The peaks of the Taygetus Mountains were the first glimpse of Lacedaemon that I ever laid my eyes upon. They were as sharp as the fangs of a dragon, steep as the gulf of Hades, and although it was early springtime, they were still decked with shining fields of ice and snow.

As we sailed in toward them they rose higher from the sea, and we saw their lower slopes were verdant with tall forests. Closer still the shores were revealed to us, fortified with cliffs of gray rock. The serried ranks of waves marched in upon them like legions of attacking warriors and one after the other spent their fury upon them in thunderous creaming surf.

We entered the mouth of a deep bay many leagues

wide. This was the Bay of Githion. Here the waves were more subdued and contained. We were able to approach the shore more closely. We sailed past the mouth of a wide river running down from the mountains.

"The Hurotas River," Hui told me. "Named after somebody with whom you are well acquainted."

"Where is his citadel?" I wanted to know.

"Almost four leagues inland," Hui answered. "We have deliberately concealed it from the sea to discourage unwelcome visitors."

"Then where is your fleet anchored? Surely it would be difficult to hide such an array of war galleys as I know that you possess?"

"Look around you, Taita," Hui suggested. "They are hidden in plain sight."

I have very sharp eyesight, but I was unable to pick out what Hui was challenging me to discover. This irritated me. I do not enjoy being ridiculed. He must have sensed it because he relented and gave me a hint.

"Look over there where the mountains run down to the sea." Then of course it all jumped into focus and I realized that what I had presumed to be a few dead trees scattered along the shoreline were rather too straight and lacking branches and foliage.

"Are those not the bare masts of a number of war

galleys? But they seem to be beached ashore, for I cannot make out their hulls."

"Excellent, Taita!" Hui applauded me generously, allaying my irritation with his childish guessing games. "The hulls of our galleys are hidden behind the seawall of the harbor we have built for them. Only a few of them have their masts still stepped. Most of them have lowered theirs, which makes them ever more difficult to detect."

"They are cunningly concealed," I conceded magnanimously.

We headed toward the hidden harbor with the *Memnon* following us. When we were as close as half a bowshot offshore, the entrance was abruptly revealed to us. It was doubled back upon itself to conceal it from seaward. As we entered it we lowered our own sails and plied the oars to carry us into the passage. We passed through the final bend, and the inner harbor was revealed to us with the entire Lacedaemon fleet tied up to their berths along the seawall. This concealed harbor was a hive of industry. On every ship men were busy preparing for sea: repairing sails and hulls or carrying aboard fresh supplies of food, equipment and weapons.

However, all this industry came to an abrupt hiatus as our two galleys came through the entrance. The *Memnon* caused a stir among the men ashore. I doubt they had ever seen anything like her afloat, but then something else happened to divert their attention from even such a magnificent sight as Rameses' flagship. The men switched their attention back to the leading trireme: Hui's *Bekatha*. They began pointing at our small group of officers on the poop deck. They started calling to one another and I heard my name—"Taita"— being bandied back and forth.

Of course most of them knew me well, not only as an erstwhile companion in arms and a person of exceptional and striking appearance but for another reason eminently more memorable to the common sailor or charioteer.

Before I had parted from them after the capture of the city of Memphis, the defeat of Khamudi and the annihilation of the Hyksos hordes, I had asked King Hurotas to distribute a small part of my share of the booty to his troops in recognition of the part they had played in the battle. This amounted to a mere lakh of silver out of the ten lakhs that were mine, the equivalent of approximately ten silver coins of five debens' weight for each man. Of course, this is a trifling amount for you and me, or any other nobleman, but for the common herd it is almost two years' salary; in other words, it is a veritable fortune. They remembered it and would probably continue to do so until their dying day.

"It is Lord Taita!" they called to one another, pointing me out.

"Taita! Taita!" Others took up the chant, and they swarmed down to the jetty to welcome me. They tried to touch me as I came ashore, and some of them even had the temerity to attempt to slap me on my back. I was nearly knocked off my feet a number of times until Hui and Rameses formed a bodyguard for me with twenty of their own men to protect my person. They hustled me through the hubbub to where horses were waiting to carry us up the valley to the site where King Hurotas and Queen Sparta were building their citadel.

Once we left the coast the countryside became lovelier with every league we traveled. The constant backdrop of the snow-clad mountains was always in full sight to remind us of the winter just past. The meadows beneath them were a luscious green, waist deep in fresh grass and myriad gorgeous flowers nodding their heads to the light breeze bustling down from the Taygetus heights. For a while we rode along the bank of the Hurotas River. Its waters were still swollen by the snow-melt, but clear enough to make out the shapes of the large fish lying deep and nose-on to the current. There were half-naked men and women wading chest deep in the icy waters, dragging long loops of woven netting between them, sweeping up these fish and piling them in glittering heaps upon the bank. Hui stopped for a few minutes to bargain for fifty of the largest of these delicious creatures and have them delivered to the kitchens of the royal citadel.

Apart from these river denizens, there were small boys along the roadside selling bunches of pigeon and partridges that they had trapped, and stalls at which were displayed the carcasses of wild oxen and deer. There were herds of domesticated animals at pasture in the fields: cattle and goats, sheep and horses. All these were in good condition, plump and sturdy with glossy coats. The men and women working the fields were mostly very young or very old, but all of them seemed equally contented. They shouted cheery greetings to us as we passed.

Only once we approached the citadel did the aspect of the population begin to change. They were younger, most of them of military age. They were living in well-built and expansive barracks and engaged in training and exercising battle tactics. Their chariots, armor and weapons seemed to be of the best and most modern type, including the recurved bow and the light but sturdy chariots each drawn by a team of four horses.

We paused more than once to watch them at their drill, and it was immediately apparent that these were first-rate battle-ready troops, at the peak of their training. This was only to be expected with Hurotas and Hui as their commanding officers.

We had been climbing gradually ever since we left the coast. Finally after a ride of four leagues, we topped another wooded rise and paused again, this time in amazement, as the citadel was laid out before us in the center of a wide basin of open ground surrounded by the high ramparts of the mountains.

The Hurotas River ran through the middle of this basin. But it was split into two strong streams of fast-running water, in the center of which rose the citadel. The river formed a natural moat around it. Then the streams were reunited on the lower side to continue their course to the sea at the port of Githion.

The citadel was formed by an upthrust of volcanic rock from the earth's center. When after the passage of many centuries the denizens of the citadel grew disenchanted with it and abandoned it, it was then appropriated by the savage and primitive tribe of the Neglints who lived in the Taygetus Mountains. In their turn the Neglints were defeated and enslaved more recently by King Hurotas and Admiral Hui.

Hurotas and Hui had used the newly captured slaves to strengthen the fortifications of the citadel until they were nigh on impregnable, and the interior was not only commodious but also extremely comfortable. Hurotas was determined to make this the capital city of his new nation.

I wasted very little time examining the citadel from afar and listening to Hui reciting its history. A first-rate admiral he may very well be, but as a raconteur he makes a fine pedant. I shook up my steed and gave him a touch of my spurs, leading the party at a gallop down into the bowl and on toward the citadel. When I was still some distance off, I saw the drawbridge being lowered and no sooner than it had touched the near bank but two riders came across it at full pelt, their faint squeals of excitement and high-pitched cries of joy increasing in volume as they approached.

I recognized the leading rider at once. Tehuti led the way as she has always done. Her hair flew out like a flag in the wind behind her. When last I had seen her, it was a lovely russet color, but now it was pure white and glistening in the sunlight like the snowy peaks of the Taygetus Mountains behind her. But even at this distance I could see she was as slim as the young girl I remembered so lovingly.

She was followed at a much more sedate pace by an older and larger lady whom I was certain I had never previously laid eyes on.

Tehuti and I came together still shouting endearments at each other. We both dismounted while our mounts were at almost full gallop and maintained our footing when we hit the ground, but used our residual impetus to come together in a ferocious embrace.

Tehuti was laughing and weeping simultaneously. "Where have you been hiding all these years, you naughty man? I thought I would never see you again!" Tears of joy streamed down her cheeks and dripped from the tip of her chin.

My face was wet also. Of course the moisture was not my own. I had received it secondhand from the woman I was hugging. There was so much I wanted to say to her, but the words jammed in my throat. I could only clasp her to my bosom and pray for us never to be parted again.

Then her companion trotted up to where we were involved. She dismounted carefully, and then she came to where we stood with both her arms extended.

"Taita! I have missed you so bitterly. I thank Hathor and all the other gods and goddesses that they have allowed you to return to us," she said in that lovely musical voice which had come down unaltered through all the years, and which I remembered with sudden guilty delight.

"Bekatha!" I cried instead and rushed to seize her in my embrace. But I kept Tehuti firmly in the circle of my other arm as I hugged her little sister, who no longer merited that diminutive adjective.

The three of us clung together sobbing and gabbling joyous nonsense at each other, thereby trying to expunge the memory of all the years that we had been separated.

Suddenly Tehuti, who had always been the more observant of the two, said, "It really is uncanny, Tata, my lovely old darling, but you have not changed an iota since I waved good-bye to you all those years ago. If anything, you seem to have grown younger and more beautiful."

Of course I made dissenting noises, but Tehuti has always had the knack of choosing the most appropriate description of any subject.

"Both of you are far more lovely than ever I remember you," I countered. "You must know that I have recently heard much about you from your doting husbands, but that was only sufficient to whet my appetite rather than assuage it. I have met all four of your sons, Bekatha, when they came to Egypt to help free the homeland from the Hyksos domination. But it was only a brief meeting, and now I want to learn everything about them from you." For any mother her whelps are the most fascinating objects in creation, and so Bekatha regaled us all the way back to the citadel with a minute account of the virtues of her four sons.

"They are not quite as perfect as my sister paints them." Tehuti gave me a surreptitious wink. "But then no man alive is."

"That's pure jealousy," Bekatha interjected complacently. "You see, my poor sister has only one child, and that is a girl." Tehuti took the gibe with equanimity. Obviously it had grown stale with overusage.

Despite her silver mane of hair, or probably because of it, Tehuti was still a magnificent-looking woman. Her countenance was unlined by time or the elements. Her limbs were lean but elegantly sculpted from hard muscle. Her raiment was not festooned with ribbons and flowers and feminine frippery; instead she wore a military officer's dress tunic. She moved with feminine grace and elegance, but also with masculine power and purpose. She laughed easily but not loudly or without ample reason. Her teeth were white and even. Her gaze was deep and searching. She smelled like a fruiting apple tree. And I loved her.

When I turned back to Bekatha, I saw she was the diametric opposite to her elder sister. If Tehuti was Athena the goddess of war, then Bekatha was the earth goddess Gaia personified. She was plump and rosy. Even her face was rounded like the full moon, but more highly colored, pink and glossy. She laughed often and loudly, for no good reason other than the joy of life itself. I remembered her as a pretty little slip of a girl just coming into puberty, half the size of Hui her husband. But now that she had grown large with repeated childbirth, he still adored her, and I soon discovered that I did also.

The three of us rode well ahead of the rest of the party. Hui and Rameses hung back tactfully to let the two sisters and me resume our very singular relationship. There was so much for us to recall and delight in that the time was not enough before we found ourselves in front of the main gates of the citadel of Sparta, the Loveliest One.

Although an army of slaves had been laboring upon it for many decades, it was not yet completed, but I judged that its mighty walls and systems of moats and fortifications would be able to repel the greatest and most determined army of any potential enemy of which I was aware. I reined in my horse in order to admire it in detail, and while I was doing so Hui and Rameses rode up to join us.

Both Tehuti and Bekatha immediately transferred their attention from me to Rameses. I did not resent this. They had given me more than my full share, and Rameses was truly a striking-looking man. In all fairness I knew of no other to match him; well, perhaps that is not strictly correct but modesty precludes me from further comparisons. So I retired gracefully into the background.

"And who might you be, young sir?" Bekatha was never one to hang back. She studied Rameses boldly.

"I am not anybody of particular account, Your Royal Highness." Rameses dismissed her query with a modest smile. "I am merely the captain of the ship that brought Lord Taita to visit you on your lovely island. I am named Captain Rammy." He and I had agreed not to prattle about his close links to the throne of Egypt. We were both fully aware that Pharaoh Utteric Turo the Great had his spies in high and unlikely places.

Tehuti was studying Rameses with an intensity that was much more telling than her little sister's eager prattle.

"You are a member of the Egyptian royalty." When she spoke, Tehuti made it sound like an accusation and a challenge.

"How did you know that, Your Majesty?" Rameses was nonplussed.

"When you speak, your accent is unmistakable." Tehuti went on studying his face a few moments longer, and then she said with certainty, "You remind me of somebody I knew well but whom I have not seen in many a long year. Let me think!" Then her expression changed again, becoming more eager and fascinated. "You remind me of my brother, Pharaoh Tamose—" She broke off and stared at her reluctant relative. "Rammy! Yes, of course! You are my nephew Rameses." She turned away from him and focused her disapproval on me, but her censure was alleviated by the sparkle of happiness in her eyes and the barely suppressed laughter on her lips. "You naughty, naughty man, Tata! Whatever gave you the notion of trying to dupe me? As if I would not have known my own flesh and blood. I taught this little hellion his first swear words. Don't you remember, Rameses?"

"Shit and corruption! And bugger me sideways! I remember them so well." Rameses merged his laughter with hers. "I was only about three or four years old at the time and you were an old lady of sixteen or seventeen, but I will never forget those sweet words of wisdom."

Tehuti leaped from the back of her mount and spread her arms wide in invitation. "Come and give your old auntie a kiss, you horrid child!"

I watched the two of them embrace with pleasure; and this was not solely because I was no longer obliged to leap from the end of the earth into eternity to make good my pledge to Rameses. It took some time for the greeting ceremony to run its course because naturally Bekatha felt obliged to add her considerable weight to the occasion, but finally we were free to mount up again and continue on our way to the citadel. The two sisters rode within touching distance of Rameses, one on each side of him.

The gates were thrown wide open as we approached the citadel, and King Hurotas scrambled down the scaffolding that still covered part of the new fortifications and on which he had been directing the builders. In appearance he seemed more like a workman himself than a king, covered as he was by dust and grime. Of course he had recognized me from afar. I am not a person who is easy to overlook, even in a crowd. And then he had been intrigued to see his own wife and her sister clinging adoringly to the young stranger who rode between them.

"This is my nephew Rameses!" Tehuti yelled at her husband when they were still separated by fifty paces.

"He is our brother Tamose's second-eldest son," Bekatha endorsed the relationship. She was making absolutely certain there was no misunderstanding as to what was meant by the word *nephew*. "And he is next in line to the throne of Egypt after you and Taita have ridded the world of Utteric." I was a little taken aback at her assumption of our future role as kingmakers.

However, Hurotas was obviously inured to her flights of fantasy. He came on readily to embrace Rameses and transfer to his admiral's uniform a liberal portion of the builder's muck that covered his royal personage.

At last he drew back and announced every bit as loudly as Bekatha had done, "This calls for a celebration to welcome Prince Rameses. Tell the chefs that I am hosting a banquet this evening, with the best wine and good food for everybody."

That evening the inner courtyard of the citadel was lit by a dozen large bonfires and trestle tables sufficient to seat several hundred of the most important nobles of Lacedaemon. The king and his immediate family sat in the center of a raised dais where they were visible to all the lesser creatures in creation. Of course I sat between my two former charges, Tehuti and Bekatha. Directly below us were seated the sons of Bekatha and Hui. These were the four splendid young men who had accompanied their father to Egypt on the campaign to rid the world of King Khamudi. Although I had met them only briefly at that time, I am an infallible judge of humanity. I knew that Bekatha had bred true to her line of Pharaohs and that her sons were choice specimens of the Egyptian nobility. Two of her boys were already married and their pretty little wives sat with them. They were all close in age to Rameses, and they were treating him like the honored guest he so clearly was. I expressed my approval of them to Bekatha, their mother, and she took it as nothing more than their due.

"In fact, I had hoped that one of my boys would marry their cousin, Serrena," she confided in me. I was by this time aware that Serrena was the name of Tehuti's mysterious and elusive daughter, whose empty chair awaited her arrival to sit beside her father, King Hurotas, at the head of the festive table. Bekatha went on speaking with barely a pause for breath: "All four of them pressed their suits to her, one after the other. But she turned them down prettily with the excuse that she could not marry someone with whom she had bathed naked as a child and had discussed their differing genital structures while sharing the same piss pot. I wonder what excuse she had for the hundred and one other suitors who have come in a constant stream from the ends of the earth to ask for her hand in marriage."

"I look forward to meeting her. I gather that she is a very handsome young lady," I acknowledged, and Bekatha went on enlarging on the subject.

"Everybody and their uncles say that she is the most

beautiful girl in creation, a fitting rival to the goddess
Aphrodite; but I cannot see it myself. Anyway, Serrena
is so fussy in her choice of a husband that she will most
probably die an old spinster." Bekatha shot a teasing
glance at her sister on the other side of me. Tehuti had
followed our conversation, but she did not deign to
reply and merely stuck out the tip of her pink tongue in
Bekatha's direction.

"Where is this paragon of feminine pulchritude?" I
demanded. None of this was news to me, but I thought
it best to divert the two of them from their discussion
before it boiled over from fun into fury. "Will she be
joining us this evening?"

"Do you see an empty stool anywhere in the courtyard?" Bekatha asked, and she looked pointedly in the
direction of King Hurotas who was sitting across the
table from us. The seat at his left hand was the only one
in the packed courtyard that was presently unoccu-
pied. Bekatha grinned and answered her own question
before her elder sister could reply, "Princess Serrena of
Sparta marches to the beat of her own drum, which she
alone can hear."

She said it in a jocular tone, almost as though she
meant it as a compliment rather than an accusation.
But King Hurotas, who had been following the conversation, leaned forward quickly and intervened: "When

a beautiful woman is only an hour late, it is because she is making a particular effort to be on time."

Bekatha subsided immediately, and I realized who truly ruled this kingdom and where his devotions lay. There was an almost immediate lull in the clamor of festivities, and I thought for an instant that the rest of the company was reacting to the king's rebuke, but then I realized that very few of them could have over-heard it, and that they were paying no heed to Hurotas or anyone else in the courtyard. Instead every head was turning toward the main doors opening out into the courtyard from the citadel.

Through them walked a young woman. This is an inaccurate description of her entrance into my life, and that of Rameses. Princess Serrena did not walk; she glided without appearing to move any part of her body, for the long skirts she wore screened her legs and lower parts from her hips downward. Her hair was piled high on her head, a crown of dense shimmering gold. The lightly suntanned skin of her arms and shoulders was as unblemished and glossy as polished marble or freshly woven silk. She was tall, but her body was perfectly proportioned.

She was not pretty, because that adjective suggests a simpering vacuity. She was simply magnificent. Every facet of her face was perfection. When taken together,

her features exceed my powers of description. As she moved they changed subtly, perfection surpassing perfection. She captivated every person who looked upon her. However, her single most striking feature—if it were possible to distinguish it—was her eyes. These were enormous but in perfect harmony with the rest of her face. They were a particular shade of green that was brighter than any emerald. They were also piercing and perceptive, but at the same time clement and forgiving.

There were only two other women I have known who came even close to her in beauty. One was Queen Lostris, she who had been my first love. Then there was the woman who sat beside me at this moment: Queen Tehuti, who had been and was still my second love. They were the mother and the grandmother of this young woman.

However, Princess Serrena was far and away the loveliest person, living or dead, whom I had ever laid my eyes upon.

She picked out her mother sitting beside me and she turned toward us with her smile blossoming. Then at the far end of the table Rameses came to his feet, and this movement switched Serrena's attention to him. The smile on Serrena's face faded to an expression of awe. She froze with one foot raised, the toe of a dainty slipper peeping from under her skirts. The splendid couple stared at each other for a long moment during which nobody else existed in the world for either of them. Eventually Serrena lowered her foot to the ground. But her eyes were still locked to his. Then she blushed softly, a rosy glow that lit her face and, impossibly, made it even more beautiful than it already was.

"Are you not my cousin Rameses? My mother told me you had come to visit us," she asked in a gorgeous lilting voice that was only slightly breathless. It carried clearly to every corner of the silent courtyard. There was a light in her eyes that reminded me sharply of the way that Tehuti had looked at Zaras on their first meeting almost thirty years previously. Rameses bowed deeply but speechlessly to her question, never taking his eyes from her ineffably lovely features.

Tehuti was sitting close to me, but nobody in the citadel courtyard was watching us as she reached out surreptitiously beneath the tabletop and squeezed my fingers. "Yes!" she whispered softly but vehemently, and again, "Yes!"

She had recognized from her own experience that enchanted moment when her daughter had, at the advanced age of twenty years, found her soul mate.

The days and weeks and months that followed were some of the happiest that I can ever remember.

The first delight for me was when King Hurotas and his queen invited me as their guest to visit the newly dug treasure chambers in the depths of the citadel dungeons. We climbed down many successive flights of stone steps with ten heavily armed guards preceding us and another ten following us. Every one of them was holding aloft a burning torch to light our way. When we reached the bottom of the deepest flight, Hurotas used a heavy bronze key to unlock the massive door that confronted us. Then three of the guards strained to swing it open.

I followed the king through into the royal treasure

chamber and looked around me eagerly. Although not a word had been said about the purpose of this expedition to the depths of the earth, I thought I knew what to expect. Both Hurotas and Tehuti were watching me with eyes that sparkled with anticipation. Almost at once I spotted what I was searching for. There were almost two dozen large cedarwood chests stacked head high in a corner of the wall of heavy granite blocks. Although I am usually able to restrain myself from abandoned behavior, on this occasion I made an exception and I let out a shout of excitement. Then I rushed across the room and tried to lift down one of the chests from the stack. I was unsuccessful. I required three of the guards to assist me before we could set it down on the flooring slabs. Then they levered the lid open with their sword blades and stepped back.

I am not an avaricious man. But you must remember that very recently I had been deprived by Pharaoh Utteric Turo of every cubit of land and every deben of silver that I had ever owned. When you possess a lakh of silver, you hardly ever think about it. When the amount is reduced to a single deben, you can hardly ever think of anything else.

"I thought I should never again look upon such a glorious sight." I spoke aloud to no one in particular as I squinted my eyes against the reflection of the torch flames off the blocks of closely packed precious metals, both silver and gold. Then I wiped the tears from my cheeks with the palm of my hand and turned back to King Hurotas. I went to him and knelt at his feet. "Thank you, Your Majesty," I whispered and bowed forward to kiss his feet. But he was too quick for me, and with a hand on each of my shoulders, he lifted me up and gazed into my eyes.

"What is a single kindness when weighed against the hundreds you have shown me and Tehuti?" he asked.

It took me, with a dozen slaves to assist me, the next three days to unpack, weigh, and then repack this plethora of riches. Tehuti made a rapid calculation that this should be sufficient to sustain me in opulence for unnumbered years.

"Always provided you can live that long," she qualified her estimate.

"That offers no real challenge," I assured her, "but it's the second five hundred years that gives me pause."

Hui's four sons formed a close family alliance. However, by reason of her superior age, beauty, enchanting personality, and the special favor of her father the king, Serrena was the undisputed leader of the pack. She could dance like a whirlwind and ride like a fury. She could play every musical instrument known to mankind and sing like the sirens that lure seamen onto the rocks with the sweet sound of their voices. But her voice was joyful and not doom laden.

She could riddle and rhyme and make others laugh with just a smile or one kind word.

Rich and powerful men came from all the ends of the earth to seek her hand in marriage, but she turned them away so gracefully and sweetly that not a single heart was broken, and they departed as happily as if she had done them the greatest favor.

Like her mother she was a formidable archer and an exponent of all the edged weapons. She was the only one who was permitted by Tehuti to handle the blue sword with the ruby pommel. This was an almost mythical weapon, with a highly convoluted provenance. I had first seen it many years before when it belonged to Lord Tanus, who had been the faithful but clandestine lover of Queen Lostris for most of her life. On his deathbed, he bequeathed the sword to Prince Memnon, who was Lostris' son. He was also the son of Tanus, although I was the only person who was aware of this fact apart from both the parents. When Lostris passed away, Memnon succeeded her to the throne of Pharaoh and became Pharaoh Tamose in his turn. He was the elder brother of my darlings Tehuti and Bekatha, and thus the grandfather of Serrena herself.

It was Tamose who, with some assistance from me, negotiated the marriage of his two sisters to the mighty Minos of Crete. As a wedding gift Pharaoh gave the blue sword with the ruby pommel to his elder sister, Tehuti. When the Minos and his island kingdom were almost totally destroyed in that massive volcanic eruption, the two widowed sisters eloped with their lovers, Hui and Zaras, and sailed away into the north to build a kingdom of their own here in Lacedaemon. Of course I assisted the two sisters to elope with their lovers, rather than return to Egypt. And of course the fabulous sword went with Tehuti.

As a passionately dedicated swordswoman, Tehuti was enchanted by the blue sword. There was no other blade like it in existence, and in her hands it became the ultimate weapon. It was probably the only gift that might have compensated her for her exile to Crete.

Tehuti allowed no one else to touch the enchanted blue blade, not even King Hurotas, her husband. Tehuti alone washed her enemy's clotted blood from the gleaming cerulean metal. Tehuti was the only one who polished and honed the cutting edges of the weapon to deadly perfection, becoming an expert metalworker in the process.

However, this day on the bank of the Hurotas River was one of rare magic. It was the day that Princess Serrena turned fourteen years of age, the day she was transformed from a girl into a woman. No gift was too extravagant for her to receive.

Of course, I was not with them in person on that day. Tehuti related the following incident to me only after I arrived with Rameses in Lacedaemon, by which time Serrena had reached the age of twenty years.

As was their custom and pleasure, the two of them,

mother and daughter, had ridden to their secret pool in the Hurotas River upstream from the citadel. They handed over their mounts to the grooms before they reached it and ran holding hands the last hundred cubits to the royal lodge built on the riverbank below the waterfall. The grooms and servants knew better than to follow them. They would wait with the horses until the two royal women returned.

Tehuti wore the blue sword on her hip, but that was unremarkable, for she wore it more often than not. Their servants and slaves had visited the lodge earlier in the morning and cleaned it immaculately. They had placed fresh flowers in the enormous copper vases, so that the main room overlooking the pool was transformed into a garden of delight. They had covered the couches with tanned elk skins and silken pillows. They had lit the fire on the hearth in the center of the floor, for winter was still lingering. Then they laid out a sumptuous meal that would have fed ten hungry men, knowing full well that what was left over would be passed on to them.

Tehuti and Serrena began stripping off their clothing almost as soon as they entered this sanctuary. Tehuti unbuckled the blue sword from around her waist and laid it reverently on the table in the center of the room facing the fireplace. They tossed the rest of their clothing onto the elk-skin-covered cushions. Then, stark naked and holding hands once again, they left the lodge and ran down to the riverbank. They plunged into the limpid waters, kicking up a cloud of flying spray. They squealed at the shock of the cold, for there were great lumps of ice washed down from the mountains floating on the surface of the river. They splashed each other with handfuls of river water until Tehuti broke away and tried to escape further punishment. Serrena chased her mother, and when she caught her, she dragged her under the tumbling water of the falls and held her there until she pleaded for mercy. Strong as she was, Tehuti had to exert herself to the utmost to match her daughter. It seemed that Serrena's body was carved not from human flesh and bone, but from some divine substance as adamantine as the blue metal of the fabulous sword.

But neither of these two magnificent women were proof to the cold of mountain ice melt. When they waded to the bank, waist deep and locked in each other's arms, they were shivering as uncontrollably as victims of the ague. Their buttocks and bellies were glowing bright pink with the cold. In the lodge they threw logs of wood on the dying coals in the hearth, and when these burst into flames they stood almost close enough to scald themselves, scrubbing each other with the dry towels the servants had laid out for them.

When they had warmed sufficiently to control their shivering, Tehuti placed a large jug of red wine on the coals, and as it began to bubble she threw a double handful of dried herbs into the brew and stirred it vigorously. When they were warm and dry, they donned their clothing and reclined side by side on the couch in front of the fire. They passed the steaming jug back and forth between them, delighting in the comfort of the mulled wine and each other's company.

Tehuti had placed the blue sword still in its jeweled scabbard across her lap. She leaned closer to her daughter and with her free arm hugged her around the shoulders. Serrena reciprocated by kissing her mother's cheek and whispering to her, "Thank you for this wondrous day, my beloved mother. You make me the happiest girl in the world."

"You are no longer a girl, my darling. You are a woman grown so lovely as to surpass the telling of it. But your birthday has not yet passed. I have one more gift for you."

"You have already given me far more than enough . . ." Serrena started and then broke off and stared at her mother speechlessly. Tehuti had lifted the blue sword from her own lap and laid it across her daughter's. Then she took Serrena's hand and folded her fingers around the jeweled hilt.

"This is my gift to you, Serrena," she said. "Use it only wisely and with care, but when you must, do not hesitate but strike to the heart of your enemy."

"It is too much." Serrena placed both her hands behind her back and shook her head, staring down at the weapon lying in her lap. "I know how much it means to you. I cannot accept it."

"But I have given it to you with my love, so I cannot take one back without taking back the other also," Tehuti told her.

Serrena tore her eyes away from the sword and stared at her mother's face as she grappled with this conundrum. It was a play on words and something that both of them enjoyed; then she beamed as the solution came to her. "The blue sword is a part of you, is it not?" she demanded, and Tehuti nodded grudgingly.

"Yes, I suppose it is." She accepted the point.

"But I am also part of you, and you are part of me, are we not?"

Tehuti saw in which direction she was headed, and her solemn expression gave way to a delighted smile.

"Then it follows that all three of us are a single entity, the sword is part of both of us, and thus all three of us belong to each other." As Serrena closed her fingers around the hilt of the sword again and drew the blade from its bejeweled scabbard, she added simply,

"It is the greatest honor for me to share this magnificent weapon with you, my darling mother."

Then she came to her feet and held the blade aloft like a burning torch. It seemed to light the whole room with its blue reflected flame. She began the exercise of arms that Tehuti had drilled into her ever since she was old enough and strong enough to lift a toy weapon. She began with the twelve parries, and then the cuts and lunges all rendered in unhurried perfection.

Tehuti applauded her, keeping the time with her hands clapping as gradually Serrena increased the tempo until the blade seemed to dissolve into a glittering and ethereal gleam of light, like a hummingbird's wing when it hovers before a bloom. Her arm became part of the same wing, changing shape in constant mutability. Her entire body danced to the rhythm set by the gleaming blade. Then she began to whirl, and her feet moved with the speed of flickering summer lightning. With every revolution she pruned the tallest bloom in one of the copper flower vases, snipping it off so neatly that it seemed not to realize it had been detached, but hovered for a second before it fell to the floor; by which time Serrena had cut loose three or four more blossoms. They fell as thick as snowflakes in a winter storm until every stalk was left denuded, and Serrena stopped dancing as abruptly as she had begun with the blue blade held aloft like a torch once more.

It was such a wonderful exhibition of swordsmanship that Tehuti would remember it always. It was she who described it to me when I remarked on the blue sword hanging from Serrena's belt.

If these were happy days for me, then for Rameses and Serrena they were paradisiacal. I have heard it said that there is no such thing as love at first sight, but this couple gave the lie to such nonsense.

They made no attempt to conceal their mutual fascination and attraction. They touched each other at every opportunity and hung on each other's words when one of them was speaking, or just sat silent gazing deeply into each other's eyes for minutes at a time.

Tehuti's first delight at their evident mutual attraction soon turned into alarm. She extracted a solemn oath of chastity from her daughter and then complained to me, "She doesn't mean a word of it. She is as hot as a young filly coming into her first season. I can smell it on her as soon as she sees him. You have to help me, Tata."

I feigned innocence. "Do you mean the same way I helped you guard your virginity against Zaras' forays?"

She recoiled and then flared at me, "I feel very sorry for you. You have got such a dirty mind."

"When?" I asked. "Then when it was you and Zaras, or now when it's Rameses and Serrena?" And she threw her hands up in frustration and then collapsed with laughter.

"There is a big difference," she explained to me seriously as soon as she had recovered her poise. "Zaras and I were never given a chance by my brother, the Pharaoh. I was being given away to a horrible old man in a political arrangement. I wanted just once in my life to be with the man I loved. Now with Serrena and Rameses they have everybody's wholehearted approval. We just want them to be a little patient."

"I think that you and your daughter may have different estimates of how much is a little patience. But I will do my best to keep Rameses on a short leash for you."

It was not an idle promise I made to Tehuti. I knew as well as she did just how impetuous and irresistible the passions of young love are. King Hurotas and Tehuti were both strongly in favor of the union of Rameses and Serrena, but it was also a matter of high state. To their minds it was essential that the rulers of all the numerous kingdoms that surrounded Lacedaemon, both near and far, should be present at the wedding. King Hurotas and Queen Sparta Tehuti were determined to make the utmost political capital out of the union.

They estimated that it would take almost a year to send the wedding invitations to all the potential political allies whose favor they were cementing, and then to juggle the near impossible task of assembling all of them in the citadel of Lacedaemon simultaneously.

"A year!" Rameses protested in an agony of impatience. "I could grow old and die in that time." But to my astonishment Serrena was much more sensible and practical.

"If you love me as much as you say you do," she told Rameses in my presence and that of her own parents, "then you will agree to what my father and mother ask of us. As the heirs to the throne of this marvelous country that I love, we have a duty to our nation that takes precedence over our own petty desires. Besides which, our love can only grow stronger with time and sacrifice." She won him over almost immediately with that simple but formidable logic.

Up until this time I had looked upon her simply as a beautiful young woman, but from that day on I began to realize what an extraordinary person she truly was. Her talents and strengths were concealed from most of us by the superficial screen of her beauty. But if you could look beyond that façade, as I was able to do, you discovered an intelligence and a steely core that was uncanny.

Although they spent a great deal of their time together so that their mutual feelings were obvious to all the world, Serrena took care not to hide from view so that prurient minds would have nothing to feast upon. In fact, both of the lovers seem to be strongly drawn to the company of other men and women of exceptional minds, and Serrena in particular enjoyed erudite discussion. She would seek me out nearly every day for at least a few hours of discussion on matters varying as widely as the shape of our world or what moved the tides of the ocean and the nature of the substances that made up the moon and the sun.

I looked forward eagerly to our arguments and discussions, and within a very few months of our first meeting, I realized that I loved Serrena as much if not more than I did her mother Tehuti. No matter that she stubbornly resisted my carefully reasoned logic and would not concede that the earth was flat, that the tides were the consequence of the insatiable thirst of Poseidon, the god of the sea, drinking deeply twice a day from the ocean. Nor that the moon and the sun are one and the same heavenly body, which is composed of a flammable substance that consumes itself in flame during the course of the day and then regenerates itself during the night. She had her own theories, which were so risible as hardly to bear repetition. I mean, if the world were truly round as a pumpkin, as she mooted, how would people be able to cling to the underside without falling off?

Over the next few months the realization gradually dawned upon me that Serrena was not the child of two ordinary human beings, but that one of her parents at least must be a divine. Such beauty and intelligence were of a higher plane. I know because I also am similarly afflicted, or blessed. I know not how best to describe it.

I have the highest possible regard for King Hurotas, the putative sire of Serrena. He is a resourceful and courageous soldier, and a dear and loyal friend. He is even a fine king, the best I have ever met after Pharaoh Tamose, but nobody in their right mind would mistake him for a god.

However, there could be no possible doubt which of them had carried Serrena in her womb, for only one of them was suitably equipped for that task. So it seemed to me obvious that Tehuti must have strayed more than a little from the narrow path of fidelity.

However, just to make assurance doubly sure I was determined to put Serrena's provenance to the test, not because I am a busybody as some people tend to think, but because of my genuinely deep affection for all those involved.

There are a number of infallible tests of divinity, one of which is the ability to understand and speak the arcane language of the Adepts and the Magi, passed on to us by the god Hermes, or Mercury as he is also known. Hermes is the son of Thundering Zeus, who gave his favorite son many roles to play in the history and evolution of mankind. Among the most important are those of generating speech, language, learning and eloquence. On the other hand, Zeus also made Hermes the god of mendacity, and the author of crafty and devious words. As a part of these multiple duties Hermes created the language of the divines, which he designated the Tenmass.

I did not have to wait too long. Most evenings the female members of the royal family, Tehuti, Bekatha and Serrena, went out on the horses for a long ride, either along the riverbank, up into the Taygetus Mountains or along the golden sands of the beach that ran along the northern side of the island. Of course Rameses and I were invited to join them. Like me, Serrena was fascinated by the sea creatures that abounded in the waters that surrounded us, and the birds and wild animals that inhabit the mountains and forests. She collected the eggs of the birds that nested in the mountains and forests and the shells of the various mollusks that were washed up on the shore. She made up her own fantastical names for each species and was overjoyed whenever she discovered something new or previously unknown to her. Rameses, like most soldiers and men of action, was not much interested in these natural subjects, but wherever Serrena led him he followed dutifully.

This particular day as we rode along the edge of the ocean, the tide had run out farther than usual.

Serrena put forward the preposterous theory that this was because of the fact that the sun and moon were aligned in some mysterious manner and exerting an aggravated pull on the waters, not because Poseidon was more thirsty than usual and thus drinking more deeply.

Now, like all those learned men who have studied the heavenly bodies, I am fully aware of the fact that the sun and the moon are actually one and the same entity. It becomes the sun when it is fully charged during the day, and then it becomes the moon during the night when its flames are burned out and recharging, at which time it becomes a mere shadow of its fiery self.

When I explained this to Serrena, she immediately challenged me. "How can they be the same heavenly body when I have seen both the sun and the moon in the sky at one and the same time?" she demanded of me in the tones of one who has settled a subject once and for all.

I reined in my horse to a halt, forcing her to do the same. "Make your hand into a fist, Serrena," I instructed her. But I changed smoothly into the Tenmass language, and when she obeyed, I told her, "Now hold it up to the sun."

"Do you mean like this?" she asked in the Tenmass. She enunciated it perfectly but was obviously unaware that she had done so.

"Now look at the ground below you, and tell me what you see there," I instructed her.

"I see nothing except my own shadow," she replied in the Tenmass, looking slightly puzzled.

"What is that round dark shape?" I asked her, leaning from the saddle as I pointed it out.

"That's the shadow of my hand."

"So do you mean that we are seeing both your hand

and the shadow of your hand at the same time, just as we can often see both the sun and its shadow, which we call the moon, at the same time?" I asked, and she opened her pretty mouth to argue further, then she closed it and we rode on in silence. Strangely enough we have never addressed the subject of the sun and the moon again since that day.

However, we often converse in the Tenmass when we are alone together, although Serrena is not aware that we are speaking an alien language. It gives me great pleasure to do so because it provides me with incontrovertible proof that she is one of the divines.

I thought long and earnestly on how to address the only person on this earth who could endorse the details of how this miraculous birth had come to pass. Even my special relationship with the main human character in this drama did not grant me the privilege of an outright confrontation. This would require all my subtlety and cunning to come at the truth without creating a dangerous furor. I even considered the wisdom of letting the truth of the matter lie undiscovered. I want to make it abundantly clear that it was not sordid curiosity on my part, but a genuine concern for the well-being of everybody concerned that drove me on.

The first time I had allowed Tehuti and her sister, Bekatha, a taste of the fruit of the vine had been a long,

long time ago when they were no more than fifteen or sixteen years old and I was escorting them from Egypt to Crete to be married to the mighty Minos. On the long voyage they had both pleaded with me to let them kill themselves rather than go through with the wedding, and I had given them wine to alleviate their distress. It worked, for that had been the last time they had ever contemplated suicide—to my knowledge. Since being reunited with them here in Lacedaemon I had noticed that the years had not lessened their penchant for the juice of the grape to any great extent. The only difference was that they had become more particular and demanding in their taste, and they sipped from only the most carefully chosen amphorae filled with the produce of the royal vineyards, as was their right.

I waited my opportunity with the patience of the hunter at the watering hole of his quarry. Then at last the potentate of one of the mysterious kingdoms that lay far to the east made a state visit to Lacedaemon, ostensibly to bolster trade relations, but in reality to inquire after the hand of Princess Serrena in marriage. Descriptions of her beauty had been bruited far and wide, but few had yet learned of her betrothal.

I was the only person in Lacedaemon who spoke Persian. Thus it was left to me to tactfully inform King Simashki, for that was the suitor's name, of Serrena's unavailability. His Majesty expressed his disappointment in such beautifully poetical language that Serrena was reduced to tears. Then he kissed both Rameses and Serrena on their cheeks and presented the happy couple with a wedding gift of twenty large amphorae of the red wine from his own vineyards.

When Tehuti sampled this wine for the first time, she remarked to her husband, "For another twenty amphorae of this marvelous nectar I would allow Simashki to marry me."

King Hurotas sipped a mouthful from his own cup, rolled it around his tongue, and then nodded. "And for twenty more I would let him have you."

I thought it fortuitous that our guest spoke not a word of Egyptian and merely raised his cup to them and joined in the general mirth that followed this exchange with a slightly puzzled expression.

It was Tehuti's self-imposed rule to limit her evening intake of wine to two large cups. "Just sufficient to make me happy, but still able to get to my bed with only two of my maids to help me," as she put it.

In the confusion and bonhomie of the banquet I managed surreptitiously to raise her consumption to four or five, simply by filling her cup from my own every time she turned away from me to kiss or caress her husband. Thus when she at last decided to leave the gathering, she had to grab my arm for support when she tried to stand up. I dismissed her maids and carried her up the stairs to her bedchamber, while she clung with both arms around my neck and giggled happily.

I undressed her and put her between the sheets just as I used to do, so long ago, when she was a little girl. Then I sat on the mattress beside her and we chatted and laughed together. But all the while I was directing the conversation in the direction I had chosen.

"So why have you had only one child while Bekatha has four, and why did it take you so long?" I demanded.

"The good gods alone know the answer to that question," she replied. "Zaras and I have hardly missed a single night in thirty years, even when I am flying the red flag. He is insatiable, and I am almost as randy as he is. I wanted a baby so badly. And, as you remarked, my little sister, Bekatha, was popping them out of her oven one after the other, just like baking pies. I almost hated her for it. I used to pray to Taweret, the goddess of childbirth, and make sacrifice every night before Zaras came to my bed. But that didn't work." Then she smiled knowingly. "How can you trust a goddess that looks like a hippopotamus standing on her back legs. She just gobbled up all my offerings and never gave me another thought, let alone a baby of my own."

"So what did you do?" I asked, but her response was oblique and obfuscated.

"You don't mind if I use the pot while I think about it, do you, Tata?" She hopped out of bed and perched herself on her chamber pot, which stood in a corner of the room. For a while we both listened respectfully to the tinkle of her liquid into the receptacle beneath her, and then Tehuti demanded, "If I tell you, do you promise you won't tell anybody else, Tata?" Her diction was only slightly skewed by her surfeit of the grape.

"May the gods strike me down if ever I do," I replied dutifully, and she gave a squeak of horror.

"You shouldn't say things like that, Tata. Take it back at once. You must never provoke the gods!" She made the sign against the evil eye.

I took up her challenge and warned the hovering pantheon of immortals who were probably listening from the shadows of the room, "Don't you dare touch me, any of you nasty old gods, or else Queen Tehuti will jump up from her potty and pee in your ear hole!"

Tehuti burst into fresh fits of giggles. "That isn't funny!" she told me, trying unsuccessfully to keep a straight face. "You must never make jokes about the gods. They have no sense of humor, none at all—unless the jokes are the ones that they play on us."

"No more jokes," I promised. "However, tell me

what you did to get yourself pregnant. I am agog to hear the secret, and I repeat my promise not to tell anyone."

"I did what I should have done in the beginning. I appealed to a male god, not a female one. I sacrificed an ox to him and I prayed to him on my knees for half the night."

"What did King Hurotas, your husband, think about that?"

"He never knew. He was away waging war on our neighbors at the time, and I never bothered to tell him when he returned home."

"And did the male god respond to your entreaties?"

"When at last I fell asleep he came to me in a dream." She dropped her voice to a whisper, and she blushed pinkly and lowered the lashes over her lovely dark eyes. "It was only a dream, I swear to you, Taita. I have always been a good girl. Zaras is my husband. I have ever been true to him."

"Who was the god? Did he tell you who he was?" I asked, and she blushed more brightly and hung her head, unable to look me in the eye. She was silent for a while, and then she spoke so softly that I could not be sure of what she said.

"Speak up please, Tehuti. Who was it?" I demanded again.

She looked up at me and repeated clearly, "He said

he was Apollo, the god of fecundity, music, truth and healing. I believed him, for he was so beautiful."

I nodded sagely. Of course, I could have added to that shortlist of his virtues that she recited to me. Apollo is also the god of lust and anger, wine and drunkenness, disease and falsehoods among countless other virtues and vices.

"Of course, you and Apollo coupled with each other." I framed it as a statement of fact, not a question. She blanched deathly white.

"It was a dream, don't you understand, Tata?" Her voice rose in a shrill of agony. "None of it was real. Serrena is my husband's daughter, and I am his chaste wife. I love my husband, and I love my daughter, not some phantom from Olympus or the netherworld."

I looked at her with silent compassion, deepened by love. She sprang to her feet and ran to me. She threw herself at my feet and clasped my knees in her arms, burying her face in my lap.

"Forgive me, my darling Tata." Her voice was muffled by the skirts of my robe. "It was all a dream and I had no control over what happened. It was magic and witchcraft. I was a feather swept up in the holocaust. It was terrible and it was magnificent. He filled every part of my body and my mind with unbearable pain and unbelievable pleasure, with blinding golden light and the darkness of the void. He was beautiful beyond words, but terrifying and hideous as sin. It lasted only an instant and a thousand years. I felt him place the miracle that was Serrena in my womb and I rejoiced at it. But it was not reality. Will you ever be able to forgive me for my wickedness, Taita?"

I stroked her hair gently, and it felt like silk under my fingers as I whispered to her, "There is nothing to forgive, Tehuti. Your husband and your daughter are all of reality and everything else is shadows. Hold them close to your heart and cherish them, and tell no other person of your weird and fantastical dreams. Forget that you even told me."

The preparations for the wedding of Rameses and Serrena took even longer than Hurotas had anticipated. We had two unexpected little wars to fight in the interim. It was the ambition of Hurotas and Hui to subjugate all the islands and lands surrounding the Cyclades and the south Aegean Sea, but after thirty years of almost continual warfare, the task was not yet half completed. No sooner was one archipelago brought under control than another came out in rebellion at the opposite end of King Hurotas' empire. In addition, the Persians were perpetually complicating and confusing the issue. Wherever they detected weakness they were quick to sneak in and cut a few throats, then fill their ships with loot and disappear as suddenly as they had arrived, back into their vast and mysterious domain that tottered on the eastern brink of the world.

"They are nothing more than uneducated savages and ruthless pirates," Hurotas told me in outraged tones.

"They probably say the same thing about us," I pointed out reasonably.

"We are pioneers and empire builders," he contradicted me loftily. "It is our destiny to civilize and rule the world in the name of the true gods whom we worship."

"But you and your men love a good fight as much as any savage," I replied. "You told me so yourself."

"There is only one thing my people enjoy more than a good fight, and that is a good revel," Hurotas acknowledged. "It is my intention to give them the biggest, the wildest and the most famous wedding that any one of them has ever dreamed of, and that no man will ever want to miss."

I nodded my approval. "Then while your guests are still recovering from a surfeit of good wine and rich food you can quietly usurp their kingdoms."

"My dear Taita, I have always admired your political acumen." Hurotas stroked his beard and smiled noncommittally.

So I went on, "If your lovely daughter, Serrena, had

chosen one of the island chieftains as a husband, she would have made enemies of the other fifteen, but this way all sixteen of them become your allies and vassals. Although she is so young, she is wise far beyond her years."

"I can only repeat my last statement about you, Taita." Hurotas kept on smiling. "You have always been able to see the way forward with great clarity."

Even though the two of us were alone, I dropped my voice so that Hurotas was obliged to lean closer to hear what I had to say next. "With those sixteen allies behind you, an annexation of our very Egypt and the punishment of the tyrant Utteric Turo becomes feasible."

"I must admit that I have thought about that possibility. Who would you suggest replace Utteric as Pharaoh in Luxor, Taita?"

"You are the obvious choice," I answered without hesitation, but he chuckled.

"I have no particular wish to return to Egypt on a permanent basis. I am very comfortable in my new citadel here in Lacedaemon. I have put a lot of effort into building it. Besides, my memories of Egypt are not particularly happy ones. But who else could I send to do the job?" he asked and I pondered his question for a moment.

"The name Pharaoh Rameses has a fine ring to it," I hazarded and Hurotas' expression changed. He looked dubious. I realized my error and recovered smoothly. "On the other hand, even though as far as I am aware there has never been a woman ruler of Egypt, the name of Pharaohin Serrena has an even more noble resonance to my ear," and Hurotas smiled again. "They could rule as a joint triumvirate, or perhaps more accurately as a biumvirate." Now Hurotas burst out laughing.

"You never fail to amuse me, Taita. Where do you get these ideas from? Very well, a biumvirate it shall be."

It had only been a very few months since I had arrived in Lacedaemon, but already my position was very nearly unassailable. Thirty years previously Hurotas had taken his instructions from me. Very little had changed in the interim, except that these days my instructions were more diplomatically phrased as suggestions.

I could not at this stage push Rameses' promotion too rapidly above Hui and his sons, but tactfully I saw to it that he was placed in the center of military and naval affairs of Lacedaemon, and that he still had command of the mighty warship the *Memnon* in which the two of us had escaped from Utteric and Egypt. He was officially ranked as rear admiral, directly below Admiral Hui. His royal bloodline and his betrothal to Princess

Serrena gave him high status, but he was wise enough, despite his youth, not to flaunt it. He was already a favorite of Hui's own family. When she entertained him, which was often, Princess Bekatha sat him beside her at her ample table and fed him liberally. She referred to him as "Rammy darling." Her sons accepted him into the family with not the slightest show of rancour or jealousy, and their burgeoning brood of young children were delighted to have another uncle to bully and beg sweetmeats from, and to pester to tell them stories and to carry them upon his back.

Of course, King Hurotas and Queen Tehuti were delighted by the prospect of him fathering their own grandchildren in due course, once the formalities had been taken care of. They gave Rameses his own suite of rooms in the citadel next door to my own, at the farthest end of the massive building from Serrena's apartments. The number of sentries guarding the princess royal was unobtrusively doubled, as though my own surveillance was insufficient to ensure that her chastity was not prematurely terminated.

The quarters provided for me were almost as grand as those of King Hurotas and Queen Tehuti, but I had good reason to believe that the queen herself was directly responsible for this. Not a day passed that she did not appear uninvited in my private dining room with sufficient provisions to supply a hundred men or more, and enough wine to keep me drunk for a year. Or to wake me after midnight in her nightdress carrying a candle as she hopped up on my bed with the assurance of, "I won't be more than a few minutes, I promise you, Tata. But I just have to ask you something very important, and, no, it can't wait until tomorrow."

Several hours later when I carried her back asleep in my arms to her own bed, her husband grumbled at me, "Can't you remember to lock your door to keep her out, Taita?"

"She has her own key."

"Then keep her there with you."

"Sometimes she snores."

Hurotas shook his head despairingly. "Do you think you are telling me something I don't know?"

However, the hours of lost sleep were a small price to pay for the comfort and utility that these magnificent quarters afforded me. From my terrace on the top floor of the monumental building I could look out at the snow-clad mountain peaks and down the wide valley to the bay. I could monitor the comings and goings of the army and all the activity of the shipping. I love wild birds, and every morning I laid out food for the different species on this terrace, and the pleasure they gave me was intense. I used one of the larger rooms as my library and headquarters. Soon the shelves were filled with my scrolls, and the overflow was stacked head high in the corners of the room.

Captain Weneg, to whom I owed a heavy debt of gratitude for my escape from the Gates of Torment and Sorrow and the brutal ministrations of the dreaded Doog, was out of place here in Lacedaemon. He came to ask me for occupation commensurate with his rank, experience and ability. Within a very short time I made all the preparations for Weneg and his small group of men to return surreptitiously to Egypt, and there to set up an intelligence unit to supply me with up-to-date information as to what travails and tribulations my sorry Egyptian homeland was suffering under the yoke of Pharaoh Utteric Turo.

I saw to it that Weneg was supplied with sufficient silver deben to pay his informers and allies, and I purchased three small but fast trading vessels to carry him and his men on their mission. It was after midnight when they sailed from Port Githion, and of course I was on the wharf to see them off and send my good wishes with them on their southern voyage.

Under a false name and with a dense curling beard disguising his handsome features, Weneg had within a very short time set up his headquarters in a wineshop almost in the shadow of the walls of Utteric's palace in Luxor.

Of course I had supplied him with a number of crates, each containing numerous homing pigeons. All of them had been hatched in the coops of the royal loft by King Hurotas' pigeon handler in Lacedaemon. Weneg smuggled these birds with him into Egypt. Within a few months his network was firmly established in Luxor and operating smoothly and efficiently, and I was receiving regular dispatches carried across the northern sea by Weneg's pigeons. The average time it took these doughty birds to make the journey was less than four days. The value of the information they brought me was incalculable.

From the pigeon mail I learned almost as soon as it happened that Utteric had changed his name to Pharaoh Utteric Bubastis, in celebration of his ascension to the pantheon of the gods. Bubastis was the god of masculine beauty and valor among his other numerous attributes. The only one of which I was truly envious was that Bubastis was reputed to be able to stretch his erect penis to the length of one hundred cubits, to catch off her guard any female who took his fancy.

The god Bubastis was often depicted as either a male or female cat. Apparently he was able to change his sexual orientation at will—which perhaps explains Utteric's attraction to that particular deity.

I also learned from Weneg that Pharaoh Utteric Bubastis was building an elaborate temple to himself on an island in the Nile downstream from Luxor. He was spending on this enterprise almost the entire ten lakhs of the silver that I had won for him from Khamudi at Memphis.

This was followed within a short time by the news that Pharaoh Utteric Bubastis' agents had traced the mighty war trireme the *Memnon* in which Rameses and I had fled from Egypt to its new anchorage in Port Githion. Weneg reported that Pharaoh's naval officers had been given the task of retrieving the ship and returning with it to Luxor. Their orders were to make certain that the traitor Taita was on board and in chains when the *Memnon* returned to Egypt. Pharaoh had placed a reward of half a lakh of silver on my head. Clearly he had neither forgotten nor forgiven me.

Recently I had become rather lax in my personal safety. I had believed that I was secure in my elaborate and comfortable quarters in the citadel, but this news shook me out of my torpor. Up to this point Rameses had allowed a skeleton crew to moor the *Memnon* in the center of the Githion harbor in full view of anyone with evil intentions toward her. Now at my orders she was brought alongside the harbor wall, and beneath the surface of the water she was secured with ropes as thick as my wrist attached to ringbolts set into the stonework of the wharf. At all times she had a picket of twenty heavily armed seamen aboard, and this was changed every six hours. Another fifty men were billeted in a stone building on the wharf only thirty paces from the *Memnon*'s gangplank. They could be deployed at the first hint of a hostile party coming ashore to try and seize the ship and work her out to sea.

Within two weeks I received another pigeon from Weneg in Luxor. The message this bird carried was that a crew of approximately fifteen to twenty men on a small and unobtrusive fishing boat had left the mouth of the Nile. It seemed highly likely that they were on their way to attempt the retrieval of the *Memnon*. Weneg had even given me the name of the lieutenant in command of the expedition. He was a slippery fellow named Panmasi, whom both Rameses and I knew by sight. He had become one of Utteric's favorites. He was a mere twenty-five years of age but had already earned himself a reputation as a hard man. He was recognizable by a scar on his right cheek, and by the limp he had received from another war wound, which forced him to drag his right leg slightly with each step.

Not long afterward our lookouts on the heights of

the Taygetus Mountains reported a strange fishing boat lurking far out in the great Bay of Githion. She appeared to be busy casting her fishing nets, but it was too late in the evening and too far offshore to be certain. When word of this sighting reached Rameses and me in the citadel, we immediately saddled up and rode at full gallop down to the port. Our men guarding the *Memnon* there reported that all seemed quiet. However, I placed them on full alert, and we all took up our battle stations and settled down to wait. I was almost certain that Panmasi would not make his attempt at seizing the *Memnon* until the small hours of the morning, when he hoped that the attention and the energies of our guards would be at their lowest ebb. In the event I was proven right, as is so often the case. An hour or so before first light I heard a nightjar call in the forest above the harbor, or rather I heard somebody give an amateurish approximation of the nightjar's call. It is one of my favorite birds and the imitation did not deceive me. Quietly I passed the word to my ambush party to be ready.

There was a short lull. We discovered afterward that this was while Panmasi's thugs were creeping up on the sentries at the gates to the harbor and silencing them either by slitting their throats or beating in their skulls with clubs. Then there was an almost silent rush

of dark figures from among the warehouses. Brandishing their weapons, they raced across the stone wharf
toward the side of the *Memnon,* where I had ordered
the gangplank to be left down, in a tacit invitation to
the intruders to come on board.

I had also placed a number of water barrels and
cargo crates on the jetty as if for loading as soon as work
began the next morning. Behind them were concealed
my archers and pikemen. I recognized Panmasi at the
head of his bunch of pirates. However, I waited until
he had led his men out into the open and he had almost
reached the inviting gangway up to the *Memnon's*
deck, and their backs were presented to us, before I
gave the order to my lads to engage. They sprang up
from where they had been hiding behind the barrels
and crates. Every one of them had an arrow already
nocked, and in unison they let them fly. The range was
point-blank, and almost every arrow thumped home.
To shouts of pain and surprise almost half of Panmasi's
men went down, and the others turned to confront us.

But the element of surprise was in our favor, and
the fight was over almost immediately. The surviving enemy threw down their weapons and fell to their
knees, sniveling and howling for quarter with their
hands held high. There had been twenty-five men in
the raiding party, but only sixteen of them had sur-

vived the volley of arrows. I was pleased that Panmasi was one of the survivors. I wanted to see him punished fittingly for his arrogance and treachery. But I was soon to be disappointed, and from a totally unexpected quarter.

Rameses' men had the slave chains ready for our prisoners. First they were stripped down to their underskirts, and their wrists were pinioned behind their backs and their ankles were shackled together so that they were limited to taking short hobbling steps. Then they were loaded aboard two large dung carts, and the teams of oxen dragged them up the valley to the citadel.

I sent men ahead to alert the population to the capture of the pirates and they turned out to line the road and mock the prisoners and pelt them with mud and ordure as they passed on their way to captivity, trial and certain execution for their crimes.

It was three days later that King Hurotas found time to try the pirates in the courtyard of the citadel. Of course the verdict was a foregone conclusion. However, there was a fine turnout of spectators for the occasion. This included Queen Tehuti and her daughter, Serrena, who sat on a pile of cushions at her mother's feet.

I gave evidence for the prosecution and a fair and balanced recitation of the facts, which nevertheless was all that was needed to condemn Panmasi and his rogues out of hand. It was not really necessary for the king to hear any evidence for the defense, but Hurotas was a generous man.

"Does the leader of this band of rascals have anything to say before I pass sentence upon the whole bunch of them?" the king demanded.

Panmasi, who had been kneeling facing the throne with his forehead pressed to the ground and his men behind him in the same attitude of penance, now rose to his feet. I have already hinted at what a slippery scoundrel he was, but now he surprised and amused me with just what a gifted actor he turned out to be.

His expression was the epitome of abject misery and repentance for his crimes. He made great play with dragging his damaged leg to gain sympathy. Snot and tears ran down his cheeks and dripped from his chin. His voice quavered as he described the family he had left behind him in Egypt: his three wives who were all heavy with child; his twelve starving children and the crippled little daughter whom he adored. It was all so preposterous that I had difficulty containing my laughter. I knew for a fact that Panmasi owned four thriving brothels in Luxor, and that he was his own best customer. He beat his wives just for the pleasure of hearing them squeal, and his daughter was crippled only because of the blow to the head with a spade that he had given her before she had learned to walk properly. When he came to the end of his recital, choking back his sobs, the king glanced at me for my opinion. I shook my head, and he nodded to have his own verdict endorsed.

"The prisoners will all rise to hear my verdict," he intoned. The miscreants shambled to their feet and stood facing him, but still with their eyes downcast. I think they knew very well what punishment they were about to receive.

"Sixty days hence is the marriage of my daughter, Serrena, to Prince Rameses of the noble house of Egypt. On that joyous occasion all sixteen of the prisoners are to be sacrificed to Hera, the goddess of marriage and marital bliss, to secure my daughter's future happiness. Before they die, their entrails are to be drawn out through their fundaments with fishing hooks. Then they are to be beheaded. Finally their remains are to be burned to ashes and thrown into the sea on an outgoing tide while prayers are sung by the priestesses of Hera in celebration of my daughter's future marital happiness."

I nodded my head in agreement with King Hurotas' verdict. It seemed to me to be fair and completely equitable, bearing in mind the scope and nature of the crimes they had committed.

"No!"

The cry startled us all, including the king and even me. We were all struck dumb, and we turned as one toward Princess Serrena, who had sprung to her feet to confront her father.

"No!" she repeated. "One hundred times, no!"

Hurotas was the first one to recover from this surprise attack by his one and only child, who was probably also his only weakness. "Why ever not, my darling daughter?" I could see he was making a mighty effort to keep his temper under control. "I am doing it for your sake, for your own happiness."

"I love you dearly, Father. But sixteen headless corpses lain out in a row will bring me little pleasure or happiness."

Like everybody else in the courtyard, Panmasi and all his men had lifted their heads for the first time and were staring at the princess, and I saw the dawn of hope in their expressions. But more than that there was astonishment bordering on disbelief as they gazed upon Serrena's beauty. This was emphasized by her animation: by the high color of her cheeks, the flash of her eyes, and the tremor of her lovely lips. Her voice rang like some heavenly musical instrument, captivating and beguiling all her audience, even me who was accustomed to it.

"What would you have me do with these rogues, then?" Hurotas demanded in exasperation. "I could have them chained to the rowing benches of one of the galleys, or send them to the copper mines . . ."

"Send them back to their loving wives and families in Egypt," Serrena interposed. "You will make many people happy with such clemency and compassion, including and especially me on my wedding day, my darling Papa."

Hurotas opened his mouth to speak, and I saw the sparks of anger crackling in his eyes. Then he closed his mouth, and, as so many people do when they are in dire straits, he looked around at me. I wanted to laugh; it was amusing to see the grizzled hero of so many bitter conflicts driven from the field in rout by a young girl.

Long ago I had taught him to read my lips, and I flashed him a single silent word now. *Capitulate!* I advised him silently.

He smothered his grin as he turned back to confront Serrena. "That is sheer stupidity," he told her sternly. "I will have no part of it. I give these rogues to you as part of your wedding gift from me. Do with them whatever you wish."

A search of the shore on the far side of the island revealed the small fishing boat that had carried Panmasi and his men up from the mouth of the Nile. They had drawn it up the beach and covered it with dead fronds and branches. It must have been more sturdy and sea-worthy than it looked to have brought so many men so far and so swiftly. In response to the wishes of Princess Serrena, my men bundled Panmasi and the remnants of his crew back on board, sans weapons and sans sus-tenance, and I pointed out the way to the south and the mouth of Mother Nile.

"We are without food or water," Panmasi pleaded with me. "We will all die of thirst or hunger. Have mercy, good Taita, I beg of you."

"I can give you only good advice, but not food or drink, which is costly and in short supply. You should remember to keep your piss cool. It is much more pal-atable when drunk that way," I told him affably. "I will give you a start of twenty-four hours, and then I will send a war trireme after you to speed you on your way. Farewell, good Panmasi. Give my respects to Pharaoh Utteric when—or rather if—you ever reach Egypt again." I nodded to my men who were guarding the re-leased prisoners and they dismounted from their horses and prepared to shove the fishing boat off the beach. But they were stopped by a lyrical cry in a familiar voice.

"Wait, Taita! Do not let them go yet!" With a sigh of resignation, I turned to face Princess Serrena of

Lacedaemon at the head of a line of half a dozen pack-horses, which were laden with food baskets and water-skins as they came down the path through the forest onto the golden sand of the beach. "You forgot the provisions for these poor creatures, you silly man. They would have died of starvation or thirst before they ever reached Egypt."

"That was my fervent hope," I muttered, but she pretended not to hear me. To add to my chagrin I saw that she had included two large skins of her father's excellent red wine in the survival stores she was providing for them. This was to my mind the ultimate folly.

Panmasi came and groveled at Serrena's feet, praising her beauty, her mercy, and her generosity and calling down the blessings of all the gods upon her, but I saw the way he looked at her under his eyelids and it made me uneasy. I walked up behind him and gave him a kick between the buttocks that doubled him over, and I told him, "Get you gone, you piece of stinking offal, and never come back or I will make sure you stay forever, buried deep belowground."

He limped back to his boat massaging his aching organs and screeching abuse at his own men. They plied the oars with alacrity, and as soon as they passed the reef they hoisted a sail and bore away southward. Panmasi and I watched each other until the distance between us was too great, and then I turned away and rode with my beloved princess back toward the citadel. But I expected that it was not the last I would ever see of that abysmal rogue, not by a long arrow shot.

The nasty premonition lingered on in the back of my mind even during the busy and joyous days that followed. More than once I was on the point of breaking my promise to Serrena and pursuing Panmasi in the *Memnon* to settle the matter decisively. I knew that I could convince Rameses to accompany me. But I am a man of honor, and my word is sacred to me.

It is little solace to me to know that if I had broken it on this single occasion, I would have saved the lives of a thousand brave and honorable men, to say nothing of the heartache and misery I would have spared myself and those who are dear to me.

The organization of the wedding of Prince Rameses of Egypt and Princess Serrena of Sparta had been made my responsibility almost entirely. This translated as meaning that if things went well, all praise would go to King Hurotas and Queen Tehuti of Sparta. However, should disaster, debacle or calamity occur, then all heads would turn immediately in my direction.

The preliminary festivities would run for a month prior to the actual marriage ceremony, and for another month thereafter. At the request of Queen Tehuti they would be dedicated to Apollo, the god of fecundity among many other things, including infidelity.

They would include feasting and reveling, worship of the 150 principal gods and goddesses, chariot- and boat-racing, more dancing and copious wine-drinking, wrestling, contests in singing oratory and archery, music and dancing and horse-racing, all with large prizes in gold and silver for the winners.

In addition, I had to supervise the building of appropriate accommodations for the sixteen visiting petty kings and their retinues whom King Hurotas and his queen had invited to attend the jollifications.

I digress for a moment to explain Hurotas' relationship to these petty chieftains or kings. When Hurotas had first landed at Port Githion almost thirty years previously, after escaping from Crete with his new bride, Tehuti, and seeking a place in the world where he could rule and grow powerful, he had taken the territory that was now Lacedaemon from the incumbent King Clydese, by the simple expedient of turning his own disaffected subjects against him and defeating him in a ferocious battle that had raged for three days along the banks of the River Hurotas.

Clydese had as his allies the three chieftains to the north of his kingdom. All three of them had died sword in hand in the conflict alongside Clydese, but their eldest sons had surrendered to the new King Hurotas. Instead of executing the three of them out of hand as they had been anticipating, Hurotas had demanded that they swear an oath of fealty to him. This they agreed to do with the utmost alacrity, having very much in mind the alternative. Hurotas then returned to them the territories on the northern side of the Taygetus Mountains that he had seized from their deceased fathers, retaining for himself only that which had belonged to Clydese.

Naturally they had also sworn to pay him a substantial tribute on all the income that accrued to them and their heirs from any source whatsoever, in perpetuity. It was an arrangement from which all of them benefited—some more than others.

The three chieftains kept their lives and nominal control of their fathers' kingdoms, whereas Hurotas was relieved of the tiresome chore of having to keep under his heel a plethora of savage tribes who did not understand even the fundamentals of allegiance and loyalty. Over the ensuing years, all sixteen of the petty chieftains of the surrounding archipelago had been recruited by Hurotas under the same terms: an offer of fealty or oblivion. Hurotas was the only one who had the ferocity and the cunning to keep all of them in order. Without him to crack the whip, they would have been at each other's throats endlessly. As it was they maintained an uneasy truce with each other, and feelings of awe and respect toward Hurotas so deep that they never queried a command of his or forgot to pay him his tribute, usually well ahead of the agreed date.

Thus it was that thirty-odd years later Hurotas invited all sixteen of his petty chieftains, or those who had succeeded them, to his daughter's wedding, and I was duty bound to assist with the preparations.

All had to be in readiness thirty days before the commencement of the season of Shomu, which is the low-water period of the Nile River and high summer in our very Egypt. Although Lacedaemon is a separate kingdom, we still followed the Egyptian calendar faithfully, for that was where Hurotas and his wife, Tehuti, had been born, and Egyptian was their mother tongue.

The first day of Shomu was the date chosen by Queen Tehuti and Princess Serrena for the wedding ceremony after they had carefully calculated the date of the bride's red moon and allowed ten days for its passage to make certain she would be ready to accord her new husband a right royal welcome on the first occasion that he visited her bridal couch.

This meant that the guests would begin to arrive and the festivities begin in the month before Shomu, which of course was Renwet, the last month in the "Emergence" of the Nile high-water period.

We all worked like slaves under the lash for time was fleeting and my two darlings, Tehuti and Serrena, kept dreaming up fresh entertainments for me to arrange for our guests, each one more elaborate and complicated than the one that preceded it.

"We know that you can do it easily, Tata darling. You are an absolute genius. Nothing is beyond your talents. You would never let me down. After all, it is Serrena's wedding," Tehuti encouraged me and kissed my cheek to spur me onward.

It was a near-run thing, but as the longships of our guests began appearing on the horizon from every direction and headed into the great Bay of Githion, there were companies of our warriors headed up by their officers to welcome them ashore and then to escort them up the River Hurotas to the citadel, where sumptuous quarters stood ready to receive them. This was in itself a complicated business, especially if more than one shipload of royalty arrived simultaneously. Our guests were very sensitive to their seniority. They were ready to defend their order of precedence with bared teeth and drawn swords, and it tested my diplomacy to the limit not to give offense to any of them.

However, my abundant charms soothed the heated tempers, and my exquisite sense of protocol prevailed to prevent a riot.

As soon as they came ashore the principal guests and their wives and concubines were handed up on to the platforms of the waiting line of chariots and escorted by mounted cavalry and blaring bands. The road was lined by cheering crowds and dancing girls and strewn with flowers all the way from the wharf of the Githion harbor to the gates of the citadel.

Here King Hurotas and Queen Tehuti were waiting to receive them. They were supported by Prince Rameses and his prospective bride. Very few of the arriving guests had ever laid eyes on Serrena previously, and although they must have been apprised of her extraordinary beauty, none of them seemed to be prepared for its actuality. Even those who had previously traveled to Lacedaemon to press their suit with her seemed to have forgotten how beautiful she truly was, and they were smitten anew. One after the other they were struck dumb and could only gawk at her in wonderment. But within a few minutes Serrena had broken the spell with her warm and easy manner and her radiant smile.

This was one of the many virtues she evinced; she seemed to be unaware of the splendor of her own appearance and was totally lacking in vanity. Of course, that only made it more effective. I could follow her progress by the ripple of excitement that she engendered, and the animation of those who crowded around her to bask in her beauty. The strange thing was that she seemed never to evoke envy and jealousy among the other women. It was as if they never considered themselves to be in contest with her; she was as unreachable as a shooting star. Rather, they took a pride in her as the pinnacle and epitome of their own sex. Her beauty was reflected in all of them, and they loved her for it.

Thus we began the run-up to the royal wedding, and as the day drew nearer the guests became more excited and filled with joyous anticipation. It was as if all of nature was aware of the importance of the occasion and contributed wholeheartedly to it. It rained, but only during the night. The sound of it on the rooftops was lulling and reassuring. Then the clouds cleared with the dawn, and the sun beamed upon us all benevolently. The winds dropped to a gentle zephyr from out of the south, just strong enough to ruffle the waters and to carry the ships of the last wedding guests sedately into Port Githion.

There was only one lingering concern that cast a pall over the festivities, and that was the unsuccessful attempt by the agents of Pharaoh Utteric to cut the war trireme *Memnon* out of Port Githion, and the threat to the safety of Prince Rameses and to his bride that this act implied.

By this time all the civilized world had learned that Pharaoh Utteric was a madman with a large army and navy at his beck and call, and that he did not hesitate to use it with little or no provocation.

Although King Hurotas truly loved his daughter, Serrena, and the wedding festivities were primarily in her honor, behind the scenes he was quite happy to use the occasion to further affairs of state. Every day at noon he called a clandestine meeting behind the closed doors of his council chamber of all the heads of state gathered in Lacedaemon. The timing of these gatherings was deliberate. Later in the day, once the festivities were renewed and the consumption of the superb wines from King Hurotas' vineyards got under way, was not a suitable time to discuss a pact of mutual protection.

Over a fortnight before the date set down for the wedding of Prince Rameses of Egypt and Princess Serrena of Lacedaemon, the eighteen heads of state, which number included Hurotas and Prince Rameses, assembled in the council chamber of the citadel.

The previous day the council had voted not to recognize Utteric as Pharaoh of Egypt, owing to his manifest insanity. They had elected Rameses as Utteric's replacement.

Once all the members were seated Hurotas called them to order. "The Council of the North is now in session, and I call upon Lord Taita, the secretary of the council, to read the Pact of Mutual Protection that has been placed before us for ratification by the Tyrant of Kallipolis, King Tyndarcus."

Tyndarcus, Rameses, and King Hurotas were the only members of the council who were able to read. I was the only one in the chamber who did not have to move my lips when doing so. That was why Hurotas had chosen Tyndarcus to present the papyrus scroll and me to read it out loud. It consisted of just over five hundred words, but it obliged all present member states of the Council of the North to come to the aid of any member of the council whose country or citizens were placed under threat by a third party.

There was some trivial discussion after I had read the document to them, but then they all signed it or made their mark at the foot of the scroll. The mood of the council members was jovial and flippant. They trooped out of the council chamber into the courtyard where King Hurotas had a magnificent black stallion tethered.

Each of them was presented with a silver flagon, and they gathered around the horse. Hurotas hefted his battle-ax and with a single blow cleaved the stallion's skull, killing it instantly. Then one after another the rulers and kings came forward and scooped up a flagon of the fresh spurting blood and raised it high before intoning solemnly: "If I break my solemn oath, may my own blood flow as freely." Then they swallowed the contents of the flagon. Some of them roared with laughter, but others gagged at the taste of raw blood. However, I am certain that not one of them dreamed that they would be called upon to make good their oath before the end of the month.

The festivities prior to the marriage of Rameses and Serrena built up to a crescendo as the date approached. With only fourteen days left before the wedding Hurotas declared a hunt for the Laconian boar. This was an animal with a long history and was a particular bugbear of his.

After Zaras and Tehuti had arrived in Lacedaemon all those years ago and Zaras became King Hurotas, one of his innovations was to plant the first vineyards and make the first wines from the grapes he grew.

Then King Hurotas made a grave error. When he consecrated his vineyards to the gods, he forgot to include the goddess Artemis in the honors list. Among her numerous other duties, Artemis is the goddess of the forests and of all wild animals. Hurotas chopped down the forests to make room for his vines, and he drove away or killed the animals, including the wild boars that might destroy his fields. The wild boar is one of Artemis' favorite creatures, and she was incensed by his arrogant and high-handed behavior.

She sent the Laconian boar to tear up his vineyards and to teach him humility. This animal was no ordinary wild pig. Only a divine being or someone born to be king was able to dispatch it, and then only after a gargantuan struggle. No matter how often the Laconian boar was killed, Artemis saw to its rebirth every year and sent it back to plague Hurotas. Each year the animal the goddess sent was larger and more ferocious and formidable than the previous one.

The last boar that Artemis had sent to confront Hurotas was reputed to stand six cubits high at the shoulder, as tall as a man. It weighed five hundred deben, as hefty as a large horse.

It lived in the dense forests high in the Taygetus Mountains and emerged only at night to ravage the fields of the men who farmed the valleys. Thus few people had ever laid eyes upon it. It could devour the annual planting of five or six struggling smallholders in a single night. What it did not eat it trampled into the mud.

Its tusks were as long as a warrior's sword. With them it could rip the entrails out of a horse with a toss of its hideous head. Its hide was so tough and thick, and the wiry hair that covered it was so dense, that it would turn the head of all but the most skillfully and powerfully thrown spear. Its hooves were so sharp that it could disembowel a warhorse with a single kick. It was not surprising that two of Serrena's erstwhile suitors declined the invitation to the hunt, one of them pleading his advanced age and the other his very recently deteriorating health. Nevertheless, both of them accepted the invitation to watch the hunt from afar or from the top of a high tree.

There was an air of nervous excitement about those who accepted the challenge as they rode out to do battle with the monster. Naturally, King Hurotas led the hunt with Admiral Hui, his boon companion, as his right hand. Very recently Hurotas had seen me fight in the battle of Luxor against the Hyksos hordes that had overrun Egypt, thus it was no surprise to anyone that I was chosen to ride at his other hand.

Hurotas ordered his wife and his equally beloved daughter to remain well back in the hunt, and Prince Rameses to ride with them as their principal protector. If he had asked my advice, I could have saved him a great deal of aggravation and loss of dignity. As it was, he was faced immediately with ferocious opposition from all three of them. Queen Tehuti led the retaliation with the skill of a barrack-room lawyer and all the authority of over thirty years of marriage.

"When was the first time I ever saved your life, my darling?" she asked Hurotas sweetly. "Was it not before we were even married? Yes, I remember now. You were still the lowly captain named Zaras. You and Taita came to rescue me from the bandit Al Hawsawi who had kidnapped me, but you were stabbed in the stomach by the bandit before you got around to performing your noble mission. In the end, it was Taita and I who had to rescue *you*!" She placed such particular emphasis on the last word that Hurotas paled with outrage. Even I was flabbergasted by the manner in which she had manipulated her account of this particular incident, but before either of us could find the words to protest, she raced on, "That was only the first of many times I saved your life . . ." And she proceeded to remind him of several more.

Then Serrena came in so smoothly at this cue that they might have rehearsed it a dozen times and not hit it so perfectly: "And Mama and I have made a pact to share the blue sword that her father gave to her." Her lovely voice quivered with mawkish sentiment. "If we are not together for this hunt, it will mean that one of us will be deprived of the weapon that might save her life, or yours. You cannot allow one of us to be delivered unarmed to the mercy of this murderous pig, can you now, Papa?" Hurotas swung round to face her before he had even replied to his wife, but Prince Rameses cut neatly across his bows before he could protest.

"It is my duty to protect my future wife, Serrena, from dreadful danger, Your Majesty. I must be by her side when we encounter this ravening beast."

King Hurotas glared at the three of them, but they stood shoulder to shoulder against him. He looked around for support, and of course he saw me hovering discreetly in the background. "Taita, explain to these idiots that this is an extremely dangerous animal we are hunting. All of them will be in mortal danger when we encounter it."

"Your Majesty, only a fool keeps on arguing when he is outnumbered and outwitted. I am here to bear witness that you are no fool. I suggest that you accept the inevitable," I replied, and he stared at me, a furious scowl vying with the twinkle of laughter in his eyes as he realized that he was without even my support. Then he turned away and strode to where two grooms were holding his charger. He swung up onto its back and gathered up the reins. Then he glared down at all of us.

"Come along then! If you are absolutely determined

to die, follow me. And may Artemis and all the other gods have mercy on your stupidity, although I believe that to be unlikely."

The area that we had to cover was immense, and the terrain was mountainous and thickly forested, with the vineyards strewn along the foot of the high ground. The pace that Hurotas set was designed to punish his wife and daughter for their earlier impudence in defying his orders. However, they matched him readily. It goes without saying that I was also at the forefront of the hunt, keeping a length behind the two royal ladies. The rest of the hunting party, almost a hundred of them, were strung out behind us over several leagues of hard going. However, they were all in jovial mood, most of them believing the accounts of the quarry were exaggerated, and that the Laconian boar was the average innocuous creature that could be dispatched with a dozen arrows and the thrust of a lance. Most of them were much more interested in the wine flagons that were being passed freely from hand to hand.

Those few of us in the vanguard found abundant evidence of the presence of the boar. Large areas of vines had been wantonly uprooted, and the irrigation channels that had been laboriously constructed by the peasant farmers had been torn up. The water was pouring away down the mountainside and back into the river in the valley whence it had originated and from there it was carried straight out to sea. Those vines which had not been ravaged by the boar were brown and leafless, and dying of thirst. The peasants who were charged with maintaining the water furrows were too terrified of the boar to work the fields, and they cowered in their hovels, more afraid of the monstrous animal than even they were of Hurotas.

The goddess Artemis could not have chosen a more vulnerable or hurtful area of Hurotas' empire than his wine lands on which to wreak her punishment for his arrogance. The king loved his wine almost as much as he loved the contents of his treasure chambers, and when he had a flagon of the liquid red magic in his hand and another under his belt, he was a man replete. Although he had been informed by his land managers of the extent of the destruction, he had not yet been able to visualize it. Hearing about it was one thing, but actually looking upon it was another thing entirely.

He rode ahead of our hunting party, waving his hunting spear over his head and railing at the goddess and her minion. I shuddered to hear such insults aimed at a daughter of Zeus. The mildest of these epithets was "horrible and hideous hag-whore." The worst was to blatantly accuse her of unnatural relations with her own wild boar. The picture it conjured up in my mind was too terrible to contemplate, but both Tehuti and her beloved daughter, Serrena, thought it inordinately amusing.

Then suddenly their peals of merry laughter were cut off abruptly by another more dreadful sound, which almost deafened us all. Hurotas reined in his steed and peered about him with a startled expression, and I confess that even I who am not readily alarmed was taken aback.

I have only once heard anything as threatening before in my life, and that was on the banks of the Nile River in Ethiopia. It was a sound that would have raised the hair on the back of a brave man's neck and might even have loosened both the valve of his bladder and that of his bunghole. It was the roaring of a black-maned male lion, only much louder than in nature. Seemingly of its own accord my head swiveled in the direction from which the thunderous sound emanated.

From the edge of the forest at the top end of the vineyard emerged an enormous squat head that seemed to belong to a creature from mythology. It was covered with curling tar-black hair. Its huge ears were sharp-pointed and pricked forward. Its eyes were bright and porcine vicious. Its snout was flattened at the tip, and its nostrils snuffled our scent. Its tusks were so long and curved that the razor-sharp tips almost met above the beast's massive head.

It uttered another lionlike bellow and I realized that this was the creation of a goddess's whim, not something from nature. This monster could probably scream like an eagle, or bleat like a goat if it so chose. The trees of the forest buckled and toppled over as it pushed them carelessly aside and emerged into the open. Its hindquarters were heavily muscled, and its back rose into a shaggy hump between its shoulders. It tore up the ground with hooves that were many times larger than those of the wild buffalo, which I had also hunted on the headwaters of the Nile. They raised a dense cloud of brown dust, which shrouded the boar and endowed it with a mystic presence that emphasized its menace. Then suddenly it hurled its great bulk into a charge down the slope of open vineyard directly at Hurotas, singling him out as though it recognized him as the principal enemy of its mistress Artemis.

Immediately Hurotas couched his spear and rode to meet the boar's headlong rush. He shouted a wild war cry, probably more to bolster his own courage than to frighten the beast, which answered him with a deafening cacophony of roars and grunts.

The boar had the advantage of a downhill attack. Its

bulk was as irresistible as an avalanche of rock down a mountain slope shattered by an earthquake. As they came together Hurotas rose in his stirrups and hefted his heavy hunting spear. He hurled it at the beast with all the strength of his right arm, which had been toughened and tempered in the furnace of many battles. The throw was perfection. The spear flew true and half its length drove through the beast's shaggy coat and thick hide and buried itself deep in its chest cavity. I could only believe that it must have pierced its heart and other vital organs through and through.

Yet the boar showed not the slightest reaction to the deep and terrible wound that Hurotas had inflicted upon it. It did not stagger or miss a stride. Its speed was uninterrupted; the bellowing of its fury was even more deafening as it swung its hideous head with all the skill and power of an executioner wielding his ax. The great curved white tusks gleamed and flashed in the air and then buried themselves in the stallion's chest. They ripped through hide, flesh, and bone in a single ghastly wound that laid the horse open from the center of its chest, through its rib cage and shoulder bone, and down its flank so all its vital organs and its guts spilled out from the wound; then the boar's tusks ripped apart the stifle joint of its back leg. The horse collapsed with two of its offside legs severed. Hurotas should also have lost a leg, but the savagery of the original impact hurled him from the saddle the instant before the tusks sliced his mount asunder. He was thrown well clear, but he landed on his head and despite his helmet he was knocked unconscious.

The boar fixated on the downed horse and continued to gore it furiously. I was flogging my own horse up the steep incline, but Tehuti was well ahead of me, charging in on the great boar and the downed horse without the least concern for her own safety. Serrena and Rameses were half a length behind her. Everyone was screaming wildly. Tehuti was cursing the boar for killing her husband and threatening it with its own demise, brandishing the blue sword over her head. Rameses and Serrena were urging each other on, maddened with excitement, all their powers of reason thrown to the winds of war. I was shouting to all three of them to have a care, to back off from the beast and leave it to me to deal with. As usual, none of them took the slightest notice of my commands.

Tehuti rode straight up behind the boar and leaned out from the saddle to slash at the tendon in its back legs. At the same moment the boar kicked back viciously and its hoof caught the wrist of Tehuti's sword hand. It cracked the bone and sent the blue sword spinning from her grip. The pain must have been intense for Tehuti lost her seat and tumbled from the saddle. She fell under the milling hooves of the great boar, clutching her injured wrist with her good hand. Rameses, who was riding close behind her, realized her predicament and swung down from his own saddle. Good lad that he is, he used his momentum to charge forward and scoop Tehuti up in his arms and roll down the slope of the field out of reach of the boar's gnashing tusks and flying hooves.

Serrena was so concerned for her mother's safety that she was momentarily distracted, and when the boar charged at her horse and the animal shied under her, she was thrown from the saddle. She managed to land on her feet, but she had lost the lance she was bearing and she looked around her wildly for another weapon, or at least for escape from her predicament.

Meanwhile I had seen where the blue sword had fallen in the mud amid the scattered and torn vines. The blade of that magical silver metal glinting like a fresh-caught tuna fish had caught my eye.

With the pressure of my knees I steered my horse to where it lay, and I leaned far out from the saddle at full gallop. My fingers closed over the jeweled hilt. As I came upright in the saddle again I shouted at her, "Serrena!," and my voice carried over the uproar of screams and wild shouts, the thunder of galloping hooves and the enraged roars of the great hog of the goddess Artemis.

Serrena switched her eyes toward the sound of my voice, and I swung the blue sword once around my head. "Here, Serrena! Catch it!"

With all my strength I hurled the weapon high. It spun once as it fell toward where she stood. Serrena pivoted gracefully under it and then snatched it out of the air. Now that the marvelous weapon was in the right hand of a demigoddess, the conundrum set for us by Artemis was on the point of reaching a solution. Serrena ran to meet the boar's next charge. I watched her with my heart pounding, caught up in a contradictory surge of pride and terror. Pride in her beauty and courage; terror at the danger she was running into.

The boar must have sensed her approach, for it left the horse it was savaging and spun around to face Serrena. The instant its eyes fixed on her, it launched into its charge. Serrena stopped and balanced on the tips of her toes, flaunting herself before the great pig, but at the last possible moment, she pirouetted aside. As it passed her the boar slashed at her with those wicked tusks with which it had so effortlessly disemboweled King Hurotas' horse. One of the ivory points snagged in the folds of her tunic, but it tore free without upsetting her balance.

Then as the beast barged past her, she cut back-handed at it with the silver-blue blade. The bright edge caught the joint of the boar's nearside back leg and severed it cleanly. The truncated limb remained upright, with its hoof buried in the clinging mud and its severed muscles twitching and jerking.

However, on its three remaining legs the boar was almost as agile as it had been on four. It spun around, using its one remaining rear leg as a pivot. It was no longer bellowing, but now it was chattering its jaws so that its tusks clashed together like castanets: a terrifying sound. Again Serrena let it come in close as it charged at her, then she whirled aside once more and the blade in her hand seemed to dissolve into a streak of quicksilver as it slashed across the boar's front right elbow joint and sliced through it as if it was a stem of boiled asparagus.

Deprived of two of its legs, the boar tumbled head-first to the earth and somersaulted over on to its back. In a wild attempt to regain its balance, it stretched its neck out along the muddy ground. Its neck was as thick as a tree trunk. Serrena stood over it, and with both hands on the hilt of the blue sword she swung it high over her head and then brought it down again in a glistening arc. The blade whistled sharply through the air with the power behind the stroke. The boar's colossal head seemed to leap off its humped shoulders. Its mouth was wide open, and it uttered a mournful sound as it hit the ground, partly a howl of rage and partly a death lament. A fountain of dark blood spurted up out of its severed throat and drenched the skirts of Serrena's tunic as she stood over it in an attitude of triumph.

I shouted with wild approbation, and immediately a hundred other voices joined with mine. Rameses ran forward to embrace her with relief. Tehuti dragged herself to her feet, and mastering the agony of her shattered wrist, which she still clutched to her bosom, she rushed to join him. The foreign kings and generals, led by Admiral Hui at the head of his Spartans, came swarming up the vineyard to laud and extol Serrena's courage and warlike skills. One after the other they dropped to their knees before her and heaped their praise and adulation upon her. She acknowledged them all with a sweeping gesture, then placed one arm around Tehuti's shoulders and helped her to where King Hurotas still lay unconscious.

Within a very short time they had revived him, and he sat up and looked around him blearily. Only then did the two women I loved more than anything in this creation turn toward me in unison and smile their gratitude over the heads of the clamorous multitude.

With that simple acknowledgment I was replete.

B er Argolid of Boeotia in Thebes, the man known as "Strong-arm" for the weight of the sword he wields, was the most important and powerful of the petty chieftains. He had ordered his minions to bring his throne to the hunting field for his comfort, but more importantly to emphasize his importance. Now, however, he insisted that Serrena should take her seat upon the throne in recognition of her feat of arms in killing the great boar. Not to be outdone, the other visiting kings and chieftains demonstrated their respect by carrying her on the throne in a procession of honor. Eight at a time, they took turns to hoist her onto their shoulders, and singing her praises, they marched with her down from the Taygetus Mountains to the citadel.

The news of her marvelous kill had preceded her by word of mouth, so what seemed to me to be the entire population of Lacedaemon had turned out to line the roadway, cheering her and pelting her with flower petals and wild acclaim. I walked at her left-hand side, the position of honor. My inherent modesty dictated that I should not thrust myself forward, but Princess Serrena insisted.

The return home took most of the rest of the day, and the sun was lowering toward the horizon when the portable throne was finally placed upon the dais in the courtyard of the citadel. Even then Serrena was not allowed to descend from it.

Her father, King Hurotas, had by this time completely recovered from his brush with the great boar, and, always the opportunist, he seized the opportunity to confirm and weld the loyalty of the sixteen petty chieftains to the standard of Spartan Lacedaemon.

The importance and excitement of the occasion were irresistible. If Serrena's beauty had been dazzling before, it was now ineffable as she glowed with the adulation that was being heaped upon her. Nobody— man or woman, old or young, noble or commoner— was able to resist it. The royal visitors and Serrena's erstwhile suitors were carried along with it as helplessly as the rest of us.

When King Hurotas stood to address them with his wounded queen beside him, looking noble and brave with her damaged hand in a sling that I had prepared for her, and his lovely daughter at his other hand, they hung on every word he uttered and they cheered him at the end of each sentence he emoted. Most of the kings had by this time equipped themselves with flagons of Hurotas' good red wine, which they were treating with respectful attention. Slaves were standing ready to refill the vessels before they were half empty.

Hurotas told the assembled kings and dignitaries how he had come to look upon them as his brothers, united by a common cause and a mutual respect. This raised an exceptionally loud and enthusiastic burst of applause. When it eventually died down, King Ber Argolid rose to his feet determined not to be outdone by Hurotas' extravagant oratory.

"From now onward, an offense to one of our number is an offense to all of us equally," he cried. "We have already ratified and signed a pact of mutual protection, so let us now join hands and swear an oath."

"Who will hear our oath?" demanded Hurotas.

"Who else but the most beautiful woman in the world?" Ber Argolid answered him. "Who else but the bravest woman alive who slew the Laconian boar?"

So one after the other, in no particular order, the

sixteen kings came forward and bent the knee before Princess Serrena and swore the Oath of the Great Boar. The ceremony and the celebration that accompanied it went on long after nightfall. One might have thought that the company would have been exhausted by this time, but it was only a beginning. The dancing, drinking and carousing had only just begun, and Serrena was the most tireless of us all. She danced with all the kings, including her own father and Rameses who was not yet a king. She even danced with me more than once and complimented me that I was the lightest on my feet of all the men who had been her partners, except for Rameses. But then she was duty bound to say that because she was betrothed to him, was she not?

When Hurotas challenged Ber Strong-arm Argolid to a bout of single-handed wrestling, most of the men left the dance floor to place their bets on the outcome of the contest. The amounts they wagered were ruinous, and their excitement was commensurate as they bellowed encouragement to their favorites. Stripped to their loincloths, the protagonists faced each other across the oaken feasting table and grunted and groaned and sweated as they tried to rip each other's arms off at the shoulders.

I was probably the only one present whose hearing was acute enough to discern anything above the pandemonium they and their audience were creating. But I gradually became aware of the faint strains of sweet singing emanating from beyond the citadel walls.

I left the contest and climbed to the parapet of the outer wall and looked down on an array of no fewer than fifty women, all dressed in ankle-length white robes, and with their faces also painted a deathly hue with white lead, and their eyes circled with black kohl. They were climbing the causeway to the citadel gates, each carrying a lighted lantern and chanting an ode to Artemis. I recognized by their makeup and religious robes that they were acolytes of the goddess. I knew that Hurotas and his stalwarts would not look kindly on having their revels curtailed by Artemis' minions whining and wailing about the death of their favorite pig. So I rushed down the stairway to the main gates of the citadel to warn the guards to deny them entry, only to find that I was too late. The guards had recognized the procession of priestesses and had thrown the gates open to welcome them.

Fifty priestesses of Artemis and twice as many armed guards had jammed the passageway into the citadel, which had been designed to be defensively narrow. I was forced back by their multitude and found myself once more in the courtyard where I was immediately embroiled with Hurotas and his new allies, the petty chieftains headed up by Ber Strong-arm Argolid. Everybody was shouting, including me. But none of us were listening.

Then quite unexpectedly a clearer and more lyrical voice cut through the uproar. It was so compelling that silence immediately descended upon us all. All heads turned toward the sound of it, and an opening appeared in the serried ranks confronting each other, through which stepped the lithe and lovely form of Princess Serrena.

"Reverend Mother!" She genuflected to the high priestess. "You are welcome here in my father's citadel."

"My lovely child, I bring you greetings and a message from the goddess Artemis. Are you willing to accept her holy word? If you are, then I beg you please kneel to receive it," answered Sister Hagne, who was the reverend mother of the Order of the Sisters of the Golden Bow. The Golden Bow was one of the many symbols of the goddess Artemis.

King Hurotas started forward at this, his expression bellicose and his eyes aglow with pugnacity. "We'll see about that . . ." he started. But fortunately I was close enough to him to seize his naked arm, all greasy with the sweat of his recent exertions.

"Restrain yourself, Zaras," I whispered so he alone could hear me. I used his former name, exerting my dominance over him from long ago. At once he checked himself and subsided. Our minor contretemps went unnoticed in the religious intensity of the moment.

Serrena sank obediently to her knees before the high priestess, who with her forefinger drew the symbol of the bow upon her forehead and then began to speak again in more profound and awesome tones, which even raised the goose pimples on my forearms: "The goddess Artemis recognizes you as her sister of blood and bone . . ."

I could not prevent myself from glancing at Tehuti where she stood beside her husband, clinging to his other arm. Like me she was trying to restrain his temper. Instinctively she returned my look as soon as she felt my eyes on her. She flushed and dropped her eyes as we both remembered what she had told me of her dream, her very real and palpable dream of the conception of this her only child. Then I switched my attention back to the high priestess. Like everyone else present I was anxious to hear what she had to say.

"Artemis recognizes and applauds the blow you struck today for the exaltation and prestige of all womankind. You have proven that we females are fully equal to the men who would seek to dominate and subjugate us." As she said this I saw Hurotas open his mouth to protest with renewed outrage and vigor. However,

Tehuti kicked his shin to prevent him from blaspheming. It was a shrewd blow for I heard the power behind it, and Hurotas bellowed with the pain.

"Oh, woman! Are you trying to maim me for life?"

I shouted with him, and I was closer to where the priestess stood so my words overrode his: "Oh, woman, you have saved the king's life!"

The sixteen kings joined in the adulation. "The Princess Serrena has saved the king's life! All hail to her!"

The high priestess, who was misnamed Hagne, which means the Pure One, was delighted with this endorsement, and I saw her eyes light up, despite the kohl that dulled much of their luster, as they settled on King Ber Argolid for the first time.

The goddess Artemis was a virgin, and no animal, man, or god would ever be allowed to violate her. She and her body were sacrosanct. She would wreak a terrible revenge on any male who even attempted to gain carnal knowledge of her. However, one of the most important duties of the priestesses of Artemis was to act as erogenous surrogates for their beloved goddess. They are sanctioned by her to have sexual congress with any creature on this earth, be it man, woman, human or animal, fish, fowl or beast. All the physical sensations they experienced in this manner were capable of being transmitted in their entirety to Artemis. However, the goddess herself would remain forever pure and unsullied by even the most unnatural conjunctions of diverse flesh, organs or apertures that were visited on her surrogates. It was an arrangement that has always fascinated me. It promises limitless possibilities even for one as physically deprived as myself.

All fifty of Artemis' priestesses followed their high priestess into the main hall of the citadel. Their demeanor was gracious and formal, but there was an underlying rapacity in all of them that reminded me of a shoal of tiger fish in the Nile River that has sensed blood in the water. Within the hour all pretense of modesty had been abandoned by our visitors along with most of their clothing. The dancing became little short of copulatory, but I admit that most of them had the forbearance to retire to the surrounding chambers before taking the final steps along the primrose path.

I was also relieved to see that Bekatha and Tehuti kept their husbands and female offspring well under their eagle eyes for the entire evening. Bekatha was more lenient, however, when it came to her four sons. I overheard an exchange between Serrena and her youngest cousin when he returned from a brief sojourn in one of the outer chambers.

"Where have you been, Palmys, and what have you

been doing?" Serrena demanded of him. "I wanted you to dance with me."

"I was making a sacrifice to Artemis," the boy told her smugly.

"I thought you were strictly an Apollo worshipper."

"Sometimes it's a good thing to bet on two chariots in the same race."

"Will you show me how you make a sacrifice to one of the divines?" Serrena asked naively.

"I offered to show you once, but you refused. More fool, you. So now you will just have to wait until Rameses gets around to teaching you the trick of it."

She stared at him for a moment while she pondered his reply, then her green eyes seemed to double in size and their intensity of green as she caught the sense of his allusion. "You have always been a dirty little boy, haven't you, Palmys?" she said sweetly. "But now it seems that you are growing up to be an even dirtier old man." And she swatted him behind the ear, so unexpectedly and so hard that he howled a protest.

Not all the associations that evening were so ill fated. King Ber Argolid returned much later from wherever he had been conducting his liaison with the High Priestess Hagne with a louche expression on his face and a lascivious sparkle in his eye. He went directly to his host King Hurotas to announce his betrothal to Hagne, who, it seemed, had very recently resigned from her position of reverend mother of the Order of the Sisters of the Golden Bow.

"Did I misunderstand you when you said that you already had ten lovely wives on your home island of Minoan Rhodes?" Hurotas could hardly refrain from grinning.

"The correct figure is actually thirteen, my dear Hurotas. But as you are no doubt aware that is the most ill-fated number in our lexicon of numerology, whereas fourteen is extremely propitious."

They were married that very afternoon by Hurotas, and it was another excellent cause for further celebration. However, the following day was the thirteenth day before the wedding of Serrena and Rameses, but I thought nothing of that at the time.

I awoke the next morning with a headache and a sense of the utmost foreboding. I lay upon my mattress and tried to fathom the reason for my sudden change of mood from the previous day. I sent one of my servants to make inquiry of the previous day's bride and groom, King Ber Argolid and Reverend Mother Hagne, but he returned to inform me that they were still ensconced in their sleeping chamber. However, judging by the squeals of feminine delight and other sounds suggestive of heavy furniture being moved about vigorously or perhaps even being broken into small pieces, they were not actually sleeping. In addition, all the other wives and offspring, including Princess Serrena, were well and none of them had been struck down by disease or any other misfortune; in fact, as the servant was reporting his findings to me, I heard happy cries and the laughter of young voices coming up through the windows of my rooms from the courtyard below. I went across to the windows and looked down.

I was mightily relieved to see that Rameses and Princess Serrena were mounted on their favorite steeds, and accompanied by two of Serrena's handmaidens and a number of Rameses' armed retainers, they were riding out through the gates of the citadel on some pleasure excursion. I smiled to myself as I realized that my sense of impending doom was probably the result of the two or three additional flagons of excellent red wine that Hurotas had pressed upon me the previous evening—contrary to my better judgment.

I went down to the river and swam naked in the cold waters, a sovereign cure for the unpleasant aftereffects of the fermented grape. Then, with my head and conscience clear, I returned to the citadel and went to join Hurotas and Hui in the council chamber, with twelve of their sixteen royal allies. The other four had sent their apologies, but they were all indisposed.

A short while after noon, Rameses returned to the citadel alone and came up to join us in our warlike preparations.

"Where is the Princess Serrena?" was my very first question to him.

"I left her on north beach, at the Blue Pool."

I knew it well. "You did not leave her alone, I hope?"

"Almost alone." He regarded me with an air of long-suffering. "With only two of her handmaidens and eight of my best warriors. I think she should be safe enough for the next few hours. I felt it was my duty to join your discussion as your plans involve the participation of my ship and my men. You should bear in mind that Serrena isn't an infant any longer, Taita. She is very well capable of taking care of herself. She promised to return here four hours after noon."

"Rameses is right." Uninvited, Hurotas joined our private discussion. "She is well protected."

Of course, then Hui had to poke his long nose in where it was not particularly welcome. "One of her bodyguards is Palmys, my youngest son. He may be young, but he is fierce," he boasted.

I felt my mood turning gloomy again, but the others had dismissed the subject and moved on with their deliberations. When I tried to remain aloof, they kept pestering me and insisting on involving me in their planning. It was difficult to ignore them, and despite myself I was gradually drawn into the debate. In fact, it was such a challenging discussion that I gradually lost all sense of the passage of time.

Then eventually two slave girls entered the chamber quietly and began lighting the oil lamps from burning tapers. I was surprised by this, until I glanced out the windows to a splendid view of the Taygetus Mountains and saw the sinking sun slipping below the jagged crests.

"In the name of mighty Zeus!" I blasphemed with surprise as I sprang to my feet. "What hour is it?"

Hui stood up and crossed to the water clock that stood on the table in the far corner. He tapped the counter with his forefinger. "This clock must be wrongly adjusted. It is dripping too fast. It shows eight hours past noon. Surely that is wrong?"

"Look out the window at the sun. That is never wrong," I answered, but then I turned to Rameses. "What time did you arrange that Serrena and the rest of her party should return?"

Rameses jumped to his feet with a guilt-stricken expression. "I am sure they must already be back in the citadel. They would have returned several hours ago. But Serrena would not want to disturb us. Hurotas left strict instructions . . ."

I did not wait to hear any more of his airy suppositions, but I was halfway out of the chamber doors when

Hurotas called after me, "Come back, Taita. Where do you think you are going?"

"To the main gates. The sentries will know if Serrena has returned or not," I shouted over my shoulder. I could hardly recognize my own voice, shrill with panic, ringing in my ears. I have no idea why I was so agitated, but suddenly all my earlier gloomy premonitions were hovering over me on vulture's wings, and the stink of disaster was rank in my nostrils. I ran like a stag pursued by hounds, and I heard the clatter of boots on the stairs as the others chased after me. I burst into the courtyard and was yelling at the guards from a distance of a hundred paces, "Has the Princess Serrena yet returned to the citadel?" I had to repeat myself before one of them understood me.

"Not yet, my Lord Taita," he shouted back at me. "We have been waiting . . ."

I could not bear to listen to more of his piffle. I brushed past him and kept running toward the stables. I remembered that I had left my sword hanging in the council chamber, but I could not go back to retrieve it, not now. I knew with the utmost certainty that something terrible had happened to Serrena. She needed me desperately.

I slipped the bit between the teeth of my favorite mount, a beautiful chestnut mare that Tehuti had given me. Then, without wasting time saddling her, I swung up on her bare back and drove my heels into her ribs.

"Hi up, Summer!" I called to her, and we flew out of the stable yard and took the road that crossed the pass in the mountains and led down to the north coast. I looked back once and saw the others led by Rameses, Hurotas and Hui far behind me but riding hard in a futile attempt to catch up with me.

The daylight was starting to fade by the time I reached the narrow path that led down to the beach and the Blue Pool. I was still pushing Summer, when suddenly she shied so wildly from the path that a less accomplished horseman would have been thrown from her back. But I clamped her between my knees and brought her down to a head-tossing halt. I looked back at the object lying in the path that had disturbed my mare. Then, with a surge of dismay, I realized that it was a human cadaver. I slid down from Summer's back and led her jibbing and tossing her head to where the body lay facedown. It was soaked with gouts of blood. I went down on one knee and gently rolled it onto its back. I recognized it at once.

It was Palmys: Hui and Bekatha's boy. He was stark naked. His murderers had sported with him before they cut his throat. They had sliced open his belly and drawn out his entrails. They had hacked off his manly parts and stabbed his eyes, leaving the sockets empty pits. He was no longer a fine-looking young man, and I felt a bitter pang of compassion for his parents.

When I stood again and looked around me, I saw why they had tortured him once they had subdued him. Palmys had placed a bitterly high price on his own life. There were the bodies of four of his assailants scattered in the undergrowth nearby, those whom he had taken with him on his journey to Anubis in the underworld.

I cursed them in the most virulent terms, but words cannot succor the dead. My full attention switched to those still living—if there were any. How many assailants had there been? I wondered, for the path had been trampled by many feet. I estimated that there must have been thirty at the least, including those four that Palmys had taken with him.

But in the forefront of my mind, overshadowing all else, was the image of Serrena. How had they dealt with her? When they stripped off her clothing, would any of them have been able to resist her naked beauty? I could almost hear their lascivious clamor as they held her down and waited for their turn to mount her. I felt the tears run down my face, tears of anger, horror and compassion. I scrambled up on to Summer's back and in wild despair sent her flying down the path toward the Blue Pool.

There were seven other corpses littered along the path. All of them were male and most of them hideously mutilated. They were those Rameses had detailed to guard Serrena. I wasted no more time in stopping to examine them. Despite myself I felt a glimmer of hope, for I had found no sign of Serrena or her two handmaidens. Perhaps the intruders were saving the women. Perhaps they knew the value of Serrena at ransom if she had not been ravaged and raped.

I came out through the forest above the beach and halted again. The daylight was failing swiftly. However, I could see the footprints the intruders had left on the golden beach sands leading down to the edge of the water. But before my eyes the horizon faded into the murk and gloom. I was unable to make out any trace of a strange ship on the darkling sea. My first impulse was to ride down to the water's edge, but with an effort I restrained myself when I realized that by doing so I might wipe out valuable signs that the marauders had left in the soft sand.

I dismounted and swiftly tethered Summer by her reins to a sturdy branch at the edge of the forest. Then I followed the tracks in the sand, keeping wide of them so as not to spoil them. Within the first few yards, I noticed something that repaid my diligence in full. There was one series of regular drag marks superimposed on the ruck of many other feet. I recognized them almost immediately.

I had already fixed my mind on the idea that the assailants were a gang of pirates who had come upon Serrena and her companions completely by random chance. But now I realized this was not the case. However, I was distracted at that moment by the sound of hoofbeats and voices shouting my name from the pathway through the forest above the beach. I recognized Rameses' voice and also that of Hurotas.

"Here!" I answered them.

They rode out of the forest into the open. The instant they spotted me they urged their mount toward where I stood, both of them shouting desperate questions at me.

"Serrena! Have you found her?"

"Is she here?"

"No! She is gone, but I think I know where she must be," I called back.

"In the name of gentle Artemis!" Rameses pleaded. "Whoever these outlaws are, they have murdered Palmys and all our men. We left Hui with the body of his son. He is totally destroyed by the loss. I beg of you, don't let them have done the same thing to my Serrena."

Riding at Rameses' left hand, Hurotas was working

himself into an ungovernable rage, bellowing savage
oaths and threats. "I will find whoever it is that has
done this monstrous thing if it takes me the rest of my
life," he roared. "And when I catch them, I will give
them such a death as will astound the very gods."

They reined their mounts in alongside me. "Who
was it, Taita? You know everything." Rameses swung
down from his horse's saddle and seized me by my
shoulders. He began shaking me wildly.

"Unhand me, and calm yourself!" I shouted back
at him, and with an effort managed to free myself.
"There! Look for yourself!" I pointed out the tracks in
the sand.

"I don't understand . . ." Hurotas yelled at me.
"What are you trying to show us?"

"Look at those prints there in the center of the
track. See how whoever made them is dragging his
right foot."

"Panmasi!" Rameses screamed the name as he realized what I was telling him. "The one Serrena herself
forced us to release. The filthy ungrateful bastard came
straight back here to seize her and spirit her away to
Utteric's lair."

"Well, at the very least, we now know that there is
an excellent chance that Serrena is still alive. Utteric
would never allow Panmasi to kill such an invalu-

able hostage," I tried to console both Hurotas and Rameses.

"I pray that you are right, Taita. But we must go after them at once." Rameses spoke like a man stretched on the torture rack. "We have to wrest Serrena from their clutches."

"This is my daughter, my only child, that these rogues have stolen from me. Rameses is right. We must go after her immediately." Hurotas was also consumed with rage and despair. "With the favor of the gods, we might just be able to catch them before they reach the mouth of the Nile, for that is certainly where they are taking her."

I was not in a much better state than either of them, but I was able to contain my emotions more firmly. "We must waste no more time here wailing and beating our breasts." I spoke harshly, trying to rally them. "By the time we have ridden back to Port Githion and prepared our ships for sea, Panmasi will have almost a full ten hours' start on us. Added to that, we have no idea in what type of vessel he has spirited her away." I pointed out the marks of a ship's bow in the sand at the edge of the beach. "The signs are that it is a small trading barque. But the sea between here and Egypt is littered with such vessels. As soon as each one spots us they will take us for pirates and run from us. We will have to chase down every vessel we sight: a long, dreary business. In the meantime, Panmasi will be running for the Nile with every sail set and every oar double-manned."

That was sufficient for them to worry about at present, so I did not point out the possibility that Panmasi would not head directly for the mouth of the Nile. He might have arranged for chariots to be waiting at one of the many tiny ports on the North African coast to carry him and his captive overland to Luxor. Once Panmasi entered the Nile River or even the territory of Egypt, he would be beyond our reach.

"Hurotas is right," I said with all the force I could muster. "Every moment is precious. We must ride for Port Githion immediately. We have to get out to sea and attempt to pick up Panmasi's scent before it fades."

Despite my bravado the darkness of the moonless night hampered us, and it was well after midnight before we reached the harbor.

While Rameses, Hurotas and Hui were preparing their ships for sea with desperate haste I was given the hateful task of riding to the citadel to break the news to Tehuti and Bekatha of the loss of their children. It is probably unkind of me to suggest that neither Hurotas nor Hui had the courage to do this for themselves.

However, by now I was inured to the horrors that had been inflicted upon all of us.

I went first to deliver the mutilated corpse of Palmys to Bekatha. When her maids had awakened her from her bed, I held her in my arms and tried to explain to her the dreadful fate that had overtaken her youngest son. I think she was still befuddled by the wine she had imbibed earlier. She kept assuring me that Palmys had taken his dinner and was already asleep in his bed.

Gently I led her through to the antechamber where my men had laid him. Despite my efforts to cover up his injuries—washing the blood from his face and combing out his hair, then closing the lids of his empty eye sockets and binding up his disemboweled stomach—he was still a terrible sight for any mother to be presented with. She recoiled from him and clung to me for a few moments and then threw herself upon his body, wailing and shaking with despair.

After a while, I was able to persuade Bekatha to drink a powerful sedative that I had prepared from my medicine chest and waited with her until it took effect. Then I summoned one of her other sons to take over her care from me, and I went to find Tehuti.

This was even more harrowing for me than her younger sister's display of grief.

I sent her maids away to wait in one of the outer rooms, and then I went through to her bedchamber. She was asleep on top of her blankets, lying on her back wearing an ankle-length nightdress. Her lovely long hair was combed out and shining like the snows on the peaks of the Taygetus in the light of the moon streaming through the high windows. She looked like a young girl again. I lay down beside her and took her in my arms.

"Taita!" she whispered without opening her eyes. "I know it is you. You always smell so good."

"You are right, Tehuti. It is I."

"I am so afraid," she said. "I had a terrible dream."

"You must be brave, Tehuti, as brave as you always are."

She rolled over in my arms to face me. "You have sad news for me, and I can sense it. It is Serrena, isn't it?"

"I am so sorry, my darling." I choked on the words.

"Tell me, Taita. Don't try to shield me from the truth."

She listened to me in abject silence, pale-faced and stony-eyed in the glow from her night-lamp, which she kept lit to scare away the hobgoblins. When I had stumbled my way into silence, she asked me quietly, "You say it is Utteric who did this?"

"It can only be him."

"Will he hurt her?"

"No!" My voice rose in vehement denial to cover my uncertainty. Utteric was mad. He did not act or think like other men. "She has no value to him if she is killed or mutilated." I crossed the fingers of my left hand as I said it. I did not want to annoy the gods by making sweeping assertions.

"Will you find my baby and bring her back to me, Tata?"

"Yes, Tehuti. You know I will."

"Thank you," she whispered. "It is best that you go now, before I make a complete idiot of myself."

"You are the bravest woman I know."

"Bekatha will need me. I must go to her." She kissed me. Then she stood up and donned the cloak that lay on the table beside the bed and walked from the room with dignity. But as she closed the door behind her I thought that I heard a muffled sob; however, I might have been mistaken, for Tehuti was not one much given to weeping.

The top edge of the sun had cleared the horizon before I finally reached Port Githion again. I found that Hurotas was aboard his flagship in the harbor, and when I too went aboard to report to him, he was just finishing a conference with the sixteen petty chieftains of the alliance. All of them had affirmed their oaths and their pledge to him: *An offense to one is an offense to all.*

Every one of them had undertaken to set sail during the next few days for their homelands and there to muster their separate armies in readiness for the campaign that loomed ahead for all of us. This was momentous news indeed. I, for one, had expected two or three of our sworn allies to renege on their obligations if they were ever called upon to make good on them. I congratulated Hurotas and Hui, and then I told them that I had informed their wives of the abduction of Serrena and the murder of Palmys. They were as grateful to me and as ashamed of themselves as I expected them to be—in that neither of them had shown the courage to deliver the terrible news to their spouses and to face the first waves of their grief and despair.

"Well and good," I told them. "But now we must go after Panmasi. The time for talking is over. The killing time is close at hand."

At last I was free to hurry along the wharf to where the *Memnon* was shortening up her mooring lines, in preparation to casting off.

"I thought you would never be ready to leave," Rameses told me grimly as I clambered on board. "Where in the honor and dignity of the great god Zeus have you been hiding yourself, Taita?"

"Is that an accusation of cowardice?" I asked him in a tone that made him blanch and recoil a step.

"Forgive me, Taita. I should never have said that to you, of all people alive. But I am half mad with anguish."

"So am I, Rameses. That is why I never heard you say what you just did." I went on at once: "Have you brought my pigeons on board?"

"A full cage of twelve of them; all of them female because they are the strongest, fastest and most determined, like all women, as you have remarked to me more than once." At that I heard the familiar cooing coming up the companionway from the lower deck. Rameses smiled faintly, probably for the first time since he had lost Serrena.

"They heard your voice. They love you, Tata, as we all do."

"Then prove it to me by getting this ship under way immediately, if not sooner," I said sternly and went below to my beauties.

Beside the birdcage in my cabin I found my writing case on the desk where it should have been, and a roll of papyrus beside it. I immediately set about composing a short but lucid message to send to Weneg in his wineshop in the shadow of the walls of Utteric's palace in Luxor. I told him I was entirely certain that it was Utteric who had ordered the abduction of Serrena; however, it was Panmasi who had carried out the deed.

Panmasi was on his way to Egypt and we were in pursuit, but he had more than a twelve hours' head start on us. There was a strong chance that we would be unable to catch him before he reached Egypt. If this turned out to be the case, then Utteric would almost certainly hold Serrena either at the palace of Luxor or within the Gates of Torment and Sorrow. I asked him to confirm my evaluation of the crisis, and to keep me informed of anything further that might be of value to us in our attempts to find and rescue the princess.

Once I was satisfied with my composition I wrote it out on three separate copies of lightweight papyrus paper. I always repeat my messages thrice. This is to ensure that at least one copy is received in good order. The skies are a dangerous place for plump young pigeons, for they are patrolled zealously by hawks and kestrels; but past experience had convinced me that at least one out of three of my birds would manage to return safely to the coop in which it had been hatched.

Thus I selected three of the strongest birds from the cage and secured an identical message to each of their legs. Then I carried one of these up to the poop deck under my arm and left the other two in their cage.

As I came out on deck I was relieved to see that we had cleared the harbor and were headed into the open sea. I then released my first bird into the wind. It circled the ship three times and then winged away on a southerly heading. At intervals of an hour I released the remaining two birds and watched them disappear over the horizon. We followed them more sedately in the *Memnon*.

The wind was fresh out of the northwest, so we ran

before it on a broad reach, our best point of sailing. We raised the island of Crete in six days of sailing and then the African coast in five days more. During this time we stopped and boarded nine strange vessels to search them. All of them took us for pirates and tried to escape us. So, as I had predicted, we had to run each one down in a stern chase. This accounted in a large measure for the time it took us to make the southern run from Port Githion to the mouth of the Nile River. It was no surprise to me that Serrena was not on board any one of the vessels that we intercepted, but Rameses and I could not take the chance of missing her.

I prayed to Artemis that if Serrena were already locked behind the Gates of Torment and Sorrow, the goddess would not allow the dreaded Doog to have his way with her. It was no comfort to me to know that Pharaoh himself would not choose to take that route with her. He preferred to follow paths not so sweetly perfumed as hers.

Once we reached the mouth of the Nile River we patrolled it for three more days. We kept below the horizon during the daylight hours but closed with the land during the hours of darkness. On the fourth day Rameses and I were both agreed that it was futile to remain any longer on station here. We knew that by this time Serrena was almost certainly in Egypt, given how long it had been since she had been abducted. So we turned back to the northwesterly heading and re-traced our route to Port Githion in Lacedaemon. The wind was no longer in our favor. The days dwindled away with infuriating sluggishness.

When we were finally in sight of Port Githion, we were hailed by a fishing vessel coming out from the harbor. We heaved to and waited for the trawler to come alongside. The person who had stopped us turned out to be another one of Admiral Hui's sons, a strapping and engaging lad named Huisson.

"Uncle Tata!" he shouted as soon as he was close enough for his voice to carry. "We have had news of Serrena. She is safe and well." He continued shouting his message as our vessels closed. "A Levantine trader plying to Egypt delivered a message from the court of Utteric in Luxor to our good king, Hurotas. Utteric boasts that his agents have seized our cousin, Princess Serrena, and that he is holding her hostage in Luxor. He is offering to arrange an exchange for her, but on his own terms."

I felt a great surge of relief at these tidings, followed almost immediately by a plunge of despair. The relief was for the fact that Serrena was alive. My despair was that Utteric was holding such a vital bargaining counter in his slimy paws.

Huisson came on board the *Memnon* and we sailed into Port Githion, discussing all the implications of these developments with anxiety and trepidation. As soon as we had moored our ship, I told Rameses and Huisson to wait for me while I went to collect the messages that my pigeon-handler's birds had brought him. He ran to meet me with a sheath of papyrus slips in his hand, all of them sent by Weneg in Luxor. They made bitter reading for me, and I was in tears when I had finished.

According to Weneg, Panmasi and his captive, Princess Serrena, had reached Luxor eighteen days previously. That was three days before we on the *Memnon* had reached the mouth of the Nile in pursuit of him.

Weneg had been a spectator in the crowd of several hundred citizens that had assembled on the docks, by order of Pharaoh Utteric Bubastis, when Serrena had been marched ashore stark naked and with her feet unshod and the glorious tresses of her hair hanging to her waist, but not so low as to cover her pudendum.

Weneg recorded how the citizens of Luxor had been reduced to silence by her beauty, and by the shock at the humiliating treatment being accorded her. Of course, none of the spectators had any idea as to who this stranger might be.

On the jetty her captors forced Serrena to her knees while one of the royal grooms sheared off the tresses of her glorious hair. A low hum of protest rose from the watchers.

Utteric glared at them, trying to ascertain which of them were defying him. This forced them to silence. Then Utteric turned and beckoned to Doog, the royal tormentor and executioner. He came forward with alacrity, followed by a band of his masked henchmen who were leading a team of oxen pulling a dung cart. They lifted Serrena to her feet and heaved her into the body of the cart. They pinioned her to an upright beam there, so she was unable to cover her nudity. Then with a drummer leading the way, they paraded her through the streets of Luxor where the populace lined the route and were incited by Doog's men to shower her with insults and ordure. Finally they led her up into hills to the Gates of Torment and Sorrow. She disappeared through the gates and they slammed shut behind her. Weneg had not seen her since.

When I had finished reading Weneg's account of her humiliation, I left Port Githion and climbed to the summit of the Taygetus Mountains. I ran most of the way to subdue my distress with hard physical effort. From the mountain peak I shouted my outrage to the gods on Mount Olympus and warned them that unless they took better care of their daughter I would have to assume that responsibility from them.

Perhaps it was just the climb to the mountain peak, but I was feeling much more certain of myself and what I had to do when I descended and found Rameses and Huisson waiting for me with the horses saddled. We set off immediately for the citadel. When we reached it we hurried to the council chamber where we found that King Hurotas and Admiral Hui were in earnest conclave with three of the petty chieftains. Hurotas jumped up and rushed to me as soon as I entered the chamber.

"Have you heard the news?" he cried. "We have received a message directly from Utteric, brought by a Levantine trader. You were right, Taita! It was indeed Panmasi, Utteric's underling, who seized my Serrena. He gloats on it without shame. She was the one who saved his life, and this is how this pig-swine has repaid her. But now we know the worst of it, and we know where they are holding her. But the most important thing by far is that they have not injured her. They have only humiliated her in the most loathsome manner."

"Yes." I embraced Hurotas to reassure him. "Huisson has told me as much. He says Utteric is offering to trade."

"I do not trust him. Utteric is a venomous snake. In the end we will almost certainly have to go to war with him," Hurotas declared. "We will have to see what price he is demanding. It will not be cheap, that is the only thing we can be very certain of. But by silver and by blood I will pay him what he deserves," he promised me grimly and then turned to the three petty chieftains at the council table. "These are the chieftains Faas, Parviz and Poe."

"Yes, I know them well." I greeted the three of them.

"Of course, I had forgotten." Hurotas looked slightly abashed. "But I am distracted by the news about my Serrena. Forgive me, Taita."

"Have you relayed the good news to Tehuti?" I demanded.

"Not yet," Hurotas admitted. "I myself only heard less than an hour ago. Anyway, she has gone out riding, and I don't know where to look for her." Hurotas paused expectantly, and of course I knew what he wanted of me.

"I think I know where she is. With your permission I will go to her," I suggested.

"Yes! Go at once, Taita. Her heart has been broken. You, of all people alive, know how to lighten her mood."

I rode to the royal lodge on the bank of the Hurotas River. I left my horse at the hitching rack and walked through the empty rooms calling her name, but all of them were deserted. So I left the building and went down to the riverbank.

I heard the splash of water before I reached the pool in which the two of them, mother and daughter, had spent so much of their time swimming. I came round the river bend and I saw her head, with her dense hair slicked down on her skull, as she swam into the current. She had not seen me, so I found a seat on a boulder at the water's edge and watched her with pleasure. I knew that she was subjugating her inner pain with hard physical exertion, just as I had done by climbing to the summit of the Taygetus.

Back and forth she swam across the flood until I felt my own muscles aching. Then she came close to the bank below me and stood to her full height in the shallows. She was naked, but her body was as sleek and muscled as I remembered it thirty years previously. She waded to the bank; she had still not seen me sitting quietly on my rock.

Then I stood up and she saw me. She stopped and stared up at me with trepidation. Then I smiled down at her, and instantly her lovely face echoed mine with delight. She ran toward me, bursting the surface of the river into foam.

"Thank you! Thank you, Taita!" She laughed through her tears of relief.

I laughed with her. "How did you know that I brought glad tidings?"

"By your face! By your beautiful smiling face!" She ran up the bank and threw her cold wet body into my arms. We hugged each other and she demanded, "Where is she?"

"She is a captive in Utteric's prison." I did not want to pronounce the name "Torment and Sorrow."

The smile fled from her face. "In Luxor?" she asked.

"She is well and unhurt," I assured her. "Utteric is willing to negotiate her release."

"Oh, how I wish I could go to her!" Her voice dropped to a whisper. I shook my head.

"No! You would never come back, but Serrena will. It may take time, but I swear to you that I will bring her back to you," I said simply. "I will leave just as soon as I can make the final arrangements. I do not think I will be able to get to her where she is being held, but even if somehow I can let her know that I am close, it will bolster her courage and alleviate her suffering a little."

"All of us owe you so much, Taita. How can we ever repay you?"

"A smile and a kiss is all I ask from you, Tehuti. Now I must go to your sister. She also needs me."

"I will come with you. Tomorrow is the day that she and her husband will entomb their youngest son, Palmys. Yet another victim of foul Utteric."

Palmys had been a popular and well-beloved lad, and several hundred mourners walked with us up into the Taygetus Mountains to the cave complex where all the relatives and close companions of King Hurotas and Admiral Hui were interred. The mummy case that contained Palmys' remains was drawn on a wooden sledge by ten black oxen.

Bekatha walked behind it, with her grim-visaged husband, Hui, supporting her on one hand and Tehuti on the other. She was wailing inconsolably. Her three surviving sons pressed close behind her with the men of their regiment coming up behind them. They were all in full armor, singing the tunes of glory, the battle songs of their regiment. It was a splendid display and a fine tribute to a gallant young warrior whose life had been so cruelly cut short.

Even I who have seen countless young men entombed or burned to ashes on the funeral fires could not help but be moved by the occasion. I hungered and thirsted for the day of vengeance. We entered the valley of Ares: the son of Zeus, who is the god of the violent and cruel face of war.

The cliffs on each side rose sheer into the sky, leaving the depths of the valley in somber shadows. The oxen dragged the mummy case to the entrance of the tomb, a deep and jagged crack in the face of the mountain. They could go no farther, and the teams were released and driven back the way they had come. Now the comrades of Palmys came forward and manhandled the sarcophagus into its final resting place. Bekatha threw herself on top of the mummy case, sobbing and wailing her grief, until Tehuti and Hui between them could draw her away. They led her back to the citadel the way we had come.

Much too slowly for my battle-eager heart the petty chieftains began to assemble their battalions, arriving from every direction and sailing into the Bay of Githion in their flotillas. Flecking the azure waters with their frosty white sails, they dropped their anchors off the foreshore. The port of Githion was by now so packed with shipping that it was possible to stroll from one side to the other across their decks, stepping over the narrow gaps that separated their hulls.

Gradually the open fields along the banks of the Hurotas River filled with the tents and shelters of the multitudes of armed warriors that came ashore, and the valley echoed with the clash of sword on shield and hel-

mets and the cries of the drillmasters as they extorted
their legions to greater endeavor.

I spent hours each day on the mountain heights scanning the waters for one set of sails among the throng:
those of the Levantine trader's barque returning from
the south and bearing the demands of Pharaoh Utteric.
There were more weeks of waiting before I finally
picked out the distinctive blue-dyed sails far out on the
waters of the bay. This coloration is derived from the
juices of a rare sea snail and possesses powers of protection from hazardous seas and even more dangerous
corsairs. I hoped against hope that this sighting was a
good omen, but I doubted that this was the case, bearing in mind whence it came.

The harbor was too congested to allow access to the
Levanter. I had to row out in a small fishing boat to
meet him. Ben Zaken, for that was his name, conceded
that he bore a message from Pharaoh Utteric Bubastis
the Great and Good—another of Utteric's misnomers.
However, he refused to hand it over to me. He insisted
on delivering it in person to King Hurotas as was his
solemn and sworn duty. I knew that he considered it
was also his solemn duty to collect every deben of his
reward from Hurotas. I tried to argue with him that
he should let me have a look at the message, so that I
might convey the most distressing parts of it to Huro-

tas and Tehuti in a gentle and diplomatic manner, but he was adamant.

Ben Zaken and I rode up the valley to the citadel where we found both of Serrena's parents waiting impatiently. There was a short delay while Ben Zaken counted out and then argued over the amount of his reward, but Hurotas turned his full fury upon him and he retired with a pained expression and muttered complaints at such harsh treatment.

When Hurotas, Tehuti, and I were alone in the council chamber, Hurotas broke the seal on the small alabaster receptacle that Utteric had sent us. It contained a papyrus scroll and a sealed vial of opaque green glass, such as those in which I, and other learned physicians, keep our most rare and valuable medications or specimens.

Hurotas placed these apparently mundane objects in the center of the table, and we stared at them in silence for a while. Then Tehuti spoke softly: "This terrifies me. I don't want to know what is in them. But I can sense the evil they contain."

Neither Hurotas nor I answered her, but I knew that all of us felt the same way.

Finally Hurotas seemed to shake himself as though he was waking from a nightmare. He wiped his face with his open hand and blinked his eyes as if to clear them. He reached for the scroll of papyrus and examined the wax seal that secured it. Then he drew his dagger from the sheath on his belt and ran the point under the seal, splitting it from the papyrus. The scroll crackled stiffly as he unrolled it and held it up to the light from the high window. Hurotas' lips moved as he began to read the hieroglyphics upon the page to himself.

"No!" Tehuti spoke sharply. "Read it aloud. I must also know what its contents are."

Hurotas balked at her demand. "I was trying to shield you."

"Read it!" Tehuti repeated, and he grimaced but then capitulated and began to read aloud.

To Zaras and Hui:

The craven deserters from the Glorious Army of Egypt.

I have the little harlot named Serrena. She is in my deepest dungeon where you will never find her. However, I am willing to exchange her for the following considerations.

Item One. You will repay to me the amount of three hundred lakhs of silver. This is the precise amount that you, as junior officers in the army of my father, Pharaoh Tamose, have stolen from me over the years since you deserted from the armed forces of this very Egypt.

Item Two. You will hand over to me the person whom you erroneously refer to as Prince Rameses. This criminal is in fact a lowly slave who pretends to royal Egyptian blood. He has deserted his post in the army of Egypt. He must be delivered into my hands to be punished with extreme prejudice.

Item Three. You will also hand over to me the person whom you erroneously refer to as Lord Taita. This creature is in fact a necromancer and a practitioner of the dark and evil arts of witchcraft. He is in addition a lowly slave who has absconded from his master. He must be delivered to me to be punished with extreme prejudice.

You have one month to respond to these my demands in full. Every month in which you fail to meet this my deadline I will send you a reminder. I enclose the first of these reminders in the green glass vial herewith.

Pharaoh Utteric Bubastis of Egypt (also known as the Invincible)

All three of us turned our eyes upon the innocuous-seeming green glass vial that the alabaster jar contained. It was Tehuti who broke the dreadful silence that had all of us in its thrall.

"I don't think I can bear much more of this. I knew this creature, Utteric. He was the firstborn child of my brother, Pharaoh Tamose, which makes him my nephew. He was a sickly and timid child, so I thought he was innocuous. How sadly I misjudged him. He is the epitome of all evil." She spoke in a whisper, which was broken up by her choking sobs, so it was barely possible to make sense of the words. But she never took her eyes off the green glass vial. "I shudder to think what he has sent us. Will you open it please, Taita?"

"One of us must," I agreed and I took up the vial and examined the stopper. I saw it was carved from soft wood and had been sealed into the mouth of the vial with beeswax. I twisted it carefully to break the seal, and the stopper popped out of its own accord with a soft hiss as though driven by gas. I tipped out the contents on to the tabletop and the three of us stared at it in dread silence.

It was a human forefinger. It had been severed at the third joint. It was slim and elegant in shape and the skin was smooth and unblemished: the finger of a young noblewoman unmarred by labor or neglect.

Tehuti let out a keening wail of despair and recoiled against the chamber wall, staring at the gruesome object in horror as she realized what it was.

"Utteric has begun to dismember my darling Serrena. Is nothing too obscene for him?" She turned and fled from the chamber, while Hurotas and I stared after her in dismay.

I broke the silence at last. "You must go after her," I told Hurotas. "Although she may not recognize it herself, she needs you now, as never before. Go after her. Give her comfort. I will wait for you here." He nodded agreement and hurried from the chamber, leaving the door ajar as he went.

After a few moments while my wits recovered from the horrifying shock, I approached the table again. I leaned over it to examine the disjointed finger more closely and dispassionately. I could see no reason to doubt what it purported to be: the finger of a young female, probably of aristocratic breeding. I had never examined Serrena's hands meticulously, but this digit appeared to belong to her, except . . . there was something incongruous about it. I puzzled over it for a while before I remembered the soft hiss of escaping gas when I had removed the stopper from the glass vial. I leaned closer to the severed finger and sniffed. Despite the

light frosting of salt that had been applied as a preser-
vative, there was the unmistakable odor of putrefaction
issuing from it.

I was so intent on the enigma that I had discovered
that I did not hear Hurotas return through the open
doorway, and I was totally unaware of his presence
until he spoke softly behind me.

"Divine flesh does not rot," he said.

I spun around and stared at him in consternation.
"What did you say?" I demanded inanely.

"I think you heard me well enough, old friend." He
nodded at me sympathetically.

"Yes. I heard you," I agreed in confusion. "But what
did you mean by . . . what you said?"

"Divine flesh does not rot," he repeated, and then
he said something else: "That finger cannot possibly
belong to Serrena." He nodded at the sorry remnant
that lay on the table. "For Serrena is divine."

"You knew!" I exclaimed, and he nodded a third
time. "How did you know?" I insisted.

"I also had a dream," Hurotas explained. "The goddess Artemis came to me in that dream and told me
how Serrena had been conceived." He paused, and he
was as subdued as I had never seen him before. "Artemis told me: *Your wife bears the child of your heart,
but not the child of your loins.*"

"Have you told Tehuti about this?" I asked, and he shook his head.

"No, I would never do that. It might destroy our trust in each other and our happiness. That is why I have come back to you. I want you to tell her why you know that this is just another disgusting subterfuge of Utteric's. I want you to preserve our trust in each other, me and Tehuti." He took my arm and shook it, but gently. "Will you do it for me, for us?"

"Of course!" I assured him, and I went out into the sunlit garden where I knew I would find Tehuti. She was sitting by the fish pool, which was one of her favorite haunts. She looked up at me as I stood over her. Her expression was desolate.

"What am I to do, Taita? I cannot give you and my nephew Rameses over to the clutches of that monster, and yet I cannot let him dismember my only daughter."

"You need not make either of those two fatal decisions." I sat beside her and placed my arm around her shoulders and hugged her. "You see, my darling Tehuti, divine flesh never decomposes."

She shook her head. "I don't understand."

"That finger is rotting, despite the salt in which it has been packed. It is not divine flesh; therefore, it does not belong to Serrena. Utteric has had it severed from some other unfortunate young woman."

She stared at me and her shoulders straightened and squared with renewed strength and determination. "You are right, Taita. I smelled it when you opened the vial. But I thought little of it. But now you have explained it, it makes positive proof."

"Yes, but we must never let Utteric have any inkling that we have not been taken in by this ruse of his."

"Of course not!" she agreed. "However, what about my husband? Promise me that you will never tell Hurotas who is truly the father of Serrena."

"Your husband is a lovely man and a great king, but I doubt he knows a god from a goat. He would never suspect that it is possible to fall pregnant in a dream. Furthermore, he trusts you without reservation," I assured her. I am a glib and fluent liar when forced to it.

I hesitated before I made the decision whether or not I should tell Rameses of my firm intention to enter Egypt clandestinely in an attempt to reach Serrena and afford her comfort and support, even if I was unable to procure her release from vile captivity. Finally I went to his quarters in the citadel and, after searching them to make certain we were completely alone, I blurted it out. I ended with an injunction to him not to breathe a word of my plan to another living soul.

Rameses listened to me in silence; and when I finished speaking, he shook his head ruefully.

"I have also made exactly the same resolution. But I was not going to tell even you," he confessed.

"Does that mean that you are coming with me?" I

pretended to be taken aback, although that had been my intention.

"What a frivolous question, Tata." He hugged me briefly. "When do we leave?"

"The sooner the quicker!" I retorted.

I released my customary trio of pigeons to Weneg in his wineshop in Luxor to warn him of our impending arrival in Luxor. Then Rameses and I went to say our farewells to King Hurotas and Queen Tehuti. Both of them were much heartened to hear of our plans to go to the succor of Serrena. Tehuti gave me an extraordinary and valuable gift to give to her daughter if and when we were able to reach her. I promised to guard it with my very life and to pass it over to Serrena at the first opportunity.

Then Rameses and I sailed on the *Memnon*. During the southward voyage, we rehearsed the roles we had agreed upon. I became a bumbling simple-minded buffoon, and Rameses was my unkempt keeper. He led me around on the end of a shepherd's crook. My speech was garbled and my gait stumbling and unbalanced. We procured our costumes from a couple of beggars at the gates of Port Githion. One of my servants negotiated the purchase, so they were not associated with us. However, they were authentically ragged, filthy and malodorous. Fortunately, we were not called upon to don them until we came in sight of the Egyptian coastline.

We in the *Memnon* hovered on the horizon until night fell; and then we ran in darkness southward again until we were able to make out the loom of the land. When this happened, we launched the small felucca that we carried as deck cargo on board the *Memnon*. Finally we said our farewells to the crew and left them to make their way back to the island of Spartan Lacedaemon, while the two of us dressed in our rags sailed our felucca into Wadi Tumilat, one of most insignificant of the seven mouths of the mighty River Nile.

When dawn broke, we were already four or five leagues upriver, just one of dozens of small craft that thronged the Egyptian waters. However, the flow of the river was against us, and so it was many more weary days before we reached the golden city of Luxor. By this time our disheveled and unshaven appearance was completely authentic, rather than merely contrived, so that when Rameses led me by my staff, with my head nodding, eyes rolling and feet shuffling, into Weneg's wineshop, that worthy did not recognize either of us, and he tried to shoo us back the way we had come. When we were finally able to convince him of our true identity, Weneg was at first astonished and then overjoyed. We sat up most of that first night, discussing

Princess Serrena's possible and probable whereabouts, and sampling the wares of the wineshop, which were a credit to our host's good taste. At the same time I took the opportunity to hide, under a pile of wine jugs in the cellar beneath the wineshop, the gift that I had brought from Queen Tehuti to be given to her daughter at the very first opportunity.

After considering all the other possibilities, we finally agreed that Serrena was most probably the guest of the horrible Doog. She had last been seen in his company, being paraded through the streets of Luxor. Of course, there was always the possibility that this was exactly what Utteric and his minions wanted us to believe, while they were holding her elsewhere in one of the numerous other prisons that had sprung up since Utteric had ascended to the throne of Pharaoh. However, the chances were that Utteric favored the Gates of Torment and Sorrow for his most illustrious guests, if only for the appeal of the name. I was the only one of our company ever to have had the good fortune to have entered those salubrious premises. Thus I was given the task of drawing up a map of the interior from memory.

My eyesight is also famously acute. Always providing that the light is good, I am able to recognize without difficulty the features of any person at a distance of up to a league, which is the distance a man can walk in an hour. Thus I was further allotted the task of keeping watch over Doog's establishment during the day from the surrounding hilltops. If the truth be told, I selected this particular task for myself. I longed to catch even a distant glimpse of the divine female whom I loved so dearly, if only to bolster my own resolution and determination to wrest her from the clutches of those foul creatures, Utteric and Doog.

Through friends of his, Weneg was able to provide me with a flock of a dozen or so scruffy black sheep. Each morning, brandishing my shepherd's crook, I drove these animals out into the hills that overlooked the road between the city of Luxor and the prison. From this vantage point I spent most of the daylight hours keeping watch over my sheep and, surreptitiously, over all the traffic that passed along the road. I soon noticed that almost all the passengers conveyed to the prison were on a one-way ride. They never returned from the Gates of Torment and Sorrow. In this respect I was able to count myself extremely fortunate to be the exception.

Of course, Rameses wanted to accompany me on these daily expeditions. But I deterred him by asking him two simple questions: "Have you ever seen a pair of shepherds guarding a single flock of a dozen sheep? And if you ever did, wouldn't you be a trifle suspicious?"

He threw up his hands with frustration. "How does it feel to always be right, Taita?"

"Strange at first; however, one eventually becomes accustomed to it," I assured him.

On the twentieth day of my vigil I drove my flock out through the south gate of the city as soon as the guards opened them, which was at sunrise. By this time I was a familiar figure, and they waved me through with barely a glance. My curly-horned ram knew the road up into the hills and he led us out of the city precincts. This particular road was usually avoided by the citizenry of Luxor, who considered it bad luck, for they knew whither it led. My flock and I had the hills to ourselves, until we reached the first sharp bend, which was surrounded by thick forest on both sides. We were given very little warning: just the clatter of hooves and the rumble of bronze-clad wheels, before a column of five chariots came charging at us around the bend. They were heading in the opposite direction to us, back toward the city of Luxor. The leading vehicle ran into my sheep at a gallop, breaking the neck of my ram and killing him outright, but also shattering the front legs of one of my ewes. The poor beast was down and bleating piteously. I had grown rather fond of my little flock, and I ran forward to protest and give full vent to my outrage.

However, the driver of the leading chariot was cursing me and my "filthy animals," and laying about him with his rawhide whip. When I appeared he threw the hood of his black gown back over his shoulders to reveal the hideous features of Doog the Terrible. He had not recognized me with my scruffy beard and long snarled hair, and my filthy and tattered attire, but to be certain I turned my face away from him and set about dragging the carcass of my ram out of the road and dispatching the wounded ewe with a rock that I picked up from the roadside. Once the road was clear, Doog drove his chariot past, giving me another lash with his whip over my seminaked back. I whimpered pathetically as the second chariot in line raced by me. But then I gawked at the passenger in the third chariot as it came level with me.

Her head was shaven, and she had been beaten until her face was swollen and bruised, and her one eye was almost closed. She wore a short tunic that was torn and stained with dried blood and other indeterminate filth. But she was still far and away the most beautiful woman I have ever laid eyes upon.

Serrena glanced at me where I stood beside the path. We were separated by merely two or three arm's lengths. For a brief instant she did not recognize me in my ragged disguise, but then her expression changed abruptly. Both her eyes widened with shock and joy, even the one with the swollen lid. Her lips formed my name, but without uttering a sound. I frowned a subtle warning at her, and she instantly restrained herself and cast her eyes down. Then the chariot in which she rode was past. Serrena did not look back at me or give any further sign of recognition, except that her shoulders no longer drooped with despair and her shaven head was held higher. An aura of renewed hope seemed to enfold her, which was apparent even from this distance.

My own spirits were uplifted, not least by the glimpse I had caught of her unfettered hands. For every one of her fingers was patently intact and undamaged. Utteric's attempted deception was exposed. Furthermore, I knew the damage that had been inflicted on her lovely face would soon heal miraculously, for hers is divine flesh.

I stood in an attitude of meek and hopeless submission until Doog's convoy of chariots disappeared over the next ridge, then I let out a great shout of joy and pranced around in a circle like a lunatic, hurling my shepherd's crook into the air. It took me a short while to regain my poise, and then I retrieved my crook from where I had thrown it and set off at a run back toward the city. My borrowed flock of sheep panicked at my sudden departure and they ran after me, bleating with distress. But I was the first to get back to Weneg's wineshop, beating my flock by a good length.

I found Weneg and Rameses in the secret basement beneath the wine store, where Weneg kept the equipment associated with his true purpose for remaining in Luxor, so close to Utteric's royal palace. These included the cages of pigeons that carried our messages to and fro between Lacedaemon and Luxor and a large supply of bows, arrows, and various other weapons.

"I have found her!" I shouted as I burst in upon the two of them.

They looked up at me in astonishment and demanded in unison as they sprang to their feet: "Who?"

"Serrena!" I exulted. "Who else is there?"

"Tell me." Rameses rushed toward me. "Where is she?" He seized me by the shoulders and shook me. "Is she well? Have they hurt her? How soon can . . ."

I had to wait for the uproar to subside before I could make myself heard. "Doog has her in the Gates of Torment. He was transporting her in a convoy of chariots in this direction . . ." Quickly I explained that Doog was in all probability escorting her to Utteric's palace here in Luxor for further harsh questioning. Then I went on to give my informed opinion as to what future they would have in store for Serrena.

"They have beaten and maltreated her. Her face and

arms are bruised and battered, but they don't seem to have inflicted permanent damage on her. Contrary to their threats, they don't seem to have amputated any of her fingers or any other bodily parts. There is nothing the matter with her eyesight or her mind. She is alert and in full control of all her faculties. This all makes sense, because she is much too valuable to Utteric as a hostage for him ever to allow his thugs to inflict real damage on her." I managed to placate Rameses and Weneg and to quitet them down so they were ready to listen to my good sense.

"This is probably the best, if not the only, opportunity we will ever get to free Serrena from captivity— and to get her away to a place of safety. Once she is locked behind the Gates of Torment and Sorrow, she will be completely beyond our reach. You can take my word on this. I have been there and I know!" Neither of them gave me an argument, but Rameses' expression was riven with a strange mixture of hope and foreboding.

"Tell us what we must do," he pleaded.

"This is how I see it," I put it to them. "We know that at this moment Serrena is outside the prison. For whatever reasons his crazed mind has dreamed up, or probably just to gloat over her and humiliate her further, Utteric has ordered Doog to bring her to his palace. Almost certainly Doog is planning to have her back behind the Gates of Torment and Sorrow before nightfall this evening. So at some time between noon and sunset today, Doog will be returning along the same road to his lair as the one on which he and I met this morning." I turned back to Weneg and asked him, "How many good and reliable men can you bring me before noon today?"

Weneg pondered my question for no longer than a few moments, counting silently on his fingers. Then he was ready with a reply. "Twelve for certain," he said. "Fifteen with a little luck, but all of them are deadly enemies of Utteric and good hard fighters. However, I don't know how many of them will have their own horses."

I nodded. "As long as they have weapons, I know where we will be able to find the horses. So we will be fairly evenly matched with Doog's ruffians, but we will have the vital element of surprise in our favor."

"One thing is for sure, we will achieve nothing by sitting here and chattering to each other like a gaggle of old women." Rameses was pacing the floor of the cellar in his agitation. He was almost as distressed by Serrena's predicament and excited by the prospect of her release to freedom as I was. However, I lingered a little longer to retrieve from under the pile of wine jugs where I had secreted it the gift I had brought with me from Tehuti in the citadel of Lacedaemon to be given to her beloved daughter. I strapped it to my back beneath the tattered and filthy folds of my tunic where it would be hidden from casual scrutiny.

I gave Weneg a list of essential items that he and his recruits must bring with them. Then we agreed to meet at the stone bridge over the stream where it ran down from the hills half a league beyond the point where I had enjoyed my recent encounter with Doog. I impressed upon him that every one of our party must be there at the very latest an hour before noon. I knew this was an impossible deadline for them to meet, but I set it so as to dissuade them from dawdling along the way.

The remainder of my faithful flock of sheep were waiting for me in the yard behind the wineshop, and we set off once more through the south gate of the city at a leisurely pace. Of course I and my sheep were the first to reach the appointed rendezvous at the bridge over the stream, but it was not too long after that the rest of Weneg's warriors began to arrive. As I had required of him, they came singly or in pairs so as not to draw particular attention to themselves. Of course, they were all fully armed as was only judicious and prudent for small parties traveling abroad in these turbulent times.

Naturally enough, not all of them made the deadline I had set. It was midafternoon before the last of them arrived at the assembly point. But finally I had a total of thirteen armed and formidable warriors concealed in the forest on each side of the road leading up to the stone bridge over the stream.

All these men had served under me in at least one of the campaigns that we had fought against the Hyksos, and every one of them recognized me at once and expressed their delight at our reunion. It was not necessary to rehearse them more than once in their part in the forthcoming ambush. They had done it all before, and that right well.

I had taken up my own position at a vantage point from where I had a fine view back along the road to the city of Luxor. I admit that I was becoming restless when at last we saw below us the dust cloud thrown up by the approaching column of chariots as they left the city and climbed the foothills toward where we waited. They passed the spot lower down where Doog and I had exchanged pleasantries that morning, and when they came on, it was with increased speed and assurance. I knew that this was because in the back of his suspicious mind, Doog had probably been troubled by our earlier encounter. But now he was reassured, and his guard was lowered. I had taken this into consideration when I made my dispositions. Careful forethought is often the hallmark of the true genius.

They came into my trap at a trot, shouting repartee at each other and encouragement to their horses. I saw that they were once again carrying Serrena in the third chariot. I was depending on that, and I had placed myself farther back in my line of attack so I could be one of the first to reach her.

The first vehicle passed us with its occupants looking ahead. They were oblivious to our presence in the thick undergrowth that lined the verges of the road. Doog, dressed in his black cloak, followed it onto the bridge in the second vehicle. Then Serrena drew level with me in the third chariot, and my heart raced as she passed so close to me without being aware of my presence. Finally, the fourth and last chariot rumbled out onto the flimsy structure of the bridge.

Now they were all committed. There was no space on the narrow causeway for any of the four chariots to make a one-eighty-degree turn and try to escape the trap that I had laid for them.

Using two fingers between my lips, I let out the shrill whistle, which was my agreed attack signal. It is a sound that I have perfected. At close quarters it is deafening. But even in the uproar of battle, it can be clearly heard at extraordinary distances. My men had been expecting it. They reacted instantly.

I had placed my two hammer men on the far side

of the bridge. They were crouching below the super-structure, one on each side of the causeway. At my whistle they jumped out of hiding and darted forward, the massive flint-stone hammers with which they were armed poised. With one or two heavy blows they shattered the spokes in both the wheels of the leading chariot. The wheels collapsed. The driver and his crew were taken completely by surprise and hurled from the carriage. The wreckage of their vehicle blocked egress from the bridge. All three of the following chariots piled up behind each other.

I led the charge onto the bridge. Our war cries further confused the drivers and startled their horses. They reared wildly and tangled the carriage traces. One animal lost its footing, crashed through the railing and fell over the side of the bridge. It dangled in space, kicking and squealing shrilly with terror and anchoring the other animals in its team. The charioteers were bellowing at one another to clear the bridge, but Doog bellowed loudest of them all. All of them were plunged into pandemonium and panic.

In my right hand, I had the gift that Queen Tehuti had given me to convey to her daughter. I had drawn it from its sheath, and the blue metal of its blade glinted in the sunlight, sharper than any other metal in existence and as deadly as doom itself.

"Serrena!" I screamed her name above the uproar. She spun around and saw me.

"Tata!" she cried. "I knew you would come." Her beauty seemed to take wing, and it galvanized me.

"Catch!" I swung the blue sword once around my head and then let it fly. She reached up to the full stretch of her right arm and snatched it out of the air as it passed above her. Then she placed her free hand on the coaming of the chariot and swung her legs out over the side. She dropped to the narrow causeway of the bridge as lightly as a sunbird settling on a bloom and darted forward.

"Doog!" she called to him, giving that obscenely ugly name a beautiful lilting cadence. Doog could not help himself but turn to look back at her. She ran at him lightly, her bare feet scarcely brushing the ground. Doog saw the bright steel in her hand and he knew he could never draw his own weapon in time to defend himself. He knew it was death he saw coming at him. He cowered down behind the coaming of his chariot, treacherous coward to the end. She jumped high in the air, and at the top of her leap she stabbed down over the coaming into his back. I saw the blue blade slip half its length into the black robe that he wore. Doog uttered a great shout of agony and involuntarily threw back his head. His face was contorted, making it even uglier than I had ever seen it before.

With a graceful gesture Serrena withdrew the blade of the blue sword from the wound. It was dulled with Doog's blood for half its length. But now she had it perfectly poised for the backhand stroke. She pirouetted, and the blade in her hand seemed to dissolve in a blur of sunlight.

Doog's head leaped from his shoulders and tumbled to the floorboards of the chariot. For a long moment his headless corpse remained kneeling, and then abruptly a fountain of bright blood erupted from the stump of his neck. Doog's headless corpse collapsed behind the coaming of the chariot.

"Come on, lads!" I shouted at my stalwarts who were still paralyzed with shock at Serrena's magical swordplay. "Let's deal with the rest of this scum." I pointed my blade at the surviving chariot crews.

"No, Taita!" Serrena stopped me with her urgent cry. "Leave them be! They are good and honorable men. They saved me from the unspeakable atrocities that Doog would have had them perpetrate upon me."

I saw the relief blossom on the faces of our captives. They knew just how close they had come to death.

"You scoundrels should give humble thanks to Her Royal Highness for every day you remain alive," I scolded them, but with a faint smile on my lips to mitigate the severity of my words. Then there was a mighty shout of her name from the rear of the column.

"Serrena! I know it is you! I heard your voice. I would recognize it anywhere, at any time!" And Prince Rameses came running forward from his battle station at the rear of the column.

Serrena, the mighty swordswoman who moments before had dispatched the dreaded Doog, squealed as though she had stood on a live coals with her bare feet: "Rameses! Rameses! I thought that you must still be in Lacedaemon. Oh, I give humble thanks to Horus and Hathor that you have come to rescue and protect me!"

The lovers rushed together and embraced with such fervor and disregard of ought else in this world that the blades of their weapons clashed together and their teeth were probably subjected to the same impetuous treatment. I was mortified but not surprised to see that Serrena was unashamedly weeping and Rameses was not far from tears. I turned away and left them to get themselves under control, while I readied the others for the next phase of our offensive.

I disposed of Doog's corpse by the simple expedient of heaving it over the bridge rail into the river below. However, I retained his severed head, which I stuffed into a horse's nosebag to be dealt with later. Of course, I kept his hooded black robes for immediate use. These were too commodious for my lean, well-proportioned body; however, I bulked them out with his undergarments, which were still wet with the blood Serrena had tapped from him. We were obliged to abandon the one chariot with the smashed wheel spokes; thus, the remaining three vehicles were heavily laden when we set off once more for the Gates of Torment and Sorrow. Added to the original crews, we were now carrying Weneg's thirteen together with myself and Rameses.

Fortunately we were not far from our destination, and when the gradient became severe, there were plenty of willing hands to get down and push.

We reached the prison as the sun was just touching the western horizon. I sat on the cross bench of the leading chariot with my arms folded pompously across my chest and the black hood drawn down to mask my features. Close behind me stood Serrena in her prison garb, with her wrists tied ostentatiously in front of her. She is a consummate actress and appeared thoroughly forlorn and desolate. However, the slip knot that bound her wrists could be released in an instant with a tug of her sharp white teeth; and the blue sword lay at her feet, concealed under a layer of loose straw. Rameses stood close behind both of us, with his sword sheathed and his face concealed by a bronze war helmet borrowed from one of our friendly guards. His handsome features were well remembered and beloved in Egypt as the favorite of Pharaoh Tamose's many offspring, but now was not the time to display them abroad.

I had timed our arrival at the Gates of Torment and Sorrow for the setting of the sun when visibility was minimal. The gates were not immediately opened to us by the guards, who were mainly the brothers, sons and nephews of the now departed Doog. They shouted suspicious questions down at us about the discrepancy between the numbers of the men and vehicles that had driven out that morning and those returning now. Several members of our party tried simultaneously to explain the loss of one of our chariots in the gorge, the number of men who had died in that disaster, and the additional men that Pharaoh Utteric had supposedly sent from Luxor to increase the garrison owing to the importance of the recently captured prisoner: namely, Princess Serrena of Lacedaemon.

I had deliberately instigated this commotion and misunderstanding to attract as many of the prison warders and guards as possible to the battlements and the entry courtyard, so that we could deal with them in a single concentrated mass without having to pursue individuals through the maze of buildings, interlinking courtyards, and dungeons within the walls.

When I estimated that my ruse had succeeded and at least thirty of the prison warders were lining the ramparts above us, I rose to my feet in the leading chariot and gave a convincing imitation of Doog throwing one of his tantrums. The black hood concealed my face as I shouted curses and threats at the men on the walls, addressing some of them by name, and my extensive and foulmouthed vocabulary was convincing. My gestures and mannerisms were perfected from the original. I have often thought that I could have been a celebrated thespian if I had chosen that career. As it was, these close relatives of his were totally duped into believing they were speaking to Doog in person.

One of them gabbled the traditional welcome— "Enter at your peril. But know ye, all enemies of Pharaoh and Egypt are eternally doomed once they are within these walls!"—while the rest of them trooped down the staircase and crowded into the entry courtyard to welcome their illustrious relative home.

Only half of them carried weapons. The rest of them had not bothered to retrieve their arms, lest they miss the excitement of the proceedings. This total lack of discipline was typical of the lackadaisical behavior of the troops of the new regime under Utteric Turo.

I recognized Doog's elder brother, who was named Gambio, as he hurried to welcome me home. He was an exception to the rule, in that he was a shrewd and clever warrior and a dangerous adversary but even more hideous than his younger brother. I knew that if I let him get even a hint of the real situation, it would be only seconds before we were involved in a serious struggle. I lumbered down from the chariot and waddled to meet him in imitation of his younger brother. My sword was still in its sheath, but my dagger was in my left hand, concealed in the folds of my robes. As we came together I seized Gambio's outstretched right hand in a steely grip and jerked him off balance. I saw the flare of terror in his eyes as he finally recognized me. In that instant he knew that he was doomed. I stabbed the point of my dagger up under his ribs and into his heart and then locked him in an embrace with my left arm. His death cry was drowned out by the general uproar that surrounded us. As I waited for him to bleed out, I dedicated his soul to the memory of the hundreds of innocents in whose suffering and demise he had taken such intense pleasure.

The other denizens of the prison were slow to realize what was taking place. They crowded around the leading chariot, beginning to taunt and threaten Serrena and trying to drag her down from the carriage. All their attention was focused on the beautiful female prisoner. I knew that they were eager to strip her naked again. Our companions in the two following vehicles jumped down and quickly moved forward to surround the leading chariot, at the same time unsheathing their blades. Silently they went to work, not alerting their enemies with any war cry. Half the garrison warders were cut down before the others became aware of the peril that had engulfed them. In the end, the last of them threw down their weapons and went down on their knees to plead for mercy. This was another unwise decision.

They were dragged away by their heels to the funeral pyres, which burned for the rest of that night.

Our first concern once we had secured the fortifications was to release the prisoners from the dungeons belowground. There were just over 120 of these, of which 30 or so were women. It was not possible for Serrena and me to count the exact numbers, because they were dying almost as rapidly as we were able to bring them to the surface. The causes of death were mostly starvation or thirst, but other factors were prolonged whippings, gouging out of one or both eyes, drawing out of the intestines, skinning alive, insertion of heated metal rods into their anuses and other ingenious procedures dreamed up by Doog and his brethren.

The reason why Rameses and I had returned to Egypt was simply to ascertain where Utteric was holding Serrena; and if it were at all possible to provide her with strength and encouragement to survive the terrible ordeal with which she was confronted. I had never even vaguely anticipated an attempt by the two of us to rescue her from Utteric's clutches. Now that we had succeeded in both these unlikely, if not impossible, endeavors, my sole concern was to spirit her out of Africa and get her safely home to her loving family in Lacedaemon as soon as was humanly or divinely possible. I am certain that if Rameses had been given any say in the matter, he would have agreed wholeheartedly with me. Neither of us had taken into account the opinion and wishes of Princess Serrena herself.

She allowed the two of us a few short hours of rest from our not insignificant actions, and then she called a council of war. At first I thought she meant a council to determine the swiftest, easiest and most expedient way to get back to her home and mother.

In the dawn the four of us gathered on the ramparts of the Gates of Torment and Sorrow. I say *the four of us* because Serrena had summoned Weneg to attend her council.

"Well, we have achieved our first goal, which is a secure base from which to operate. For this I owe my full thanks to the three of you," she opened the meeting. I glanced at Rameses and Weneg and saw that they were every bit as mystified by this announcement as I was. "Our next priority is to open communications with my father in Sparta," she continued.

"I am sure you mean that our next priority is to get you out of Egypt and across the sea to Lacedaemon and into your father's loving care as soon as possible," I cut in on her. She stared at me in astonishment.

"I am sorry, my darling Tata. I don't understand what you are talking about. What you have achieved here is an act of genius. No! It's much more than that. You have worked a miracle. You have opened a base in the middle of enemy-held territory. We are completely isolated here."

"You mean until word of our present whereabouts gets back to Utteric in Luxor." I pointed out the silhouette of the golden palace, which was clearly visible on the horizon to the south of us, no more than five or six leagues distant . . . or ten at the most.

She gave me her lovely wide-eyed look of pretended innocence. "Who is going to convey the news to him?"

"One of the prison warders—" I began and then broke off. Since yesterday evening all the warders were dead and burned. I corrected myself: "I mean any of Utteric's underlings bringing supplies or prisoners from Luxor."

"No one is allowed beyond the Gates of Torment and Sorrow," Serrena pointed out. "All supplies and new prisoners are deposited in the entrance courtyard, where you will greet them with your celebrated impersonation of Doog in his black hood." Then she changed her voice: "Know ye, all enemies of Pharaoh and Egypt are eternally doomed once they are within these walls!"

Although her imitation was very convincing, I refused to be fobbed off and I managed to keep a straight face as I put my next question to her. "What about when Utteric next summons you to Luxor for a meeting? What do you want me, in my role of Doog, to tell him?"

"I have Utteric's solemn oath that he never wants to see me again. He really is a very stupid boy, and so easy to ridicule. All his pretty boys were giggling at him every time I bested him in an exchange. He wanted to have me executed on the spot, but I pointed out that I was of no value to him if I were dead. In the end he actually burst into tears of frustration. I almost felt sorry for him. He swore an oath before all the gods that he never wanted to lay eyes on me again and flounced out of his own throne room."

I could not contain my glee, and I burst out laughing at her description. But still I made a last effort. "What about the local farmers? The shepherds grazing their flocks?" I knew it was a doomed effort, but I soldiered on.

Serrena stamped her foot on the battlements. "These walls are fairly rugged," she said. "Even the most vigilant shepherd will not be able to see through them. Besides which, the only shepherd to come anywhere near this place of terrifying reputation was a naughty old darling named Taita. Not even Pharaoh Utteric the Invincible will come anywhere near it. That's why he sent his minions to fetch me."

"What about your loving parents? They are desperate to see you again." I would try anything to get her back to the safety of Lacedaemon.

"My father and mother won't see me again until they come to Egypt," she told me firmly.

"Why ever not?" Once again she had taken me by surprise.

"Because Egypt is now my home. My future husband is destined to be the Pharaoh of Egypt, and I am to be his queen. I have even chosen my title. I shall be known as Queen Cleopatra. Which, as I am sure you know, means 'the Glory of her Father.' Papa should be placated by that."

Rameses laughed. "And so shall I!"

I recognize a hopeless cause when I meet one. So I went down on one knee before her. "All hail to Queen Cleopatra!" I capitulated.

"Now shall we try to be serious?" she asked sweetly. "We have work to do." She turned back to confront Weneg. "How many pigeons do you have in your wineshop and how soon can you smuggle them out from under Utteric's nose and bring them back here to the Gates of . . ." She stopped herself uttering the awful name that Utteric had given to his prison and thought for a few seconds. ". . . the Garden of Joy! That's it!" Her expression became blissful. "That's the new name for our headquarters here! And the first thing I want is to get rid of all those skulls at the entrance. We will give them all a decent and respectful burial."

"I should like to keep one particular skull at the entrance, if it pleases Your Majesty. You can bury or burn the rest of them," I protested.

"Which one is that?" she demanded suspiciously.

"The dreaded Doog," I told her and she tinkled with laughter.

"Only you could have thought of that, Taita. But I agree that it is highly appropriate."

Weneg reverted to his role of wine merchant once more and entered the main gates of Luxor that same evening. Doog had been a regular customer of his, so it was unremarkable when the following morning he emerged through the same gates with five donkey loads of wine flagons. At the bottom of each donkey load was concealed a basket containing a dozen or so pigeons. Each of the birds was blindfolded to discourage them from cooing while they passed through the city gates in the presence of the guards.

While Weneg was absent on this mission Serrena and I composed our message for her father, King Hurotas. These papyruses were too bulky to be carried by a single bird, so when Weneg returned, we dispatched them in serial form. Our one complete message required five birds to carry it.

It contained the news of Serrena's rescue by Rameses and me from Utteric and Doog. Of course, we received no acknowledgment or any reply from Hurotas, for he had no pigeons that had been hatched in the city of Luxor or in the Garden of Joy. So we could only imagine the relief and happiness the tidings occasioned in the citadel of Hurotas.

We continued to send birds every few days. Our subsequent messages were much more succinct and consisted mostly of details of Utteric's troop movements and informed estimates of the numbers of his war galleys, chariots, and regiments and their dispositions.

I suggested to Weneg a more satisfactory method to open reciprocal communications between the citadel of Lacedaemon and the Garden of Joy. Every time he returned from his visits to his wineshop, he brought with him a number of birds, both male and female, who were sufficiently mature for mating. We explained to Princess Serrena our intentions of breeding birds in the Garden of Joy and sending them by land and sea to Lacedaemon, so that when they were released there they would return immediately to their birthplace, coincidently bearing messages from her father, King Hurotas.

"Pigeons are wonderful creatures," Weneg explained to her. "Among their other virtues, they are monogamous."

She looked slightly mystified, so I explained to her: "They are faithful to each other for life, with no feathered concubines lurking in the background."

"Now that is so sweet . . ." She turned to Rameses and gave him a telling glance. "So very sweet!" He shot back a silent protest that made her green eyes twinkle.

When Weneg and I introduced a male pigeon to the coop he had built that already held six female birds, there was great excitement among the hens, who fluttered about in theatrical panic. It took some time for the male to make his choice, but when he had done so Weneg removed the five rejected females from the coop and left the male to pursue his courtship with the hen he had selected.

"Now watch the male bird—" Weneg continued his explanation.

"Hold on a minute, Weneg." Serrena stopped him. "You can't go on calling him that. He is not just the male bird. He should have a real name."

"Of course, you are absolutely right, as always, Your Highness. I should have thought of that. What should we call him?" Weneg asked. "How about Lord Fine Feathers?"

"No!" Serrena thought for a moment. "Look at him! Doesn't he think that he is just the greatest lover, and we want him to father plenty of little ones, do we not? There is only one name for him. Uncle Hui! We shall call him Uncle Hui!"

The three of us burst into delighted laughter, and it took us a while to recover. Weneg eventually called us to order. "See how he puffs out his chest and struts around her. Of course she runs away from him."

"But not very far and not very fast," I pointed out.

"Of course not," Serrena agreed. "She is a female, so she isn't stupid."

"Now he chases her spreading out his tail and dragging it along the ground. But she keeps just ahead of him."

"Of course she does! She is a clever girl!" Serrena clapped her hands. "She does not want to make it too easy for him."

"At last she turns back to him, and he opens his beak for her," I observed.

"Why would he do that?" Serrena demanded.

"It's called 'billing.' He is inviting her to be his single special friend." I took over the explanations from Weneg, because I know a great deal more about pigeons than he does.

"Now, don't let him dupe you," Serrena cautioned

the female bird sharply. "Remember what your mama told you. Never trust a male." But the female pigeon ignored her advice and thrust her entire head down the male's throat. After a pause, she withdrew her head and sank belly down to the ground.

"You will be sorry!" Serrena sighed softly as the male bird hopped up onto her back and clapped his wings sharply, then spread his tail feathers to cover her nether regions. "Or perhaps you won't," she amended her warning and reached out shyly for Rameses' hand.

I pretended not to notice the side play and went on with my explanation: "Now, in about ten days' time she will lay two or three eggs, which will hatch about another eighteen days later. The chicks will mature and be ready for the long flight from wherever we send them back here to the Garden of Joy in another month and a half."

"That's such a long time," Serrena mused regretfully. "You have no idea just how I long to hear from my father and mother." She shook her head sadly, but then seemed to brace herself. "But now we have to find a way to send the mature birds to Lacedaemon to fly back with the messages from my loved ones . . ."

Before I could reply, there was a trumpet blast from

the high tower, a warning signal from the sentries, and I broke off the discussion. "That means that there are strangers on the road up from Luxor. All of you know your roles and stations for any eventuality. I have to get myself into my Doog costume," I told them and hurried away.

I was more than a little anxious, for this had been the first sighting of strangers since Serrena had returned from her last visit to Utteric. I dreaded the thought that he had changed his mind and sent for her to be brought to his palace again to torment her. I ran all the way back to the central courtyard, and then, without pausing for breath, I climbed the long staircase and came out on the high battlements of the tower. I immediately saw the dust cloud raised by running chariots. They were coming up the road that led from Luxor.

"How many chariots?" I asked the sentry, and he shrugged.

"Quite a few, about ten or a dozen is my guess. They are being driven hard."

I felt a gust of relief. Utteric would not have sent that number if he wanted them merely to fetch Serrena to Luxor for further sport with her. "Do you recognize any of them?"

"They are still too far off, but almost certainly they

are prisoners and their escorts," he confirmed my evaluation of the situation.

"Hold them at the entrance gate as usual. I am going to change my costume."

By the time I returned and made my way to the portcullis above the main gates there were eleven dusty war chariots drawn up in front of them. Every carriage was loaded with passengers, the majority of them in chains.

"Who are you? Who sent you? And what is your business?" I challenged them in the tones of Doog from the top of the walls.

"We are royal charioteers of Pharaoh Utteric the Invincible! We are sent by Pharaoh to deliver thirty-one prisoners to you for punishment and execution with extreme prejudice."

At my command the prisoners were disembarked from the chariots, and, chained together by the ankles, they shuffled through the gates into the entrance courtyard, where the empty eye sockets in the skull of Doog stared down upon them from the niche high above. I used Doog's hieroglyph to sign the papyrus receipt for the prisoners; then the escorting charioteers retired through the main gates, mounted their now almost empty chariots and set off back down the road to Luxor. The long file of prisoners was led through the inner gates into Princess Serrena's freshly planted gardens. As they entered, the waiting band burst into merry and welcoming music.

The prisoners were roused out of their lethargic despair as they looked around them with astonishment. Very few of the shrubs and plants were as yet in full flower; however, the gibbets and gallows that they were expecting to see were gone. Instead three blacksmiths stood ready at their anvils with flint-headed hammers and chisels in hand, and they hacked the chains from the ankles of the prisoners as each of them came forward. Then to their further astonishment, each of the condemned men was given a clay pot of frothing beer, a loaf of bread and a large dried sausage to bolster their spirits. One of the persons who distributed this largesse they recognized immediately as Prince Rameses, whom rumor had counted as long dead. The prisoners cheered him ecstatically, and once they were freed of their chains and had wolfed down the food that they had been given, they crowded around the prince, making deep obeisance and showering him with their loyal sentiments and congratulations on his return from among the dead. Of course, they knew me as well, if not better, than any claimant to the title of Pharaoh. I also came in for my share of gratitude and praise.

My sergeants marshaled them into good order. However, the stench that emanated from them was eye-watering. They had worn the same vestments since their arrest by Utteric's special police several months previously. On my orders they were marched away to the fresh water wells below the kitchens, where they were ordered to strip naked and wash themselves and their clothing with lye. This they did with the alacrity and hilarity engendered by almost hysterical relief at the sudden change in their treatment and circumstances.

Once they had been cleansed and clothed, Rameses and I recognized twelve of them. These were all the heads of the leading families of Egypt and had been intimates of Pharaoh Tamose before his death. They had all been fabulously wealthy. When we questioned them, we discovered that in every case without exception they had been charged with high treason, found guilty and condemned to death. Naturally all their assets had been confiscated and added to the royal treasury of Pharaoh. Utteric had never been too bashful to help himself.

Apart from the wealthy elite of Egyptian society, some of the most popular and successful administrative officials and army officers in Egypt were among the prisoners. When their identities had been established, I made a welcoming speech to them. I assured them that they were just the sort of citizens that Rameses and I

were delighted to welcome into our company. I com-
miserated with them on the treatment they had suffered at the hands of the false Pharaoh, but I assured
them that we had suffered at the hands of Utteric to an
equal extent. I invited them to join our faction, which
looked upon Rameses as the only rightful Pharaoh of
Egypt. I assured them that their sentences had been set
aside, and they were once again full and free citizens of
this great country; and furthermore that Rameses and
I would be honored to listen to their opinions on the
subject.

It seemed that every single one of them had strong
views, and they all wanted to express them simultaneously; the resulting uproar would very soon have
gotten completely out of hand had not Princess Serrena
chosen that moment to enter the conference hall. In all
truth, it was I who had arranged for her presence at
this critical moment.

The clamor and the shouting sank swiftly into a
stunned silence as these scions of the nobility looked
upon her for the first time. We should remember that
these were men who had not laid eyes upon any member
of the opposite sex for the many months that they had
been incarcerated by Utteric.

Now they were experiencing an almost religious
revelation of beauty, the moment when mere flesh be-

comes divine in the eyes of the beholder. And that her divine blood had made her lustrous tresses grow back even more shining than before was something quite amazing to behold.

Rameses took her hand and led her forward to present her to them. "This is the woman who has promised to become my wife. She is the Princess Serrena of Spartan Lacedaemon," he told them and a sound swept through their ranks. It was partly a sigh of yearning and the other part a paean of adulation.

I am never one to miss an opportunity. I raised both of my hands in a silent but unmistakable invitation to them to give their assent, and I was almost swept away by the thunder of their united voices.

"All hail to Rameses and Serrena! Pharaoh and queen of our very Egypt!"

I t seemed that the obtuse and uneducated Utteric had by some strange chance selected the thirty-two men for execution *with extreme prejudice* who almost perfectly made up a superior government cabinet ideally suited to assist and advise Pharaoh Rameses on the administration of greater Egypt.

Included in their ranks were experts and innovators in the fields of agriculture, food, animal welfare, education, fisheries and forestry, mining of metals, building, wealth and taxation, water supplies, and—most valuable of all—the army and the navy and the art of waging war. They took to the roles they were offered by Pharaoh with gusto and mostly good sense. My life was not made easier and more relaxed by the fact that these acknowledged experts appealed to me for my advice at every turn of the road, especially if that turn led them to a dead end.

Every now and then new prisoners arrived at the gates of the Garden of Joy, consigned to us by Utteric the Invincible for summary execution. Very soon we had several hundred recruits from this source. From among their ranks Weneg and I selected carpenters and boat builders. We set them to work on the manufacture of four fast sloops and a pair of cutters from designs drawn up by me. These vessels were to be used to communicate with King Hurotas and our allies in Lacedaemon. As we were making the first of these boats ready to put to sea Serrena sought me out in great excitement with the tidings that the three pigeon eggs that had been produced by the female, with a little assistance from the bird she had named Uncle Hui, had now hatched. In a few weeks the chicks would have matured and learned to fly so strongly that they could be dispatched to Serrena's parents in Lacedaemon to commence their life's work of ferrying messages back and forth between our two camps.

Serrena herself was busy every night until long after most of the rest of us were asleep. She was compiling what she referred to as her *Codis Brevus,* a form of writing that was twelve times shorter than the traditional hieroglyphics and totally secure. It comprised a single symbol for the two hundred basic words of our Egyptian language, sufficient to formulate most messages. For other rarer words there was a code to replicate the sound. When she explained the basic principles of the code to me, I was immediately intrigued by the simple beauty of the system and appalled by the fact that I had not thought to develop it for myself. With me to assist her, we had a first draft to send to her parents in Lacedaemon with the initial shipment of pigeons. Two superior minds working in unison are often more effective than fifty working individually.

We launched the first of our sloops, which we named *Artemis' Promise*, a little after midnight, when the full moon had slipped below the horizon and only the stars gave light for navigation of the river. The crew comprised half a dozen of the most skilled sailors we could find, who had made the voyage from Egypt to Lacedaemon on numerous occasions. The captain of this little craft was an experienced seaman by the name of Pentu. I trusted him both as a man and a seaman. The captain and crew carried thirty-six pigeons in cages on board. This was the total number of birds that we had been able to hatch in the Garden of Joy and bring to maturity. They were strong enough to make the long flight over open water and savvy enough to have a chance of avoiding the attentions of the fish eagles and other raptors that patrolled the skies above them.

In addition to these birds, they carried almost a hundred papyrus scrolls filled with the artistic hieroglyphs of Princess Serrena's brush and addressed to King Hurotas and Queen Tehuti.

Late the following evening, there was a light tap on the door of my chambers, and when I opened it a cautious crack, I discovered the royal couple huddled on the threshold, bundled up against the chill.

"Are we disturbing you, Magus? May we come in?" Rameses only used that form of address when he wanted something excessive from me. Warily I opened the door a little wider.

"Sweet Hathor, of course not and of course you may! Or vice versa." I made my reply sufficiently ambiguous not to commit myself, but I stood aside to let them in.

They sat side by side in embarrassed silence for a while, and then Rameses roused himself and showed his metal. "We thought you might like to pray with us."

"What an odd thought!" I looked astonished. "The gods make their own decisions without consulting us. In fact, very often they prefer to do exactly the opposite to what we request, just to demonstrate their own superiority."

Rameses sighed and glanced at Serrena with an "I

told you so" expression. Her lovely eyes grew enormous and then to my consternation began to fill with tears. I know what a consummate actress she is, but I sighed with resignation.

"Very well then," I capitulated. Rameses' dour expression changed to a grin and at the same time Serrena's tears dried up miraculously. "What is to be the substance of our prayers? What is our request to the gods? As if I didn't know."

"We want the most benevolent deities to keep a safe watch over *Artemis' Promise* and take her safely to her moorings in Port Githion," Serrena told me earnestly. "Then we want them to look after our pigeons and to guide them all safely back to us, with the messages from my mother and father intact."

"As simple as that?" I asked. "Very well. Shall we form a circle and hold hands?" Serrena has lovely soft hands, and I enjoy holding them.

Each of us worked out an estimate or rather a hopeful guess at the time it would take for *Artemis' Promise* to make the voyage down the Nile to the sea and then across half the great Middle Sea to Port Githion, then for Hurotas and Tehuti to read and reply to our letters in Serrena's new *Codis Brevus*, and finally to launch the pigeons and for them to make the hazardous return flight back to the Garden of Joy. Serrena's estimate was fifteen days, Rameses was a more realistic twenty and mine was twenty-three days, but only if the gods were in a compliant mood.

The days passed with all the speed of crippled tortoises; first Serrena's estimate was exceeded and then Rameses' twenty days with clear skies overhead. Even I was becoming a little despondent and my nightmares were filled with clouds of bedraggled feathers from slaughtered birds. But on precisely the twenty-third morning after the sloop's departure, the gods finally relented and the sky above the castle seemed to turn blue and purple with returning pigeons. We counted them aloud as one after another they fluttered into their welcoming coops.

We anticipated that Hurotas and Tehuti would have released them sparingly, perhaps two or three whenever there was something important to report. But our astonishment mounted in step with our actual bird count, until we reached the number of thirty-six and we stared at one another speechlessly.

There were two elements that amazed us. First, Hurotas and Tehuti had dispatched all thirty-six birds back to us in one mighty wave; and, second, every single one of them had survived the hazards of their flight.

"Only my darling mother could have ignored my request and written so fulsomely." Serrena spoke in awed tones. Naturally, I felt duty bound to rise to the defense of the woman I love.

"Come now, Serrena. Don't you think you are being a little unfair to the splendid woman who gave you birth?"

"Compare my mother's pages against the number sent by my father!" she challenged me. So I did.

Thirty-two pages were painted in Tehuti's beautiful multicolored hieroglyphics. She had airily ignored her daughter's suggestions as to brevity. A great deal of her response was in rhyming poetry, and I was forced to concede that much of it was really rather clever. It celebrated the fact that her daughter, Serrena, had survived the harrowing kidnapping by Panmasi and her subsequent imprisonment and humiliation by Utteric. She extolled Serrena's courage and fortitude and eagerly anticipated their reunion. She asked if naughty old Taita had remembered to give Serrena the blue sword that she had sent; and she charged her to keep the blade sharp, with suggestions on how to do so. She reassured Serrena that the dress for her wedding to Rameses had finally been completed and was truly splendid. She longed to see her wearing it. Then she gave her a number of recipes for songbirds baked in honey and glazed eels, which she wanted Serrena's permission to serve to the wedding guests. Finally she ended by bemoaning the lack of space on the itty-bitty papyrus sheets for further news, and repeating her love and heartfelt wishes for her daughter's continued safety and flourishing good health. Last, she demanded that Serrena should send her many more pigeons, because there was so much more vital news that she simply had to relate, including the fact that Huisson's wife had given birth to a baby boy.

In contrast the four pages sent by Hurotas were masterpieces of brevity and clarity, the work of a great and experienced soldier. They were written in the *Codis Brevus* developed by Serrena and further improved upon by myself.

On these four pages that Tehuti allowed to Hurotas, he was able to lay out for me his order of battle against Utteric. This would be in two phases: seaborne and land-based. As was customary Admiral Hui would command the fleet and Hurotas himself would command the chariots and the footsoldiers.

At the beginning of the campaign the chariots would originally be based at the port of Sazzatu. This was situated thirty-five leagues to the east of the point where the Nile empties into the great Middle Sea. It was the ideal place from which to launch the land invasion of Mother Egypt. Already Hurotas had ferried 260 war chariots and their crews to Sazzatu and left them there, to seize the town and surrounding area. The fleet had returned to Lacedaemon to take on board another shipment of men and chariots. The eventual number of chariots assembled at Sazzatu would be on the order of nine hundred. This would make it the largest and most formidable cavalry unit in history.

Once the cavalry had a foothold on the African mainland, the navy would be free to launch its attack up the River Nile. Hui would drive initially for the city of Memphis. There he and Hurotas would link up. Once they had consolidated their hold on that city, they could commence the long approach march on Luxor.

Hurotas ended with the single word of greeting and farewell between brothers in arms. This was the cryptic symbol "SWORDS." The meaning was understood between us as: *Your companion in arms to the end.*

"Four pages against thirty-two." Serrena cocked her head at me. "Do you still think I am prejudiced?"

"I never used that word." I dismissed her protest with dignity and turned to Rameses. "Hurotas expresses himself very succinctly."

"He makes it sound very easy," Rameses protested; so I turned back to Serrena satisfied that I had confused and obscured the object of discussion.

"What do you think?" She smiled and spread her hands in a gesture of defeat.

"When he realizes that he is up against you and my father, I think Utteric's feet will be slipping in whatever foul-smelling substance he deposits beneath himself as he heads south for the jungles of darkest Africa where he can hide among his peers, the apes."

"I admire the picturesque manner in which you express yourself, my dear princess!" I put my arm around her shoulders and squeezed to show my approval, and also because I find her so eminently squeezable.

"You are always so kind, Taita dear," she purred.

Rameses smiled as he watched us. "You are a lucky girl, Serrena. You have two fine men who love you."

"I know about Taita, but tell me, please, who is the second one you are referring to?"

Weneg and my other spies in Luxor reported that there was no indication of any sudden military stir in the city of Luxor, but I warned them that it was impending and would be the sign Utteric had become aware that Hurotas and his sixteen allies had begun their expeditionary onslaught on his dictatorship here in Egypt.

I expected Utteric to respond by hastily assembling all his available forces and hurrying northward to Memphis and the coast to bolster and reinforce his regiments there and resist and attempt to repel King Hurotas' invasion.

Rameses was eager to begin our offensive immediately, even before Utteric made his move from Luxor downriver to Memphis and the delta. He argued that we had surreptitiously assembled an elite force of almost four hundred highly trained men in the Garden of Joy: men who had suffered grotesquely at the behest of Utteric and his brutes and were eager to take their revenge.

"What damage do you suggest our little force of four hundred men might inflict on Utteric's army of over four thousand?" I asked him.

"If we attacked after midnight, we should be able to set fire to most of the ships that Utteric has moored in the harbor and also burn the warehouses along the riverfront where he has stored many of his weapons and other supplies," he declared.

"At the same time we would also disclose our existence. As it stands Utteric believes that Serrena is in solitary confinement behind the Gates of Torment and Sorrow, and that all the prisoners he sends to the same place have been faithfully executed by Doog, and that you and I are somewhere at the far northern end of the world. Do we want to disillusion him just yet?" I asked and he looked abashed.

"I thought—" he began, but I interrupted him.

"You didn't think far enough. What we need to do is to get in contact with Hurotas, either by pigeon or by special courier, so we are able to coordinate our strategy. But in the meantime, we must restrain our noble instincts until such time as we are able to inflict the greatest desolation and despair upon Utteric the Utter Prick."

Serrena, who had been listening avidly to our conversation, clapped her hands with delight. "Oh Taita, that's a lovely name for him. Why did you not tell it to me before?"

"It was your father's quip and not mine, and I never steal other people's jokes," I explained with a sober expression before I turned back to Rameses. "I can see by your expression you agree with me, Rameses."

So we sharpened our swords and waited impatiently as the days became weeks. Then in the dark of the moon, the intrepid Pentu sailed the little sloop *Artemis' Promise* back into her hidden mooring on the river below the Garden of Joy. I felt that she had justified the name we had given her by safely completing such a hazardous double voyage in such short order. Her hold was packed with gifts from Queen Tehuti to her daughter. These included a dozen bottles of Serrena's favorite perfume, a plethora of dresses in various magnificent hues sewn and embroidered by her favorite dressmakers, a pair of sandals to match each dress, a large selection of silver and gold jewelry studded with brilliant stones, and numerous rolls of papyrus covered with magnificent hieroglyphics.

In one of these weighty epistles, Tehuti explained in detail how worried she, Tehuti, had been all this time by one particular aspect of her daughter's incarceration. "There is no suffering, not even childbirth, that a woman is forced to endure that is as agonizing as being deprived of appropriate apparel to wear," was how she phrased it.

As deck cargo the *Artemis' Promise* carried almost fifty cages of pigeons that had been bred in the citadel of Lacedaemon and therefore were conditioned by their nature to return there at their very first opportunity to take to the skies. Clearly Hurotas and Tehuti were determined to remain in contact with us.

Before the rise of the sun I had written three messages in the *Codis Brevus* addressed to Hurotas. I sealed them in the silken carrying pouches attached to the breasts of the pigeons. They seemed as eager to return to where they had been hatched as I was to see them on their way. But I kept them waiting a little longer while I wrote a separate note in which I confirmed that *Artemis' Promise* had returned safely to her moorings, and that all the communications from Hurotas and Tehuti that it had carried were well received and agreed upon. As the first rays of the morning sun dispersed the shades of night, I kissed the heads of each of the three birds and threw them into the air. They climbed into the sky on eager wings and made two or three circuits of the fortress before they flew away on a northerly heading.

Then we settled down to wait with all the patience we were able to muster. Weneg and his spies kept a day and night watch on the palace of Luxor and the harbor for the first sign of any unusual activity. I knew that we would not have much longer to wait, for Pentu informed me that Hurotas was almost on the point of following him when he left Port Githion. In the event it was a mere twelve days before Weneg hurried up the road from the city. From the top of the main tower of the Garden of Joy I watched him come. Even at a distance of almost half a league I could make out the excited expression on his face. When he saw me he stood in the stirrups and waved both hands above his head.

I rushed down the staircase to meet him at the front gates. "The entire city of Luxor is in an uproar!" he shouted as soon as we were close enough to hear each other. "Drums beating and horns blowing! Utteric is girding his loins for war, or should I say girding the loins of his men for war while he hides under the bed."

"This must mean that Hurotas and Hui are at last approaching this very Egypt, with their allies. Find Rameses! An hour ago he was in the garden with the princess. Tell him that we are going into Luxor to assess the scale of Utteric's warlike preparations and try to suss out his intentions. We will don the same old rags that we wore on our first visit to your wineshop. I will meet him at the main gates as soon as he is ready."

I had deliberately left my own disguise unwashed and sealed in a wooden box, to prevent the lively stench that it emitted from evaporating. This was still sufficiently powerful to bring tears to my eyes when I sniffed them. I daubed my face and hands with soot and placed on my head a wig made up of an assortment of various types of hair, both human and animal. This was also unwashed and infested with vermin. The vermin served to deter the unwelcome attention of strangers.

As I passed the stables I paused to examine my reflection in the water of the horse trough and saw that I looked sufficiently repulsive. I hurried on to the main gates where Rameses was already waiting for me. He was also untouchable in appearance and robust in odor, but in a more regal manner than I was or, for that matter, than the elderly crone who accompanied him. She was grossly overweight and her facial features were hidden behind a tangled mat of greasy gray hair. She waddled forward to greet me, and when I realized it was her intention to embrace me, I backed away in alarm.

"Kindly unhand me, madam!" I warned her off. "I

must caution you that I am riddled with both leprosy and the black pox."

"Both of them? How greedy you are, Tata! But I am not fussy. From you I will take either one you can spare." She tinkled with her own enchanting laughter. "Stand still so I can give you a kiss."

"Serrena!" I cried. "How did you put on so much weight so suddenly?"

"Just a few of the dresses that Mama sent me, packed around my waist. I learned the trick from you. But I must commend you: I just adore your hairstyle."

The three of us slipped through the back gate of the fortress on the side farthest from the city, then under cover of the forest we circled back and came to Luxor from another direction entirely. Long before we were in sight of the city walls we heard the martial music: the drums, the fifes, and the trumpets echoing up from the valley. Then when we were able to look down from the surrounding hills, the first thing that caught our attention was the fleet of transports and warships anchored in the Nile River. There seemed to be several hundred of them, too many of them to count. They were moored so closely together that they made the great river look like solid ground.

Although their sails were furled, all the masts and rigging were festooned with flags of every conceivable shape, size and color. Hundreds of smaller rowing boats threaded the narrow lanes of open water between them. These were piled high with the barrels and baggage being ferried out to the larger vessels. My heart beat faster and the blood within it was fired by this warlike display.

Most people look upon me as a sage and a philosopher, a man of noble spirit and an essentially gentle and forgiving nature. However, beneath the veneer lurks the revenging warrior and the ruthless man of action. At that moment the hatred that I bore Pharaoh Utteric was so intense that it seemed to scald my very soul.

When we looked down on the city that stood between us and the riverbank, we saw that within its walls the excitement and the warlike preparations were every bit as intense as those on the river itself. Every turret and tower, every rooftop and the encircling walls of the city itself were decked with flags.

Outside the city walls every road and footpath was packed solidly with traffic. There were chariots, carriages and carts drawn by men and horses and oxen and even by goats. This entire throng was converging on Luxor. The three of us started down through the dense forest that covered the hillside, disappearing into it until we met one of the tracks leading to the rear gates of the city. One at a time we left the screen of vegetation, adjusting our ludicrous clothing as though we had been attending to a call of nature in the bushes, and we joined the column trundling down to Luxor. No one took the least notice of us, and nobody questioned us when we reached the city gates. We were swept through them by the multitudes.

The streets of the city were even more densely packed with people than the country roads had been. The only persons who could move with any purpose were the squadrons and platoons of heavily armed men marching in endless ranks down to the docks to board their transports. Sergeants with whips went ahead of them, cursing the crowds and lashing out at those who blocked the way.

As soon as the soldiers passed, the separated crowd closed up again, so that we could only shuffle along, jammed shoulder to shoulder and belly to back. Of course, both Rameses and I knew the layout of the city intimately; at one time it had been home to both of us. We managed to duck out of the main thoroughfares and into the alleyways and subterranean tunnels between the buildings and under them. Some of these passages were so narrow and dark that we had to move in single file, sucking in our bellies and turning sideways in the more constricted places. We held aloft burning candles or tapers to make out the way ahead.

We steeled ourselves to the knowledge that the rickety buildings above us were prone to collapse, and close around us under the rubble lay the crushed corpses of hundreds of unfortunates who had been killed by the frequent cave-ins.

The tunnels we were following led with no or very little warning into caverns and chambers of various sizes and heights. All these rooms were filled with traders who were busily employed selling or buying any of the myriad objects on offer.

Among some of the more unusual wares that I noted were bottles of the goddess Hathor's urine. I offered one of these as a gift to the princess because they were very reasonably priced. However, she declined on the grounds that she quite capable of producing her own.

One of the vendors, a creature with a heavily painted face and of indeterminate gender, accosted me with the salutation, "Hello, darling boy, how about a bit of to-ing and fro-ing, or if you prefer it inning and outing?"

"Too early for me, I am afraid. I have not yet digested my breakfast. It will give me hiccups," I declined politely.

He, she or it stared at me suspiciously and then challenged me, "You remind me of the famous Lord Taita, the seer and sage. Except that you are older and much uglier."

"I doubt you ever met Taita," I returned the challenge.

"Oh, yes, I did." He waggled his forefinger under my nose. "I knew him well."

"Then tell me something about him that nobody else knows."

"He had a pleasure post that was longer than an elephant's proboscis and thicker than the wanker of a whale. But he is dead now."

"No, that was his twin brother you are thinking of. The real Lord Taita was left-handed. That is the only way you could tell them apart," I explained.

He looked perplexed and picked his nose. Then he shook his head and mumbled, "That's strange! I never even suspected that Lord Taita had a twin." He wandered away still picking his nose. Both Rameses and Serrena lifted the hair of their wigs that hung down over their eyes and stared at me.

"I wish I was able to lie with a straight face like that," Rameses told me wistfully.

"What is your twin brother's name? If he is prettier than you are, I would like to meet him," Serrena asked me seriously, and Rameses pinched her buttock so she squeaked.

Rameses and I continued working our way through the subterranean labyrinth toward the surface. Finally we climbed up a derelict sewer and came out in a corner of the parade ground behind the pile of ancient rubble that concealed an open-air latrine that was popular with both sexes. A number of patrons were engrossed with their business when we emerged among them. We took little notice of each other, and all of us continued unperturbed with what we were about.

On that memorable day the parade ground was the busiest and most crowded part of the entire city. We would not have been able to force our way into the amphitheater if we had attempted the usual route. As previously arranged we found Weneg and four of his ruffians waiting to welcome us at the exit from the informal latrine. They gathered up the three of us, forming a protective cocoon to shield us from being trodden by the multitude, and we forced our way up the stone tiers until we reached a ledge near the summit from where we had a splendid view over the stadium. This was packed with what seemed to be the entire population of Luxor.

Only the center of the stadium was bare. It was roped off and protected from being engulfed by the masses of humanity by guards standing in alignment facing outward with drawn blades. Below our perch was a raised wooden saluting podium. However, for the moment it

was also empty. In front of the podium was a bandstand on which a fifty-piece band was belting out lusty
marching tunes and patriotic airs.

The tumult mounted steadily until with a final clash
of cymbals the band fell silent and the drum major
turned to face the audience with his arms held high.
Slowly the din subsided.

Then in the silence a tall figure stepped onto the
bandstand. It was a figure of pure gold. From head to
feet it was covered with the glittering metal. Golden
helmet and faceplate, golden cuirass, and golden greaves
and sandals. The sunlight played full upon it, dazzling
the eyes. It was a skillful display of showmanship.

Then once again the band burst into a full-throated
anthem. I recognized it as the epic created by Utteric to
his own glory, to which he had given the modest title
"The Invincible." This was the signal for a regiment of
Royal Guards to take to the field. They marched out
a thousand strong, beating their swords against their
shields and singing the chorus of the anthem:

Ten thousand dead upon the field,
But the Invincible lives on!
Ten thousand years pass by,
But still the Invincible persists!

Listening to the inane and ridiculous assertions of the chorus, I felt my rage and my hatred flaring afresh for the monster who now ruled Egypt. His madness was enhanced by the cunning and shrewdness with which he leavened it. I glanced at Serrena where she sat beside me. She was instantly aware of my eyes upon her. She replied to my unspoken comment without taking her eyes from the golden figure.

"You are right, Taita. Utteric is mad but clever. He is slaughtering his own aristocracy, the great body of men whom his father, Pharaoh Tamose, trained to perfection, the army that defeated the Hyksos and drove them from this land of Egypt, because they are his father's men. It is because their loyalty lies with his father in his tomb. In the view of Utteric they are all yesterday's men. Men like you and Rameses. He knows all of you despise him, so he wants you destroyed and replaced with men like Panmasi who worship him."

Now she turned her head and looked at me for the first time, and she smiled. "Of course, you know that Panmasi who captured me is now a general in Utteric's new army? In fact, he commands the Royal Guards: the regiment that you see out there." She pointed with her chin; she was much too canny to use her forefinger and so draw attention to herself. "That is Panmasi standing behind Pharaoh on the reviewing podium."

I had not recognized him until Serrena drew my attention to him. His helmet had obscured his features, and he was partially hidden by those others who surrounded him.

"And you?" I asked her. "Don't you feel anger when you see those two together, Utteric and Panmasi: the ones who humiliated and tortured you?"

She thought about my question for a few seconds and then she replied softly, "No, not anger; that is too mild a term for it. What I feel is a boiling sense of fury."

I was unable to see her expression behind the dangling strands of the wig that she wore, but her tone was completely convincing. At that moment the marching guards came to a halt with one last stamp of their feet and held the bare blades of their weapons aloft in salute to Utteric in his golden armor. The abrupt silence that gripped all of us, both spectators and participants, was so profound that it was almost palpable.

Then the gold-clad figure of Pharaoh stepped to the front of the podium. Slowly and deliberately he stripped the glove from his right hand and held his bare hand aloft. I felt Serrena stiffen beside me, but I could see no reason for this reaction of hers. It was not unusual for even Pharaoh to bare his right hand in this manner when saluting his troops.

However, the next thing that happened was totally unexpected.

On the far end of the parade ground facing the podium was a hillock that was a favorite vantage point from which privileged spectators were allowed to view the martial display. It was a distance of less than two hundred paces from the crest of the hillock to the front edge of the podium.

Abruptly a small, dark object took flight from among the crowd on the distant hillock. I have exceptionally acute eyesight, and even against the dense mass of humanity I picked it out the very instant it was launched into flight. At first I thought it was a bird, but almost immediately I saw my mistake.

"Look at that!" I exclaimed. "Somebody has shot an arrow!"

"Where?" Rameses demanded, but Serrena had picked it out just an instant after me.

"There, above the hillock." She pointed it out as it reached the zenith of its flight and began the drop. "It's coming straight toward us."

I made the calculation. "It won't reach us. It has been lofted too high. But it is dropping straight toward Utteric." I scrambled to my feet. I was suddenly appalled by the fact that it was Utteric, my deadly enemy, who was in danger. If the arrow killed him, I would be deprived of my revenge for all the suffering he had inflicted upon me and those persons dearest to me. I wanted to shout a warning to him, but the arrow was dropping too fast for any call from me to be effective. Utteric still stood with his right hand upraised. His golden helmet and the cuirass that covered his chest were a shining beacon to which the arrow flew relentlessly. It was as though Utteric was welcoming death.

I saw the heavy arrowhead was fashioned from chiseled flint, designed especially to penetrate armor. It would tear through the malleable breastplate as though it were papyrus. Time seemed to slow down. Everyone, including Utteric's staff and especially me, seemed to be frozen, unable to move. The arrow blurred with its velocity over the final few feet and then with a metallic clang like that of a great bell it struck. Utteric was hurled backward. But in the fleeting instant while he was still on his feet, I saw the head of the arrow and half the shaft protruding from between his collarbones. It had transfixed him completely.

Then Utteric crashed into the wooden boards of the podium with such force that some of them splintered. He lay without further movement, pierced through his evil heart and killed instantly.

The silence that followed was utter and complete. It was as if the whole world held its breath, and then as one released it in a cry of terrible dismay, a mighty keen of mourning as though the world had lost its father. Utteric's military staff rushed forward. They were headed up by General Panmasi and a number of his other sycophants and toadies. One of them produced a blanket in which they wrapped up the body, making no effort to remove the flint arrowhead from Utteric's vitals, or the armor that masked his head and torso.

Then a dozen of them hefted the corpse and carried it down the stairs that led from the podium to the stone-walled building below. The band started to play a lament. The masses seemed confused and uncertain how they should react. Some of them were weeping and wailing ostentatiously, and tearing out fistfuls of their own hair. However, many of them were having difficulty containing their joy. They were trying to hide it with the skirts of their robes and by rubbing their eyes vigorously to make their tears flow.

I was perhaps one of the few in that multitude who was truly saddened to see Utteric killed. I hugged both Rameses and Serrena to me for my own solace, but I was not far from sincere and heartfelt tears.

"It should never have ended like this," I whispered

to them. "Utteric has escaped the punishment he deserved for his cruelty and monstrous evil."

On the other hand, Rameses was elated. "At least he is gone, once and forever." Of course, he was next in line to the throne of Pharaoh. "I wonder who shot the arrow. I should like to give him my sincere thanks and reward him for his courage."

There was a movement among the crowds; hesitantly and uncertainly they edged toward the exit gates. The three of us joined them. However, we did not get very far before we were confronted by the armed guards stationed there. Their harsh commands carried clearly to where we were shuffling along wedged in by the multitudes.

"Back! All of you must remain in your seats. Nobody is to leave the stadium until the assassin is found." They reversed their spears, and with the shafts prodded and drove the crowds back from the gates. "We know who it was that shot the arrow that killed Pharaoh Utteric the invincible."

Grumbling and protesting, we moved back to our original positions.

Serrena sat close to me. Her face was turned away from Rameses, who was still complaining to his neighbor on his far side. She spoke softly, barely moving her lips. Her voice was just audible to me. "It was not him," she said.

"I don't understand. Who wasn't who?" I asked just as softly, taking my cue from her.

"That figure in gold armor wasn't Utteric. It was not Utteric who was arrowed," she repeated. "That was an impersonator, a double."

"How do you know that? He was completely masked." I seized her arm and drew her closer. I felt a surge of relief that I might still be able to have my retribution on the living Utteric.

"I saw his right hand," Serrena said simply.

"I still don't understand," I protested. "What does his hand have to do—?" I broke off my protest and stared at her. I am not usually so slow. "You recognized that the hand we saw with the glove removed was not Utteric's?"

"Exactly!" she answered me. "Utteric has smooth unblemished hands. Almost like those of a young girl. He is inordinately proud of them. His intimates say that he washes them in coconut milk three times a day."

"How do you know this, Serrena?" I persisted. "When did you get to study his hands?"

"Every time he raised them to hit me in my face. Whenever he tried to twist my nose off. Every time he dug his fingers into my vagina or thrust them up my anus to make his pretty boyfriends giggle," she said bitterly, her tone emphasizing her lingering outrage. "The man in the golden mask who was struck down by that arrow had rough and calloused hands, like those of a farmer. It was not Utteric."

"Yes, what you say makes good sense. But I am sorry that I made you reveal such intimate and disgusting details of the humiliation he inflicted upon you."

"Just as long as Rameses does not learn about what they did to me. I would not want him to know that. Promise me that you will never tell him."

"I give you my solemn promise." I knew the words were trite, but I squeezed her hand hard to give them weight.

We waited one hour and then another. The only relief, for what it was worth, were the solemn dirges played endlessly by the band to mourn Pharaoh's passing. By that time, muttering in the crowd had turned to anger. I heard remarks made openly that bordered on treason. Now that Pharaoh was dead, those citizens who were usually very careful of expressing their opinions of him were much less discreet.

Then suddenly and unexpectedly the band changed its tune into bright and joyous music, in contrast to that which they had previously been playing. The crowd's grumbling dwindled to bemused silence. I could see the men and women who during the past two hours had expressed intemperate opinions regarding Pharaoh and his death looking about them anxiously, trying to judge who else had heard them, and regretting their words.

General Panmasi and four other high-ranked officers in Pharaoh's army marched together up the stairs from the building below to where only two hours previously they had carried Pharaoh's blanket-wrapped corpse. The band welcomed them with a sprightly fanfare as the five of them stood beside one another at the front of the podium. When the band at last fell silent, General Panmasi stepped forward and began to speak through the voice trumpet that he carried. With this instrument his voice carried across the parade ground. Other more junior military officers were stationed at intervals to relay Panmasi's speech to those near the rear of the crowd.

"Loyal and true citizens of mighty Egypt, I bear joyous tidings for you. Our well-beloved Pharaoh Utteric, whom we all saw struck down by a traitor's arrow, has proven true to his appellation of the Invincible. He has cheated death! He is with us still! He lives on eternally."

A doubtful silence greeted this revelation. They had all seen the arrow that transfixed Utteric's corpse.

They had seen with their own eyes that it was a mortal stroke. They were wary that this was some sort of ruse to make them betray themselves. They cast their eyes down and shuffled their feet, trying to avoid exchanging glances with their neighbors or making any other incriminating gesture.

Panmasi turned back to the head of the stairway and fell to his knees in obeisance. The other four senior officers immediately followed his example, beating their foreheads on the planking of the podium.

The same figure in armor of gold that we had seen earlier being carried away in a blood-soaked blanket now emerged from the stairwell. He walked tall, proud, and bold. He showed no evidence of the fatal wound that had been inflicted upon him, except for the smears of dried blood on his armor and the gaping hole that had been torn in the front of his golden cuirass by the assassin's arrow. He marched to the front of the podium and lifted his helmet from his head to reveal the veritable features of Pharaoh Utteric that the populace had come to recognize so well.

The same persons in the crowd who had earlier covertly applauded his death now prostrated themselves with loyal fervor, wriggling like puppies and mouthing their extravagant joy at his miraculous return from the dead.

Utteric surveyed them haughtily; his features—enhanced by the makeup he wore—were proud, sneering, and effeminately pretty. He was obviously enjoying their wild adulation. At last he held up his hands for silence.

I whispered to Serrena, "You were quite right. He does have girlish hands."

She nodded at me in agreement.

"Who was killed by the arrow?" I wondered.

"We will never know," Serrena assured me. "He is already burned to ashes, or deep in the Nile with weights attached to his feet." And then she shushed me to silence with the rest of the congregation as Pharaoh began to speak.

"My beloved people, my loyal subjects, I have come back to you! I have returned from the dark place to which I was sent by the assassin's arrow." The crowds roared their joy at his survival. Then Pharaoh held up his hands once more, and they fell silent immediately.

"Now we all know that there are traitors abroad!" Utteric continued, with his voice turning suddenly accusing and angry. "There are those who plotted my assassination and tried to carry out their evil designs." The masses moaned with anguish at the very thought of such treachery.

"I know who they are, these murderous traitors.

My loyal guards have arrested all thirty of them. They will all meet the fate they so richly deserve." Led by General Panmasi, the spectators burst into wild cheers and protestations of patriotic loyalty. When this finally abated, Pharaoh continued, "The first and foremost of these villains is the man who shot the arrow that was meant to kill me. He is one of my senior ministers in whom I placed my complete trust. My guards saw him draw the bow that launched the arrow which struck me but could not kill me." He raised his voice to a shout: "Bring forth the traitor Irus."

"Not Minister Irus!" Rameses protested in a horrified whisper. "He is an old man, but noble and good. He would never commit murder. I doubt he is still robust enough to draw a compound bow."

Serrena took his hand to quiet him and prevent him from rising to his feet. "Irus is beyond salvation, my darling," she whispered. "The man who launched the assassin's arrow is more than likely the same man who is leading Irus to the block. His name is Orcos and he is one of Utteric's most ruthless henchmen. But he also has the reputation of being a formidable archer."

Rameses nodded sorrowfully. "I know Orcos well. I also know that Irus has tried to oppose some of Utteric's most savage and cruel judgments. This is the price he must pay for those indiscretions."

"Utteric is playing one of his master strokes here today. First he is asserting his claim to immortality. His subjects saw him killed. Now he has returned from the dead, to destroy those who seek to oppose him." Serrena spoke quietly, but with conviction. "Men like Irus. Utteric is setting out to silence the voices of all honest and honorable men in Egypt. He has learned that my father is on the sea with his fleet and his chariots and those of all his vassal kings. He is securing his rear before he marches to oppose my father's invasion. There is nothing we can do until they arrive here in Egypt. We can only wait. Perhaps Utteric will send Irus and the other accused to the Gates of Torment and Sorrow; if so, we can take care of them."

The royal guards led Irus and the other prisoners up on to the podium with their hands tied together in front of them. It was clear at a glance that they had all been beaten and treated harshly. Most of them were bleeding, and Irus their putative leader was only half conscious. His once handsome face was so swollen and bruised that I could barely recognize him. His long white locks were matted with his own drying blood. He had been stripped of his clothing, all except a brief loincloth, and whip welts covered his naked back. It took two of the royal guards to steady him and keep him on his feet when they dragged him to face Pharaoh.

Immediately Utteric launched a verbal assault on him. In the process, he was lashing himself into one of his maniacal rages. I have seldom heard the likes of the filth that spluttered from his lips mixed with flying spittle. He had a riding whip in his right hand. He used it to emphasize his tirade: slashing it across the old man's face, swinging it back and forth until more blood dribbled down his beard and his legs collapsed under him. The two guards hoisted him upright to keep him facing his tormentor and enduring every blow of his punishment.

Finally Utteric stepped back. He was panting wildly, and sweat ran in rivulets down his cheeks. He dropped the riding whip with which he had beaten Irus, and he drew his sword from the sheath on his belt.

"Let him go," he said, panting at the guards. "Let him fall to his knees in an attitude of supplication. Cut the bonds from his wrists so he can hold out his hands and plead with me for mercy." Obviously the guards had done this many times before with other prisoners. They grinned with anticipation as they carried out Pharaoh's orders.

"Hold out your hands, you poisonous traitor. Beg

me for my royal mercy, you ancient stinking turd," he shrieked at Irus. The old man was too far gone to respond; he shook his head in bewilderment, and the blood drops splattered the boards under him.

"Make him do it!" Utteric shouted at the guards. Still grinning they stepped forward and seized the rope ends that they had deliberately left tied around his wrists. They heaved back on these and Irus was pulled facedown on the boards of the podium, but his arms were extended to their full stretch in front of him.

Utteric stepped forward with the naked blade of his sword poised. He tapped it lightly on Irus' forearm to measure the distance and then he lifted it above his head and swung down from on high. The bronze blade sheared through Irus' left arm, flesh and bone, without a check. The guard heaving on the rope fell back and blood spurted from the severed stump in a jet. Irus gave a weak little cry and the watching crowds echoed it, half of them in horror and the other half in approbation.

Once again Utteric raised his blade and measured the stroke with a swordsman's eye. Then he swung and hacked cleanly through Irus' other arm. Shorn of both his arms, Irus lay whimpering in a puddle of his own blood.

General Panmasi stepped forward at Utteric's left hand and signaled for one of the waiting chariots to come forward. The charioteer brought his vehicle up to the base of the podium, with all four of his horses prancing and skittering at the stench of blood. In the meantime the two guards had tied lengths of rope to Irus' ankles. They passed the ends of these to the charioteer who made them fast to the rings at the rear of his vehicle. Pharaoh then jumped down from the podium and took up the driver's position in the chariot that the driver vacated for him. Utteric shook up the reins, and the team of four started forward at a trot, dragging Irus' mutilated body behind the vehicle. Irus cried out with the agony of being dragged and at first he tried desperately to balance his naked and mutilated body over the bare ground and fend off the rocks and other obstacles that littered the perimeter of the stadium with the bloody stumps of his arms. But on the second circuit of the stadium he gradually grew weaker until he could no longer defend himself. His head bumped and jolted against the earth until the last flicker of life was extinguished. Pharaoh Utteric hauled his corpse back to the podium and jumped down from the chariot.

"Invincible Pharaoh, what should we do with this other filth?" General Panmasi asked as Utteric mounted the podium again. With his drawn sword, he indicated the other twenty-nine prisoners who knelt, trussed like pigs for slaughter.

Utteric gave them a dismissive glance. "I have done enough hard work for one day. Send the whole treacherous brood of them out to the Gates of Torment and Sorrow. Let the experts there deal with them appropriately."

"We will have to hurry to get back to the Garden of Joy in order to welcome Utteric's prisoners there," I warned Serrena and Rameses as Pharaoh and his entourage remounted their chariots and drove out of the stadium in the direction of the golden palace.

We had to push our way through the crowded street, but as soon as we reached the city gates, we ran most of the way back through the hills, taking shortcuts, wading through the streams and climbing the steep rock faces that were too sheer for the horses towing the heavily laden chariots we knew were not far behind us. Once again I was amazed how well Serrena kept up with Rameses and me; she was often first to reach the top of the harsher climbs. Of course she was much lighter on her feet than either of us.

We arrived at the Garden of Joy not much more than an hour ahead of the convoy of chariots bringing the condemned prisoners up from the city of Luxor; in fact, I was still busy with my makeup and donning my Doog costume when there were shouts from the sentries in the lookout towers warning of the approach of many vehicles along the road from the city.

I hurried through to the main gates just in time to greet the new arrivals with the usual gloomy rigmarole of question and answer and usher them through to Serrena's delightful Garden of Joy. No sooner had they recovered from the shock of finding themselves in paradise compared to what they had been expecting than I divested myself of my Doog costume and introduced them to Rameses. They knew me and Rameses well by sight since we had lived in Luxor and both of us had been men of substance and stature. However, they had been informed by Utteric that both of us were long dead, so their astonishment and delight were boundless. They surrounded us and clamored for the chance to embrace both of us and express their infinite gratitude for lifting from them the threat and shadow of death.

It took only the barest minimum of suggestion from me for all of them to suddenly recognize in Rameses the future Pharaoh of Egypt and the replacement for the loathsome creature who had arrogated that title and sentenced all of them to a torturous death.

First in ones and twos they began to go down on their knees before Rameses and hail him as Pharaoh, and then in a rush they were all chanting his praises and swearing fealty to him. I let their fervor reach boiling point and then begin to abate before I played my winning trick.

Serrena had been awaiting my summons in the pavilion close at hand and at the exactly apposite moment she appeared. The freed prisoners turned to her with curious expressions, which swiftly turned to silent stupefaction. I had impressed upon her the need to present the most winning appearance in her power. But even I had not expected her to improve upon perfection.

She was wearing the most striking dress of all those sent to her by her mother, Tehuti. It was a heavenly shade of green that changed miraculously to all the other colors of the rainbow as she moved and the light played upon it. It suggested the tantalizing shape of her body beneath the cloth. Her arms were bare and her skin was burnished to perfection. Her head balanced on the long elegant neck was proud and ineffably lovely. The green of her eyes was brighter than any precious emerald and mesmerized the beholder with their perspicacity.

I went to her, took her hand in mine, and led her back to where Rameses waited to receive her. She glimmered and glided by my side, and the smile she laid upon her spectators seemed to captivate them all anew. Rameses held out his hand to welcome her. Then I turned back to our guests and addressed them again.

"I take infinite pleasure in presenting to you the daughter of King Hurotas and his wife, Queen Tehuti. This is the Princess Royal of Lacedaemon. Serrena is her name. She is betrothed to our Pharaoh Rameses. He has rescued her from captivity in the hands of the false Pharaoh Utteric. She is to become your queen. My lords, please pay her your respects, I beg of you!"

One after the other they pressed forward and made obeisance to Serrena and she gave each of them such a smile that I am certain turned them immediately into her admirers and followers for their lifetimes. In this way I was instrumental in making certain of Rameses' ascension to the throne of Egypt, and of my own place as his chancellor and adviser.

I gave our new recruits very little time to find their places in our ranks. I knew by name and usually by face those of them who were truly valuable to our cause, and I wasted no time in introducing them to the others who had preceded them. Then I slotted each of them into the position in which they would be most effective in our plans.

My first real concern was to learn from them everything that they knew about Utteric and his convoluted machinations, so that we would be in a stronger position to fight and destroy him. Much of that which they were able to tell me I already knew. But I was fascinated to hear from them how Utteric had succeeded in turning himself into an elusive personality only superficially attached to reality. He had conceived a number of identities or aliases, such as the person who had been shot down by an arrow on the podium of the stadium and then returned as the living Utteric a few hours later. According to my new informants, those persons fulfilling the role of Pharaoh in public were more often than not impostors. These included those commanding his armies in the field, who were almost exclusively surrogates. This was also a fine ruse for him to avoid the hazards of the battlefield while earning all the plaudits of victory and avoiding the ignominy of defeat. Of course, this made it considerably more difficult for us to bring him down. We could never be absolutely certain we were striking at the real Utteric, or at his surrogate.

I also learned from these sources that the armies of Hurotas and his allies had at last fully landed in Egypt. They had swept in from the great Middle Sea and staged almost a thousand of their chariots at Sazzatu only thirty-five leagues to the east of where the Nile debouched into the sea. While these chariots commanded by General Hui drove overland for the city of Abu Naskos, the ships stormed into the multiple mouths of the Nile itself and fought their way southward to lay siege to the same city, taking it in a forked attack from both land and river.

Abu Naskos had replaced Memphis as Utteric's

northern capital. Memphis itself had suffered irreparable damage during the earlier siege by Hurotas and me when we mined the walls to defeat Khamudi, the Hyksos leader. Utteric had built a new city and formidable capital at Abu Naskos forty leagues farther north. This was on the site of the ruins of another ancient city, whose origins were lost in the mists of antiquity.

With all this very much in the forefront of my mind, I decided that I must judge for myself if it was the real Utteric who was taking the bulk of his army northward or if one of his impostors was assuming the role. If it was Utteric at the head of his army, then we would be justified in attempting to seize the city of Luxor from the depleted divisions he had left to garrison it, even though we were a mere four hundred strong holed up in the Garden of Joy. We must hope to be able to turn the remaining defendants of the city to our banner. I was determined to go alone and witness for myself Utteric's departure from Luxor, not taking even Weneg or Rameses to accompany me. I warned the sentries on the main gates not to bruit the news of my leaving abroad, and in the hour after midnight, the stillest hour of the night, I slipped through the gates of the Garden of Joy into the darkness and headed down the hills toward the city of Luxor.

The moon was still high and full and the dawn hours

away when I reached my destination and looked down on the Nile from the high ground. The harbor was lit up almost as bright as day by the flares. A constant stream of stevedores were tramping down the dock under heavy burdens to load them into the holds of the ships. As each vessel was filled, it battened down its hatches and pushed off from the dock, turned its bows down the current and disappeared into the darkness toward the city of Abu Naskos.

Then as the sky lightened and the rim of the sun pushed above the eastern horizon, a small party of horsemen galloped through the gates of the harbor and reined in their mounts beside one of the moored war galleys. The riders dismounted and in a group climbed the gangway to the ship's top deck. They were all dressed in the style that had become popular with the upper classes since the ascension of Utteric to the throne. These included wide-brimmed hats that concealed their features. The crew of the galley pushed off from the jetty. And as the ship swung across the current, one of the passengers lifted his hat and stooped to kiss his male companion on his open mouth. Then as he turned away and donned the hat once more, I caught a brief glimpse of his features. I sighed with satisfaction. They were unmistakably those of Utteric the Invincible. My vigil had been fully rewarded.

I hurried back to the Garden of Joy and summoned the war council to an urgent session to plan our next move. I wanted to take full advantage of the fact that Utteric had left Luxor and rushed away to the defense of his northern city, which was more obviously menaced by King Hurotas' onslaught. It was a measured and well-reasoned debate that lasted most of the remainder of the day.

We finally decided to wait a further five full days in order to give Utteric time to get well on his way into the north before we made an open onslaught on the forces that he had left in Luxor. We had no way of knowing accurately how numerous these were. Of course, Utteric was an inexperienced commander, but in extenuation of his mistakes he had no way of knowing what a stronghold we had managed to build out of the Garden of Joy with the superior men he had sent to us for execution. There was an excellent chance that he had reduced his garrison in Luxor to a perilous degree. In essence, what we had to ascertain was whom he had left in command and what force he had placed at the disposal of the person he had appointed.

In the interim, we decided that some of us who were known and well regarded in Luxor, despite the enmity of Utteric and the fact that we were rumored to have been obliterated by Doog and his tormentors, should

nevertheless go into the city and attempt to make contact with those citizens we knew were well disposed to
our cause. We should warn them of our intentions and
try to enlist their sympathies for the elevation of Rameses to Pharaoh in the place of Utteric.

As if all these anxieties and incipient disasters were not sufficient for me to worry over, that very same evening, just as I was opening a jug of red wine to soothe my frayed nerves, I was visited unexpectedly in my quarters in the southern tower by Rameses and Serrena. Their demeanor was unusual and immediately put me on alert. First they knocked timidly on my door rather than entering unannounced. They were holding hands, but neither of them looked me directly in the eyes. Nevertheless, they expressed the fervent hope that they were not disturbing me in any way. When I assured them that this was not the case, the conversation came to an abrupt hiatus. I broke the silence by offering each of them a mug of my wine, notwithstanding the fact that it was my last jug. They both accepted with gratitude and there was silence once again as we all tasted the wine with fierce concentration.

I finally broke the silence by inquiring if there was any other way that I might be able to assist them. At this they exchanged silent but significant glances, and then Serrena took the plunge.

"We have to be married," she said. This took me aback.

"I am not sure what you mean by that," I replied cautiously. "Do you mean that you have been naughty, playing the beast with two backs, and now you have to be married to avoid the consequences?"

"No! No! Don't be daft, darling Tata. We have just had our first real fight because we have not been naughty."

"Now I am really confused," I admitted. "You will have to explain this to me."

"We have just had our first fight because I want to and Rameses won't do it. He says he has given his word to my mother not to do it with me until we are married."

"Didn't you also give your word, Serrena?" I asked.

"Yes, but I didn't think it meant forever," she said wistfully. "I have waited a year already, and that is long enough. I can't wait another day. I am very sorry, Tata, but you have to marry us tonight!"

"How about tomorrow?" I procrastinated. "Give me a chance to get accustomed to the idea?"

She shook her head. "Tonight!" she repeated.

"Will you allow me to finish my wine?"

She nodded. "Of course I will! After you marry us."

"Where have you chosen for that auspicious event?"

"In my garden, where all the gods can see us and give us their approval."

"Very well," I capitulated. "It will be a great honor for me to officiate!"

I made it a lovely ceremony. I reduced all three of us to happy tears with the beauty of my words. When I pronounced the fatal words, "Now in the sight of all the gods I pronounce you man and wife," the two of them disappeared like smoke in a high wind. I did not see them again for some time. When at last I did, they were still holding hands, but I am not suggesting that is all they had been doing during the two intervening days.

"Well?" I asked. "I hope you are satisfied at last?"

"If only I had had any inkling of just how marvelous it really is, I would have married Rameses the very same day I met him," she replied seriously. "Thank you ten thousand times, Tata. It surpassed all of my most extravagant expectations."

On the third day after Utteric had left Luxor, I deemed that it was safe for us to make a reconnaissance of the city. From those who had taken shelter in the Garden of Joy, Rameses and I selected ten men we knew well and trusted completely. We all took a vow of secrecy in the event of our capture. We would go to our deaths without surrendering any information. Then we split up and approached the city gates individually. Almost immediately I was alarmed by the attitude of the guards. They were much more alert than I had ever seen them previously. So much so that Rameses and I decided when we were still some distance away that we should not take the chance of trying to enter the city. We took one of the tracks that bypassed the gates where a crowd had gathered seeking entrance but were being meticulously checked and minutely searched by the guards before they were allowed in.

From a safe distance we lingered among the idlers outside the walls and watched the proceedings. We saw one of our companions seized and marched away by the sentries. They had obviously recognized him as one of those who had been arrested at the city stadium on the day when Utteric had proven his invincibility by surviving assassination by the hidden archer. Yet we saw two of our other companions pass by the guards and allowed to enter the city. Nevertheless, we decided not to take any further chances and we recalled our companions who were still waiting in line to enter the city. Then all of us withdrew discreetly and, still moving individually, made our way back to the Garden of Joy. Here we waited anxiously for our two companions who had managed to pass the scrutiny of the guards to return to the garden. This they managed to do just before sundown when the city gates closed. Nevertheless, we still lost one of our best men. We never saw him again, and we could only presume that he was tortured and executed out of hand by Panmasi's thugs. If this was his fate, he did not betray us, and we were never placed in peril by his confessions to his captors.

The two men who returned safely from the city

were also fine fellows. They were brothers named Shehab and Mohab. They had been able to contact their friends, relatives, and compatriots in the city and from them garnered vital information. The person Utteric had left in command during his absence was none other than General Panmasi: the same felon and outlaw who had captured Serrena and spirited her out of Lacedaemon. However, I was given pause by the fact that he was indubitably also a cunning and devious adversary.

From the two brothers we learned that General Panmasi probably had no more than three or four hundred men under his command. Utteric had taken the rest of his army north with him to Abu Naskos to oppose Hurotas' invasion. This indicated that Panmasi and Utteric had no reasonable idea of the numbers of the men we had liberated from their grasp. They must be convinced that their execution orders had been carried out to the letter by the dreaded Doog. They clearly had not the least notion that Doog was no longer in a position to slaughter any more innocents, and that his polished skull now decorated the portcullis of the Garden of Joy.

I looked forward to disillusioning Panmasi at the very first opportunity.

We began our planning within minutes of receiving the report of the two stalwart brothers, Shehab and Mohab. They had learned exactly where Panmasi had his men barracked and how many guards were placed on the city gates during the night when they were closed. Furthermore, and most importantly, they had learned that Rameses' legend lived on and he and I were still fondly remembered in Upper Egypt, especially in Luxor, for we were both sons of that city. So we were both determined to make the most of our popularity and use it to evict Panmasi without waiting for Hurotas' army to capture Abu Naskos and then fight their way up the Nile to reach us in Luxor. This could take several months or even years.

In the Garden of Joy we had been able to muster 382 men whom we had rescued from Utteric's clutches. But most unfortunately, we had very few weapons with which to arm them. However, our two spies had learned that before leaving Luxor, Utteric had ordered his men to seize all the weapons that they could find in a house-to-house search of the city, other than those in the hands of his own troops. These illicit weapons were locked away and guarded by his men under Panmasi in a secure warehouse in the dock area, outside the main city walls.

Included in this weapons cache were several hundred compound bows, and an appropriate number of long arrows with flint heads that were matched to the limbs of the bows. There were also a large number of bronze-bladed swords and daggers and over a hundred battle-axes stored with the bows in the warehouse.

On the night that we chose for our attack on the city of Luxor, the moon was, most obligingly, reduced to a waning crescent that was due to set a little after midnight. This suited our purpose admirably. It gave us ample light for our approach march on the harbor warehouse, and then it set when we needed utter darkness for our ultimate attack. Our raiding party was divided into platoons, each linked together by a rope of appropriate length to prevent them becoming separated in the darkness. The two men leading each platoon were armed with sledgehammers to smash open the doors to the warehouses when we reached them. The docks were a sufficient distance from the city walls not to alert the guards there with the sounds of the hammer blows, and these were further muffled by the intervening hillock.

We set off from the Garden of Joy an hour after the sunset. The platoons followed each other at short intervals, maintaining a steady pace so as to arrive at our goal in good order. When we reached the docks, we threw off the linking ropes and crept up silently on the doors of the storehouse. When the word was quietly passed back that all three teams were in position, I gave my notoriously piercing two-fingered whistle. This was followed immediately by the thudding of muffled sledgehammers, the crashes of the warehouse doors being burst open and the confused shouts of the sentries within, rudely awakened from their slumbers and just as swiftly being returned to oblivion by the blows of the same hammers.

When the last sentry was silenced, we waited anxiously with heads cocked and ears pricked for the sounds of further alarm and panic from an enemy that we may have overlooked. But gradually we relaxed as the silence persisted and was then replaced by the scraping of flints as we lit our oil lamps. The wicks flared and we looked about us; we found ourselves in a long room filled with the weapons of war that had been hurriedly stacked in untidy piles down the full length of the floor.

"Help yourselves, my friends, but be quick about it. We have a long night's work ahead of us," I told them, and the men spread out down the length of the room gathering up war bows and edged weapons from the piles of equipment, testing the tension of the bow limbs before they strung them with cat gut or trying the cutting edges of the swords against their thumbs. In the meantime Rameses and I kept on urging them to hurry and make their selections.

Within a very short space of time the men trooped

out of the storeroom with recurved bows strung, bulging quivers of arrows slung across both of their shoulders, and gleaming sidearms sheathed on their sword belts. At the whispered orders of our sergeants and captains they extinguished the oil lamps and fell into their formations once more. Then in close order we started up the cobbled street toward the main gates of the city. When we reached them they were locked and cross-bolted but apparently deserted. The men who followed Rameses and me took cover in the drainage ditch down both sides of the road, while we went forward and I pressed my ear to the door to listen. The silence continued. I drew my dagger from its sheath and knocked lightly with the hilt on the woodwork using the agreed call sign: three sets of three knocks repeated thrice.

It was answered at once. I moved across to the peep-hole and waited until the cover over the aperture was lifted from the far side and one of Shehab's bright yellow eyes caught the starlight and flashed as he peered out at me.

"How are our mutual friends?" I asked softly.

"Sleeping!" he replied as softly and closed the cover in my face. I heard him fiddling with the locking bar on the inside of the wicket. The wicket door finally swung open. It was a narrow single entrance, just large enough to admit one man at a time if he ducked his head

368 · WILBUR SMITH

and kept the bow slung on his shoulder clear. I glanced beyond Shehab's grinning face, and by the dim light of the few oil lamps set in the woodwork of the portcullis I could make out the somnolent figures of the gate guards. One or two of them were snoring peacefully. Another was holding one of the red wine jugs that I had given to Shehab the previous day. However, the jug was now empty, and the guard held it upside down clutched to his chest. Like the rest of his comrades he was showing no interest in any of his surroundings. The juice of the Red Sheppen with which I had spiked the wine is a potent soporific.

To the first five of my men who followed me through the wicket I delegated the task of trussing up and gagging the comatose gate guards, using the guide ropes and strips of the prisoners' own tunics stuffed into their mouths. I directed the men who followed the first five to go to the winches in the portcullis. They seized the handles and wound them up with a will. The massive gates groaned and squeaked as they lifted in their channels. As soon as they were high enough, the rest of our men poured under them in a solid stream, carrying their newly acquired weapons at the ready, but true to my strict instructions keeping as silent as was possible. They uttered no war cries, and the sergeants gave their orders in hoarse whispers. But, nevertheless, the stamping of their bronze-shod sandals and the rattle of their weapons was significant. Inevitably, before all our men were through the gates and in the city, we were challenged by Panmasi's guards, who were patrolling the inner streets of the city. They came running to investigate the sounds of metal on metal and marching feet and ran headlong into our phalanxes. The quiet streets were transformed within seconds into a bloody battleground. The bellows of the respective war cries became continuous. The shouts of "Long live Utteric the Invincible!" were met immediately by "Rameses forever!"

Our men were generally much older than the low-born country boys with which Utteric had filled his regiments, presumably because they were more malleable and bore no allegiance to Tamose and the previous regime. Neither were our men any longer as fit and strong as once they had been. But they were experienced in all the arts of war, canny and disciplined warriors who knew every street and back alley of the city in which they had lived most of their lives. In the beginning we were heavily outnumbered by the fresh young troops that came swarming out of their barracks. But my men knew how to endure. They closed their ranks, locked shields and hacked away grimly at Utteric's legions. We sang our war songs, and the population of Luxor was roused from sleep and they heard us. They heard the name Rameses and their blood stirred. Grizzle-bearded old warriors of thirty-five and even forty years of age heard the name and they remembered that they had fought for Tamose, the father of this man Rameses, and that he had been a great and good Pharaoh.

They also knew well enough the name Utteric, who still ruled them with a heavy hand. They paid the extortionate taxes he imposed upon them to fund the temples to his own glory, and they ate the stale bread that was all they could afford in place of the good red meat and wine that had once been their lot. They had remained silent when their old companions were herded together and sent up the hills to the Gates of Torment and Sorrow, never to return.

Now when they heard the name Rameses, they knew this was their last chance to make a stand for what they knew was their right. They threw aside their scrolls and the chessboards with which they had filled their empty days and shouted to their wives to bring their arms and armor from the cupboard below the stairs and to pay no heed to the red rust that bloomed upon them. Then they sallied out into the darkened streets of the city in groups of five or ten and listened for the war cry "Rameses forever." When they heard it they limped, hobbled or ran to join their old companions and took their proud place in the shield wall alongside us once more.

We fought for the rest of that first night, and all the day that followed, but by the evening we knew we were winning and we fought harder still, and the shield walls of Panmasi's legions began to buckle before us and then to crumble, and his men began to defect in droves to Rameses' standard when they realized he was an Egyptian Pharaoh and an attractive alternative to Utteric. Then when darkness fell the remnants of the army of Panmasi collapsed and they fled the city.

Princess Serrena was the first person to greet us as we debouched through the open gates in pursuit of Panmasi and his shattered legions.

When Rameses and I had decided to attack Panmasi and his minions in their stronghold behind the walls of Luxor, I had used all my influence and wiles to convince Serrena that she owed it to Rameses and the rest of her family to remain safely in the Garden of Joy and to stay well clear of the battlefield. I had unashamedly pointed out that she was now a married woman and, considering the gusto with which she had assumed her matrimonial duties, there was every chance that she was now a mother-to-be. The battlefield was no longer her fiefdom. Henceforth, her sole concern must be the contents of her womb. Of course, she had argued with me bitterly, employing all her considerable wiles to try to win a place at Rameses' right hand in the assault on the city of Luxor. But to my surprise, Rameses joined the argument on my side, demanding of his wife that she keep herself and her future offspring safely behind the walls of the Garden of Joy. At this point I expected to witness a protracted argument between these two notoriously stubborn creatures. But to my astonishment, Serrena capitulated almost immediately to her new husband. I had never expected Serrena to take her maternal obligations so seriously. She had avoided the battlefield for the time being, but here she was waiting to take over at the very first sign of masculine incompetence. In retrospect, I should have expected no less of her.

By the time of this reunion the moon was just a thin sliver in the midnight sky and the darkness was almost complete. It was impossible for us to follow the trail left by Panmasi and his surviving horsemen by its light. But I knew that if I allowed Panmasi a full twelve hours' head start we would never catch him again. I wanted him. I wanted my vengeance on him more than I have wanted anything in my life. I recalled every act of treachery and cruelty he had ever perpetrated upon me and the persons dear to me. I remembered the mutilated body of Palmys after Panmasi and his men had finished with him, and the grief of Hui and Bekatha as they laid their son to rest. But most of all I remembered how he had beaten and humiliated Serrena, and I longed to feel him squirming on the point of my sword as I ran it into his guts.

But Panmasi was gone, and all of us were almost played out. We had fought relentlessly for a long night and a *longer* day, and most of us were not young anymore. Nearly all of us were wounded. Even though most of our injuries were superficial, they were still painful and debilitating. And I was tired, tired to the very marrow of my bones. Without realizing why I was doing it, I glanced at Serrena. She must have seen something in my eyes that she read as an appeal— mistakenly, of course.

"Panmasi is nothing but a whipped cur dog running back to its master," she said to me, and I realized at once that she had solved the conundrum for us. We did not have to follow the trail left by Panmasi. We knew exactly where he was going. And suddenly I was no longer exhausted.

However, we still needed horses if we were to catch Panmasi before he reached Abu Naskos to rejoin his master. It seemed that he had taken all the horses that he needed for his men and himself to escape. Those animals that were superfluous to his needs he had crippled so as to deny them to us. Few sights are more harrowing than a beautiful horse with the ligaments of its fetlock joints hacked through on both its hind legs. It was typical of the man that he preferred to inflict agony on these lovely creatures to taunt us rather than driving them away or killing them outright. It was one more score for me to settle with him when we finally met again.

I was so angered I almost reminded Serrena that it

was she who had insisted we free Panmasi when her father and I had that treacherous rogue in our power and were on the point of dealing with him to ensure that he would cause us no further anguish. But I could not bring myself to be so cruel to one I love so dearly. I even sent her to bring down those horses that we had stabled within the Garden of Joy. While she was away I put the poor creatures that Panmasi had crippled out of their agony with a sword blow between the ears.

In addition to those from the Garden of Joy, we found a few uninjured animals that had been overlooked by Panmasi's henchman in their haste to fly the city. Thus we gathered mounts for twenty-two of my men to take up the chase to bring Panmasi to justice.

Naturally enough, both Rameses and I protested anew when Serrena announced that she was determined to join us in the final hunt for Panmasi and his escaping henchmen. We used the same old rhetoric regarding the poor little mite cowering in her womb who might suffer injury and even death if its mother were so cruel as to inflict the hardship of a long and harrowing ride upon it.

Serrena listened to both of us with a sweet smile on her face, nodding her head as if in agreement with our pleas and protests. When we finally ran out of words and were gazing at her expectantly, she shook her head.

"I only wish everything you are telling me were true, but the goddess Artemis has different ideas," she told us. "Almost the moment you left me in the Garden of Joy, she sent me my red moon."

"What on earth is that?" Rameses looked mystified. He was still very naive when it came to the mysteries of the female body.

"Tell him, please, Tata," Serrena appealed to me.

"It's the goddess Artemis' way of saying, *Not good enough. Try again,*" I explained.

Rameses thought about it for a few seconds, then he smiled happily. "Tell the goddess I accept her challenge only with the greatest of pleasure!"

Within the hour we had completed our preparations for the long ride and were ready to pursue Panmasi and attempt to prevent him reaching Utteric in the city of Abu Naskos in the north.

Naturally enough there was no further argument. Red moon or not, Serrena was no longer to be denied. She was coming with us.

Long ago I had perfected the trick of sleeping in the saddle with my feet tied together under my mount's chest and a reliable groom to lead us both. I awoke an hour before dawn and took only a moment to orientate myself. I felt totally rested and eager for the first sight of the chase.

"Have we crossed the Sattakin River yet?" I called to my lead groom. The Sattakin was one of the only significant tributaries running into Mother Nile to the north of Luxor.

"Not yet." He looked up to check the stars. "I reckon still about half a league to go."

"Any sign of Panmasi's horses ahead of us?"

"It is too dark to read tracks without dismounting, my lord. Do you want me to check?" he asked.

"No, we are committed. Don't waste another minute. Keep going!" I ordered.

I looked back and could just make out the dark shapes of Serrena and Rameses following me closely. Rameses was sleeping in the saddle just as I had been, and she was holding him so he did not slide off his mount's back. I would not waken him yet. I could hear the hooves of the other horses following us. Although there were many of them, I could not make out any in the darkness. There was no point in increasing the pace until it was light enough to see well ahead, other than increasing the risk of running into an ambush set by Panmasi.

I restrung my war bow, wedging the lower limb in the pommel of my saddle to get the tension on it. Then I slung it over my shoulder and drew five arrows from my quiver and lodged them in my belt, ready to be launched in quick succession. I glanced back and saw that Rameses was now awake. Serrena must have roused him. He was also busy with his weapons, preparing them for instant use.

He looked up at me and I could make out his features clearly: the dawn light was coming on apace. Now I could see the horses and the riders that followed him. I counted them quickly and all twenty-two of them were present. Then I glanced down at the pathway beneath my mount, and my heart tripped and then beat faster. It was light enough to see that the dry surface of the track had been pounded into powder by the passage of many hooves. The tracks were less than an hour old. Even as I watched, one of the hoofprints collapsed upon itself in a run of dry dust.

I held up my hand. The men following me bunched up behind me and sat their horses quietly. Rameses and Serrena came up level with me, one on each side, with our boots almost touching, so I was able to speak in a whisper.

"I think I recognize where we are. Ahead of us the ground dips sharply into the gorge of the Sattakin River. Judging by his tracks, Panmasi is not more than half an hour ahead of us. We were in danger of running into his rearguard in the darkness. However, I am almost certain Panmasi has now halted his troop in the gorge to rest and water their horses. They will obviously have posted pickets to cover their back trail, but we are still concealed from them by those folds of the ground there—and there." I pointed them out, and then I turned and looked back the way we had come.

"Our best alternative is to retreat, and then make a wide circle to get well ahead of him while his men are resting. Then when they start moving again, they will still be watching their back trail, but we will be lying up ahead of them."

There was no demur from any of them, not even Serrena. So we turned and retraced our steps for a considerable distance southward. Then we swung in a wide semicircle toward the east and swam the horses across the Sattakin River before it entered the gorge and ran down to join waters with the Nile.

We continued our semicircle and at last came within sight of the rough track that ran from Luxor along the east bank of the Nile. We approached it cautiously, and when we were within a few hundred yards of it I went forward alone on foot, leaving the rest of our contingent concealed in a convenient wadi. When I reached the road I was relieved but not surprised to find no tracks or other signs of recent human passage upon it.

The Nile River lay only a mile or so to the west and was by far the most popular route for most traffic between Luxor and Abu Naskos. As I had hoped, Panmasi was still lingering at the crossing of the Sattakin River, secure in the belief that he was not being followed. We had succeeded in getting ahead of him. I ran along the verge of the road, hopping from tussocks of grass to clumps of weeds to cover my footprints as I searched for an inconspicuous ravine to serve as an ambuscade. This was difficult because the hills along the Sattakin River were almost entirely denuded of trees, and the grass was sparse and seldom more than knee high.

However, the gods favored me, as they so often do. I discovered a shallow ravine running parallel to the road that was almost unnoticeable from a distance of fifty paces, which was approximately the distance that separated the road from the ravine. It was also a perfect killing range for our recurved bows. Behind our ravine was an inconspicuous outcrop of rocks, which provided almost perfect concealment for our horses. They required only two of our number to tend them. The rest of us were lying up in the ravine, each with an arrow nocked in our bows, and follow-up arrows ready to our right hands.

The rising sun was hardly four fingers' width above the horizon when we heard the sounds of many hooves clattering along the rocky surface of the road climbing up the escarpment from the Sattakin River. I had arranged a clump of grass on the lip of the ravine to mask my eyes and the top of my head as I peered out. Every other man in the ambush had his head well below the lip and his face pressed to the bottom of the ravine. I deliberately differentiate between the sexes of those who were obeying my instructions and those who were not.

Serrena was directly behind me and therefore out of my line of vision. All my concentration was focused on the track ahead of me and the column of men approaching along it. I had no idea that her head was up and that she was using me and my clump of grass as cover. She had already adopted the classical archer's squat, with an arrow nocked and her eyes bright as an eagle's as it focuses on its prey the moment before it begins its stoop.

I let Panmasi lead his men deep into my trap before I opened my mouth to shout the command to my men to let their arrows fly, but I was shocked into silence by the unmistakable sound of a heavy recurved bow, one with a forty-deben draw weight, releasing its arrow only inches from my left ear. This was a sound akin to the crack of a heavy bullwhip lash magnified many times by its proximity. The arrow flew past my ear in a liquid blur of sunlight. Only an eye as sharp as mine was capable of following the flight of that arrow.

At the head of the approaching column of horsemen, Panmasi was bare to the waist. His helmet and breastplate were tied to the back of his saddle. As were most of the men that followed him, he was sweating heavily in the heat of the early sunlight. Serrena's arrow struck him just below the juncture of his ribs and three finger widths above the umbilical scar in the center of his belly. It buried itself up to the fletching, and the force of it lifted him out of the saddle and hurled him backward. He twisted in the air, and I saw the arrowhead protruding from the center of his back. It must have severed his spinal column, and he was screaming with the shock and agony of the wound. It was a mortal stroke, but I judged from the site of the wound and the angle of the arrow shaft that it would take a while for him to die. Serrena had aimed her shot to kill inevitably, but also to kill slowly and remorselessly.

I realized she was taking full retribution for the torment and suffering that Panmasi had visited upon her, and others of her clan such as Palmys. I could not grudge it to her even if it meant she was flouting my orders. I was at least accustomed to the occasional disobedience from her.

Panmasi's men seemed not to realize what was happening. Almost none of them had seen him struck by Serrena's arrow. Most of them rode with eyes downcast, and their forward vision was blocked by the horsemen riding ahead of them. When he was unseated and thrown bodily from the saddle, it brought down the men following directly behind him. Within seconds the entire column was plunged into chaos. Very few of the riders had strung their bows, and not one of them had nocked an arrow. Most of them were too busy trying to stay in the saddle to even realize they were under attack.

While this was all happening Serrena released three more arrows in quick succession. I saw each one of them fly true and three more of the enemy riders were knocked from their saddles and trampled by their mounts. Unlike the arrow that she had aimed at Panmasi, every one of these ripped through the chest cavity, piercing heart or lungs or both organs, killing almost instantly.

"Nock! Draw! Loose!" I screamed as I brought up my own bow, trying to catch up with Serrena's initiative. The rest of our men sprang to their feet and started letting fly a hail of their arrows into the column of enemy horsemen. With the first few volleys I saw at least fifteen of the enemy knocked down, bristling with arrows. And others continued to drop, as the subsequent volleys swept over them.

I had estimated when I first saw them from a distance that their total numbers did not exceed sixty men. Thus we had reduced their numbers to a par with our own with less than a dozen volleys of arrows. But now they had realized the predicament they were in and were dismounting and trying to string their bows to enable them to retaliate to our salvos.

Nonetheless, I was very much aware of the fact that these were Egyptians whom we were killing, mis-guided Egyptians for sure, but Egyptians nonetheless. Very soon I could take no more of the slaughter and I shouted across to them, "Throw down your bows at once, or face annihilation." Then I turned to our own men. "Hold your arrows. Give them a chance to ca-pitulate." Slowly a silence fell over the field. Nobody moved at first. Then abruptly one of the opposing ar-chers broke ranks and stepped forward.

"I know who you are, Lord Taita. I fought beside you in the ranks of Pharaoh Tamose's legions against the Hyksos, in the field of Signium. You stood over me when I was wounded, and you carried me from the field when those Hyksos bastards broke and ran."

His features were vaguely familiar but much older than any that I remembered. We stared at each other and it seemed that all of creation held its breath. Then I smiled at last as my memory caught up with me. "Do not ask me to carry you from the field again, Merimose. For I swear you have doubled or trebled your weight since our last meeting."

Merimose let out a hearty guffaw and then dropped to his knees in obeisance. "All hail, Lord Taita. You should have been made Pharaoh in place of the one who now desecrates the throne of Upper and Lower Egypt."

It always amuses me to learn just how fickle the common man can be. Merimose had changed his allegiance in the time it takes to nock an arrow and loose it.

"Nay, Merimose! I give you Pharaoh Rameses and Pharaohin Princess Serrena of Lacedaemon whose duty and honor that now is, rather than mine."

A murmur of awe ran through their ranks as they recognized the names. First one and then another and finally all of them threw down their weapons and fell to their knees, pressing their foreheads to the ground.

I summoned Rameses and Serrena to me and led them across the now quiescent field of battle and down the capitulated ranks of our erstwhile enemies. As we came to each of them I made them state their name and rank and swear an oath of fealty to the royal couple. There were only thirty-two of them who had survived the encounter. However, every one of them declared himself to be an ardent convert to the reign of the new Pharaoh.

We came at last to General Panmasi who was still lying where Serrena's arrow had felled him. No one had attended to his injuries. His erstwhile loyal warriors were paying scant attention to his moaning and raving and delirious pleas for water to drink. They were all keeping well clear of him. But they watched the three of us with fascination as we went to stand over him.

I have told you how bitterly I hated him. However, there are limits even to my hatred. I wondered if I was not reducing myself to the same base level by allowing him to endure the outer limits of agony, when I had in my power the means to end it cleanly and quickly. I felt myself wavering. Almost of its own accord my right hand reached down for the hilt of the dagger that hung on my belt. I had honed the edge on the blade that very morning as we waited in ambush. As an accomplished surgeon I knew precisely where the main arteries in the neck were situated. Furthermore I knew how quick it would be and almost completely painless for a man in Panmasi's condition. But this was not for the sake of Panmasi, who was an unregenerate villain. This was for myself and my own self-esteem.

Before my fingers touched the hilt of my dagger, I felt another set of fingers close around my wrist. They were warm and smooth, but hard as polished marble or the blade of the blue sword that they wielded so skilfully.

Slowly I turned my head and looked at the woman who held me. She did not return my gaze, but she spoke so quietly that no one else could hear her, except her husband who stood at her other hand.

"No!" she said.

"Why?" I asked.

"I want him to suffer," she replied.

"I have no choice," I answered her.

"Why?" she asked.

"So that I do not descend to his level," I said simply.

She was silent for twenty beats of my heart. And then her fingers opened, and my hand was freed. Even now she still did not look at me, but she closed her eyes and nodded her head in an infinitesimal gesture of acquiescence.

I drew my dagger from its sheath and stooped to take a handful of Panmasi's beard in my other hand. I pulled back his chin to expose the full length of his throat. I placed the razor edge of my blade behind his ear and cut down so deeply that the metal rasped against his vertebrae and his blood pumped in sullen jets from the carotid artery. His final breath hissed out of his ruptured larynx. His body convulsed for the last time and he died.

"Thank you," she said softly. "You did the right thing, as always, Tata. You have become my councillor and my conscience."

We left Panmasi where he died: food for the jackals and the birds. We retraced our route to the ford over the Sattakin River, taking with us Merimose and his companions who had so recently changed their allegiance. I decided to stop there and rest our horses and our men until the following day. That evening as we sat around the fire, eating our frugal dinner and washing it down with a jug of red wine, the three of us had deliberately separated from the other ranks to enable us to converse freely.

We touched lightly on the passing of Panmasi, which left us brooding quietly for a while, but then Serrena dramatically changed the subject in her inimitable fashion.

"So why are we returning to Luxor?" she asked.

"Because it is the loveliest city in Egypt." Her question took me so much aback that my response was equally vacuous.

"My father and my mother are probably in Abu Naskos by now," Serrena said wistfully. "Not to mention my uncle Hui and my aunt Bekatha and all my cousins. They will have come to rescue me from Utteric."

"I agree that your entire family is probably camped on the bank of the Nile, busily feeding the mosquitoes with their blood, while Utteric and all his sycophants are comfortably ensconced inside the walls of the city." I could see where this conversation was bound, and I was trying to head it off. "Any way you look at it, it is a long ride from here to Abu Naskos . . ."

"I was not suggesting that we ride. We have over fifty fine ships that we captured from Panmasi lying in the Luxor docks," she reminded me. "If we push our horses, we can be back in Luxor before sunrise tomorrow morning. Then in a fast cutter with twin masts, a team of stout slaves on the oars, and a good river pilot at the helm, we could be in Abu Naskos two or three days later. Now explain to me where I have gone wrong in my calculations, I beg of you, my darling Tata."

I always try to avoid argument with a pretty woman, especially a smart one. "That is precisely what I was about to suggest," I agreed. "But I thought it was your plan to rest here tonight and only begin the journey back to Luxor in the morning."

"All good plans are subject to change at short notice," she said seriously. I sighed with resignation. She was not even giving me the opportunity to finish the contents of my wine jug.

We rode through the night and reached Luxor the following morning just as the dawn was breaking. The guards at the gates recognized us immediately and ushered us into the city with the utmost respect and ceremony. They formed an escort around Rameses and led us to the golden palace of Luxor, where Weneg was already in conclave with the Interim Governing Committee, which was composed almost completely of those men we had assembled in the Garden of Joy. Many of them wore bloody bandages like badges of honor, and they seemed rejuvenated by their recent warlike endeavors.

They were overjoyed to welcome us to their midst. Their first official act was to unanimously ratify the ascension of Pharaoh Rameses I to the throne of Upper and Lower Egypt. Rameses formally accepted the honor and swore the royal oath from the throne. He then declared the Interim to be his final and fully legitimate committee. He also announced that he had chosen Lord Taita to act as the first and senior minister of his new parliament.

While Rameses was occupied with these commonplace proceedings, his wife was engaged with the more significant aspects of our existence, such as requisitioning a fast ship to convey us down the Nile to a reunion with her family. To be fair to Serrena, her marriage to Rameses was a secret shared only by the three of us. Her state wedding could only be celebrated once certain other trivialities had been taken care of, such as the presence of her father's royal allies to witness the proceedings. So it was wiser and more diplomatic that Serrena make no public or official appearances until those aims were achieved.

Late that same afternoon I placed my personal hieroglyphic on an official document appointing Weneg to act in my absence in the capacity of senior first minister. Then Rameses and I melted into the background, only to reappear a short time later in the dock area of the river harbor, where we unobtrusively boarded a twin-masted cutter named the *Four Winds*, which immediately cast off her moorings and headed out into the current, bearing away on a northerly heading toward Abu Naskos and the Middle Sea.

Serrena remained belowdecks in the master cabin until the lights of Luxor merged with the darkness behind us. Then she appeared on the deck as mysteriously and as beautifully as the evening star above her. She laughed with joy to see us both, kissed me on both my cheeks, and then disappeared belowdecks again. Rameses went with her, and I saw neither of them again until morning. There followed three of the happiest and most peaceful days I can remember as the *Four Winds* ran north for Abu Naskos with the current driving her on apace.

On the third night, I woke a little before midnight. I knew that we should arrive at our destination early the next morning. So for me further sleep was no longer possible. I went to sit in the bows and wait for the dawn. The ship's pilot, whose name was Ganord, came forward to join me, and as always I was grateful for his company. He was an elderly man with a countenance the same texture as that of one of the river crocodiles. He possessed a pair of deep-set eyes the indeterminate brown of river pebbles that missed nothing, and a luxuriant and creamy beard that flowed down to his waist. He had spent his entire life since early childhood plying the river and the shores of the great northern sea.

He knew these waters as did no other, not even I. He knew the names of the river sprites and water gnomes, even those that had disappeared back in antiquity with the passing of the ancient tribes. He had traveled from the source of the Nile where it tumbled down from the sky to its culmination where it poured through the rocky Gates of Hathor and cascaded into the abyss, falling away through all eternity.

This night Ganord spoke about the river where it flowed past the city of Abu Naskos, for that was our final destination. According to him, the city was inhabited for the first time approximately a thousand years ago by a superior tribe of people; Ganord referred to them as a race of demigods. They were accomplished in most of the higher skills such as building, reading and writing, and horticulture. They irrigated both banks of the Nile and built fortifications to protect themselves from the savage peoples who surrounded them. It seemed that they had developed the means of crossing swiftly from one bank of the river to the other, probably on a system of bridges, although Ganord suggested it was by witchcraft. According to him, there was still much evidence of their former presence in the multiple layers of ruins beneath the present city, Abu Naskos.

This presence ended abruptly around five hundred years ago, probably as a result of a cataclysmic series of earthquakes. It seems that the surviving population moved away from the Nile and disappeared in a northeasterly direction toward the Euphrates River and Babylon. Abu Naskos remained deserted for five hundred years thereafter.

Ganord realized that I found his discourse fascinating, and he went belowdecks and returned with a souvenir of these demigods, which he gave me as a gift. This was a small bright green tile, no wider than the span of my own hand, which depicted a strange fish with long flowing fins and a golden head. He claimed to have found the tile in the rubble of the ancient city ruins. He told me that it was the only remaining relic of the original tribe.

I felt mildly cheated when our discussion was terminated by the sunrise and the arrival on deck of my two most favorite people. It seemed to me that they might so easily have occupied themselves in their cabin for another short while without suffering any serious discomfort.

However, Ganord excused himself the moment they appeared; backing and bowing, he hurried away to join the captain of the *Four Winds* at the stern where he immediately ordered a shortening of sail, and we tacked across the river to anticipate the final bend before the city of Abu Naskos opened ahead of us.

The sun rose at almost the same time, so we had a fine view of the city stretched out before us along the western bank of the Nile. At this point the river was well over a league wide, which is the distance that a man can walk in an hour. Thus the tops of its walls were well out of arrow range from the opposite bank.

They were built of massive slabs of golden-yellow sandstone, which were tall and intricately turreted in the style of the Hyksos who had rebuilt the city after seizing it from us Egyptians. It had taken almost a century for us to drive out the invader and to take back what was rightfully our heritage, only to lose it again to a mad and tyrannical Pharaoh who was now ensconced behind that formidable structure.

I must have seen a hundred or more battlefields during my lifetime, but this one will remain forever in my memory. It seemed to epitomize both the grandeur and the folly of men caught up in the mindless fury of war.

The walls of the city were separated from the waters of the Nile by a narrow strip of sand upon which Utteric had beached the ships of his fleet. I counted these as we drew closer. There were almost a hundred flat-bottomed vessels, each capable of carrying thirty or forty men. The stone battlements of the city walls hung almost directly over the ships. At a glance I could make out the piles of rocks on top of the walls, which could be hurled down on an enemy coming ashore to seize, burn or plunder any of the vessels lying there.

There were no gates in the wall facing the river; no openings through which even the most determined invader could press his attack and gain access. The loopholes and arrow slits were halfway up the wall, over one hundred cubits above ground level.

Utteric's troops marched and countermarched along the parapets, their helmets and breastplates glinting in the sunlight, obviously hoping by their presence to deter our assault troops. Above them stood a forest of flag posts upon which waved and fluttered the flags and colors of Utteric's regiments. They were a flagrant challenge and warning to the armies of Hurotas that faced them from across the river.

The bulk of Utteric's army was hidden by the massive castle walls, and their numbers could only be estimated by their vessels and flags and the herds of horses that grazed on the hillside behind the city walls. Whereas on the opposing bank of the river Hurotas' legions with their multitudinous equipment and accoutrements were clear for all to see.

The Laconian fleet was moored along the eastern shore of the river with heavy cables anchoring them to the bank. These were to prevent the enemy from cutting them out in a sneak night attack. Anchor watches, armed and alert, guarded their decks. Their masts and rigging were decked out with an array of colored flags to challenge those on the battlements of the castle of Abu Naskos facing them across the river.

On the eastern bank occupied by Hurotas and his allies there were no fortress walls or permanent structures. It did my heart good to see the camp of my old friend and ally. Open forest spread over the low rolling hills as far as the eye could see. But now this was covered by hundreds of tents and pavilions. These had been laid out in neat blocks, keeping the barracks and command posts for each of the sixteen invading armies separate. Beyond these there were the stables for the horses, and the parking grounds for almost a thousand chariots, and even more numerous heavy luggage wagons.

On the outskirts of this huge agglomeration of warriors were the huts and hovels of those who barely qualified for the title of human. These were the whores and vagabonds, the misfits and the ne'er-do-wells, and all the other riffraff that follow an army of warriors into battle—if only to scavenge and loot the corpses.

"There is my father's battle flag!" Suddenly Serrena was dancing beside me, pounding my shoulder with her clenched fists, presumably to focus my attention. She has a powerful and painful punch.

"Which one is his? Point it out to me," I pleaded, mainly to induce her to discontinue the punishment.

"There! That one with the red Laconian boar." My ploy worked. Now she was pointing rather than pounding.

Of course, Hurotas' standard was the tallest on the field and the closest to the bank of the river, just as his headquarters tent was the largest in the entire battle array. I shaded my eyes with both hands the better to appraise the tall and lissom feminine figure that at that moment stooped out of the entrance of Hurotas' tent. Then as I recognized her I could not restrain my excitement, and my voice matched Serrena's for volume: "And there is your mother, coming out from your father's tent!"

At that Serrena shrieked incoherently, leaping up and down on the deck and waving both arms above her head. Tehuti straightened up and stared across the water at us in astonishment. Then she recognized her daughter, and she hurled aside the basket she was carrying.

"My baby!" she wailed in a tone that sounded more

like abject despair than joy. She began to run. She
shoved aside anyone who stood between her and the
riverbank with a force that sent them sprawling.

We were standing in the stern of the cutter. I
grabbed the whipstaff out of Ganord's hand and put
the tiller hard over, turning the bows in toward the
land. Serrena ceased her shrieking and took off running down the deck like a deer pursued by a wolf pack.
When she reached the bows of the cutter, she made no
effort to check her speed but dived headfirst overboard
and with a tall splash disappeared beneath the surface
of the Nile.

My heart skipped several beats, but then her head
popped out again and she began swimming frantically
toward the shore. She was swinging both arms in alternative overhead strokes. Her hair dissolved in stream-
ers over her face like that of a water vole, and she left a
creaming wake on the surface of the river behind her.

Only seconds behind her daughter Tehuti reached
the bank and she also dived in. I had almost forgotten
what accomplished swimmers the two of them were.
This was a rare sight indeed; in fact it is almost unheard
of to see two females of high birth involved in such an
extraordinary performance. Those very few who are
able to swim do so alone and in secret; and usually in

the nude as a ritual sacrifice to Isis, the goddess of love whose vulva is appropriately shaped like a seashell.

Mother and daughter came together in deep water and seized each other in such a rigorous embrace that they sank below the surface. They surfaced again still locked together, laughing and weeping and gasping for breath. When they sank for the third time, the crowd upon the riverbank crowded forward in ghoulish anticipation of disaster.

Even I was alarmed, and I told Rameses, "We don't want them disturbing the crocodiles. We have to get those two idiotic women out of there." The two of us stripped down to our loincloths and plunged overboard. When we reached them, we found it impossible to separate them. We towed them back to the cutter as a single entity. Ganord and the crew helped us drag them in over the gunwale to the cheers and merriment of the multitudinous onlookers on the riverbank.

"What in the name of foul Seth and all the other gods of death is happening out there?" a familiar voice bellowed from the bank. The crowds parted once again, and King Hurotas marched to the edge of the river, scowling like an ogre until he realized that the two bedraggled and sodden females being manhandled by the crew of a small river cutter were the dearest loves of his life. The tone of his voice changed, becoming immediately soppy and mawkish. "That's my darling Serrena!" He opened his arms wide. They were massively muscled from wielding the weapons of war and tattooed with ghastly images to terrify his enemies. "Come to your papa, my little one!"

By this time Serrena had run out of wind with which to shriek, but she still had more than sufficient with which to run and swim. She tore herself out of my solicitous hands and repeated the whole wild performance. She charged down the deck of the *Four Winds,* splashing it liberally with Nile water and pursued hotly by her mother. In quick succession the two of them threw themselves overboard once more and set off for the shore.

"Is it worth rescuing them again, do you think?" Rameses asked me solemnly. "Or should we just let them take their chances?"

Serrena had a head start on Tehuti for the final lap from the *Four Winds* to the eastern bank of the river so she was the first to reach her father. He picked her up and threw her high in the air, just as he must have done when she was a small child. He caught her as she descended and smothered her with his beard and his kisses. Then Tehuti reached them; Hurotas picked her up with his free hand and, hugging both women to his chest, marched with them into his campaign tent.

Rameses and I dried ourselves hurriedly and pulled on our discarded clothing as Ganord steered the *Four Winds* into the riverbank. As soon as our bows touched land, we jumped ashore and fought our way through the excited throng to the tent into which Hurotas had disappeared with his two women. This was not a simple process for it seemed that everyone present wanted to praise and congratulate us for rescuing Serrena from the clutches of Utteric. We were hugged and kissed by men and women indiscriminately. But finally we found ourselves inside Hurotas' campaign tent.

Like most things that belonged to Hurotas, the interior of his tent was exceedingly large and imposing. In fact, it vied in size with the assembly hall in the citadel of Sparta, which was just as well, since his guests that day comprised almost half the entire expeditionary force, or so it seemed to me. These included the courtiers and concubines of all sixteen of the royal courts who had accompanied Hurotas from Lacedaemon, together with the senior military officers and ministers.

As soon as Rameses and I entered their midst, King Hurotas waved at me from the far side of the campaign tent to get my attention and then he said, "Tehuti and

Serrena have gone to change their wet costumes, so they could be some time, possibly even days."

I grinned at his brand of humor and then I placed one arm around Rameses' neck and with my lips an inch from his ear repeated what Hurotas had said. The throng that surrounded us was several hundred strong and it seemed that every one of them had a wine jug in his fist and was shouting at his immediate neighbor to make himself heard. In addition, there were four or five bands playing at full volume.

Rameses looked back at me with a solemn but resigned expression. "In the name of Dolos, the imp of trickery and deception, how do you do that, Taita?" When we first met he used to test the accuracy of my interpretation, but he no longer bothered. I supposed one day he would learn about reading lips, but until he did it amused me to confound him.

It took some time for us to cross the crowded tent, but when we reached Hurotas, he embraced both of us long and heartily and then drew us aside and led us through a doorway to a small and secluded compartment. Here Hurotas immediately rounded on Rameses. "I have had only a short time to discuss with Serrena the urgency of her marriage to you. She agrees with me for once. It is vital that we present Utteric to the world at large as a villain who abducted an innocent virgin from her home and family and subjected her to untold and brutal torment."

"Your Majesty," Rameses intervened at once, "I must make it clear that Utteric tortured and humiliated your daughter. He beat her and imprisoned her; however, he refrained from deflowering her virginity and he did not allow any of his followers to do so."

"I give eternal thanks to all the gods and goddesses in the panoply of heaven that this is indeed the case," Hurotas conceded. "However, in all the nations of the world there will be those who cast slanders and calumnies on my daughter. There is only one way we can turn these aside."

"It will be my honor to take Serrena to wife as soon as this is possible. You need say no more, mighty King Hurotas." Rameses did not look in my direction; however, I understood that the nuptials I had performed for them previously were to remain a secret between the three of us for all time.

"I am delighted that we are in total accord. I will count it a great privilege to have you as my only son." Hurotas stood up and glanced at me. "Good Taita, perhaps we should see if I maligned my two darlings by suggesting to you that they might take several days to change their sodden clothing."

Rameses blinked once and then shot a question at

his future father-in-law: "When did you first make this suggestion to Taita, Your Majesty?"

"A short while ago when the two of you first walked into my tent."

"I did not hear you say it." He looked puzzled. "There was so much noise."

"Then you should ask Taita to teach you how to hear with your eyes. He is the only one I know of who has the trick of it."

Rameses stared at me, and his expression slowly changed from mystification to accusation as he worked it out. I knew that there would soon be two of us who were able to read lips; Rameses would see to that. I shrugged in apology for having duped him. Perhaps it was just as well that he learned the art, for I could not keep it to myself forever. In the years ahead it was bound to come in extremely useful for both of us. It was by now apparent to me that our futures were inextricably intertwined.

E ven in our determination to show to all the world that Rameses and Serrena were husband and wife and the future Pharaoh and Pharaohin of Egypt, we all had to proceed with dignity and observe established protocol.

The task was not made any easier by the fact that we were at the same time engaged in waging a war that boded fair to become the most savage and relentless in the history of Egypt or any other nation on this earth.

With my usual good sense and understanding, I determined not to be drawn into the essentially female domain of marriage and matrimony, and to apply myself totally to the masculine aspect of war and dominance. In this regard I had the very best of company in my old and trusty companions Zaras and Hui, and my more recent cohorts Rameses and the other kings both greater and lesser.

As always I was guided by the old adage of any superior warrior: *Know your enemy.*

My enemy was Utteric Bubastis, but I did not know him. He was a figment who seemed to change shape and profile with every breath he drew. I was not even certain he was still a single entity. For the next two days after Rameses and I arrived in Hurotas' camp, we watched the battlements of the fortress on the far bank of the Nile and I saw many who could have been Utteric, sometimes as many as two or three of them together. Some of them reminded me of the Utteric who had burst into tears when threatened, or who was able to whip himself into screaming, frothing tantrums.

However, we were in no hurry to commence hostilities. This was a period of consolidation and preparation. Hurotas had only finished setting up his camp five days before we came downriver from Luxor to join him. As yet not all the petty kings had arrived from the north. Every day new flotillas sailed south up the Nile to join us. It would be rash of us to commence our onslaught before our forces were fully assembled. This was a complex movement of troops, made no easier by the sudden decision of Bekatha to assume command.

Fortunately this happened at a private family dinner given by King Hurotas to celebrate the escape of his only daughter, Serrena, from her captors at the Gates of Torment and Sorrow. It was also intended as a focus of all the warlike instincts of the family on the humiliation and suffering inflicted upon them gratuitously by the abduction and torture of Serrena.

The evening began well with belligerent speeches from Hurotas and Hui. Then Bekatha's three remaining sons joined in the speechifying. By this time Tehuti and Bekatha had partaken of more than their fair share of the excellent Laconian wine. Bekatha listened to the bloodthirsty boasts of her sons, and suddenly and unexpectedly she burst into a flood of tears. The mood of the revelers changed in an instant.

All the women present sprang to their feet and clustered around Bekatha uttering endearments and commiserations, while the men looked at one another in bewilderment. Then all of us turned in unison to Hui. We said nothing but the message was clear: *This is nothing to do with us. She is your wife. You fix it!*

Reluctantly Hui came to his feet, but he was fortunate. Before he could reach his wife's side she uttered a cry of abysmal distress, "Why do I have to send all my babies to be slaughtered?"

In that instant the devoted and united family was divided into sects and segments.

Tehuti came in instantly on the side of her little sister. "Bekatha is absolutely right. We have Serrena back. We don't have to fight a pointless little war now."

"Pointless?" shouted Hurotas. "Did I hear you say *pointless,* my darling wife? Did I also hear you use the word *little?* Do you have any idea what it has cost me to raise an army and bring it here to Egypt? Somebody has to pay for it, and that somebody is not going to be me."

"Be fair to us, Mama," cried Sostratus, Bekatha's second-oldest boy. "We are only just starting out on our careers. Don't send us home in disgrace. All the world will say we were too cowardly to stay and do battle with Utteric the impostor."

I was watching Serrena. I knew that the outcome depended on her alone. Hurotas would do exactly what she wanted and so would Tehuti. They might put up a show of resistance, but Serrena was the one who would make the final decision. I saw her glance at her father, and a shadow of doubt clouded her gaze. Then she looked at her mother and her aunt Bekatha, and I saw her make her decision. I knew that I had to be quick to forestall it, otherwise we would all be on our way north to Lacedaemon again, possibly even as soon as the morrow.

"I think it cruel to force Serrena to spend the rest of her life in this country that she so obviously detests. I think Bekatha and Tehuti are absolutely right. We should all go back home to Lacedaemon and leave this blighted country to Utteric. I am sure that our allies, the petty kings, will understand our position and will not expect compensation for bringing their armies to our assistance and then sailing home empty-handed. Serrena will be perfectly happy in the land of her birth, living in some pretty little cottage with Rameses and a dozen lovely brats on the banks of the Hurotas River. I am sure she will understand that the family fortune was spent in good faith. Not for her the silly and pretentious name, Queen Cleopatra . . ." By this time my oratory had taken wings. My audience were agog, especially Serrena.

Then I saw Serrena reverse the final decision she had made only minutes before, as smoothly as she had made it.

"All is true that you say, darling Tata. But there are always two sides to every question. I have always been taught that a wife must accept without complaint the decrees of the gods and support her husband in the task they set out before him. In time I know I shall also learn to accept the name Cleopatra, trite as it may be. If Rameses and I stay here in Egypt as Pharaoh and Pharaohin, we will have sufficient funds for my darling mother to visit me whenever she chooses. We will both learn to cherish the beauty and abundance of this very Egypt. What is more, my father will not be reduced to penury for my sake."

A stunned silence followed this declaration, and then Bekatha's boys hugged one another. Bekatha burst out weeping anew, but I refilled her wine mug and she had to stop her lamentations to sample the brew.

Hurotas looked solemn and said, "You have made a bitterly hard decision, my darling daughter; however, 'tis the right one." He glanced at me, still solemnly, but he lowered his right eyelid in a congratulatory wink. We had triumphed once again, but it had been a close-run thing.

The following night Rameses and I set out to reconnoiter the west bank, the side on which Utteric had sited his fortress of Abu Naskos. Utteric had built no gates facing the river. I had of course received descriptions of them but had never laid eyes upon them. I knew it was essential for me to do so. We took only fifteen of our own men with us. The moon rose after midnight, so we used the dark period to cross the Nile and hide our boats in the reeds. Then as soon as it was light enough to make out the ground, we moved out quietly toward the fortress. We had not gone more than a few hundred cubits before we came upon a herd of Utteric's horses grazing by the light of the moon. We rounded them up and sent two of our men to drive them back to where we had left our boats. We repeated this maneuver three times, gradually accumulating a herd of over 150 beautiful chariot horses.

The moonlight shone magnificently on the western walls of the fortress, affording me a fine view of the two gates from a safe distance. I was able to estimate the substantial size and rugged construction of both gates and note the defensive walls and ditches lined with sharpened stakes that supported them.

After a discreet period had elapsed, we withdrew. When we reached the spot where we had left our boats, we found that in accord with my orders two of the boats had been used to drive the horses across the river. We followed them in the remaining skiff. It was a long swim for the poor creatures; the Nile is over one and a half leagues wide at this point. But when we finally reached the eastern bank below Hurotas' camp, Rameses and I were delighted to discover that all the animals had crossed safely ahead of us with no casualties.

Thus emboldened with success, four nights later, against my better judgment, I allowed Rameses to convince me to attempt a repetition of our raid. It pains me to have to relate that we were not as successful the second time. Utteric's men, who had driven away the remaining horses, were lying in ambush for us. We fought desperately to get back to where we had hidden our boats. When we finally reached them, we found that the men we had left to guard them had been massacred, and the bottoms had been knocked out of our boats. Half our men were not able to swim. Frantically we broke the damaged boats down to their individual planks. At the same time we fended off the determined enemy pursuit. Then we retreated into the river. We gave each nonswimmer a plank for flotation and then we pushed and dragged them out into the flow. With the enemy shouting insults at us from the bank and launching volleys of arrows after us, we allowed the current to bear us away. We suffered further losses of five of our men who were either drowned or taken by the crocodiles. This meant that only six of us survived and were washed up on the eastern bank of the Nile. I have noted in my celebrated tome *The History of Warfare* that down through the ages every military commander of merit and illustrious achievement has survived at least one defeat during his career. It matters only that he should survive it, not how he describes it.

Fortunately, the last of the petty kings arrived on the eastern bank at exactly the same time as us. This was Ber Strong-arm Argolid, king of Boeotia in Thebes. He had seven ships in his flotilla. Between them they carried 630 fighting men, and ten of his numerous wives, including Queen Hagne, who was formerly the reverend mother of the Order of the Sisters of the Golden Bow before she was swept off her feet by Strong-arm.

They came sailing up the Nile from the delta in line astern. They were astonished to find Pharaoh Rameses and his chief minister, Lord Taita, half naked and coated with mud, floundering chin deep in the Nile and clinging to a few broken planks of wreckage. Their surprise swiftly gave way to hilarity as we were hoisted aboard Ber Argolid's flagship.

When she saw my sorry state of attire, Queen Hagne took me aside and removed her regal gown. Then she offered it to me with the assurance, "You need it more than I do, Minister Taita."

I accepted graciously, more because I wished to appraise her naked bosom than for any other reason. I discovered that Strong-arm Argolid had excellent taste in mammaries; and in retrospect the gown was comfortable and the color suited that of my eyes, although the sleeves and the hem were a little short. Then Strong-arm and all his officers and wives gathered around us with expressions of the utmost anticipation to hear our tale of woe and disaster. Fortunately I had anticipated this inquisition and I had cautioned my men, including Rameses, to discretion.

"It was nothing to speak of really," I protested with

an air of modesty when the question was put to me by Strong-arm.

"I am sure it was another triumph for you, my lord." Queen Hagne batted her eyes at me, leaving me no alternative but to exaggerate a little.

"Pharaoh Rameses and I decided to cross the river to cut out as many of Utteric's horses as we could to reduce the number of chariots that he will be capable of fielding, and of course to increase our own numbers." I saw Rameses blink and open his mouth to correct me. Then he closed it and nodded cautious agreement.

"Did you manage to get any of his horses?" Strong-arm demanded. "It doesn't seem like it to me." At this point he guffawed vulgarly.

"We got a few," I demurred with dignity.

"How many is a few?" he wanted to know. "Five? Ten?"

"A little more than that," I admitted. "Just over one hundred and fifty. But the good gods only know how many of them will reach our camp. Of course they bolted as soon as they came ashore on this bank ahead of us. We will certainly have some losses, but we should be able to retrieve most of them." I looked at Rameses inquiringly. "Do you have anything to add, Pharaoh Rameses?" He shook his head, overwhelmed by my version of the facts. But Queen Hagne interjected at the appropriate moment.

"So that's how you and your men got yourselves so wet. You had to swim back from the far side of the river with the horses?" She was a charming and sagacious lady. The more I saw of her, the more I liked her. She knew a brave and astute man when she saw one.

"You understand our predicament, Your Majesty," I agreed with her. "Of course we had to demolish our own boats. Even though they were of little value, we could not allow them to fall into the hands of the enemy."

The king of Boeotia in Thebes nodded thoughtfully, and the hovering sneer left his lips. Then he called for wine to be served to us by his stewards there on the open deck.

"This is really an excellent vintage," he told me as he abandoned the subject of Rameses' and my own ingenuity and heroism. Other people's triumphs soon pall. One's own little mishaps and miscalculations are best kept to oneself.

With the arrival of Ber Strong-arm Argolid in Hurotas' camp, all sixteen of the royal oath takers were assembled in one place, and the long-delayed second marriage of Rameses and Serrena could at last proceed. I had been the sole guest, participant, and functionary of the previous ceremony so I was determined to play as discreet a role as possible the second time around. Serrena had her entire tribe to bolster her, while Rameses had Bekatha, who had adopted him, and her sons, who looked upon him as their brother. They didn't really need me.

I was able to apply myself to a matter that had given me pause ever since we had sailed from Luxor on the *Four Winds* with Ganord as the pilot. This was his description of the tribe of superior beings who in antiquity had built and inhabited the ancient city that had once occupied the spot on the opposite bank where Abu Naskos now stood.

I searched my pockets and found the clay tablet of the fish with a golden head that Ganord had given me. I examined it once again minutely. However, it remained beautiful but totally enigmatic. I went down to the riverbank and searched for the *Four Winds* among the small boats and ships anchored here. However, the boatmen told me that the cutter had returned to Luxor while I was chasing wild horses on the western bank of the river. Nobody knew what had happened to Ganord. I showed them the golden-headed fish tile. They agreed that it was interesting, but none of them had ever seen anything like it before.

I fashioned a purse out of a tanned otter skin that fitted the tile precisely, and I suspended it on a cord around my neck so that it hung down under my tunic. It gave me pleasure to rub the tile between my fingers while I was ruminating.

Over the next few days, I took to strolling along the riverbank alone. But I was never lonely. I am a child of the Nile, but my birth date is obscure. However, I know the Nile was mine from the day of my birth, whenever that might have been. I loved it, and I sensed that it loved me in return.

I found a pleasant spot in the shade of a tree from which I had a view across the wide flow of the river to the fortress of Abu Naskos on the west bank. This was the point where several small islands formed a chain across the Nile. All of them were densely overgrown with ancient trees and lianas. Here the river was about one and a half leagues wide, so the islands were only one-quarter of a league apart. I thought that I could probably swim that distance in less than half a turn of an hourglass. I smiled to myself and shook my head; why would I want to do that?

I dismissed the thought and stood up. As usual I held the golden-headed fish tile in my right hand. But this time it stung my thumb. I exclaimed with surprise. It felt almost like a wasp sting, but not as intense. I changed the tile to my other hand and examined my thumb. There was no sign of the sting mark, no inflammation and the discomfort faded swiftly. I thought little more of it and walked back to the camp.

That evening Tehuti insisted that I join her and Hurotas for dinner. Rameses and Serrena were also with them; and I had not seen any of them for a few days.

We passed a very pleasant evening together, discussing the impending nuptials.

I was awake early the following morning before sunrise. I dressed and set off along the towpath beside the Nile. When I reached the spot opposite the chain of islands, I took my seat on the same smooth rock as the previous evening. I felt very relaxed and, without thinking about it, I pulled the fish tile out from under my tunic and began to rub it idly. There were a flock of black-headed weaver birds building their hanging nests in the branches above me. I don't know how long I watched them, but I started to feel hungry and I realized I had not yet eaten any food that morning.

I stood up and the tile stung me so sharply that I dropped it and sucked my finger. It dangled on its cord against my chest. That was when I realized for the first time that the tile was imbued with esoteric powers. I touched it again with one finger. There was no reaction at all. I rubbed it between my thumb and forefinger, anticipating another unpleasant sting. There was still no reaction. But I had lost my appetite. I was engrossed with considerations other than food.

I changed my seat so the sunlight fell directly upon the tile. I studied it as though it was the first time I had ever seen it. I counted the scales on the body of the fish. I examined the fins and flowing tail minutely. I could detect no further arcane sense or meaning. Then I examined the reverse side of the tile. There were no scratch marks or the slightest indication of hieroglyphs or cuneiform lettering. As I rotated it again I noticed something that had escaped my attention up until that moment when I turned it at an angle to the sunlight. There were a number of minute dimples in the background, behind the silhouette of the fish. They could have been made with the point of a sharp needle before the clay was fired in the oven. As I changed the angle of the light they disappeared. Then they reappeared as I moved it back in the opposite direction.

I counted these irregularities. There were four of them: two behind the fish's tail and two ahead of the nose. I pondered the significance of them, but I could still find none. This spoiled my mood. I knew that I must be missing something. It made me hungry again. I ran back to the camp and went around to the kitchen area. The cooks had some cold sausages left over from the midday meal. They were greasy and oversalted, but I ate them in defiance of the gods who I sensed were making me their buffoon, and not for the first time.

Disconsolately I wandered back to my rock beside the river, where I sat belching up the unpleasant memories of my sausage. Once again I pulled the fish tile out from under my tunic. I held it up to the sun, turning it so the four dots appeared and disappeared. I lowered the tile and looked out across the Nile River.

I stared at the string of small, almost identical islands stretched out across the green waters to the far bank. But they were unrelated to my mystery . . . or were they?

I felt a small chill of excitement, strong enough to raise the hair on my forearms as I realized that there were four almost identical islands in the river, the same number as there were dots on the ceramic tile. It was a tenuous and feeble link, but four is the magical number of Inana, and Inana is my guardian goddess. I knew that I had to pay a visit to at least one of the four islands.

I could take a boat and be on the first island in under an hour. But I knew that hostile eyes were watching from the walls of the fortress on the far side of the river. I could swim faster than I could row a boat, and seen from across the river my head would not seem much larger than that of an otter's. I began to shed my clothing before my thoughts were fully defined.

I moved up the bank of the river, keeping well back from the water's edge so I would not be noticed from the walls of Abu Naskos. When I had the nearest island directly in line with the fortress, I moved to the riverbank and slipped into the water until it reached to my chin. I paused to check my equipment. I had my knife belt strapped over my loincloth. I drew the knife from its sheath and tried the point and the edge against my thumb. It was wickedly sharp. I slipped it back into its sheath. Then I adjusted the cord of the purse that contained the ceramic tile so that it hung down my back, rather than dangled down my chest where it could wrap around my arms with every stroke I took.

I pushed off from the bank and set off for the nearest island, making sure that I never broke the surface with the stroke of my arms or a kick of my legs. I had to angle sharply upstream against the current to keep my head aligned with the island and the fortress beyond it.

When I reached the island, I grabbed hold of a liana that hung out over my head and stretched down with my feet to find the bottom. This was my first surprise. There was no bottom. The bank of the island fell vertically into the depths of the river. I hung on to the liana while I drew several deep breaths. Then I released my hold and swam down like a diving wild duck. I peered down through the limpid water, expecting at any moment to see the loom of the bottom. At last I was forced to abandon the attempt as my lungs started to ache and heave.

When I burst out through the surface, I grabbed the hanging liana again and sucked my lungs full of sweet air. When I recovered I swam across to the sheer wall of rock that made up the bank of the island. With the help of the roots and branches I scrambled up the rock wall and reached the flat top of the island. I sat there while I got my bearings and reoriented myself. Then I pushed my way through the dense undergrowth and followed the lip around until I returned to my starting point.

I realized that the island was shaped like the stump of a tree, rather than having the usual flattened pancake silhouette. Both beneath the surface and above it was straight up and down. The top was circular and flattened. It was unlike any other island I had ever known. I was intrigued by it, but the dense vegetation made it difficult to be certain of the exact shapes and dimensions. I started to cross it from side to side, clambering over fallen trees and trying to dig down with my bare hands to reach bedrock. However, the roots of the trees and plants were interwoven. I hacked at them with my knife but to little avail. They were hardened with age.

I sensed that something extraordinary had to be hidden here. The goddess Inana and I have a strange relationship, but I have learned that I can usually rely on her. She has never cheated me; or at least not to my knowledge. After another hour or so, I had to rest again. I sank down with my back to the base of a wild fig tree.

"So what did you expect to find here?" I asked myself. I often speak aloud to myself when I am alone. I pondered the question. Then I replied carefully, "I expected nothing. But I hoped for a sign or a message from the Old People." By the Old People I meant those who had lived here in antiquity.

"Like another prick on the finger?" The question was spoken in my voice, but not by me. I looked about me in wild surmise, and I saw her. She was standing among the trees at the edge of my vision. She was just another shadow among shadows. However, I knew it was she.

"Inana!" I said her name, and she laughed—as clearly as a bell and as sweetly as a nightingale. Then she spoke again, but this time in her own ineffably lovely voice.

"If you cannot see where you look, then look where you can never see." She laughed again and then she faded away. I sprang to my feet and reached out with both hands toward her, but she was gone.

I knew it was futile to run and call after her. I had done that so many times before. I sank down again on the spot where I had been sitting. I felt bereft.

Then I felt something prick me sharply. I reached behind me, between my naked buttocks. There was something hard and sharp as a shark's tooth sticking into my secret flesh. I took it between my fingers and drew it out, grimacing at the sharp pain.

Holding it gingerly, I brought it around in front of my eyes and stared at it. I felt my heart jump and my blood thrill in my veins. I reached over my shoulder and found the leather purse in which I had stowed the perfect ceramic fish tile given to me by Ganord.

I laid the undamaged tile on the palm of my hand, and then I placed the sharp fragment which I had retrieved from between my buttocks beside it. The fragment was an identical match to the corner of the whole tile.

However, where it had been broken off the point was as sharp as a needle, and wet with a smear of blood from my posterior. At the other end it widened into the head of the golden fish that I knew so well.

I placed the fragment on top of the original whole tile, and the two merged perfectly. They had been struck in the same mold, perhaps a thousand years previously.

I saw this as an indication that the Old People had been here before me and were here again. I knew that they were trying to tell me something of importance. I took the whole tile in one hand and the fragment in the other, and I focused all my attention on them. Nothing changed for a while, and then gradually the four dots in the background of the whole tile became more intense and seemed to glow like tiny stars.

"Four!" I whispered the number aloud. I knew that I was close to a solution. "Four, not one or two . . ." I broke off as I saw the meaning. "They are reminding me that there are four islands, not just one. If the solution is not on the first island I must search for it on the other three!"

I thrust the whole tile and the fragment back into the leather purse and then jumped to my feet and made my way to the western side of the tiny island. From there I peered across the river at the other three islands and the towers of the fortress of Abu Naskos. Almost immediately I ducked lower into the dense undergrowth. Two enemy guard boats were circling the island closest to mine. They had two sets of oars a side, and a pair of men on each oar. The masts of their boats were bare of sails, but they had a pair of archers in the crosstrees. These had arrows nocked and ready to loose, and they were scanning the undergrowth of the second island. Even as I watched, the nearest guard boat altered course and headed directly toward me. I crawled away, and as soon as I was screened by the vegetation,

I jumped to my feet and ran to the opposite side of the island and dived off the sheer cliff. Immediately I surfaced I struck out for Hurotas' camp. It seemed that the enemy had known I was there and were searching for me, but I could not be certain. It may have been a mere coincidence.

It was an easy swim, and I used the time to review what I had seen and learned while I was on the first island. My mind kept returning to two things that were significant. The first was the unusual shape of the island. The second was the fragment of green ceramic that had stabbed into my buttocks and that was such an exact match to part of the tile that Ganord had given me before he disappeared into the south again.

I kept turning these two anomalies over in my mind as I swam. I was about halfway back to the east bank and Hurotas' camp when the first possibility, or should I rather say when the first improbability occurred to me. It was so bizarre that I shouted the words aloud. "Could the island have been built by ancient man to a design, rather than being shaped arbitrarily by random nature?"

I swallowed a mouthful of Nile water in my excitement and had to tread water to cough it up. By that time I was ready with my second improbability: "And if that is so, then did ancient man also build the other three islands to the same plan? And if so, why did he do such a preposterous thing?"

I swam on, still pondering my third improbability. Once again Ganord gave me the answer. "Could it be because he wanted to be able to cross the river swiftly and secretly, as if by witchcraft?" I stopped swimming and trod water as I realized the enormity of my supposition. I was considering the possibility of ancient man going beneath the waters of the Nile, rather than over the top of them by boat or bridge. I am prone to odd notions such as these. I have even contemplated the possibilities of man being able to fly. I admit that I rejected that fantasy after reluctantly conceding that it would not be feasible for him to grow wings. However, I knew that I was able to dive to the bottom of the river. I had demonstrated that ability within the last hour. But even my mind balked at crossing from one bank of the Nile to the other on a single breath of air. The distance was almost one and a half leagues. Of course, it is not possible to measure accurately distance over water, or the speed of a ship, or for that matter the speed of a swimming man. I was still pondering the possibilities when I reached the eastern bank of the river just downstream from Hurotas' camp.

I was waist deep and wading ashore when I was enchanted by the melodious tones of Serrena calling my name: "Tata, do you not know that this part of the river is the haunt of crocodiles, and of men who are even more dangerous?" As ever, she knew when I needed her most. She came rushing down the bank of the Nile to rescue me. Of course, Rameses was not far behind her and equally solicitous.

Even though I had last seen them the previous day, I had missed both of them sorely. The two of them having saved my life once again, as soon as we reached dry land we could move on to more monumental events.

"We have set a day for our marriage—" Rameses began breathlessly.

"—it's for the day after tomorrow at noon!" Serrena ended for him.

"I hope it will be as good as the one I gave you."

"Nothing could be that good, ever again." She came up on tiptoe to kiss me.

All warlike endeavors were set aside until after the wedding, although if Utteric Bubastis wished to debate our decision, we were prepared to accommodate him. To this end I carried my sword on my hip as I danced with the pretty girls. I had learned the hard way never to trust Rameses' half brother. The crenelated walls of Abu Naskos on the far side of the Nile were lined with hundreds of curious heads as he and his rogues watched us and tried to work out what the marching bands and the dancing throng were playing at.

All our women wore garlands of wildflowers on their heads and the younger and prettier females were bared to the waist, which I found an agreeable condition. As the wine flagons were passed from hand to pretty little hand the dancing became more abandoned, the music louder, and the words of the chorus more risqué. Some of the more enlightened young ladies slipped away into the forest with their fancy or in some cases with their fancies and returned glowing with more than mere bonhomie.

Each of the sixteen kings made a speech wishing the bride and groom eternal happiness, and then they loaded them down with exotic and extravagant gifts. These included elephants and mahouts to ride them, ships and slaves to row them, poems and poets to sing them, trumpets and drums and musicians to play them, diamonds and sapphires and crowns to display them, fine wines and flagons of silver and gold to make them more pleasurable to drink.

However, I had chosen two hundred of our most warlike warriors and prevailed upon them to moderate the amount of wine that they imbibed during the day. Meanwhile, Hurotas, Hui, and I had picked out positions along the bank of the Nile that were the most inviting for Utteric's cutthroats to launch a sneak night attack from. When the sun set and night fell, the sounds of music and hilarity continued unabated, or rather increased substantially in volume.

Hurotas, Hui, and I quietly led our picked men out

of the camp to the ambush positions along the bank of the Nile that we had chosen during the hours of daylight. I did not inform Rameses of our intentions. I knew him as well as I knew myself by now. He would have insisted on joining us. However, I was reluctant to add her husband's corpse to the list of Serrena's wedding gifts on the morrow.

We did not have too long to wait. After an hour or so, the sounds of hilarity in the camp behind us began to abate; during the next hour, they ceased almost entirely. Utteric's captains chose their moment well; I knew that it was highly unlikely that Utteric himself would take any part in a night attack.

There was a sliver of yellow moon showing above the dark loom of the far bank, and its reflection danced on the surface of the river. It made an admirable backdrop for the mass of small boats that swarmed across the water from Abu Naskos toward where we waited.

"Right into the tiger's mouth." Hurotas chuckled softly beside me. "I couldn't have arranged it better myself."

"I don't agree," I whispered back. "They are at least three cubits too far upstream."

"About as far as a pretty girl's left leg," he pointed out. "I find that distance perfectly acceptable."

However, I let them come even a little closer, until

the men in the bows of the leading boats jumped overboard and landed waist deep, then started to pull the
boats the last few cubits to our bank.

"Yes?" I asked Hurotas.

"Yes!" he agreed, and I put my two fingers between
my lips and blew a piercing whistle. My archers were
holding their arrows nocked at full draw. At my whistle they loosed as one man and the night air was filled
with the fluting of the wind in hundreds of fletchings.
This was followed by the thumping of the arrowheads
as they slammed into human flesh and the screams of
wounded men as they went down struggling in water
that reached over their heads.

Chaos swept through Utteric's flotilla. Some of the
boats tried to turn away and collided with others who
were following close behind them. These capsized and
floundered. Men screamed briefly as the weight of their
armor pulled them under the waters. Others screamed
longer and stronger as our archers flailed them.

Then some of our men ran forward carrying burning torches and lobbed them onto the piles of dry brush
that we had piled at intervals along the riverbank. The
tinder flared at once, and the flames leaped up to light
the night and reveal in stark detail the boats and the
men aboard them. Our archers had been launching
their arrows at shadows; their salvos had been erratic.

But now their aim tightened and the slaughter was more effective. Fewer than half the enemy boats succeeded in turning back for the western bank, and even those were half filled with their wounded and the dead.

Then our men put aside their bows and waded into the shallows, unsheathing their knives to deal with the wounded who remained and make sure they were carried away by the current or taken to the bottom of the river by the weight of their armor.

We had to consider that the area was to be the scene of joyous nuptials on the morrow. We wanted to avoid the groans and whimpers of those combatants who had survived and the stench of those who had been more fortunate.

By noon on the day following all signs of the conflict had been obliterated. The ashes and the puddles of dried blood on the riverbank had been covered with white sand. The current had taken the floating corpses northward to the sea, or their armor had anchored them in the dark and deep pools where the crocodiles and other denizens of the Nile were according them their last rites.

We had thrown a cordon of bronze around our camp on the eastern bank of the Nile opposite the fortress of Abu Naskos. The horses were in the traces of the chariots; and every one of our ten thousand warriors was on full alert and armed from the studs in the soles of his sandals to the peak of his bronze helmet.

Princess Serrena had finally chosen her matrons of honor to accompany her to the altar dedicated to Isis the Egyptian goddess of love and marriage, and to the Lacedaemon goddess of love, Aphrodite. She had started out with sixteen ladies, a wife of each of the petty kings. But this had led to bitterness and acrimony, to tears and recrimination among the wives who had not been chosen. Serrena and Queen Tehuti had been forced to raise the number first to thirty-two and finally to forty-eight, but their only stipulation was that the wedding gifts were increased by the same amount. It was a solution that satisfied everyone—not least Serrena. The gifts were piled high in front of the altar to the goddesses. The massed bands of the regiments were assembled behind them, taking it in turn to belt out the battle hymns that were a challenge to our foes on the opposite bank of Mother Nile and a rallying call to our allies who stood foursquare beside us.

As the midday hour approached, the music became louder and more frenetic, the bared swords beat a tattoo on the glittering bronze shields, and ten thousand voices blended like the thunder of the heavens. Then as the hour struck, a sudden silence so complete that it was an assault to the human ear overwhelmed all the world.

The ranks of the ten thousand opened soundlessly

and the tall and commanding figure of Pharaoh Rameses, the new ruler of our very Egypt, stepped forward. He marched to take his place before the altar to the goddesses Isis and Aphrodite; then, as he turned to face the gateway to the women's camp where Serrena was secreted with her matrons of honor, he raised his right arm and the singing began.

At first it was sweet, warm and low as a summer breeze off the waves of the indolent ocean. Then it rose into a paean of joy and an ode to love. The gates to the women's camp swung open and through them danced two files of women dressed in garments of rainbow color. There were twenty-five women in each of the columns. Their feet were bare, and their hair was dressed with ribbons and flowers. They laughed and sang, clapping their hands or strumming on the lyre and cithara and other strung musical instruments. The right-hand column was led by Queen Tehuti and the left-hand column by her sister, Princess Bekatha.

Between the two ranks walked a man and two women. The man was King Hurotas decked in gold and jewels. He wore rubies in his crown and diamonds on his slippers. His gown was of purple silk and his breeches were of cream silk. His booming mirth was so infectious that his men could not restrain themselves but laughed with him.

The female figure on his right arm was tall and lithe. She reached as high as Hurotas' shoulder, but she was covered from the top of her head to the tips of her toes with cloth of gold that sparkled in the noonday sunlight. Yet she carried herself with such grace and energy that despite the fact that her face was veiled, no person who looked upon her could doubt who she was for a single instant.

Pharaoh Rameses of Egypt reached out to her with both hands and King Hurotas whirled his daughter into a pirouette and sent her twirling across the gap that separated them to end up in a deep curtsy at the feet of her bridegroom. Rameses took her hands in his and lifted her upright. Then he reached out for the cloth of gold that covered her head and with a flourish whirled it away, leaving Princess Serrena revealed in her true glory from the top of her shining head, her remarkable golden tresses dressed with gossamer and pearls, down over the rippling multihued silk that clung to every swell and hollow of her body and limbs.

Human or divine, there was not one of us present that day who did not acknowledge her as the most splendid creature we had ever laid eyes upon.

They began to dance and we danced with them. Only when the sun set and darkness fell did the bride and groom retire to the lodgings that had been prepared for them. However, the celebration continued unabated for the rest of that night.

I danced with both Tehuti and Bekatha, and then I slipped away and went back to my own tent without tasting a drop of Hurotas' excellent wine, which I confess tested my resolve to nigh on its limit. I slept until two hours before sunrise, then I roused myself in the darkest hour of the night and went down to the river, picking my way carefully around the drink-sodden carcasses that were scattered at random like the casualties of a savage battle.

With only the stars to guide me and dressed in my loincloth with my knife in its sheath and the purse containing my fish tile slung around my neck I waded out until the water reached my chin and then I began to swim. I passed the familiar first island without a pause and headed for the second. I was beginning to fear that I had missed it in the darkness when suddenly it loomed ahead of me lit by the first inkling of the dawn. I angled in to come at it from the downriver side, using the island's own bulk to break the flow of the current.

Then I dived down to the foundation of the island on the bottom of the river. By this time the light was strengthening sufficiently for me to compare the formation of this second island to the first. I was astonished to find that it was close to identical in almost every respect. It was the same size, or so close it made little difference. It was steep too, as was the first, rising sheer from the bottom of the river. Now I could be certain that both of them had been built by humans, probably by the same man or men.

It must have involved a great deal of work, and for little or no repayment or advantage. Neither of the two islands I had so far visited was high enough above water to be useful as a signal tower; in fact, they seemed to have been deliberately built low as if to escape detection. The fact that they were constructed in deep, fast water emphasized the difficulty of the work undertaken by the ancient peoples. I considered the possibility that these were the remains of a dam or lock, but they were set too far apart; and there were no indications on the bank of the river that an attempt had been made to channel water away for any purpose, such as irrigation or domestic usage.

By now it was light enough for me to see the hand- and footholds and to climb the wall to the top of the structure. As I climbed I realized that this was an identical round tower with a flat top, but not as badly weathered as the first tower. When I reached the top, I saw traces of chiseled stonework of advanced design that had weathered over the ages. I started digging and dislodging the masonry, but each stone was perfectly cut and assembled with hairline joints to its neighbor. It was a laborious task. After several hours, I had gone down only waist deep and was preparing to abandon the task, or at least to hand it over to a gang of common laborers. My fingernails were cracked and chipped. I am proud of my hands and have often been commended by the ladies for the condition in which I maintain them. I lifted what I promised myself was absolutely the final slab from the excavation, and then I was startled by the one that lay beneath it. I could see only the top edge of it, but it was unique and distinctive. I snatched the purse that hung over my shoulder, and with fingers that shook slightly, I drew out the fired clay tile that Ganord had bequeathed to me. I measured it against the buried tile, and it was an exact match for size.

At that I abandoned all thoughts of handing over this excavation to others, especially common workmen.

I drew my knife from its sheath and started gently easing the strange tile from the bed that it had occupied for countless millennia. At last it came away in my hands. I scrambled from my shallow trench and squatted with the new tile on my lap. I admit that before I settled down I glanced at the ground beneath my naked buttocks to ascertain that Inana had placed no sharp ceramic splinters beneath me. Then I could apply my full attention to my new acquisition or, rather, my new ancient acquisition.

It was identical in size and shape to my fish tile, but in all other respects it was completely different. The fish tile was green; this one was vivid blue. This tile depicted a stylized seabird—a shearwater perhaps—although it could equally have been an ostrich. The artist had not made it clear which his intention had been. In addition, this tile was demarcated by three dots rather than the four on my fish tile.

I was already starting to refer to the two islands as Fish Island and Bird Island. I glanced across the river toward the fortress of Abu Naskos and wondered if the other two islands that I had not yet explored had also been named by the ancients, perhaps Crocodile and Hippopotamus Islands. The thought made me smile.

I returned to my excavations and found a complete course of identical bird tiles running around the ancient shaft. Naturally I was intrigued by this and continued digging down in hope of further discoveries. However, within a very short distance I came up short against a fault line. There had clearly been a shift in the earth's crust that had damaged the substrata. Nothing made sense any longer.

All I had learned was that the ancient peoples had sunk two shafts, one on Fish and the other on Bird Island. I had no way of knowing how deep and to what purpose they had undertaken this tremendous amount of work. The shaft beneath my feet had been churned into rubble.

"What if Fish and Bird Islands are joined in some magical manner?" I did not say that, I did not even think it. I knew it was Inana imitating my voice. She seems to take endless pleasure in teasing me.

I tried to resist her suggestion. To what purpose would the two islands be joined? I had proven to myself that man can only exist for a very limited period beneath the surface of the water. I had dived to the bottom of the Nile River and other shallow bodies of water, but only for a very short space of time.

I looked across at Fish Island and measured the distance with my eye. My spirits quailed when I considered traveling even one-tenth so far on a single breath of air. I jumped to my feet and paced up and down in agitation. I stamped on the ground, but it was solid with no suggestion of an excavation beneath it.

"What if there was a tunnel like a rabbit's warren joining the two islands?" I mused, and immediately shook my head. "Water finds its own level." That was a truth that I had worked out for myself when I was still very young. "A rabbit's warren fills with water just like any other hole in the ground."

But I knew I had missed something. I pondered it anew. "Why don't my lungs fill with water when I dive to the bottom of the Nile?

"Because I seal them off by holding my breath.

"So if the walls of the tunnel are waterproof and the entrances of the tunnel are above water level then the tunnel is also waterproof. There is no way for water to enter.

"Ah, there is the catch! The walls of the tunnel are not waterproof. They are made from earth, and earth is porous."

"But if the ancient men had discovered another impervious substance to line the walls of their tunnel, then they would have been able to walk beneath the waves." This last was said in Inana's sweet and enchanted tones, and I looked up and saw her leaning elegantly against a tree overlooking my excavations. As usual, her reasoning was convoluted, but she had led me by a roundabout route to something like the truth.

Then she smiled and went on, "Ganord suggested to you that it was by witchcraft, but as ever he was wrong. The ancient peoples used simple common sense. As I know you do also." She straightened up from the tree against which she was leaning and walked to the edge of the cliff. Then she stepped off it and dropped lightly as a falling leaf to the surface of the river far below. She walked away across the wavelets, and the silver river mist rose in a cloud to envelop her.

"Now that we are at last all assembled, my first and only duty is to thank all sixteen of you for standing by your oath of *An offense to one is an offense to all.* We are here to overthrow a monstrous tyrant who has seized the throne of the Pharaohs . . ." Hurotas addressed all the foreign kings on the strip of greensward that lined the eastern bank of the Nile River, opposite the towering fortress of Abu Naskos.

Each one of them was clad in full battle array. Behind them were massed their troops, all ten thousand of them. They stood shoulder to shoulder in seemingly endless ranks: shield touching shield on either side, grim-faced beneath their brazen helmets, their shields aglitter and their bows as yet unstrung, but the quivers slung on each shoulder bulging with arrows.

Drawn up against the bank of the Nile facing them was their fleet, with oars shipped but all their pennants and ensigns streaming, a bold and unequivocal declaration of their warlike intent.

Hurotas ended his speech and turned to face the massed drummers. He raised his sword to demand their attention. In unison they lifted their drumsticks to their lips. Hurotas paused for a beat and then cut left and right with his blade. The drums rolled like summer thunder, and the files of armored men peeled off and marched down to where the warships waited to take them on board and ferry them across Mother Nile to death or glory.

This was an intricate and potentially hazardous maneuver. It was our intention to sail a fleet of galleys laden with chariots, horses, and men across the Nile and to land them on the opposite bank. Utteric's squadrons were holding this territory in force. The fortress of Abu Naskos was probably the most powerful citadel in Egypt or in the entire continent of Africa for that matter. We knew that Utteric had had a long time to make his warlike dispositions while Hurotas and his allies had gathered their own forces and sailed halfway across the world to confront them. We had good reason to believe that Utteric had recruited powerful allies of his own past his eastern borders, and the countries scattered farther beyond.

These probably included the Persians and the Medes and any of fifty other tribes and clans. All these were reputed to be marvelous horsemen and warriors. However, it is my experience that reputation very often falls far short of actuality and, furthermore, that Persia and Media are much farther from Abu Naskos than is Lacedaemon.

Nevertheless, I prevailed upon Hurotas and Hui to make a number of probing attacks on the western bank of the Nile before committing ourselves to an all-out assault. We were confident that our chariots were superior to those of Utteric, and we could use them to secure a beachhead upriver from the fortress of Abu Naskos from which we could envelop the citadel itself and place it under siege.

For five consecutive days we had sailed our squadrons up and down the river in a warlike display of aggression. Some of our vessels were packed with armed men, but most of them had dummies and scarecrows lining the deck rails. We watched the dust clouds thrown up by Utteric's chariots and cavalry as they followed our threatened assaults. We carefully assessed the numbers of Utteric's troops and chariots. They were far larger than we had anticipated.

Then at dawn on the sixth day we sent a large squadron downriver as a decoy, while Hurotas and I took a smaller convoy loaded with our best chariots and crews five leagues in the opposite direction. Over the previous days of juggling for position we had singled out the best landing ground within ten miles of the fortress of Abu Naskos on the western bank of the Nile. We had chosen a strip of open meadow with a gentle slope into the river. This was where a small tributary stream ran down from the forest and joined the main Nile. This stream had a firm and stony bottom in which the wheels of the chariots would not bog down as we ran them ashore and recovered them at the termination of our foray ashore.

As the rising sun crested the horizon behind us we ran two of our ships into the western bank and beached them there. Each of our vessels was carrying four chariots with the horses in the traces and our charioteers at the reins. We dropped the loading ramps in the bows, and the horse teams surged down them and splashed through the shallows and up the banks of the river. Hurotas was driving the lead chariot, and I was commanding the last vehicle in the line of eight. All our men were armed with heavy recurved bows that were strung ready for immediate action, in addition to our battle-axes and broadswords. This expedition was intended to be a reconnaissance patrol. The object was to make contact with Utteric's forces and further assess their strength and numbers. Meanwhile, our squadron of ships would anchor in the river and await our return, ready to pick us up again if we came under serious attack while we were ashore.

As yet there was no sign of Utteric's troops. Our chariots fell into close-order formation, and, with Hurotas leading, we started forward to follow the track that led across the open grassland into the forest.

We had almost reached the dense treeline when we were assailed by a tremendous burst of sound that echoed down the glade. It was totally alien; I had never heard anything like it before. However, I presumed that it was the blast of many war trumpets. Hurotas immediately raised his clenched fist in the signal for our column to halt. Meanwhile, our horses danced and tossed their heads against the curb of the bits, arched their necks and whinnied with agitation. We charioteers gazed around us in astonishment, not certain what to make of the commotion.

The uproar died away, but it was replaced by the thunder of hooves and wheels so loud that it sounded like the charge of a hundred chariots sweeping down through the forest in full battle array. Instinctively we wheeled into line to receive this charge.

To our astonishment it was a single vehicle that burst out from among the trees, but it was like nothing that any of us had encountered previously. It was hurtling straight at us, and there was no doubting its hostile intentions. It was twice as wide as one of our chariots, and half again as high. Whereas our vehicles were equipped with a single pair of running wheels, this one had four a side, a total of eight in all.

Our wheel rims were hewn from hardwood and were equipped with six heavy spokes. Each of the enemy's wheels was a single disc of polished silver metal of a type I had never seen before. From the central hub protruded a curved blade as long as a man's arm. In addition, there were four more blades sited at regular intervals around the perimeter of each wheel. All of them were spinning viciously. Although I had never seen the like before, it was obvious that they could chop into small fragments anything with which they came in contact, including the spokes of our own chariot wheels.

Each of our chariots was drawn by three horses. The enemy vehicle was drawn by eight glossy black animals that stood several hands taller at the shoulder than did any of ours. They each had a long black unicorn horn protruding from the center of their foreheads.

They matched each other stride for stride, jets of steam spurting from their nostrils.

Our vehicles carried a crew of three men each, a driver and a pair of archers. The enemy driver stood alone at the reins, leaning back to hold his team in check. He was driving straight at us.

He was a towering brute of a man. His body armor was simple and lacked ornamentation: polished silver from the throat downward, obviously designed to deflect the arrows of his enemies. He was unarmed. His unstrung bow stood in the weapons bin beside him, as did his broadsword. He held nothing in his gauntleted hands except the reins of his chariot. However, his helmet was extraordinary. It covered only the right side of his face and the top of his head. His single eye was concealed behind the narrow slit in the gleaming metal.

However, the left-hand side of his face was totally exposed and it presented a horrible sight. It was formed of gnarled and gleaming scar tissue. His mouth was puckered and twisted. The eyelid drooped sardonically, but behind it the eye itself glittered with baleful intensity.

As we raced toward each other I snatched an arrow from the quiver under my right hand and nocked it to the bowstring. In the same movement, I lifted the fletching of the arrow to my pursed lips and held my aim for the hundredth part of a second before I loosed. I saw it blur across the narrow gap that separated us, flying precisely for the bridge of the left eye in the ruined face.

He was dead. I knew it for a certainty. I expected the arrow to bury itself up to its fletching in his skull. But at the last possible moment he dropped his chin onto his chest. The point of the arrow struck the crest of his helmet at the level of his forehead and it glanced away, whining as it flew into the dense bushes behind him.

The alien charioteer did not even blink at the strike. Instead he focused his full attention on Hurotas at the head of our line of chariots, obviously attracted by the magnificence of his helmet and breastplate. He steered his team of black unicorns directly at Hurotas, who tried desperately to avoid a head-on collision and yanked the heads of his team hard over. The result was that the stranger's vehicle struck them at an oblique angle. The spinning knives on his wheels ran down one side of Hurotas' rig, chopping the legs off his horses in a pink cloud of blood and bone fragments. The maimed animals went down screaming, and the knives went on through the wheel spokes, hacking them into kindling. The vehicle dropped on its side and somersaulted, hurling Hurotas and his crew overboard. They lost their weapons as they struck the ground and rolled in the dirt.

The black unicorns charged on down the left-hand line of our chariots, striking them one after the other in rapid succession and tearing off the wheels on their near sides, sending them crashing to earth one after the other. By good fortune, I was in the right-hand column of four vehicles, so the stranger and I passed each other without me giving him an opportunity to rip off one of my wheels. However, I nocked another arrow and I hauled back and loosed it, aiming into the open visor of his helmet. He was only ten cubits from me, the width of two chariots between us. My arrow was fast enough to cheat the eye. But he lifted one gauntleted hand from the reins and swatted it aside as effortlessly as if it were a buzzing blue fly. For a hundredth part of a second he stared at me from under his drooping eyelid; it was one of the most menacing looks I have ever received. Then we had passed each other.

I dropped my bow and snatched the reins from my driver when I saw Hurotas lying ahead of me where he had been flung by his capsizing chariot. He was trying to get back on his feet, but obviously he was dazed by his fall. He had lost his helmet and his weapons and all sense of direction. One side of his face was swollen and coated with dust and dirt.

"Zaras!" I called his former name, and it had the desired effect. He squinted at me as I swerved my chariot to line up on him.

"Make me an arm!" I shouted urgently. It was something we had practiced endlessly when we were much younger. He pushed himself upright and looped his right arm against his hip, facing me. But he was swaying unsteadily on his feet.

I steered my team of three horses with the reins bunched in my left hand and, leaning far over the right-hand side of the vehicle, I drove at him, swinging my team aside at the last moment, so the right animal brushed past him. As I came level with him still at full gallop, I hooked my right arm through his. The shock of contact almost jerked me out of the carriage. However, I managed to resist it and to swing Hurotas off his feet and then haul him aboard.

Now I was using one arm to steady Hurotas, who was still groggy, and with the other hand I was steering the chariot. With a quick glance I saw that the boats that had put us ashore had now become aware of our predicament, and they had turned back toward the landing to take us on board again. However, the current was now against them and they were making slow progress of their return to our rescue. Hurotas was a big man and he was weighing down our vehicle, and the closer we approached the riverbank, the softer and muddier became the ground beneath our wheels.

I glanced back over my shoulder to check the whereabouts of our enemy and his team of horned black monsters. I did not have to look far. Having brought down half our chariots with his spinning wheel knives, he had now switched his full attention to my vehicle. I realized that he must have recognized Hurotas as my passenger, and probably he knew who I was as well. Everyone else knows my stature and standing, why not him . . . whoever he might be?

He was close behind us and catching up with us rapidly. Those great Stygian monsters of his became more menacing with every stride they gained on us. I had seen what terrible injuries they could inflict with those head horns. However, the bank of the Nile was now less than a couple of hundred paces ahead of us, and the pickup boats had broken free of the restraining current and were approaching swiftly to meet us.

I had learned that it was fruitless to launch arrows at our scar-faced assailant. Perhaps the strange beasts drawing his chariot were more vulnerable. I thrust the reins of my chariot into the hands of Hurotas, even though he was still bemused and groggy. I snatched up my bow from the bin beside me, nocked an arrow, turned, and let fly at the central animal in the team of unicorns, which was now very close behind us.

Despite the fact that the chariot under me was bouncing wildly over the rough track, my aim was true and the arrow struck the animal in the very center of its great heaving chest, and buried itself up to the fletching. I knew that I had pierced its heart. Yet the monster did not falter or miss a stride but bore down on us inexorably. It was then I realized with dismay and horror that the scar-faced charioteer and his team of monsters were from another warp of existence. They were an aberration of the dark gods.

The thought no sooner formed in my mind than Scar-face rammed his team of unicorns into our chariot and our left-hand wheel exploded in a cloud of wooden fragments. Our three horses went down in a squealing heap, blood squirting from their amputated legs. We had just reached the sheer bank of the river when this happened. Hurotas and I were hurled from the chariot like stones from a catapult. We were sent sliding and slithering down the bank into the turbulent Nile waters.

The boats were coming into the bank to rescue us. They were only twenty paces offshore, but plying the oars like berserkers and yelling at us to swim. I fished

Hurotas to the surface and began dragging him out to meet them. Both of us were impeded by our armor, and Hurotas was still dazed. However, we reached the first boat and willing hands stretched down to haul us on board. Before we were pulled aboard, I darted a quick glance behind me and saw that our adversary had halted his team of unicorns on the top of the high bank. They were pawing the ground, snorting and blowing steaming breath from their flared nostrils in protest against the restraining harness. Scar-face had snatched up his longbow from the weapons bin and was stringing it, bending the heavy weapon with practiced ease.

I stretched over my shoulder and unhooked my bronze shield from its harness. Then I swung it around in front of us to afford both Hurotas and myself some protection from the storm that I knew was about to break over us. Scar-face looked up at the struggling knot of our men around the boat, and then he lifted the bow to draw fully. He smiled, and it was the first emotion I had seen him display. It twisted the scarred half of his face into a cynical grimace as he let the arrow fly.

He was aiming at me specifically, but I was ready to receive the shot. I brought up my shield to cover both Hurotas and myself, but I braced it at the particular angle that would deflect the arrow and not allow it to penetrate even the light alloy from which I had blended it. I felt the jolt of the strike and heard the metallic twang of flint on metal, but the arrow glanced off the shield and I heard it strike the gunnel of the boat behind me. I pulled Hurotas beneath the surface of the river with me, and although he struggled to be free, I dragged him under the keel of the boat to surface on the far side of the hull. Here we were hidden from the scar-faced archer on the bank above us. However, I could hear his arrows striking fresh victims and the screams of the exposed boat crew as they died choking and kicking in puddles of their own blood.

"Come on, Zaras." I slapped his face to try and focus his attention. "Help me to swim this boat across to the far bank, but in the name of great Zeus, keep your head down behind the hull, unless you want an arrow through your eyeball."

We paddled and shoved the boat halfway back across the river before the pandemonium in the hull above us subsided and I decided to risk a glance back at the far bank, on the assumption that the range was by this time too long for even an archer of Scar-face's extraordinary skills. A quick scan reassured me that the far bank was indeed deserted of all but the corpses of our dead. Scar-face and his unicorns had disappeared back into the forest. There were an additional five dead bodies in the boat that Zaras and I were pushing. All of them were bristling with arrows.

Hurotas was suffering badly from the injury he had received to his head. His speech was garbled, and he barely had the strength to climb back into the boat when finally we reached the eastern bank. I had to get behind him and boost him over the gunnel. Then he collapsed in the bilges. I found that I was unable to row the heavy boat single-handed against the current, so I was forced to drag it along the shoreline on the end of a tow rope. This was a torturously slow business and it was little short of the Hour of the Wolf when I finally reached the camp of the sixteen kings. This is the hour precisely halfway between dusk and dawn. It is the hour when most people die, when sleep is deepest, when nightmares are most convincing. It is the hour when the sleepless are haunted by their deepest fears, when ghosts and demons are most active and powerful. The Hour of the Wolf is when we mourn our dead most bitterly.

However, our camp was fully awake to a man, and pandemonium reigned supreme. Three survivors of Scar-face's murderous assault upon us had fled the field and reached the camp far ahead of me. They carried with them the news that our entire force, including both Hurotas and myself, had been massacred to a man by the dreaded archer. This had plunged the camp, including the royal women, Tehuti and Serrena, the sixteen kings and their royal courts, all our armies and the host of camp followers into dire lamentation. They had been performing the funeral dances to the gods of death and singing the hundred dirges to the spirits of the underworld since the setting of the sun.

They had managed to sustain their strength and energies only by resorting to the copious clay amphorae of red wine that were littered through the camp. The women had torn their clothing and scratched their faces until they bled. The men stamped the ground and beat their bare chests, vowing revenge and a hundred lives for every one of ours wiped out by the foe.

Precisely on the Hour of the Wolf when the three stars of Inana reached their zenith in the sky above us, I staggered out of the darkness into the bright light of the funeral fires, bearing in my arms what was patently the corpse of King Hurotas. Our clothing was tattered and caked with river mud that resembled exactly exhumed grave dirt. Only our faces were deathly white, and our eyes were wide and staring as those of corpses who had passed through the gates of Hades.

A sudden aching silence fell upon the multitudes who gazed upon us. They shrank away from us in horror, certain that we had returned from the infernal world.

Desperately I sought out Tehuti and Serrena to reassure them and found them not far away clinging to each other between two of the funeral fires. They were both staring at us in awe. I opened my mouth to give them reassurance, but I was by that time so far gone that the only sound I emitted was a dreadful graveyard groan. Then I collapsed to the ground with Hurotas on top of me. The next thing I was aware of was being clasped in the embrace of the two most beautiful women in existence and smothered in their kisses and endearments.

I had the vivid but fleeting notion that I had died and been admitted into Paradise.

I t took Hurotas only a few days to recover his wits. I still have a sovereign cure for head injuries that had been given to me by a black witch doctor beyond the great falls of the Nile when we had journeyed there with Queen Lostris all those many years ago when we were fleeing from the Hyksos.

However, our campaign against Utteric had been thrown into confusion by the arrival of the mysterious scar-faced archer and his unicorns. We had no idea who he was and where Utteric had found him, but he dominated the western bank of the river. He effectively denied our troops access to it. No matter when or where we made our attempts to cross over and lay siege to Utteric's fortress of Abu Naskos, the archer and his unicorns confronted us. We were utterly overwhelmed by the arrows he showered upon us with such extraordinary accuracy. I managed to collect several of these projectiles that had struck our chariots and even some that had killed our men at long range. They were not much different in design or manufacture from those made by our own armorers. However, when shot from his bow they ranged almost twice the distance that ours did. I watched him shoot on a number of occasions and counted that he was able to get four or five arrows airborne at the same time. Very few of these missed their mark.

Our men, even the bravest and the best of them, were becoming despondent. Some of the petty kings were muttering about abandoning the campaign and sailing back northward to their sordid little islands and their fat and ugly wives.

Even I, the eternal optimist, was becoming desperate. I was experiencing unpleasant dreams in which Inana, my particular favorite goddess, had taken to mocking me. On the other hand, she was definitely ignoring my prayers and supplications. The scar-faced adversary was clearly from another time and place, and I desperately needed help and guidance from her. It seemed that she had taken up temporary residence on the four man-made islands in the Nile River before Abu Naskos, so I had to seek her there.

Three nights later, after I had fully recovered from my latest ordeal, I waited for the rise of the moon before I went down through the sleeping camp, whispered to the sentries who were accustomed to my midnight perambulations, then slipped into the dark Nile waters and began to swim. I passed the black silhouettes of both Bird and Fish Islands without stopping and then the third island in the chain materialized out of the night. It was backlit by the panoply of the stars. This was unfamiliar territory for me. Although it looked identical to the first two islands from afar, I was not sure what to expect.

When I swam close enough to touch the stone walls, I found that they were indeed similar to the other two: sheer and high, extremely difficult to scale except by a skilled and intrepid rock climber. However, they gave me little pause, and as I climbed I noticed that the erosion of time and the elements was not nearly as severe as on the other two islands. I was even able to discern the chisel marks of the ancient builders on some of the stone blocks. When I reached the top I found that it was paved with the same slabs. Of course these had been cracked and tumbled by the roots of the plants forcing their way through them. Similar to the first two, the top of the island was thickly covered by this dense vegetation.

By this time the moon had risen above the horizon. It was a waxing half-moon with no cloud cover to obscure its light. I pushed my way through the dense undergrowth, and when I reached the center of the tower, I was amazed to find the remnants of an ancient staircase descending into the opening of a vertical shaft. It was in defiance of all logic that the ancients had built a shaft to reach the bottom of the river. Then I realized that there was probably not just one shaft but four of them, one in each island. I scrambled down the tumbled steps, risking breaking my neck if I lost my footing, but very soon I found my way blocked by the rubble and detritus that had accumulated over the ages.

I searched for a continuation of the shaft, but all I found was another line of ceramic tiles built into the wall. These depicted creatures that surely must have been intended to be otters. Fish, bird, and otter tunnels, but none of them leading anywhere.

I swore a bitter protest to the goddess Inana for treating me so shabbily, and I kicked at the compacted rubbish that denied me access to the depths of the shaft. This was a foolhardy gesture. I thought I had broken my toe. I sat down hurriedly and nursed my injured foot in my lap. Fortunately, further examination proved my toe to be intact. I hauled myself to my feet and limped back up to the surface.

"Did I hear somebody call my name?"

I started guiltily as a familiar voice spoke close behind me. I turned to find the goddess perched on the lip of the shaft. She was as ever impossibly beautiful. Her features glowed in the moonlight with an interior radiance that exceeded that of the heavenly body in the sky above us. Her smile was more enchanting than it had ever been.

"Forgive my impudence, Exalted One. I was remonstrating with myself, not with you." I would have made obeisance, but my foot still throbbed painfully.

"So have you changed your name to the same as mine, dearest Taita? I am flattered but not entirely convinced."

Her point was well taken, so I let it pass and changed the topic of our conversation. "Where does this tunnel lead to, Beloved of Zeus?"

"To wherever your heart desires and deserves." She was still punishing me, and I accepted it as justified. She changed the subject without pause: "But that seems to be the least of your present troubles, am I correct?"

"To whom or what are you referring?" I asked cautiously.

"You do not even know his name," she mocked me sweetly. "How can you hope to prevail against him without even knowing who he is?"

"I presume we are discussing Scar-face?" I asked.

"I know nobody by that name, neither good nor evil." She was being pedantic again.

"But you do know a person with that particular affliction or distinguishing mark to his face, do you not?"

"His name is Terramesh," she agreed. "He is the son of Hecate and Phontus."

"Everybody knows Hecate is the goddess of magic, ghosts, and necromancy," I conceded. "But I do not know of anyone by the name of Phontus."

"Very few have heard of him, Taita," Inana explained to me. "He was a mortal who was among the first men on earth. He abducted Hecate and raped her. From the union she gave birth to Terramesh. Thus her son is a half-god and half-human. He is a divine but not a god. When he reached maturity, Terramesh fought a duel with his father, Phontus, to punish him for how he treated his mother. They fought for a day and a night, but eventually Terramesh slew his father. However, in return he received from Phontus what appeared to be a mortal injury to the left side of his head and face."

"If he received such an injury from his own father, how then is he still here to bring me grief and hardship?"

Inana inclined her head to acknowledge the legitimacy of my protest. "As Terramesh lay dying his mother, Hecate, came to him. She worked a spell on her son that drew him back from the threshold of death. Then Hecate decreed that her son cannot die except by an identical wound to the right side of his face. Only the weapon that inflicted the original wound to the left side can be used to deliver this fatal blow."

"Where is that weapon?" I asked eagerly. "Where can I find it?"

"Hecate has protected her son extremely carefully. The weapon is hidden in a cave in the Amaroda Desert to the north of the River Tantica."

"I know that river. It is a tributary of Mother Nile. It is only three or four days' travel from here!" I exclaimed.

"Ah! But the cave is concealed by a spell that Hecate herself placed upon it."

"Do you know how to break the spell?"

"I know everything," she said solemnly. I blinked. Even I would hesitate to make such a sweeping statement; however, her credentials are at the very least equal to mine.

"Perhaps you should tell me," I suggested.

"Perhaps you should first assemble your helpers."

"Why do I need helpers?" I protested.

"Because Hecate stipulated that at least two divines must recite the spell in unison at the entrance to her cavern for it to open, and then they must identify the fatal weapon from among several hundred others that she buried in the same spot to further confuse the issue."

"Is that all?" I heard the bitter irony in my own tone.

"Not entirely. Only a king may wield the weapon against her son, Terramesh. He does not have to be a divine, but he must utter a specific war cry as he strikes; otherwise, the blow will be turned aside."

"I believe that I can find comrades of mine who meet all those criteria."

She nodded. "I have waited down the centuries for such a one as you. The number of innocents that Terramesh has slaughtered is legend. But now his time has come to die."

"I agree with you wholeheartedly. But before we part again, I would like to discuss these islands in the river with you." I patted the tiles on which Inana was sitting. "Where do they lead to?"

"Surely over the centuries since your birth you have learned a little patience?" she chided me.

"Not really," I replied, but she had faded away, once again.

It was a long swim back to the eastern bank of the Nile, but the time passed swiftly, for Inana had given me much to think about. When I reached the shore it was still dark. I did not even waste time drying myself but ran directly to Rameses' camp. The guards at the gates tried to restrain me from disturbing the royal slumbers, but I raised my hand to silence them.

"Listen, you half-wits!" They fell silent, and we were able to hear the muted but ecstatic little cries issuing from the royal tent. "Now if that's slumbering, I wish somebody would teach me the art of it." Then I raised my voice: "Mighty Pharaoh, are you awake?"

I was answered immediately by a feminine squeal: "Tata! Is that you? Rameses and I have just this moment finished. Where have you been? We missed you at the feast last night. Come in! Come in! I want to show you what Rameses has bought for me."

When I entered the royal bed tent, they made room for me on the mattress. Serrena scolded me, "You are as cold as if you have been sleeping on the top of the Taygetus Mountains in the middle of winter." I was shivering from my swim and grateful for the camel-skin blankets the two of them piled on top of me.

We chatted away happily for a while, and then I set about the delicate task of explaining to them how we were going to triumph over the scar-faced monster. I could not tell them, or anyone else for that matter, about my special relationship with the goddess Inana.

In the tale I had prepared for them, Inana was a wise old woman who visited me from time to time. They listened avidly to my version of the story of Terramesh and how he could be defeated. I excluded only any reference to the divinity of Serrena herself, a fact of which she was still blissfully ignorant. By the time I had finished they were as eager as I was to set off to find the cave in the Amaroda Desert and to retrieve the fatal weapon that could slay Terramesh. It took the remainder of that day for us to make our arrangements for the journey.

Fortunately the Amaroda Desert is situated on the eastern bank of the Nile so it was not necessary to cross the river again and run the risk of encountering Terramesh before we had made adequate preparations to deal with him. The three of us were all the force that was needed, with supplies for no more than ten days. Water would present no problem for us and our horses. We would be following first the Nile and then the Tantica River as far as the cavern. Of course, I had to inform Hurotas and Hui of our expedition and, naturally, they wanted to join us. However, I used all my powers of persuasion and pointed out that they would be performing essential duties by remaining with the main army; not least of all they would be maintaining order among the sixteen allied kings, who managed to be difficult even when they considered that they were being at their most cooperative. Some of them were still mumbling about abandoning our venture in the face of Terramesh's arrows.

So lightly burdened the three of us were able to move extremely swiftly. On the fourth afternoon after leaving the camp opposite the fortress of Abu Naskos, we reached the headwaters of the Tantica River, which was the rendezvous that I had agreed on with Inana. I left my two companions to set up camp and to feed and water the horses from the river while I wandered away downstream in search of Inana in whatever fanciful guise she had chosen for the occasion.

I had not had an opportunity to bathe since leaving Abu Naskos, so I did so now. I was sitting on a rock beside a pool in the river drying myself in the warm breeze waiting for Inana to put in an appearance. I had already accosted a large green frog, a small brown serpent, and sundry other insects and wildlife without marked success. I was beginning to succumb to the desert stillness and to the fact that I had slept little since leaving the camp on the Nile.

"We were discussing patience at our last meeting, or rather lack of it," she said suddenly and unexpectedly. "I am pleased to see you are making progress."

I started fully awake and looked about me. A small turtle was floating in the pool close at hand. "I expected something less cold-blooded and scaly," I chided it in return.

"And no doubt you expected me to have pretty feathers?" She spoke again, but this time from behind me. I looked around quickly and there was a lovely little desert warbler sitting on the rock close to me. Her breast was creamy and sleek and her wings were a lovely auburn shade. She spread one of them and began to groom it with her beak.

"That color suits you splendidly, my dear," I told her.

"I am so glad you like it," she trilled, and I could not prevent myself from laughing.

"You are beautiful, as always." I chuckled. "But if we are to be serious, I prefer you in human guise."

"Then avert your eyes for a moment," she said, and I obeyed by looking back at the turtle in the pool. "Now you may look again."

I turned toward her once more, and she was the Inana I knew so well in all her splendor. She pirouetted once with her tresses and her skirts billowing out around her. Then she sank down beside me and hugged her knees to her chest.

"Ask me a question," she invited me. "I know that's what you are dying to do."

"Am I so obvious?"

"I am very much afraid you are, poor Taita."

"Where is Hecate's cavern from here?"

"Look to the horizon straight ahead of you. What do you see?"

"I see three conical hills on the skyline."

"At the foot of the middle one is the entrance to the cavern you seek."

"What is the password that will open the way?"

"'Open mighty Janus of two faces!' repeated three times."

"That is logical and easy to remember." I nodded. "Janus is the god of doorways and gates."

"When will you leave?"

"The horses are played out, and so are we. My plan is to rest here tonight and leave early tomorrow morning, at first light," I replied.

"I will wait for you at your destination," she promised and faded away like a lovely mirage.

We left the Tantica River before sunrise the next morning and set off across the plain. At first we rode in company with many thousands of migrating gazelle. These graceful little animals danced across the desert with horns shaped like a lyre and facial patterns outlined in delicate brown scrolls. Serrena composed a song to their beauty. When she sang it to them, they listened with ears pricked and big luminous dark eyes staring in astonishment. They must have been aware of her divinity for they allowed her to approach them so closely that she might almost have leaned from the saddle and touched one of them. They moved on en masse and disappeared over the horizon as swiftly and as silently as the wispy puffs of dust raised by their elegant little hooves.

As is so often the case with desert landscapes, the three conical hills were much farther off than they appeared to be. It was almost midday when we reined in the horses under the slope of the central hill and looked up at the peak. It was also higher than I had anticipated.

Fresh green grass was growing on the lower slopes so we pitched our rudimentary camp and hobbled the horses and turned them loose to graze.

Then the three of us set off to search the lower slopes for some clue to the entrance to Hecate's cave. I had a strong premonition of where I would find Inana. I knew she would not want to appear before all three of us, so I sent Rameses and Serrena off in the opposite direction. Then I wandered along the northern slope alone. I heard her before I saw her. She was sitting on a rock and preening her feathers again, pausing every few minutes to trill her sweet warbling song. I found a seat on the rock beside her, and she finished her song before she addressed me.

"Hecate was here," she said. "She was expecting you to arrive. She wanted to frighten you off. She wanted to interpose herself and conceal the entrance to her cavern, but I drove her away."

I was shocked by this news. I felt my skin crawling as if it was covered with poisonous insects. I glanced around expecting Hecate to materialize at any moment, hissing and spitting like a cobra. "Do you have the power to do that?" I asked her with trepidation.

"I am Inana, granddaughter of Zeus," she answered me simply. "She fled squawking and shrieking back to where she belongs." She hopped up onto my shoulder and spoke into my ear: "Remember always, Taita, that you are one of my special favorites. That's why I love to tease you. Come, let me guide you to the entrance to the horrible harridan's hiding place."

We started up the slope with Inana warbling in my ear and breaking off now and then to give me directions. We reached a sheer wall of rock at the base of the conical hill, and Inana told me to wait a while.

"Whatever for?" I wanted to know.

"The other two are coming back here," she told me. I had no idea how she knew that, but I thought it best not to argue. It was as well I didn't because within a few minutes I heard Serrena's melodious voice as she chatted cheerfully to Rameses, and his gruffer tones as he answered her. Their voices grew louder as they approached, then Inana flew off my shoulder and settled on the cliff above me. At that moment the other two came into sight around the rocky wall and waved to

me. Inana had timed it perfectly, and they had no inkling that I was in any way related to the pretty little
bird perched on the cliff above me.

"Did you find anything?" I called to them.

"No, nothing," Rameses called back. "How about
you?"

I was about to give him the same reply when I looked
up and saw something that I had not noticed until that
moment. "There is a fissure in the cliff wall over there.
It looks interesting." They quickened their pace, and
when they reached me I pointed out the opening. It
was almost hidden by the dense vegetation that choked
it, and it was obvious that no man or animal had entered it in many years.

The crack in the rock face was just wide enough
to allow three grown men to enter it simultaneously
shoulder to shoulder. I drew my sword from the sheath
on my hip and began to hack away at the bushes and
creepers that obstructed the entrance. Rameses joined
me, and Serrena hovered behind us, giving good advice,
and urging us onward. Above us the pretty little warbler fluttered from bush to bush chattering excitedly.
We worked our way into the fissure for about twenty
paces before we reached a gigantic round boulder that
was jammed in between the walls, blocking the entrance off entirely. It looked as though it had been in

place for a very long time, perhaps even for centuries. We cleared away the growth of bush in front of this obstacle and then I turned back to Serrena. "I hope that you remember the password?" I asked her.

"Yes, of course," she replied. "It's 'Open—'"

"No!" I raised my voice only slightly. "Don't say the words until we are both ready."

"You don't have to shout at me," she replied haughtily.

"It's better than throttling you," I pointed out.

"I suppose it is, when you put it like that," she agreed with a repentant grin. She proffered her hand and I took it. We stood side by side facing the rock jam, with Rameses close behind us.

The warbler flew down into the fissure and perched on top of the massive round rock that confronted us. I drew a deep breath; for some reason, I felt suddenly nervous. I squeezed Serrena's hand and we started together.

"Open mighty Janus of two faces!" we chanted in unison, and then paused.

"Open mighty Janus of two faces!" we repeated our exhortation. Then we drew breath together and did so for the third and final time: "Open mighty Janus of two faces!"

With a thunderous roar, the rock exploded into

hundreds of flying pieces. The red-winged warbler was sitting directly on top of it, and she was hurled up the spout of the fissure. Her shrieks of surprise and terror almost matched the force of the explosion. Even in my own distress, I was grateful for Inana's immortality and her invulnerability from physical harm, for without that protection she would have suffered serious injury. Serrena and I were standing well clear, but we were thrown backward off our feet and showered with rock shards and other debris. Rameses was twice as far again from the source of the explosion, but being only human, he suffered a great deal more than Serrena and I did. I was very touched by Serrena's concern for him, but I do think he was rather overplaying the dying-hero image. I left them to it and scrambled forward over the rubble to the cavern entrance that had been exposed, and I peered into it.

It did indeed appear to be the opening to the cavern that Hecate had used to store the blades and weapons, among which she had tried to conceal the one that was capable of terminating Terramesh's evil existence. However, the dense shadows and the fine dust cloud raised by the explosion almost totally obscured the interior. The three of us were forced to restrain our impatience and wait until the dust settled. By the time this happened, the sun was setting behind the conical hill.

Fortunately I had brought with us a good supply of torches made from dried reeds and resinous sticks of wood. We lit three of these from fire sticks and, holding them aloft, we made our way back to the cave entrance and peered through the opening.

The cavern that was now revealed was not particularly large. Nevertheless, it resembled the interior of a particularly slovenly quartermaster's storeroom, one that had not been cleaned out or tidied for a century or more. It was piled from wall to wall and head high with this trash. Only a few of the items could still be recognized for what they were: these were bundles of arrows, hand axes, swords and other edged weapons.

The rest of the contents of the cave consisted of hundreds upon hundreds of other amorphous items, piled upon one another and then coated with a thick layer of dust, which effectively concealed their identity. My spirits quailed as I realized we would have to bring every item out into the daylight, clean the filth off it, and then by some means or other try to arrive at a conclusion as to which was the weapon that had so grievously wounded Terramesh all those centuries ago. As a long liver and a putative divine I discovered that I had not the slightest intuitive inkling as to which it was.

I looked around for the red-winged warbler, but,

typical woman, she was nowhere in sight when she was needed most.

"Well, we had better get started, I suppose." I tried to sound enthusiastic.

"Cheer up, Tata," Serrena encouraged me. "It should take no more than a month or so at the most."

There was not the space for more than one of us to work in the cavern at the same time. Rameses and I took it in turns to do so. Whichever man was not working in the cavern joined Serrena in the entrance fissure and passed each item from hand to hand until they could be stacked outside the entrance. It was a slow and tedious procedure. Even with strips of cloth tied around our noses and mouths, the dust we stirred up choked us and could not be long endured before we had to change places.

We labored on as the moon rose and infinitely slowly traversed the sky above us. A little before midnight I had relinquished my position in the main storeroom to Rameses, and I moved back into the tunnel. On the wall above my head I had placed one of the torches of dried reeds in a bracket. It was throwing a good light.

I had lost count of the number of dusty items Rameses had passed to me to carry down to Serrena at the entrance, but then he did something that broke the rhythm and monotony. He passed me an ancient leather bag that was dry and brittle with age. As I took it from his hand the leather tore open and the contents spilled on to the floor of the fissure at my feet. I muttered an oath and then stooped to gather up the contents. These were four bronze arrowheads. Before I touched them, I stopped and stared at them. Three of them were corroded with age, black and worn until they were barely recognizable. The fourth arrowhead was as pristine as if it had that very minute come off the blacksmith's anvil. It was shining and sharp edged, so the torchlight danced on its surface.

I reached for it, but as my fingers touched it I exclaimed with surprise and jerked my hand back. It was hot, almost but not quite painful to the touch. I had my back turned to Rameses so he had not seen my reaction. Outside the cave entrance Serrena was also turned away, stacking the other items I had passed out to her. Neither of them was aware of my discovery.

I gathered up all four of the arrowheads. Now that I was ready for it, the heat of the fourth was almost comforting. I carried them to the entrance where Serrena turned back to meet me with a weary smile.

"Are we almost finished?" she asked.

"Well, almost halfway perhaps," I told her and she

rolled her eyes. I placed the three ancient and time-eroded arrowheads in her outstretched hand. She began to turn away, but I checked her.

"There is one more," I told her, and she turned back to me and proffered her other hand. I placed the fourth arrowhead in her palm. She jerked as though she had been stung by a bee. She threw the three ancient arrowheads in her other hand to the ground and cupped the fourth in both hands as if it was something exceedingly precious.

"This is it, Tata!" She brought the shining arrowhead up close to her face and stared at it. "This is the one we are searching for."

"How do you know?" I asked.

"I know. I just know. And you know too, Tata." She looked up at me in accusation. "You knew before you gave it to me, admit it."

I chuckled. "Call your friend Rameses. We ride at once for your papa's camp at Abu Naskos. And don't lose that arrowhead. Your kingdom and your husband's life may depend on it."

The three of us were mounted within the hour and reached the Tantica River before dawn. We watered the horses and then rode on until the middle of the afternoon when we rested the horses and ourselves for three hours. Then we rode on through the second night. Two of the horses broke down during this leg of the journey, but we abandoned them and rode on. We lost two more of them at the end of the following day, but we reached King Hurotas' camp opposite Abu Naskos before dawn. We had ridden from Hecate's cavern to Hurotas' camp in three days, which was a feat to be proud of. However, I was not so proud of having killed horses in the process.

We found that very little had changed in our absence. A standoff had developed between the two armies, with each side sticking to their own territory on their respective sides of the Nile. Not one of our men was prepared to cross the Nile and face the certainty of being confronted by Terramesh.

The only significant change had been the decision of two of the petty kings to renege on their oaths of *An offense to one is an offense to all.* They had boarded their ships with their particular armies and sailed back down the Nile to the Middle Sea, and from there set sail for their own kingdoms—if you could call a pestilent wind-swept rock inhabited by a few treacherous pirates a kingdom. As Hurotas pointed out, there were fewer than 150 of them in total, and every single one of them was a whiner and a coward, which included their two kings.

After greeting Hurotas and Hui, my next act was to call for Tarmacat, who was the most celebrated bow maker and fletcher in the civilized world. We were old friends, and he came at once to my summons. After we embraced and exchanged greetings, I told him, "I want you to make me the most perfect arrow in existence. The fate of the civilized world may depend on it."

"This is a summons I have waited for all my life," he replied. "Show me the bow and I will make the arrow for it."

I led him to the ivory table at the back of my tent and drew back the silken cloth that covered it. An unstrung bow lay upon it. Tarmacat approached it, and before he even touched it his expression changed to one of awe.

"I have only ever seen three other bows to match this one." He stroked with reverence the intricate bindings of gold wire that covered the grip. "All of them were the property of a king or a monarch."

"This one is no exception, good Tarmacat. It belongs to Rameses the First, Pharaoh of Upper and Lower Egypt."

"I expected as much, my Lord Taita. I will begin at once. I will not waste another hour of my life."

"I will help you," I told him. Tarmacat had a lifetime's accumulation of the finest materials at his disposal. It took another two days for us to make a selection of the best of it, and then to carve and shape four shafts to perfection. Then Tarmacat balanced them so that they would fly true to a range of two hundred paces. Finally we fitted the arrowhead that Serrena and I had discovered in Hecate's cavern into each of the perfect shafts in succession. Rameses shot each arrow once, and we chose the one that showed the least deflection, which was less than half an inch.

That evening I swam to the third of the four islands in the Nile before the fortress of Abu Naskos, and as I waited for Inana to put in an appearance I once more examined the shaft that the old people had built. I found that its purpose was still a riddle to me. I was relieved when Inana finally put in an appearance. The last time I had laid my eyes upon her was when she was chirping a pretty tune, perched in her feathered finery on top of the great rock that blocked the entrance to Hecate's cavern. I had the good sense not to remind her of that occasion.

Perhaps as a reward for my tact she came directly to me out of the dark night, and for the first time ever she kissed me on both cheeks, and then, despite the fact that I was sopping wet from the river, she perched on my lap.

"I am delighted that you and your henchman Tarmacat have been able to produce the perfect arrow," she told me without preamble.

"You never miss a thing, do you?" I was still savoring those kisses, and I was astonished by how much I enjoyed the experience. "But are we ever going to be given a chance to use that arrow?"

She ignored my quibble. "There is a hidden glade in the forest behind Utteric's fortress of Abu Naskos on the western bank of the River Nile. Hecate has fashioned it as a retreat and a refuge especially for her own son."

"How do you mean a hidden glade?" I was intrigued.

"I mean it exactly as I say it. It does not exist except to those who have the eyes to see and the ears to hear."

"Where would I get the use of such eyes and ears?"

"Only from one of us who live on Mount Olympus."

"You mean from a god? Not even from a divine?"

"Dear Taita, you amaze me with your acumen! That is precisely what I mean."

"My acumen almost matches your sarcasm." I dropped my voice as I said it.

"I am glad I did not hear that." She shrugged. "But to return to more important matters than acumen and sarcasm: Terramesh, the son of the goddess Hecate, is in this secret garden at this very moment, but he grows restless. Even I do not know if he will still be there by tomorrow morning."

"How soon can you take us there?"

"I will speak to my friend the red-winged warbler," she said, and then she smiled. "I hope she has recovered from the opening of the cavern of Hecate. The poor little thing suffered a dreadful shock."

It was not yet midnight when I parted with Inana and left her on the third island. I had warned Rameses and Serrena to be prepared to act swiftly on my return to Hurotas' camp. The two of them were sequestered in my tent, fully dressed and sleeping lightly on my bed. They responded instantly to my quiet call to awaken them. In the stables behind my tent, I had horses saddled and ready to ride.

I had also arranged for light rowing skiffs to be hidden at intervals along the riverbank, both upstream and downstream of the main camp, for as yet I had no inkling of where we must cross. As it turned out, Terramesh's hidden glade was less than two leagues downstream from us. Dawn was breaking as the three of us reached the eastern bank opposite it. We turned our mounts loose to make their own way back to the camp. Then we went down to the bank of the Nile and found the skiff hidden under a pile of driftwood and other trash. We cleared away the debris, and then Rameses and I dragged the boat down to the water's edge, while Serrena followed us carrying the long leather bow case and the other light equipment. We clambered aboard and pushed off from the bank and rowed over to Utteric's side of the river. We were concealing the skiff again under a covering of vegetation when I heard a familiar twittering and I looked up to see the red-breasted warbler fluttering impatiently in the branches of the tree above us. Rameses strung his bow and checked the contents of his quiver before we set off toward the north at an easy lolloping run. Neither of the other two realized that I was following the bird. They were not even aware of its existence

We ran for half the morning. There was no path or roadway to follow, but the warbler picked the easiest terrain for us to traverse. The hills we climbed were heavily wooded, and the forest grew denser as we forged our way deeper into it.

Suddenly without warning the warbler vanished. We came to an abrupt halt, and both Serrena and Rameses looked at me expectantly. I was as perplexed as they were, but I put on the best face possible and told them with an assumed air of confidence: "Wait here. I won't be long. I just want to check the lie of the land ahead."

I left them and pushed my way through what appeared to be an impenetrable barrier of thornbush. But despite the savage appearance of the hooked red-tipped thorns, they turned out to be amazingly accommodating. They slid over my limbs and body without snagging my flesh or clothing. However, after a very short while I found myself subject to a sudden and debilitating languor. My footsteps slowed and I came to a halt. I wanted to sit down and rest, and possibly take a short nap. My vision grew dark.

Only then did I realize I was being manipulated by an alien influence. I had run into a psychic barrier. I felt myself swaying on my feet, and my legs were growing numb and heavy under me. My mind was clouding. I could not think clearly. I could not go any farther.

Then I felt a light pressure on my shoulder, and I heard Inana's sweet voice in my ear: "Fight it, Taita! You know what it is. You can overcome it."

I took a deep breath that whistled in my throat and chest and I listened to her voice. I felt the dark cloud that was inundating my mind begin to lighten and abate. My legs firmed under me. I forced them to take another step.

"Yes, Taita. You have the power to overcome it. Be strong for yourself and for those you love. They need you now."

I took another step, and then another. The thorns brushed my face, but I knew intuitively that Inana was turning the points so they would not bite into my skin.

Then suddenly the thorns no longer brushed my face and I could see light behind my closed eyelids. I opened my eyes and I saw a wondrous landscape laid out before me. The dense hedge of fierce thornbushes had gone. Before my eyes was laid out a garden of delights. There were limpid lakes and waterfalls that glittered in the sunlight. There were forests of lovely trees, green and luxurious. Their high branches were picked out with vivid flowers that shone like rubies and sapphires. Under them were spread carpets of green velvet lawns.

From the forest across the lake emerged a herd of the beautiful sable unicorns that I had last seen drawing Terramesh's chariot with the devastating blade-edged wheels. Now they were running free, no longer in harness. They frolicked like colts as they cantered down to the edge of the lake to drink of the waters. When they had taken their fill they trotted back to the edge of the forest and disappeared in the trees.

"This is the hidden garden of Terramesh," I said

with certainty as my wits were restored to me in their entirety. The bird on my shoulder chirruped her agreement, and I felt a stab of concern. "But where is Terramesh now?"

"He is sleeping."

"Are you certain of that, Inana?"

"Don't be afraid. You are safe now with me."

"I am not afraid," I corrected her with dignity. "I was mildly concerned, and that is all." Then I moved on to more pressing matters. "How are we going to manipulate Terramesh into a position where Rameses is able get a clean shot at the undamaged side of his face?"

And so we discussed this problem in detail. Inana forsook her avian manifestation and reverted to her human form in order to make her explanation more abundantly clear. She pointed out the area of the garden that she had chosen as the killing ground. Then she explained how she intended to manipulate our victim to enter it, and where Rameses, Serrena and I must take up our positions to await Terramesh's arrival.

"He has never previously laid eyes on Serrena. He will believe that she is a surreal manifestation, a spirit provided for his pleasure by his mother or one of the other dark gods who favor him. They have done this for him countless times before. He will be expecting it and be completely off his guard." Inana turned and pointed out a single magnificent tree that grew in the middle of the lawns. "The center of that sycamore tree trunk is hollow. You and Rameses will use it as a hiding place. When Serrena has maneuvered the quarry into the correct position at precisely the agreed range, Rameses will hail him with the challenge. Then when he turns Rameses will do the rest." She looked at me with those astonishingly lovely eyes. "Is there anything that I have not made quite clear?"

"Yes, there is. How am I to get Serrena and Rameses through the thorn fence without them falling asleep on me?"

"I am sure you will think of something," she replied and I heard the echo of laughter in her voice as she mutated from goddess back to pretty little bird. "You cannot expect me to assist you. Not in my present manifestation."

I went back through the thorn hedge and found Rameses and Serrena waiting for me anxiously where I had left them on the far side. "Where have you been, Tata?" they demanded in unison. "We were getting very worried."

"The only thing you need worry about is that I have to carry each of you through this thorn hedge. Please don't argue. We are running out of time."

"But—" Rameses protested indignantly.

"No buts, my darling husband. You heard Tata. You are going first," Serrena told him firmly, and he subsided. She was by now indisputably in control as his senior wife.

Rameses wanted to carry his own bow case but I prevailed on him to leave it in Serrena's care and he reluctantly agreed. Empty-handed he managed to get halfway through the thorn hedge before his legs folded up under him and he subsided in a heap, snoring softly with a happy smile on his face. He was a big man, all muscle and bone, but I managed to drape him over one shoulder and carry him through into the hidden garden. I laid him in the shade of the giant sycamore and left the warbler perched in the foliage above him to keep watch over him.

Then I went back through the hedge to fetch Serrena. She hopped up into my arms without quibble and threw both arms around my neck.

"I have been looking forward to this," she told me happily. After her husband, she seemed light as thistledown and I was able to carry the bow case and other luggage in addition to her. When I laid her under the sycamore tree beside Rameses, she snuggled up to him without waking either him or herself. I sat and watched them for a minute or two. They were such a perfect couple that I became all mawkish.

"This is all very homely and endearing," the warbler warbled in the branches above me. "Perhaps a lullaby from me would make it perfect."

Rameses and I had both long ago agreed that sixty-five paces was the ultimate range for the most accurate shooting of his bow. At that distance he had demonstrated that he could hit a target the size of an acorn time after time, without fail. I slapped his cheeks until he woke from his slumbers, and he gazed about him, marveling at the beauty of the secret garden. His exclamations roused Serrena. Once both of them had become accustomed to their new surroundings I explained the roles that I expected them to play.

I gave Serrena the small bundle of cosmetics and other feminine accoutrements that I had carried along with the bow case, and with which she could enhance her beauty to even greater splendor. We left her to work this feminine witchcraft, while Rameses and I paced out the killing ground together, from the hollow trunk of the sycamore to the wild blue columbine flower that grew in solitary glory in the center of the lawn facing the lake.

Inana had assured us that Terramesh was asleep in the forest beyond the lake. Inana, in her manifestation as the red-winged warbler, was perched at the top of the tree under which he lay. She would keep him comatose until Rameses and I were ready to receive him. There was a causeway across the center of the lake. Inana would influence Terramesh to use it as soon as she roused him from his slumbers.

At long last the trap was baited and set. Rameses and I had taken up our positions within the hollowed-out center of the sycamore. Rameses nocked the fatal arrow to his bowstring. The metal head of the arrow shone with the peculiar patina of pure gold. He closed his eyes for a few seconds, as if in prayer. Then he opened them again and nodded at me. I stepped into the opening in the trunk of the tree and looked up the wide expanse of the lawn to where Serrena waited inconspicuously under the overhang of the thorn fence that surrounded the secret garden. She was sitting forward eagerly watching for my signal. I waved my free hand above my head, and she stood up and walked gracefully down the lawn to take up her position beside the blue flower. This was ostensibly her signal to me, but more accurately it was my signal to Inana, who I knew was watching from the treetop on the far side of the lake.

Serrena wore the silken dress that had been her wedding garment. It shimmered as she moved, showing off the sculpturing of her body in exquisite detail. But the long tresses of her hair caught the sunlight and her features glowed with the cosmetics she had applied, making all her surroundings seem drab by comparison.

I tore my eyes off her to turn and look across the lake just as the towering figure of Terramesh stepped out of the encroaching forest on the far side. There he stopped to stretch and yawn cavernously, before he walked out onto the causeway that spanned the waters. He was unarmed, carrying neither sword nor bow. He wore only a brief loincloth; thus his extraordinary physique was almost fully exposed. He seemed to be composed entirely of massive bone and bulging muscle, the one not necessarily in harmony with the other. He appeared to be more savage animal than human being.

Only the one side of his head was covered by his metal helmet. The exposed half was deprived entirely of hair, riven and wrought by scars until it resembled a parody of natural flesh and skin. In the center of this expanse of damaged flesh, his lidless eye stared un-blinkingly ahead.

He was halfway across the causeway before he became aware of Serrena standing on the lawn above him. He stopped in midstride and stared at her fixedly with his single eye.

Serrena returned his gaze just as expressionlessly. Then she lifted both hands to her breast and, beginning with the button beneath her chin, she began unhurriedly to open her bodice to her waist. Then she delicately parted the cloth so her breasts showed in the opening, large, round and creamy, tipped with ruddy nipples. She took one of her nipples between two fingers and pointed it toward Terramesh, manipulating it gently until a drop of clear liquid gleamed on the tip. At the same time she hooded her eyes in flagrant invitation, epitomizing the perfect blending of pulchritude and lust.

Terramesh raised both his hands to the fastenings of his helmet, then lifted it from his head and let it drop. The contrast between one side of his face and the other was startling. The ruin and mutilation of the left side was offset by the stern nobility of the right. And yet the eye was cruel and the line of the mouth unrelenting. He smiled with the undamaged half of his lips but it was without humor or kindness; rather, it was a sneer of lust and rapacity.

With both hands he loosed his loincloth and discarded it, so that his genitalia were exposed. They dangled flaccid and soft down to his knees. He took his penis in one hand and stroked it back and forth. His fingers barely spanned its girth as it stiffened into rigidity. His foreskin peeled back from his glans, leaving it pink and shining and the size of a ripe apple. It thrust out rigidly ahead of him by the length of his forearm.

Serrena seemed to be goaded on by this display. She shrugged out of her apparel and stood naked with both hands cupped around her mons pubis and her hips thrust forward. She smiled lewdly and it matched his for cupidity. I was startled by this display of wanton lust from her although I realized it was contrived.

Terramesh started forward. He left the causeway across the lake and marched up the slope toward where she stood. He passed close to where Rameses and I were hidden within the hollow of the sycamore, so close that I could hear his grunts of arousal like those of a great wild boar in must and smell it on him like the stench of a virulent pox.

I let him go on twenty paces up the lawn and then I touched Rameses' shoulder. In unison we stepped out of our hiding place. Rameses took three paces ahead of me to give himself a clear shot, and then he dropped naturally in the archer's stance with his bow presented and his single arrow nocked. On the greensward above us Terramesh came to a stop a few paces in front of where Serrena stood. He towered above her, almost blotting her out from our line of sight.

At the same moment Rameses called to him in a voice so thunderous that it startled even me who was entirely prepared for it, "Son of Phontus, I bring you a message from your father!"

Terramesh spun around to face us. He froze and stared down at us. Then everything seemed to happen at the same instant. Serrena dropped facedown into the grass behind him, instantly clearing the range for Rameses' shot. In a single flowing movement Rameses had lifted his bow and drawn the string back to its fullest extent, then released it with a sharp, almost musical twang of the bowstring.

Terramesh's reaction seemed instantaneous but was still far too slow to cheat the deadly arrow, which was already halfway to its mark. It reached its zenith and began the drop before he had even twitched. Both his hideous face and his massive penis were pointed to the sky from which the arrow fell like a ray of sunlight. It took him in the precise center of his staring eyeball, which exploded in a bright spray of aqueous liquid. The shaft protruded half an arm's length from Terramesh's eye socket. At that angle and depth it must certainly have transfixed his brain. I expected him to drop instantly and lie where he fell. But instead he started to run and at the same time to scream in a high, penetrating monotone. He came straight at us; at first I thought it was a deliberate attack, yet he gave no indication of seeing us. But when Rameses and I jumped out of his way he kept on straight down the hill toward the lake, blindly screaming his agony and his fury.

We drew our swords and took off in pursuit, but neither of us could catch up with him. Then, still screaming, he ran full tilt into the giant sycamore tree, which he manifestly was unable to see. The impact drove the point of the arrow completely through his skull and out of the back of his head. But he kept on his feet and staggered in small circles, still howling. Then the flesh began to fall off his head in strips as though it was rotting. The white bone of his skull gleamed in the sunlight and then it also began to crumble.

Simultaneously the meat of his arms and upper torso blackened and fell off the bone in chunks and tatters. The stench of putrefaction that his body emitted was so overpowering that we covered our mouths and noses and backed away from him as he collapsed. His body continued to writhe and convulse as it turned to pulp and became a shapeless heap of ordure. Even this crumbled into dust and began to blow away on the light

wind that swept across the lake. However, the arrowhead that had slain him lay on the spot where he had
fallen. Hesitantly Rameses went to it and stooped to
pick it up, but before his fingers touched it the metal
blackened and eroded into nothingness. Eventually
neither sign nor evidence of the previous existence of
Terramesh remained.

We stared in astonishment and awe for a while,
but finally we turned away and walked back to where
Serrena waited for us. We sat down on each side of her.
Rameses placed his arm around her shoulders and she
leaned against him. Her face beneath the cosmetics was
bereft and pale as snow, and her eyes swam with tears.

"I had to force myself to watch it. It was just too
horrible," she whispered. Then she pointed back over
the spot where he had vanished. "See what is happening to Terramesh's hidden garden."

Before our eyes the lake and the waterfalls dried up
and became nothing more than sordid muddy depressions in the earth, filled with green slime. The trees of
the forest dropped their lush vegetation and the blossoms that covered them. Their trunks and branches
turned black and dry. The grass that grew beneath
them withered away. The limbs of the giant sycamore
tree fell from the trunk and lay twisted and contorted
on the ground below like those of an amputee. The

thorn hedge that had enclosed the secret garden reappeared, stark and forbidding, but then almost immediately began to droop and fade away. There remained
no vestige of Terramesh's herd of magnificent black
unicorns. They had disappeared with rest of the secret
garden. Nothing remained but decay and devastation.
The only exception was Terramesh's helmet, which lay
where he had abandoned it. I went down to retrieve it
as a remembrance of these monumental events.

"There is no reason for us to remain here another
minute longer," I said as I returned to where they
waited. Immediately Rameses helped Serrena to her
feet and we set off toward where we had left our skiff
hidden on the bank of River Nile. None of us looked
back.

The sun was setting when we reached Hurotas' camp, and a joyous cry went up as the sentries recognized the three of us in the skiff. Some of them plunged into the river to seize our craft and drag it ashore. By the time we had disembarked half the army had gathered to welcome us. Then Hurotas and Tehuti came hurrying from their royal camp and fell upon Serrena. Hurotas seized her in his arms and carried her into his camp while Tehuti danced around them in a circle chanting her thanks to all the gods for her daughter's safe return. Rameses and I followed them at a discreet distance, waiting for our turn to have the attention of Hurotas. By fortunate chance we carried with us the sack containing our equipment and Terramesh's helmet, which I had retrieved from where he had abandoned it on the causeway across the lake.

Finally Tehuti took her daughter into her arms and, surrounded by their ladies-in-waiting, they withdrew into the women's seraglio. Hurotas came to us immediately. "Follow me!" he ordered. "I want to know exactly what happened, and particularly I want to know the whereabouts of that ravening monster."

He led us into his private conference tent and, while we found seats for ourselves, he broached a flagon of red wine and poured the contents into the enormous jugs that he reserved for special occasions: a certain sign of his approval.

"Now tell me. Tell me everything," he commanded as he dropped into his throne facing us.

Rameses looked at me. On the journey back from the secret garden we had discussed how much we should reveal to Hurotas of our encounter with Terramesh. We were worried that so much of what had happened to us was so extraordinary as to be unbelievable to anybody who had not witnessed it for themselves. We had finally agreed not to withhold any details from Hurotas, no matter how far-fetched they seemed to be. If he balked at the veracity of our description, we had as evidence the testimony of his own beloved daughter. He could never disregard that.

I took a deep breath and a large mouthful of the wine, which bolstered my resolve, and then I began to talk. I talked for a long time even by my own standards. Of course I glossed lightly over certain aspects of Serrena's role in the proceedings; after all, she was his daughter. I decided that it was unnecessary to describe her skillful distraction of Terramesh in the moments before Rameses loosed the fatal arrow. Hurotas listened avidly, at intervals nodding his understanding and acceptance of my account.

When I ended my recital Hurotas was silent for a while, and then he said, "So you brought the skull of Terramesh back with you, as irrefutable proof of this creature's demise."

"No." I corrected him mildly. "That is not what I said."

"I know what you said and of course I believe you. But why complicate matters? We have plenty of choice skulls lying around here. Any one of them could have belonged to this creature you call Terramesh. I am going to have to send our troops back across the river to capture the fortress of Abu Naskos. If there is any possibility that Terramesh is still alive and waiting for them, our troops will be more than reluctant to go back across the river. A nice clean skull, or even a filthy one, will convince them that Terramesh will not be there on the west bank to greet them."

I glanced at Rameses and he grinned back at me. "In the short time I have been married I have learned not to waste my breath by arguing with either my wife or my father-in-law."

The following morning the entire armies of Rameses I of Egypt, King Hurotas of Sparta and Lacedaemon, and the fourteen remaining petty kings who paid him homage assembled in the dawn, but well back from the river and out of sight of the lookouts on the walls of the fortress of Abu Naskos. The mood of our troops was subdued. Later I heard that a malicious rumor had been circulating through the camp since the three of us had returned the previous evening from our expedition across the Nile. In essence this was that the campaign against Utteric Turo and his new and formidable warrior, Terramesh, was to be abandoned and that Hurotas and his allies were about to quit the field and scurry back to Sparta, taking Rameses and his bride with them.

King Hurotas and Pharaoh Rameses took the reviewing stand and stood shoulder to shoulder facing the serried ranks, but there was no cheering or beating of the war shields with drawn blades.

After a solemn pause Hurotas made an imperative gesture and two slaves followed them up onto the stand. Between them they carried a large wicker basket, which they placed on the front of the stand. Then they backed away, making obeisance so deep that their foreheads touched the planking between their feet. After another pause Hurotas began to speak.

"Two days ago Pharaoh Rameses and his wife, Pharaohin Serrena Cleopatra, accompanied by Lord Taita, crossed the Nile River surreptitiously and entered rebel-held territory. They went in search of the vile creature known to all of us as the scar-faced archer."

A low, involuntary groan echoed from the massed ranks. Hurotas waved his hand to quiet them and went on speaking.

"This archer is also known as Terramesh the Indestructible. I had commanded our three intrepid heroes to hunt him down and kill him like the mad dog he is, and then to return with his severed head, but making sure to conceal it until they were able to place the head in my hands." By this time Hurotas had captured the attention of the vast majority of the men assembled before him. Their mood had lightened. Even I who had been a participant was fascinated by Hurotas' skilled manipulation of the facts. With a flourish Hurotas pointed at the wicker basket that stood before him, and every eye in the dense mass of charioteers and archers followed the gesture. Hurotas stepped forward and threw open the lid of the basket, then reached into it and brought forth a human head, which he held aloft for all to see.

Slivers of rotting skin and flesh still clung to the bone and the mouth lolled open with the swollen blue tongue hanging out of one corner. The eye sockets were empty gaping holes.

"I give to you the head of Terramesh!" he bellowed. No man in the array could doubt his word for even a fleeting second, for buckled onto the skull was the golden helmet that they all knew so well and feared so profoundly. A shout of joy and triumph went up from eight thousand throats.

"Terramesh! Terramesh! Terramesh!" As one man they drew their swords and beat upon their shields in time to the thunder of their voices.

Hurotas let them shout themselves hoarse, and then he unbuckled the helmet from the skull and held the helmet aloft.

"This trophy goes to the regiment that most distinguishes itself in the battle that lies ahead." They roared again like lions. Then in his other hand he lifted the mutilated human head with sightless eye sockets and lolling tongue. "And this trophy goes to Hades the

King of the Underworld. It will be conveyed to him by Hephaestus, the god of fire.

He marched with the head to the watch fire and threw it into the flames and we all watched with fascination while it burned to ashes. It was a decision befitting a king, I thought. No one could ever question the authenticity of the skull, for it no longer existed.

The army spent the rest of that day restringing their bows, sharpening their swords, repairing their shields and armor, and resting. Then when night fell we waited for the waxing gibbous moon to set before they fell into their regiments and marched down to the bank of the river and boarded their vessels. They showed no lights and all commands were given by the officers in whispers. The troop ships dispersed and made their separate ways upstream and down to their landing positions on the enemy bank, which had been carefully selected over the previous days and weeks.

We had hoped to take the enemy sentries off guard, and in that we were not disappointed. Utteric and his men had believed themselves secure under the protection of Terramesh. It transpired that Utteric had paid him the vast fortune of ten lakhs of silver for his protection. However, at this stage Utteric was totally unaware of the one-eyed monster's very recent demise. As a consequence half his army was billeted outside the walls of the fortress of Abu Naskos where they were employed in farming grain and vegetables, and raising goats and cattle to feed themselves and their companions during the remainder of the campaign.

We came ashore after midnight and launched our attack on them. Most of them were asleep and their sentries with them, convinced as they were that they had the protection of Terramesh. When we woke them with our war cries, they made very little effort to stand and fight but ran for the shelter of the fortress walls in pandemonium and panic. More than half of them made it. The remainder of them were cut down or taken as our prisoners.

Understandably, our men had been a little timid in their pursuit. Despite Hurotas' exhibition of the severed head and their demonstration of bravery the previous day, most of them had been half expecting Terramesh to reappear.

Nevertheless, we managed to capture over a hundred of Utteric's men. Two of them I recognized. They were good men who had been caught on the wrong side of the fence. When I took them aside for questioning, they reminded me that their names were Batur and Nasla. They were brothers who had fought under me against the Hyksos. When I opened a flagon of wine and poured each of them a mugful, they remembered what good friends we really were. And with each mugful they downed they became more accommodating.

I questioned them minutely on the conditions existing inside the fortress of Abu Naskos and they replied readily. They told me that Utteric's fortress was formidably secure against attack. There was only one entrance and that was through the massive double gates set into the walls on the opposite side to the River Nile. I asked them about scaling the walls and they replied that there were three sets of walls one within the other, and all of them were formidable in design and construction. They suggested that probably the most successful form of assault would be by tunneling under the foundations. Then I inquired if they knew of any existing subterranean works beneath the fortress, but they were adamant that there were none. It did not sound very promising, and I smiled ruefully as I realized that Utteric had chosen the easiest fortress in the whole of Egypt to defend.

Batur and Nasla then went on to inform me that

Utteric had sent most of his horses and chariots away, probably to his forts in the delta where it would be difficult for us to follow and find them. However, he had retained about forty chariots and horses, which he kept in the stables of the fortress, probably to be employed in forays against us; but even more likely they were to be used in escaping from Abu Naskos if the necessity ever arose.

I then discussed the enigma of Utteric's identity with them and they agreed with me that he was using impersonators to confuse his enemies, which of course meant Hurotas and Rameses. However, Batur and Nasla had both worked closely with Utteric and they claimed that they were able to differentiate between him and his impostors. This was a very valuable skill for us to have access to. Then they told me that with each passing day Utteric was becoming stranger and further divorced from reality, and that his fantasies were taking over reality in his mind. This came as no great surprise to me. His mind had always been unhinged.

The brothers also told me that they had lived for the past two years in the fortress of Abu Naskos and had learned most of the secret entrances and exits and the other complexities of that vast structure. When I wanted to know how the two of them had become embroiled in Utteric's web, they explained that as young men they had enlisted in the service of Pharaoh Tamose. When he was killed by the Hyksos, his eldest son, Utteric, had inherited the Hedjet Crown of Pharaoh. However, the brothers had swiftly been disenchanted by Utteric. They assured me that it was their dearest desire to defect to the standard of Pharaoh Rameses whom they both knew and admired.

I presented the two of them to Rameses and he recognized them. He told me he had a high regard for them. He agreed with me that we should employ them as secret agents and they might be used eventually to help us gain access to the fortress—in whatever way was feasible. Batur was the older brother and he agreed to return to Abu Naskos with the alibi that he had been captured by Hurotas' men but had managed to escape and work his way back through our lines to reach the gates of Abu Naskos. The younger brother was Nasla. He would stay with us outside the walls to inform and advise us on matters related to the fortress and the monster within. The two brothers had developed an intricate code of signals with which they were able to correspond clandestinely and at a distance.

I was confident that they would prove themselves to be extremely useful.

The next few weeks were occupied by the laborious business of moving our forces across the river and closing in on the fortress to begin our preparations for the final assault on Utteric's stronghold. When finally this began it soon fell into the familiar pattern of three steps advance and then two steps retreat, rather in the convoluted manner of a formal dance. Our engineers drove the trenches and tunnels toward the walls of the fortress, starting from a safe distance to avoid the arrows from the enemy archers on the tops of the walls. Then, once we were approaching the foot of the walls, Utteric's men sallied forth during the night and attempted to destroy our trenchworks. This led to bitter fighting in virtually complete darkness in which it was almost impossible to tell friend from foe.

Then the following morning we would assess the damage and begin once again the whole dreary process of repairing our earthworks and then driving them forward toward the seemingly impregnable walls. It was not a pastime that particularly appealed to me, and I left it to others with more patience and experience at breaching the walls of a citadel: men such as Hurotas and Rameses.

My thoughts returned rather to the four mysterious islands in the Nile and my pleasant and more fruitful interaction with the goddess Inana, who was so often there to greet me. I had made the most out of the three islands on the east side of the channel, and only the fourth island closest to the fortress of Abu Naskos still awaited my attention. This island lay within a long arrow shot of the tops of the fortress walls so I was compelled to approach it from the east bank where Hurotas' main camp had originally stood. However, this was an inordinately long swim even for me and the days and nights were becoming colder; so I was reduced to rowing across in the skiff during the hours of darkness when I would not make such an obvious and tempting target.

The first night I attempted this there was a gibbous

moon, which threw a good light but not good enough to make me and my skiff visible from the walls of Ut- teric's fortress. As I approached the island from the side farthest from the fortress I was struck by how closely it resembled the first three. Any lingering doubts I had about the interrelationship of all four islands were thus dispelled. When I reached it I moored my skiff to a liana that hung down from the top of the man-made wall almost to the surface of the river. The first thing that was apparent to me was that the stonework of this island was in much better state of repair than any of the other three. I was able to identify the individual blocks of stone. There were even footholds remaining in the wall that made the climb to the summit much easier. I scaled it swiftly, buoyed up by excitement, and when I reached the top I found the entrance to the vertical shaft exactly where I expected to find it in the center of the tower. However, the night was so dark that I was unable to see more than a very short way down the shaft.

I knew that I had to light one of the candles I had brought with me. These were a very recent innovation of mine to replace the common torches of reeds or grass. I had made them from beeswax, which was a superior innovation, but the clear light they threw was visible from a great distance. I decided to take the chance that it might be seen from the tops of the fortress walls. I climbed a short way down the shaft as I deemed it to be safe. Then some swift work with the fire sticks and I had a glow of wood dust that burst into flames when I applied the wick of my candle to it.

My eyes adjusted almost instantaneously to the bright clear light, and then I looked around and immediately gasped in awe. The entrance to the tunnel in which I was sitting was completely tiled with ceramic bricks in a pale green color, each one decorated around the margin with tiny images of a prick-eared desert fox.

However, unlike the first three tunnels, the walls of this one were in a remarkable state of repair. More than a quarter of the ceramic friezes had survived the ages, and the stairs beneath my feet were only slightly dished by the passage of the feet of the ancient people who had used them.

The shaft was blocked in two or three places by fallen stonework and other rubbish, but I was able to clear a way through these with my bare hands. The staircase descended into the center of the island at a steep angle. I counted the steps as I made my way down. I reached 150 and then I realized with a sudden shock that I must have descended far below the surface of the river.

I was in peril of death by drowning. At any moment a torrent of water might come rushing up the tunnel to sweep me into eternity. I turned and hurried back up the staircase, and as I went I chanted my prayers to all the gods, but more especially to Inana, to spare me from a dreadful death all alone in the depths of the earth.

I reached the entrance to the tunnel still breathing forcefully and with only my sandaled feet wet, but the rest of my body from the ankles upward dry as the dunes of the desert. I sat on the top steps of the tunnel and considered this remarkable turn of affairs. I was faced with the fact that I had made a miscalculation, which was unusual for me; it now seemed possible that not every tunnel or space beneath the surface of a river must be inundated by water.

In fairness to myself this tunnel was the first one in existence that I had ever heard about that ran beneath a river, especially such a mighty one as the Nile. I had never even remotely considered such a possibility. However, I had no option now but to review my conclusions. From this standpoint it was only a matter of minutes before I had seen the flaw in my previous reasoning.

Why does the hull of a boat not fill with water? The answer is because there is no aperture for the water to enter by. Yet if you pierce a hole in the hull it fills immediately! Like the flatness of this earth on which we stand, it all began to make sense.

I admit that I shied away from the conundrum of the vast differences in volume between the hull of a boat and a tunnel under the Nile River.

I waited impatiently for Inana to make her appearance so that I could discuss this proposition with her and hear her advice, but she was clearly in one of her contrary feminine moods and by now the dawn was breaking so I had to make my departure before I was spotted by the sentinels on the walls of the fortress.

I spent most of the following day in a frenzy of impatience waiting for nightfall. However, I had the good sense to employ part of the time searching out an assistant to work under me in my further endeavors. Nasla was my choice. Not only was he young and strong, but his knowledge of the layout of the Abu Naskos fortress was more extensive than anyone in either army. He was intrigued to hear what I had already discovered about the island and the underwater tunnel, and he was eager to accompany me.

We set off in my skiff across the river at twilight. Once we had moored at the foot of the tower and climbed to the top he exclaimed in astonishment at the entrance to the shaft and demanded excitedly, "To where does it lead, my lord?"

"I don't know yet, but we are going to find out."

"I will go first if you so wish," he offered. I shrugged

nonchalantly and stood aside for him. Not that I was in any way fearful of the consequences. I waited until his voice echoed cheerfully up the shaft, and I saw the reflection of his candle flame far below me.

"I am at the bottom, Lord Taita. Do you wish to follow me down?" he shouted up to me. It did not sound as if he was drowning, and I was pleased that my hypothesis was so far holding water, in both the literal and figurative senses. I started down to where Nasla was waiting for me at the bottom. Here the vertical shaft leveled out and became a horizontal tunnel.

"Have you explored it farther?" I demanded.

"No, my lord. I was waiting for you to take that honor."

I looked at him sharply, uncertain if he was being sarcastic; but even in the light of the candles his expression was without cynicism. "Follow me then, good Nasla." The more I saw of him, the more I liked and trusted him. I led him along the tunnel, considering the likelihood that we were the first persons who had passed this way in many centuries. To withstand the pressure of the water above us the construction of the walls had to be much more robust than elsewhere. The materials the ancients had utilized were baked red clay bricks, not the pretty ceramic tiles used nearer the surface. The joints between the bricks were so fine as to be almost invisible. I inspected them closely and found no leaks.

I then studied the horizontal tunnel in which we stood, and compared its relationship to the shaft down which we had descended from the surface. As I had expected, the tunnel seemed to run in the direction of the west bank and the fortress of Abu Naskos. However, I had no magic fish to check this assumption.

"Come along, Nasla," I ordered him and we set off along the tunnel. It ran almost dead straight for 310 paces, which I counted aloud as I paced it out. The tiles beneath our feet were dry. The air in the tunnel was cold and ancient in taste and stuffy to breathe, but sufficient to sustain life.

Then the floor of the tunnel angled upward abruptly under our feet. Nasla looked at me inquiringly over the top of his candle flame, and I explained what was taking place: "We have passed beneath the river and reached the western bank. Now we are climbing. I expect we are heading for the foundations of the fortress. Of course that is only a guess, but look at the walls now."

The walls of this part of the tunnel were once again decorated with colorful ceramic tiles, indicating that the Nile water above us was shallower or even nonexistent. There were no images printed upon the tiled walls, but they were covered with some type of flowing archaic script. I realized that these must be the inscriptions of the ancient builders. Probably they were memorials to their own genius and skill. I wasted no time in attempting to decipher them but hurried forward, anxious to learn where the tunnel came to the surface. One hundred and fifty paces farther along the ascending tunnel we were brought abruptly to a halt. It seemed that the roof had collapsed in a solid rockfall. We could go no farther. My disappointment was so intense that I had to express it in some unequivocal manner. I shouted an obscenity and drew back my fist to punch the solid wall of broken rock that confronted me.

Nasla seized my elbow from behind and prevented me breaking all the bones in my right hand. I struggled with him briefly and then I capitulated gracefully.

"Thank you," I told him. "I am grateful to you. You prevented me from doing further damage to the wall."

"That's all right, my lord. I am accustomed to it. My brother, Batur, also has an extremely foul temper." He said it in such a friendly and pleasant tone that I was forced to press my forehead against the wall and close my eyes for few seconds to control my burgeoning rage.

Then I said in a tight whisper, "I think you had better say no more, good Nasla. But take me back the way we came. I need some fresh air. Otherwise one of us might die down here."

Let no one tell you that I am unable to control my temper. By the next morning I was almost completely recovered and I realized that it was only a temporary setback. I decided that I would need the benefit of Rameses' good sense and judgment. I found him on the west bank of the river assisting Hurotas with the sapping works before the walls of Utteric's fortress. I was delighted to find that Queen Serrena Cleopatra was by his side as I had hoped and expected she would be.

She acted as my guide and led me on an extended tour of the siege works. I was amazed at the knowledge she displayed of the technique involved. By then it was time for the midday meal. We ate it together seated under the branches of a spreading elm tree from where we had a grand view over Utteric's fortress and the field of battle. In the background lay the river and the four islands that had so much occupied me. At this distance they appeared to be insignificant, but they served to get our conversation going in the right direction. Rameses and Serrena were not aware of my preoccupation with the islands. I had a conflict of interest between them and Inana. They had no idea of my special relationship with the goddess, so I had to gloss over that part of my story and attribute all my knowledge to the old ship's pilot Ganord who had given me the first ceramic tile from the tunnels and shafts beneath the islands.

At first the royal couple were only vaguely interested when I pointed out the four islands, but then I deployed my full skills as a raconteur and both of them rapidly became completely captivated by the mystery of them. When I neared the high point of my story, Serrena wriggled around on her buttocks, barely able to contain her eagerness to reach the denouement, and even Rameses' eyes glowed with anticipation. When I finally reached the point in my recital where my quest was cut short by the rockfall, neither of them would at first accept that was how it ended.

"What happened then, Tata? What did you do then?" Serrena demanded.

"Yes, Tata. Tell us what you found beyond the rock jam," Rameses joined in. "Or is all this make-believe? Are you just having a bit of fun with us?"

When they finally accepted that it was a true account of what I had discovered, they both wanted me to take them immediately to the island and its tunnel. I had some difficulty convincing them that it was only expedient to wait for darkness before we set off. We passed the time by discussing the underwater tunnel that stretched from the fourth island to the foundations of the fortress of Abu Naskos.

"When you come to think of it, it was a rather fruitless and unproductive work by the ancients," Rameses suggested.

Serrena turned on him immediately. "What do you mean, my darling husband? It was a magnificent undertaking!"

"Magnificent?" Rameses chuckled. "To build a tunnel from a man-made island in the middle of a mighty river to an underground destination? I would describe it as asinine in the extreme."

"You have missed the point entirely," she retorted. "The tunnel began on the east bank of the river where our original camp was situated. It passed below the surface of the Nile to all four of the man-made islands in succession—Fish, Bird, Otter and Fox—before it entered the foundations of the fortress that preceded Abu Naskos."

"Why?" Rameses demanded. "Why did they build four islands?"

"Because the Nile is too wide for less than that. The air in a single tunnel would become stale and poisonous. They had to let the tunnel breathe."

Rameses looked abashed. "What happened to the tunnel between the first three islands?"

"Once the Old People went away it collapsed with age and neglect," Serrena explained sweetly.

"Oh!" he said. "I see!" And so did I. I was pleased that I had not become embroiled in the discussion and been left as speechless as Rameses.

Six of us made the crossing to Fox Island. Apart from the three of us I had decided to forgive Nasla his recent indiscretions and take advantage of his knowledge of the layout of the fortress and the islands. In addition we needed two ordinary sailors to guard the boat while we went ashore.

We arrived at Fox Island two hours after dark and we went ashore immediately. Nasla had covered the entrance to the shaft with dead branches and other rubbish and this had not been disturbed during our absence. Now Nasla cleared this away and I led the rest of the party down the shaft, stopping only for Rameses and Serrena to examine the ceramic tiles and the images of desert foxes, which delighted Serrena particularly.

When we reached the bottom of the shaft and crowded into the tunnel, I explained to the couple that we were now beneath the river. Serrena looked up at the roof so close above her head with a solemn expression on her face and then edged closer to Rameses and took his hand for reassurance. As I led them on along the tunnel I told them that this was 310 paces long, almost the same as the width of the river above us. Then when the floor of the tunnel inclined upward, I explained the reason for this: "We have now reached the west bank and we are rising up toward the shore."

Rameses smiled and Serrena recovered her voice and pointed out the flowing archaic script that covered the walls from this point onward. Then to my astonishment she began to translate it fluently into the Egyptian language.

"Be it known to all peoples of this world that I, Zararand, King of Senquat and Mentania, hereby dedicate these works to the eternal glory of Ahura Mazda, the god of goodness and light . . ."

Before I could prevent myself I blurted out, "What language is that, Serrena, and where did you learn to read and speak it?"

Serrena broke off in confusion and glanced at Rameses. "I do not remember exactly." She was suddenly hesitant. "I have had so many different tutors over the years."

I was immediately vexed with myself. I had asked the question in haste. I should have realized it was part of her inherent memory as a divine, a residual echo from her previous existences that even she was unable to place accurately.

"Probably your husband taught you." I made a joke of it and Rameses looked at me aghast. I winked at him and he grinned with relief and then burst out laughing.

"I must plead guilty, Tata. Of course I taught her." He grinned. "I have taught her everything she knows." Serrena punched his shoulder and we all laughed. The awkward moment passed and I led them on along the tunnel, until abruptly we were confronted by the rock-fall that blocked our way.

I turned back to the three of them and spread my hands in a gesture of resignation. "This is far as it goes!"

"What has happened here?" Serrena demanded.

"The roof of the tunnel has collapsed in a rock jam," I explained. "We can go no farther than this. It seems that everything beyond this point remains a mystery forever."

"But can we not simply clear the fallen rocks away, just as the original miners must have done?" Serrena wanted to know. Her bitter disappointment was elo-quently expressed in the tone of her voice.

"It's a rockfall," I repeated. "There is no solid roof above it. It's a death trap. If you go in there and try to clear it, it will collapse on you again . . ."

Rameses brushed past me and went to kneel in front of the rockfall. He ran his hands over the intruded face, beginning at floor level and working his way to the top of the wall, standing on his tiptoes to reach that high. He worried a fragment of raw rock loose from the wall; then he thrust his hand into the aperture that it had left and groped upward. Finally he pulled his hand and forearm free from the wall and turned back to me, holding the fragment in his other hand and proffering it to me.

"No, Tata, for once in your life, you are wrong," he told me. "That is not a rockfall. It's a rock filling. Look at the chisel marks in this chunk! I felt the roof above where I pulled it out. It is solid and unbroken. It was worked by man! It is wall of packed rock and not a fall of rock."

I pushed past him without replying and went to the rockfall, deliberately referring to it in my own mind as such. I am taller than Rameses, so I did not have to stand on tiptoe to reach into the aperture that he had left. This time I did not hurry my examination. With an effort I removed two more pieces of rock from the top of the rockfall and examined them minutely. Indisputably they also had been marked by man-made tools. I then thrust my arm into the empty space in the wall that I had opened and felt for any joint in the rock roof above that point. There was none. It was solid. The tunnel had not been blocked by a rockfall; it had been deliberately sealed by men.

I turned back to face Rameses and steeled myself. "You are right. I was wrong." Such simple words; so difficult to say.

Rameses understood. He reached out and placed one arm around my shoulders and squeezed. "It seems that you and I have some more work to do," he said simply. He understood my foibles and tactfully made allowances for them. In that moment I loved him as much as one man can love another.

We estimated that there was space in the tunnel for no more than twenty men to work at one time. However, we had absolutely no idea how long it would take us to clear the obstruction. We decided that to begin with we could have our workforce carry the loose rock back from the face and stack it along one wall of the tunnel. If this proved to be insufficient space, then we would have to carry it up the shaft to Fox Island and dump it into the river.

There were other small problems to consider. We did not know how deep below ground level we would be working, and how clearly the noise of our labors would be transmitted to the fortress above us. Nor did we have any idea how long it would take, and how twenty men and more could live, work and sleep in such a confined space for an indefinite period.

"You will think of a way," Serrena told me blithely. "You always do, Tata."

After sixteen days even I was reaching the limits of my ingenuity and endurance. We discovered soon enough that the ancients had gone to great lengths to make a formidable project an almost impossible one. They had used a malleable substance similar to clay to bind the large rocks together; this had dried and hardened to a consistency that exceeded the rocks themselves in strength. These had to be broken into manageable pieces to be manhandled out of the rock pack. The noise of the flint-headed hammers was so deafening that the men had to plug their ears with cloth. These barriers had been alternated with an ingenious combination of pitfalls and rockfalls. Eight of our workmen were killed by these devices, and several others were badly injured. Then abruptly, without prior warning, we found ourselves out of the tunnel and into a warren of small storerooms and passageways.

We searched this area eagerly but found that there was no ingress or egress from it. It had been sealed off entirely. I called for Nasla as the acknowledged expert on the structure and layout of the fortress of Abu Naskos, which Rameses and I were convinced stood above this complex of dungeons. He was reluctant to give us advice without first consulting his elder brother. We agreed with him that this was a sensible course of action and sent him back to join Hurotas' troops, who were still laying siege to the fortress. At the same time we dismissed most of our workmen, who had rendered such sterling service in breaching the many obstacles to reach our present position. We kept only five of them, who had proven themselves to be the most sensible and hardworking.

Rameses, Serrena and I moved back up the tunnel to Fox Island and set up a temporary camp there while we waited for Nasla to return from his contact with Batur. It took three more days for this to happen. Nasla had experienced difficulties in contacting his brother, but finally he had succeeded handsomely and the two of them had exchanged long coded messages over the walls of the fortress.

The most important of these was that Batur had heard our efforts to break through the final barrier into the ancient storerooms beneath the fortress. He had been thoroughly alarmed by these noises. However, Rameses and I had restricted the loudest and most noisy work to the hours after midnight when Utteric's troops were asleep or at their posts on the battlements high above ground level. There had been no general alarm caused by the sounds of our subterranean labors, muted as they were by the intervening storerooms and stone walls.

The second-most-important news was that the two brothers had arranged means to guide us to the point where we would be able make direct contact with Batur. It had become apparent that the maze of small rooms and passageways in which we had reached a dead end were part of the original creation of the ancient ruler, Zararand, King of Senquat, who had left his details inscribed on the walls of the tunnel.

Centuries later, when the ancient Senquatian kingdom had either fled this very Egypt, or had been defeated and annihilated in battle, the fortress had been taken over by the Hyksos rulers. They were the ones who had built the present fortress over the ancient ruins. It was the Hyksos who had covered in and sealed off the original foundations and subterranean storerooms in which Rameses and I now found ourselves trapped. It became apparent to us that Utteric had no idea of what lay beneath his fortress of Abu Naskos.

Having learned this, Rameses and I were eager to move back into the subterranean complex where Nasla could guide us to make contact with his brother, Batur. It would then be up to Rameses and I to make the most of the element of surprise and rush out from Utteric's own basement in force to fall upon him and send him and his minions to the perdition they all so richly deserved. This course of action would have to be coordinated closely with King Hurotas' forces that were surrounding the fortress above ground level.

However, Rameses' and my first priority was to burrow our way through from the ancient storerooms beneath the false floor into the building above occupied by Utteric and his troops. At the midnight hour agreed with Batur we returned with Nasla and our five workmen along the tunnel under the Nile and into the sealed-off basement. We all spread out through the abandoned storerooms and passageways. I made the men extinguish their candles as there was no need to waste them. Then we settled down to wait in strict silence. The darkness was complete and the silence eerie. Even I was soon disoriented by this and I wondered how the men were faring. I considered shouting to them to give them comfort, but I thought better of it. They might have queried my own fortitude.

I lost all sense of time, but finally the abysmal silence was broken by the intermittent and barely audible sound of metal being tapped by metal somewhere above our heads. This was followed by a chorus of relieved cries and the flare of candles being relit by our waiting men. For the next hour or so we tracked the sounds down to their origin.

This was where Batur on the floor above us had inserted a metal rod into a predrilled aperture part of the way through the roof and was beating on it with a smaller rod. At this point we drilled with an auger a small hole completely up through the roof. This was a tedious and exhausting job, for the roof slab was four cubits thick. Finally Nasla applied his ear to the aperture and recognized his brother's voice whispering down it from the top end.

It remained only to enlarge this minute aperture to the size sufficient to allow a grown man in full armor and carrying all his weapons to pass through it unhampered. This took almost three days, but finally it was completed and Rameses and I, guided by Nasla, crawled up through it into the fortress of Abu Naskos proper. Here the elder brother, Batur, was waiting to greet us. The two brothers then conducted us on a tour of the lowest portions of the fortress, which were used mostly for storage and were therefore only sparsely inhabited. Batur and Nasla were well known to the few of Utteric's troops that we met, and all of us were conversant with their passwords so we raised no suspicions.

The brothers pointed out to us the passages that led up into the main fortifications of the fortress. We then returned the way we had come. Batur remained behind to conceal the opening to the freshly excavated shaft, using for this purpose a pile of sacks containing dried barley, which fortuitously were stacked in the adjoining rooms of the cellars.

Our next task was to move almost three hundred men from Hurotas' old camp on the east bank to the four ancient man-made islands where they would be comfortable but from where they could be deployed swiftly into the underwater tunnel that led into the foundations of Utteric's stronghold.

While this was happening Rameses and I assembled all the officers of rank and lectured them on the layout of the interior of the fortress and its battlements, so that when they led their men through the shaft into the vaults they would have a sense of their exact position within the massive building and be able to find their way to their battle stations. We tried to ensure that attached to each of our military detachments there was at least one man who had seen Utteric previously and would be able to recognize him if and when he saw him again. We were well aware of Utteric's slippery reputation of using many impostors and doubles to confuse his enemies.

We then rehearsed and drilled our waiting companies on transferring expeditiously from their temporary billets on the four islands to Fox Island, there to descend the shaft into the underwater tunnel to the west bank and finally to make their way through the vaults up into the main body of the fortress, mostly in utter darkness. During this transfer the men were roped together in groups of twelve, each group led by a reliable sergeant who was the only one to carry a lighted torch.

All these preparations went smoothly, but Rameses was left with one seemingly insoluble problem. This was how to persuade Queen Serrena Cleopatra not to join our nocturnal assault under the Nile, but to remain with her father aboveground, where she would be relatively safe.

"You don't understand, Tata," Rameses assured me. "If she thinks it is because she is a woman and has to be taken care of by a man, then she will just refuse to cooperate."

"I do understand, Rameses," I corrected his reasoning. "I knew your wife's mother and her grandmother before her. All of them had one thing in common. They give orders glibly but never accept them graciously. You will just have to explain it to her slightly differently. Which is that you need her to assist the senile old man who just happens to be her father to recognize

Utteric should they encounter him when they storm the walls of Abu Naskos together. Hurotas has never laid eyes upon him, whereas Serrena probably knows Utteric better than anyone else alive. Even if his face is masked, she can recognize him by his hands."

The next evening Rameses returned to Fox Island from his visit to Hurotas' camp where he had attended a final briefing by the king himself. Rameses had a flagon of excellent Spartan wine under his cloak and he grinned as he poured me a brimming cup. "Drink up, Tata. We must drown our sorrows."

"Tragic news?" I asked.

"It couldn't be better." And then he clasped his brow. "Forgive me for that slip of the tongue; of course I meant couldn't be worse. My darling wife will not be beside me in the front rank of the coming battle. I will be able to concentrate all my energy on reaching the gates of the fortress and keeping them open until we can march in in force. Serrena will be in her father's care, guiding him to find Utteric in the turmoil and the fighting. We can be certain that Hurotas will not allow his one and only daughter to get herself into trouble."

It had been a monumental enterprise made even more difficult by the dual nature of our offensive, but finally everything was in place for the assault on Abu Naskos. The royal lovers had spent the previous night together in the old camp on the east bank of the river, but in the dawn they parted. Serrena crossed the Nile to be with her father, King Hurotas, in the trenches before the fortress, and Rameses joined me in the crowded tunnel beneath the river.

Then as night fell we moved forward and finally took up our positions at the foot of the stairway that led into the basement of the fortress of Abu Naskos. The signal to begin the assault was the rise of the new moon.

This was all very well for Hurotas and the others who had a fine view of the nocturnal sky from where they were. However, Rameses and I had at least fifty cubits of rock over our heads. We had to rely on the lookouts on Fox Island to pass the message along the file of men in the tunnel beneath the Nile to where Rameses and I squatted at the head of the line.

The moon message came at last and Rameses and I stood up and began the climb to the top of the ladder where Batur and Nasla waited. The men that followed us were roped together in small gangs to keep them from losing contact with each other in the utter darkness. Only the leader of each gang carried a lighted candle.

Rameses had five of these gangs under his command. His objective was the main gate to the fortress. He and his men had to seize it, throw it open and hold it until Hurotas and Hui could race forward from their trenches at the head of the main force and consolidate the breach.

I had two of these gangs of twelve men under my personal command. I had handpicked these men, which meant that there were none better. Nasla would guide us to the top story of the fortress where Utteric's private quarters were situated. It was our main objective to capture him alive so we could be certain we had the right man. But if we encountered the slightest difficulty, it was agreed by all that he should be killed out of hand. According to Batur, Utteric had been positively identified entering his quarters only two days previously, and no one had seen him leaving the top level of the fortress since then.

From ground level the fortress stood eight stories high and each story was ten cubits tall so the climb we were faced with was about eighty cubits. There were lighted lanterns burning at intervals along the walls of the passageway, but these cast only a feeble light, so I gave the order for every man to light his torch. There was now sufficient light for me to lead them at a run even though the stairs beneath our feet were narrow and steep.

I had carefully considered our choice of arms and had finally restricted it to edged weapons: swords and long knives. Bows and arrows were too cumbersome and difficult to draw and aim in these confined spaces. We climbed the stairway with naked blades in our hands, not to be taken by surprise at the sudden appearance of an adversary. Just as we reached the sixth level of the fortress the silence was broken on the floors below us by a wild cacophony of shouts of anger and outrage, together with screams of pain and the clash of metal on metal.

"Rameses' men are engaged!" Nasla grunted close behind me.

"Keep going!" I retorted. "He has two hundred men and more to help him reach the gates."

We turned the next bend in the stairs and ran headlong into a small party of the enemy descending as fast as we were climbing. They had obviously been alerted by the sounds of battle on the lower floors but had not expected to encounter us so soon. Their sidearms were still in the sheaths. I killed the first one simply by lifting my blade until the point was lined up with his Adam's apple. When he ran onto it I felt the jar as the point parted his vertebrae, and the warm spurt of his blood over my wrist as his jugular erupted. I let his corpse slide off my blade, and now my point was perfectly aligned with the diaphragm of the man who followed him closely. This one had obviously dressed in haste, for his breastplate was unbuckled and his chest was partially exposed. My thrust buried my blade to the hilt. When he dropped I had to put my foot on his throat to stop him struggling. Then I twisted my sword to enlarge the wound and allow the blade to come away readily. By this time Nasla and the others had dealt with the remainder of the enemy. I jumped over the bodies and raced on up the stairs. Finally we came out on the top level of the building.

"Which way now?" I demanded of Nasla.

"Straight on! The first door!" He pointed with his chin. We charged it together and it burst open at our rush. There was the figure of a man at the window across the room. Obviously he had heard us coming. He turned back to confront us. He was dressed in full armor. His breastplate was of polished metal plate that might have been gold. The visor of his helmet was closed and his eyes gleamed through the slits. His sheathed sword hung at his right hip. Only his hands were bare. They were smooth and pale. Free of wrinkles and calluses, like those of a lovely young woman. When I saw them, I knew exactly who he was.

"Utteric, your time of glory has come. We are here to put your immortality to the test," I told him. He reached for the hilt of his sword and took a step toward us, but at that moment our men came pouring through the doorway behind us. Utteric hesitated no longer. He whirled away and placed one hand on the windowsill. Then he leaped high, threw his booted feet over the sill and dropped from our sight.

I felt a moment of seething anger, mixed with bitter disappointment at being cheated of my revenge yet again. I heard myself snarl like a predator deprived of its prey. This was the top floor of the castle. Neither man nor beast could survive a fall of that height.

I raced across the room to the window and leaned far out, staring down in trepidation, dreading to see Utteric's corpse sprawled in death on the earth far below.

However, the scene that met my gaze was far different from that which I had imagined. It was almost as brightly lit as daylight. Hundreds, nay, thousands of burning torches surrounded the walls as the mighty army of Hurotas surged forward toward the castle gates. These stood wide open where Rameses and his men had done their duty. If Utteric's broken body lay among them it was lost from my sight in the masses and the pandemonium.

In desperation I thrust the upper half of my body perilously farther out through the window frame. Now that the field of my vision was extended I saw that no more than two stories directly beneath me was a narrow terrace on which sprawled the armored body of the man with the feminine hands. As I watched he pushed himself into a sitting position and looked up at me through the eye slits in his helmet.

"I see you, Utteric," I called down to him. "And I am coming for you." At which he scrambled to his feet and looked around wildly, obviously seeking an escape route. I saw from the way he moved that he had damaged one of his legs in the fall. I jumped up on the windowsill, paused there for an instant and then I sprang out over him. I had hoped to land on top of him and knock him down again for all time. However, he was quicker than I had anticipated. He managed to dodge aside, and I hit the spot on which he had been standing. I landed awkwardly and the sword I had been clutching spun from my grip and clattered on the slabs just beyond my reach.

On my hands and knees I went for it, but from the corner of my eye I saw that Utteric had cleared his own sword from its scabbard and was hobbling grimly after me. I threw myself forward and just managed to reach my weapon. As my hand closed over the hilt I rolled swiftly. By this time Utteric was standing over me with legs spread wide and his own sword held in both hands above his head, poised to stab down into my chest.

Traditionally all of us Egyptians have an aperture in the crotch of our armor between the thighs, which the armorers have conveniently allowed for us to piss through. Lying on my back I could see that Utteric was no exception. I aimed a kick with my armored heel into this unprotected area and felt it land solidly.

Utteric had just begun to stab down at my chest; my kick landed while he was committed and unable to avoid it. The sudden excruciating pain threw him completely off balance and destroyed his aim. He missed my heart area with the point of his sword but drove it into the joint of my left shoulder. Then he staggered away, clutching his injured genitalia in one hand and screaming like a baby. But in a reflexive reaction he had pulled the blade of his sword out of my wound and was waving it in his other hand.

I sat up and fumbled around until I recovered my sword; then I pushed myself to my feet and turned to face Utteric. The terrace was narrow and I was standing between him and the door to the interior of the fortress. He darted a quick look over the balcony but it was a very long way down. I saw him steel himself and then turn to face me with one hand still held between his legs, nursing his crotch, and the other hefting his sword. He knew he had to fight me, and he knew it was to the death.

I had recovered swiftly from the trauma of my fall and my sword felt lithe and light in my right hand. I went after Utteric with a series of interlinked thrusts leading with my right foot and keeping him turning into his damaged leg, which he was favoring. I listened to his breathing and heard it becoming labored and hoarse. It was not only from the pain of his injury but also because he was out of condition.

I remembered the relish he had displayed when he gave Minister Irus such a painful and lingering death in the amphitheater of Luxor by lopping off both his arms and then dragging him behind his chariot until his brains were dashed out on the hard earth. I considered dealing out the same kind of brutal death to Utteric now, but then my essential humanity reasserted itself.

Abruptly I switched my angle of attack, forcing him to turn into my sword hand. He stumbled slightly as he made the change and he dropped his guard fractionally as I knew he must. My riposte was like a stroke of lightning, so fast that it cheated the eye. I drove my point into the front of his chest, through his heart and half an arm's length out through his spine. He let his sword drop from his hand and his legs collapsed under him, but I held him upright dangling on my blade with his feet dancing lightly under him, barely brushing the floor of the terrace as he died. When this happened I lowered the angle of my blade and let him slide off it and lie in a heap at my feet.

Then I stooped over him, reached down and opened the visor of his helmet. I should have known it would not be that easy. Utteric's face had haunted my dreams for a long time. And I knew then that it would continue to do so, for I was looking now into the face of a total stranger. Only the hands were still those of Utteric. This was just another of Utteric's sleights of hand. I shook my head and grimaced at the weakness of my own pun. Then I straightened up and listened to the night around me. It was filled with sounds of mortal conflict: the shouting of belligerent war cries and the screams of the wounded; the clash of edged weapons on helm and breastplate; the whining of the wounded and the whimpering of the dying.

Then the door onto the terrace behind me crashed open on its hinges and this was followed immediately by the rush of booted feet and the cries of approbation from my men who had followed the staircase down from the top floor of the fortress.

"Well done, Taita. You killed the treacherous bastard." That was Nasla and he was pounding my back.

"Yes, I got another one of them," I conceded. "But only Hathor and Tanus know which one this is. Nevertheless, we will take his armor. It seems to be authentic and will be worth good gold. Then let us go down and try again to find the one true and veritable Utteric."

We left the half-naked corpse of the stranger lying on the terrace, and I led the way down the staircase and into the pandemonium of battle.

This was exacerbated by the virtual impossibility of telling the difference between friend and foe. We all wore the same uniforms and spoke the same language with the same accents. Even more confusing was the darkness and the lack of illumination in the passageways and even the courtyards and halls of the fortress. Faces were almost impossible to recognize at any distance. Both sides in the conflict were driven to calling out the name of their leader as they ran into each other and before they made the final decision to give battle or embrace each other.

However, the gates of the fortress remained firmly in control of Hurotas' troops. I and my men fought our way down to this level through the chaos and we found King Hurotas was there with his Serrena and Rameses, the stalwarts who had been responsible for the capture of the gates. Rameses and his men had cranked the portcullis open on both gates and jammed the mechanism so that the enemy could not close them off again. Hurotas' regiments were marching in through them in close order, and although we were uncertain of the precise numbers of Utteric's men, we had to be at the point of outnumbering them. The cries of "Hurotas" began to overwhelm those of "Utteric." I knew that this meant many of Utteric's men were changing sides. I was beginning to feel that victory was finally within our grasp here in Abu Naskos and my thoughts started to turn to Luxor and the tenuous hold that Weneg and his men had on that city.

Abruptly there was a sharp change in the sounds of battle. The cheers of triumph changed to a hubbub of alarm and consternation. The ordered ranks of our troops marching in through the gates suddenly scattered in panic, leaving the gateway clear. As they ran they were looking back over their shoulders. Then suddenly I heard the unmistakable sound of moving chariots: the clatter of the hooves of the teams drawing them and the grinding of the metal rims of the wheels on the paved stone surface; the cracking of the whips and the shouts of the charioteers at the reins. The thing that puzzled me was that all this uproar issued from the open gates of the fortress and not from the direction of the river. Only then did I recall that both Batur and Nasla had mentioned to me that Utteric had retained about half a troop of chariots in the fortress when he sent the bulk of his cavalry away to his forts in the delta to evade capture by Hurotas and his petty kings.

No sooner I had thought this than a squadron of chariots came charging down the alleyway toward the open gates of the fortress. The drivers were whipping their horses mercilessly. The charioteers were loosing the arrows from their bows indiscriminately into the crowds of our men who were struggling to get out of their way. All the chariot crews were suited in full armor. Every one of their heads was covered by helms and faceplates, so it was not possible to tell one from the other. A few of Hurotas' men were too slow to get out of their way and they were knocked down and trampled by the horses and then run under and ground to bloody tatters by the bronze-covered chariot wheels. I was caught up in the struggling mass and trapped against the wall of the alleyway. But I was at least able to see over the heads of the crowd and I was in a position to count the escaping chariots as they drew level with where I stood.

They were running four abreast in ranks of ten, making up forty vehicles, which was the number that Nasla and Batur had quoted to me. As the last rank came level with where I was lurking I saw the charioteer in the nearest vehicle look at me. You will ask how I knew this. All of them including this one wore helmets that covered their heads entirely; even their eye slits were just dark apertures. But I could feel this one's eyes. They passed over me almost casually as he nocked another arrow to his bowstring. Then his head jerked back and his gaze focused upon me as he recognized me. There was not a doubt in my mind. His hatred for me was so virulent that I could feel it like a jug of boiling water thrown in my face. I knew with utter certainty that I was looking into the eyes of my sworn and dedicated enemy to the death: Utteric Turo, self-styled the Great, putative Pharaoh of Egypt.

With his right hand he lifted his bow with sudden

steely purpose and drew the fletchings back to touch the sneering slit that formed the mouth of his mask. I was pinned helplessly by the throng to the stone wall at my back, unable to even duck my head. However, his left-handed draw with the bow reminded me that Utteric was left-handed, and that therefore his arrow would have left bias. I saw and recognized the first movement of the fingers of his left hand that predicted his release of the arrow, and I rolled my head into the shot. The flight of the arrow was too fast for me to follow with the naked eye, but I felt the draft of air on my cheek as the arrowhead nicked my ear in passing. Then almost simultaneously I heard it strike the stone pillar behind my head and the shaft shiver into pieces at the impact. Almost immediately the pressure of the crowd that held me was released as they scattered and I dropped to the stone slabs.

I did not rise to my feet again immediately, not because I feared Utteric's next arrow, but because it took me a second or two to stanch the bleeding from the nick in my earlobe. When I did regain my feet, the formation of enemy chariots had burst out through the main gates and was racing away across the plain parallel to the river toward the west. They were being pursued by several hundred of Hurotas' warriors. However, these were on foot and their arrows were falling well short of

the fleeing chariots. Many of them were already starting to abandon the chase and turn back toward the fortress. By the morrow Utteric and his stalwarts would
have a lead of twenty leagues or more; but which way
would they be headed? I thought I knew.

"So which way will Utteric be headed?" Hurotas demanded of the council gathered inside the war room of the Abu Naskos fortress. Most of the other members glanced in my direction, so he turned to me. "My Lord Taita, do you have any thoughts on the subject?"

Like the rest of them Hurotas was in a rare mood. His tone was jovial, and his expression was genial. Only an hour previously he had been present when the treasure vault of the fortress had been thrown open. The royal accountants and assessors would still be busy tallying the total amount a week hence, and calculating the distribution to the gallant men who had freed this very Egypt from tyranny and had never thought of counting the cost.

"Utteric was born in Luxor," I replied to Hurotas' query. "He has spent his whole life there. He has never left this very Egypt and I cannot imagine that he ever will. I am sure that he firmly believes that city of Luxor is still in the hands of his minions. Like a small boy who has burned his fingers, he will be running for home."

"Brief and to the point"—Hurotas nodded—"as always, Tata. Now tell me, can you catch him for us?"

"That is my firm intention," I assured him. "Apart from every other incentive such as loyalty and honor and justice, Utteric still has the greater part of Egypt's treasure and wealth hidden away somewhere. What we retrieved here in the delta this day is only a very small part of it. I, for one, very much want the rest of it. I intend to leave for Luxor immediately. With your permission, naturally."

Hurotas nodded assent. "You have it."

"I need a member of royalty to accompany me and give my mission standing and prestige. I would ask that it be Pharaoh Rameses. However, he is needed here."

"Then it should be either Hurotas or Tehuti who go with Taita, but it must be a member of royalty," Rameses supported me. But now other voices rose indignantly.

"It is you, our own son-in-law, who is being crowned. We are not going traipsing off with Taita while that is happening," Hurotas protested, and Tehuti took his hand and squeezed it to confirm their family solidarity of purpose.

Serrena was the only one of all of them who had not spoken out, but now she rose to her feet and came to stand beside me. Her expression was so remote from its usual sunny and charming aspect that a sudden silence fell on everyone in the hall, and all of them watched her in trepidation as they waited for her to speak.

"I will go with Taita," she said firmly.

"No! I forbid it," Hurotas jumped to his feet and shouted.

"Why would you forbid me from performing my bounden duty, father of mine?" Serrena asked softly.

"I forbid it because you are only a woman." They were clearly the first words that came into Hurotas' head, and they were not the most convincing or tactful of any I had ever heard him utter.

"It was only this woman who slew the Laconian boar. I am only the woman who lopped the head off Doog the Terrible." Serrena stood a little taller as she replied. "I am the same woman who shot an arrow through the guts of General Panmasi. I am the Queen of Egypt and it is my duty to protect the kingdom from tyranny. Forgive me, Father, but I must go with Taita." Then Serrena turned her head toward Queen Tehuti, and she asked, "Mother?"

"I have never been more proud of you than I am at this moment, my daughter." Tehuti's voice quivered with emotion. She came to embrace her daughter, and her cheeks were wet with the tears of pride. She stepped back and unbuckled the sword belt from around her waist, and then with both hands presented it to Serrena. "I hope you never have cause to use it in anger, but if perchance you must, then thrust deep, my darling daughter." The great ruby in the hilt of the blue sword burned with a sublime fire as she buckled it around Serrena's waist.

Serrena looked beyond her mother to where Rameses stood. "My husband?" She asked him the same question, and his expression softened.

"Now you have become a queen in far more than name alone," Rameses told her. "If I cannot accompany you, then there is no other I would rather choose as your companion than Taita. The two of you go with my blessings!"

Serrena turned back to her father. "I ask your forbearance, my beloved father."

Hurotas spread his hands with a smile of resignation that was both rueful and proud at the same time. "You have my forbearance, my beloved daughter," he replied.

Hurotas gladly allowed us to choose a hundred of his best men with their forty chariots and horses; to these we added Batur and Nasla and a half-dozen other stalwarts who had known Utteric Turo and would recognize him if they saw him again. Then Serrena and I discussed how we could travel to Luxor most expeditiously. Naturally, the deciding factor was the flow rate of the Nile, which would be contrary to our direction of travel if we took a ship from the delta to Luxor. At this season of the year over this stretch of the river the flow is almost the same as a man's fast walking pace. That means that it would reduce the speed of a boat by half. However, a boat would be able to keep sailing both day and night. A horse with a rider on its back could only keep trotting for a limited time before it had to rest. Accordingly Serrena and I loaded our men and horses aboard five large riverboats that were lying beneath the walls of Abu Naskos. We had more than sufficient crew to man the oars, and to rotate them regularly. They pointed the prows into the current and we set off up-river for the city of Luxor.

The wind blew steadily out of the north both day

and night, filling our sails and thrusting us on against
the current, but it still took frustrating hours and days
of sailing and rowing until the early morning when I
climbed the peak of the mizzenmast and through the
river mist I made out the walls of the Garden of Joy
on the hills above the river. An hour later we moored
our little fleet alongside the main wharf of the Luxor
docks and Serrena and I went ashore with half a dozen
men; all of us, but most especially Serrena, wearing
disguises. We were not sure whether or not Utteric had
reached the city ahead of us. If he had done so, then it
opened up all sorts of nasty eventualities. There was
even a remote possibility that he might have been able
to reinstate himself in the city.

However, when we reached the main gates they were
already open and it seemed that business was being
conducted as usual. I even recognized three or four of
the guards. They were all Weneg's men. It was immediately clear that Utteric and his band of renegades had
not yet arrived from the north, but I knew that they
could not be very far behind us.

The city guards were delighted to see me. When I
asked Serrena to remove her disguise and show them
her face, they recognized her immediately. Beside
themselves with adulation, they prostrated themselves
at her feet. I had to deliver a few solid kicks to get them

on their own feet and have them escort us to Weneg's apartments at the golden palace. Weneg also was thrown into transports of joy by the sudden appearance of the Pharaohin. I had to remind him sharply that Utteric and a band of his villains was not far behind us.

Four hours later, when Utteric's chariots finally arrived before Luxor, it was to find the city gates locked and barred and the top of the walls deserted. A resounding silence gripped the city. He and his entourage stopped cautiously in a bunch at long arrow range from the main gates. They had very obviously ridden hard all the way from Abu Naskos. Those of their chariots that had survived the journey were dusty, battered and hard used. I had counted forty spanking new vehicles leaving the garrison of Abu Naskos, each of them drawn by a team of five matching horses in prime condition. Now the chariots had been reduced in number to twenty-nine. Eleven of them must have lost wheels or broken their axles and been abandoned along the road. The spare horses were being herded in a loose bunch by the charioteers who had been deprived of wheeled transport. They had lost condition and weight in the intervening days. Their coats were stiff with dust. Four of five of them were lame and limping.

Within the city walls Weneg's men were at their posts. Most of them were lining the tops of the walls, but at my orders keeping their heads well down behind the parapets. The rest of them were massed inside the city gates, out of sight but poised to sally forth at my order to do so.

Utteric Turo was obviously not expecting to meet resistance. He had left the city safely in the hands of General Panmasi. Now he was almost certainly expecting Panmasi to rush out to greet him. When he did not, Utteric was immediately wary. Suspicion was deeply embedded in his nature. And because I knew him so well it had infected my own thinking. I realized that I had made a mistake by ordering my men to keep out of sight.

"Can you see Utteric?" I asked Serrena, who lay at my side on the ramparts of Luxor, peering through the same niche in the parapet.

"Not yet. There is too much dust and movement," she replied. "And they are too far distant."

Utteric's men were milling around nervously, waiting for his order to approach the city gates more closely. The situation was slowly developing into a standoff.

I saw that most of Utteric's charioteers, because of the heat at this time of the day, had removed their bronze helmets and breastplates. I shaded my eyes with cupped hands and stared fixedly at the group trying to recognize any of them. Suddenly one of them lifted his helmet with both hands, preparatory to replacing it on his head. At the same time his mount turned under him and the sunlight struck full upon his raised face.

I clutched Serrena's arm. "There he is!"

"You don't have to punish me for it," she protested. Sometimes when I become excited I forget how strong I am. However, there was no doubt in my mind. It was the veritable Utteric, and his suspicions had been thoroughly aroused by our failure to show ourselves. He was preparing to run once more. I rose to my feet with the arrow nocked in my bow. I knew the range was extreme, and he was a moving target. He was hauling his mount's head around, and at the same time roweling it with his spurs. The range was much too far, but I let my arrow fly. I watched it climb into the sky and then begin the drop. It looked so good that I thought I was going to wing him at the very least and I exulted silently. But then I felt a sudden gust of wind kiss my cheek and I saw the arrow lift on the current of air and flick over his head. He ducked at the sound of it passing so close and flattened himself along the neck of his steed. The other riders and their mounts bunched up around him and they galloped away into the east, heading in the direction of the Rift Valley and the Red Sea.

I stood up and watched their dust cloud until it dispersed and then I called to Weneg, "How soon can you give me a hundred horsemen to follow Utteric?"

Weneg did not reply at once, but he scrambled to his feet and came running to me along the walkway. His expression was worried. "Do you intend to chase after Utteric?"

"Of course I do." I heard the snarl in my own voice. I abhor stupid questions.

"But he is heading straight into Shushukan territory. You dare not follow him with only a hundred men. You will need an army at your back before you attempt it."

"Shushukan?" I moderated my tone of voice slightly. "I have never heard of it. Who or what are you talking about?"

"I must apologize, Lord Taita. I should have explained more clearly. I did not know about them myself until a few weeks ago. They are a tribe of renegades and criminal outcasts. They live beyond civilization or restraint." He spread his hands in a placating gesture. "I suggest we discuss it before we make any hasty decision, my lord."

"If Utteric is riding straight into their territory, and they are as wicked as you describe them to be, then these Shushukan creatures will surely take care of him for us. It will save us a deal of trouble." I smiled, but Weneg shook his head again.

"I have heard rumors that Utteric himself is the chief of the Shushukan and the founder of their movement. Small wonder they call him the man with fifty faces."

Serrena had been listening attentively to our exchange, but now she spoke out: "I do not understand why Utteric would have gone to such extremes. Surely as Pharaoh of Egypt he has ultimate power and authority over all?"

I shook my head. "Only over the good. But even a Pharaoh does not have the right to propagate evil. If Utteric rules as Pharaoh and at the same time he is master of the Shushukan, he has both good and utmost evil at his behest."

"How very clever of him!" she said seriously, but her eyes sparkled like those of the lioness who has smelled her prey. "Surely you have closed down the good side for him. You have denied him access to Luxor and any of the other fine cities of this very Egypt. You have confined him where he belongs with access only to the Shushukan."

"We must learn all there is to know about this place of evil," I decided. "We must send our spies in to learn all about the perpetrators. Who rules and holds power there, who it is that makes the laws—although perhaps there are no laws in such an environment as that which Utteric has created."

"I have already made inquiry," Weneg assured me. "I would have reported to you earlier if I had been given the chance. But you had no sooner arrived than Utteric was breathing down your neck. The ostensible leader of Shushukan is a man who glories in the name of Mad Dog."

"That sounds appropriate," I agreed.

"They tell me that he is a foul villain, this Mad Dog. In other words, he is an excellent man for the job."

"Perhaps Mad Dog is merely one of Utteric's many assumed names," I suggested before I went on to ask, "Do you have any idea how many Shushukan Utteric has under his command?"

"I have no idea at all. But some say he has a hundred thousand men."

I blinked to hear that figure. If Utteric had even half those numbers, then he commanded the largest army in the world. "What else do they say?" I asked Weneg.

"They say Utteric has already built a mighty castle at Ghadaka on the shores of the Red Sea from which he will conquer the rest of the world."

I turned away from Weneg and paced along the parapet. I looked out to the east and saw the dust cloud of Utteric's chariots shriveling and dispersing on the light wind. I turned and went back to where Weneg waited for me.

"What you tell me is all hearsay," I pointed out to him, and he shrugged and shuffled his feet.

"It is what I have been told," he mumbled apologetically.

"I want to send scouts down immediately to check this information. They must be good and trustworthy men, working separately so if one or more are apprehended by Utteric's men, then the others still stand a good chance of getting back to us with reliable information," I told him, and he nodded.

"It makes good sense to check our information thoroughly, Lord Taita."

"There are two excellent men whom I brought with me from Abu Naskos. They are brothers by the names of Batur and Nasla. I particularly want you to send them on this reconnaissance."

"It shall be done. However, it will take several days for them to reach Ghadaka and return with their findings."

"Then the sooner you send them, the better," I pointed out and turned to Serrena. "Your Majesty, you have heard the possible odds that Utteric may be able to bring against us. I need your help to raise all the men and chariots we can lay our hands upon before we march on Utteric's lair at Ghadaka."

"Of course you need only ask, Tata."

"Thank you, my dear." I took her arm and walked her along the parapet. "I think Weneg's estimate of Utteric's military strength is wildly exaggerated. The notion that he has built a mighty castle on the Red Sea without us knowing about it becomes more preposterous the more I think about it. A building on the scale he suggests would take decades to erect, and it would require tens of thousands of workmen. I assure you that if such a fortress existed, I would have known all about it many years ago. It should not take me too long to get the facts. In the meantime we will be able to assemble the strongest force available to oppose Utteric."

When Utteric had departed from Luxor at the beginning of his conflict with Hurotas and Rameses, and moved down the Nile to the delta to seize the fortress at Abu Naskos, he stripped the city of Luxor of most of its chariots and archers. He left only the armaments that he deemed necessary for General Panmasi to quell and subdue the city in his absence. These, together with the chariots that King Hurotas had given us when we left Abu Naskos, added up to a total of 111.

These then were all the vehicles that were available to us now for the assault on Utteric's great and impregnable castle of Ghadaka, with its hundred thousand savage inmates. That night I sat with Queen Serrena Cleopatra Rameses on the walls of the city of Luxor, beside one of the watch fires eating hard cheese that we roasted on long skewers until it was runny. Then we washed it down with a red wine that we warmed on the same fire.

"So you think I am slightly demented?" I asked Her Majesty.

"That is not what I said, Tata." She shook her head primly. "I said I think you are stark raving mad!"

"You say that simply because I changed my mind?"

"No, I say that because only a crazy man mounts an attack on an impregnable fortress with a hundred-odd chariots, and no siege equipment of any kind."

"You don't have to come with me," I pointed out.

"Oh, I wouldn't miss it for anything." She smiled. "You may just succeed. Then I would never forgive myself."

We left Luxor while it was still dark the following morning. It took us three days' hard riding to reach the rim of the Great Rift Valley, which fell to the shores of the Red Sea, halfway toward the center of the earth. We had a splendid view out across the sea, which is actually a dirty blue in color. It is bounded on its eastern side by pitch-black beaches, which may be the reason why they call it the Red Sea. You would be amazed at how perverse and stupid ordinary people can be.

After we had watered the horses and fed them from

the nosebags, we started down the escarpment. However, we had not descended halfway when we spotted two riders climbing the steep path toward us. They were still a mile or more below us, but both Serrena and I recognized them: Serrena because she is a divine even if she does not know it, and I because I have superb eyesight.

Both of us gave our mounts a touch of the spurs and galloped to meet them. "Hey now, Batur! What cheer, Nasla?"

"I have learned not to argue with you, my lord," Batur said as he came level, and his younger brother agreed with him:

"It must be so boring to always be right."

"There is no castle then?" I felt jubilant at being proved correct once again.

"There is no castle," Batur concurred. "But there is something a hundred times worse. We did not dare approach it closer than half a league. You will not want to do so either. Even Utteric's men have fled and left him there alone. We spoke with them when we met them on the road. They thought that we still paid allegiance to Utteric so they spoke freely. They are returning to Luxor to place themselves at the mercy of Pharaoh Rameses."

"You try my patience, Batur!" I warned him. "If

there is no castle, where then has Utteric sequestered himself. Speak up, fellow!"

"He has taken refuge in a leper colony, my lord." He turned in the saddle and pointed back the way he had come from the sea. "There, in that tiny village named Ghadaka. He is alone, except for several hundred lepers. None of his men would stay with him. They think that he is now mad. I disagree with them. I believe that Utteric has been crazy since the day of his birth." He spoke without a smile.

I was struck dumb. It was probably the first time in my life this had ever happened to me. Without another word I dismounted from my horse and walked away down the slope until I found a convenient rock, which I settled on moodily and looked down on the settlement of Ghadaka. This was a straggle of single-room thatched huts, no more than fifty or sixty in number, spread out at intervals along a half-moon-shaped beach. Nearby the huts I made out a small gathering of human beings who were huddled in a grove of palm trees. It was impossible to tell the men from the women. They were all heavily draped with cloaks that covered their heads and faces completely. They sat as still as corpses.

I was afraid. For the first time I can ever remember I was afraid of death, of that silent and eerie type of dying I saw being played out on the beach below where

I sat. I was aware of my divine birth, but now I was uncertain, or rather I was not certain enough to act upon that notion and enter the living death of a colony of lepers.

Suddenly I was aware of the lightly perfumed presence of Serrena sitting beside me and the silken touch of her hand on my forearm.

"You and I have nothing to fear," Serrena said softly. I turned and looked into her eyes. She knew; it was as simple as that. She knew about our divine state, despite all my earnest endeavors to protect her from that knowledge. She knew, and because of that I believed again.

It was enough. I took Serrena by her hand and drew her to her feet. "You are not content to leave Utteric's punishment to the gods?" I asked her, but she shook her head.

"You know that I am not content with that. I have sworn an oath to Utteric and to myself."

"Then let the two of us go down and make good your oath."

We went back to where we had left our horses and rode to rejoin the chariots where they waited with the brothers Batur and Nasla.

Early on the morrow, Serrena and I took five chariots laden with food and the staples of life and we drove down the escarpment to the point just above the beach and the sea where a pair of dilapidated gates hung open on their hinges. To one side of them stood a signboard on which was displayed the following dire warning: "Go no further, O you who love the gods and the life they have granted you! Beyond this point you will find only sorrow and weeping."

The charioteers pulled their vehicles over and unloaded their goods in silence and unconcealed trepidation, piling the sacks of grain and dried meats in jumbled disorder on the side of the track. While they worked they cast nervous glances toward the thatched roofs of the village that stood above the beach. As soon as they were done they put the lash to their horses and galloped away up the escarpment to where the brothers were waiting to guide them back to the city of Luxor.

Serrena and I were now alone. We rode on into the village of lepers. Hooded heads with masked faces peered out at us from the doorways of the hovels as we passed. These openings were without doors, and the unpainted clay walls were without windows. Nobody hailed or called after the two of us as we rode on toward the palm grove above the beach. The silence was profound and heavy with despair.

Serrena steered her horse closer to mine until our

stirrups were touching, and she murmured just loud enough for me to catch her words: "How will we ever find Utteric if he is wearing a hood and mask like all these other inmates?"

"Don't worry about us finding him," I replied. "You and I are the two people whom he hates most in all the world. All we have to do is flaunt ourselves, and he will find us. But be alert. When he comes he will be fast and we will have almost no warning."

In the grove we found the same clusters of silent figures we had seen from the heights of the escarpment. They seemed not to have moved or shown any other signs of life, except one or two of the masked heads rotated slightly as they followed our progress through the grove. We stopped at last where their numbers seemed slightly more concentrated; by that I mean they were almost a dozen strong.

"Who is in charge here?" I asked in the graveyard tones that seemed appropriate to this setting. The silence that followed my question seemed even heavier than it had been before.

Then suddenly there was a cackle of weird laughter, and one of the hooded figures replied to my question, "Hecate, the goddess of the dead, is still fighting with Anubis, the god of the cemeteries, for that honor." I was not certain which one had answered me, but he or she raised a few bitter laughs.

"Do you have anything to eat?" I tried again.

"If you are hungry, you can eat the same coconut husks I ate last week; they should be partially digested by now!" one of the faceless creatures called out. This time the laughter was louder and more derisive. Serrena and I waited for it to abate.

"We have brought you food." Serrena stood in the stirrups and her voice carried to everyone in the grove. "Smoked pork and dried fish! Loaves of millet and sorghum! As much as you can eat!"

Immediately a deep and bitter silence fell over the grove, broken only when one of the robed figures jumped to her feet and threw back the hood that covered her face. It was a terrible and haunting sight. Her nose and ears had been eaten away by the disease, and so had her upper lip so that her mouth was fixed in a perpetual grin like that of a skull. One of her eyelids was gone while the other was tightly shut. The open eye was vividly bloodshot. The stink of her rotting flesh wafted to us on the sweet sea breeze. I felt my gorge rise, and I swallowed painfully.

"You wicked creatures," she screeched at us with tears streaming from her lidless eye down her ravaged cheek, "coming here as you have to mock our plight. Why speak to us of food when you know there is none? Have you no pity or mercy? What have we ever done to you that you should treat us so?"

Serrena turned to her and her voice throbbed with compassion. "I have brought you and all your companions food, I swear it to you in the name of the goddess Artemis! Five cartloads of food await you beside the signboard of welcome to your village. If you are too sick, I shall bring it to you and feed it to you with my own hands . . ."

An exclamation of hunger and hope went up from the throng, laughter mingled with cries of despair or pain as they dragged themselves to their feet and hopped or hobbled toward the gates to seek the miracle that Serrena had promised them.

When they fell Serrena and I came up behind them to lift them to their feet and help them up into the saddle of our horses and carry them on. The first shouts of delight and disbelief rose from the front row of the crowd as they came upon the piles of food.

They fell to their knees and ripped the sacks open with shaking fingers. Those whose fingers had already been eaten away by the disease tore them open with their teeth and stuffed the food into their mouths through tattered and bloody lips.

The outcry was heard in the cottages farther from the entrance gates and the inmates were drawn to it instinctively like hiving bees. The weakest of the lepers, those who were far gone with the disease, were knocked off their feet, but they tried to crawl on their hands and knees to find a few crumbs of bread. The stronger of them fought each other like dogs for a shred of dried sausage.

Even Serrena and I were separated in the melee: not by very far but nevertheless by too far. So she called to me urgently in the Tenmass, the secret language of the divines, "Beware! He is close."

"How do you know?" I called back in the same dialect.

"I can smell him."

I have learned not to underestimate Serrena's sense of smell. It is more acute than that of any hunting hound.

I darted a glance around and saw at once that at least four hooded figures were close to me in the press of humanity. I had two knives on my person. In a sheath on my right hip I carried my main hunting knife. This was a double-edged weapon with a blade just under a cubit in length. I could reach it with my right hand. Then at the small of my back under my cloak I had a second blade only half that length, but I was able to reach it with either hand. However, right at this very moment I was caught in a logjam of humanity—sick and stinking humanity at that—and forced to adopt an inelegant stance that left the narrow area behind my left shoulder unprotected. I struggled to free myself enough to turn and cover my back.

I called again urgently to Serrena in the Tenmass, "Is my left shoulder clear?"

"Drop!" she called back and there was a tone of urgency in her voice such as I had never heard before. Immediately I let my legs fold under me, and I slid down into the press of churning feet and legs; some of them were covered with long skirts stained with dried blood and pus; others were naked and thick with leprous sores and running ulcers. All of them were shoving and pushing at each other.

Just above my head a human hand was wielding a knife, stabbing and slashing blindly at the space where I had been standing only seconds before. I recognized the hand by the description that Serrena had given me so vividly in the amphitheater of Luxor when Utteric had been shot down by an arrow, only to arise again from the dead so miraculously. It was a lovely hand, smooth and almost femininely graceful, that belonged to the epitome of evil.

In the awkward position I found myself, I was unable to reach either of my own weapons. Utteric's knife swept past my face and went on to slash open the scabrous naked thigh of one of the others in the throng. Blood spurted from the wound, and I heard the victim scream in pain. This seemed to goad Utteric into a frenzy. He hacked and stabbed wildly, wounding another woman.

I reached up as the knife swept over my head and grabbed Utteric's wrist with my left hand, and as soon as my grip was secure I used my right hand as well to cover his on the handle of the knife. I had him in a wrist lock from which he could not escape. I twisted his wrist back upon itself until I heard the ligaments popping, and Utteric shrieking in agony.

I hoped that this cry would guide Serrena to us; and I twisted harder. He squealed again at an even more gratifying volume. Then abruptly the scream was cut off, and the tension went out of his body and limbs. He legs folded beneath him and, still in my grip, he collapsed on top of me. I rolled him over and I saw the hilt of the blue sword protruding from the small of his back with the ruby in the hilt aglow with celestial fire. It was perfectly placed to penetrate his kidneys and separate his spinal column.

Serrena dropped to her knees beside me. "Is it Utteric?" she demanded. "Please, Artemis, let it be the right one we have killed!"

"There is only one way to be certain," I answered her, and I reached out for the leper's hood that covered his head, and tore it away. Then I rolled him onto his back, and in silence we stared at the face of the dying man.

His features could have been noble like those of his brother Rameses, but they were not. They were sly and crafty.

Or they might have been kind and thoughtful like that of his brother, but they were cruel and demented.

I stood and placed my foot on Utteric's back to hold him still while I withdrew the glittering blue blade from his clinging flesh. Then I reversed my grip on the hilt and offered it to Serrena. "Do you want to finish it?" I asked her; but she shook her head and replied in a whisper:

"I have had enough bloodshed to last me a long time. You do it for me, Tata darling."

I stooped and took a handful of the thick dark curls at the back of his head. I lifted his face out of the dust so that I would not damage the blade when I hacked through his neck into the stony earth under him. With my other hand on the hilt I touched the back of his neck lightly with the edge to measure my stroke. So sharp was it that the pale skin parted in a thin red line to give me an aiming mark. Then I lifted the blade high and swung down again unhurriedly. It made a soft snicking sound as it parted the vertebrae. Utteric's corpse flopped into the puddle of his own blood, while I lifted his severed head high and spoke into his face. "May you suffer a thousand deaths for every one that you have perpetrated!"

Then I knelt and wrapped the head in the leper's hood that Utteric had used to conceal himself.

"What will you do with it?" Serrena asked as she watched me. "Will you burn it or bury it?"

"I will hang it on the entrance tower of the Garden of Joy alongside that of Doog the Terrible," I said, and she smiled again.

"My Lord Taita, you are simply incorrigible!"

S errena insisted on staying on at the leper colony of Ghadaka. She recorded the names of every one of the inmates and promised that they would be provided with food and the other essentials of life for as long as they lived. Then she tried to alleviate their suffering by all and every means she could conjure up, and she wept for them when they died. Of course she prevailed on me to remain with her.

By the time I could get her agreement to accompany me back into the other world we had left, ten days had passed. Those lepers who were still able to walk accompanied us halfway up the escarpment. They wept and shouted their gratitude to Serrena when at last they were forced to turn back to their pestilent hovels beside the sea.

When we finally reached Luxor one of the first things that Serrena did was to arrange for regular shipments of food and medications to be sent to Ghadaka. All this was despite the other demands on her time and goodwill, such as the preparations for the ascension of herself and Rameses to the thrones and crowns of the realm.

Of course King Hurotas and Queen Tehuti capitulated to the entreaties of Rameses and Serrena to remain in Luxor for the festivities leading up to the coronation. General Hui and his wife, Bekatha, decided to follow this excellent example. Then the fourteen petty kings headed up by Ber Argolid of Boeotia in Thebes decided that there was no good reason for them to hurry away to their kingdoms, especially as these were now firmly in the grip of winter.

Luxor was becoming distinctly overcrowded. Fortunately Pharaohin Serrena came up with the excellent idea of restoring to me, Lord Taita, all the properties and rights that had been confiscated from me by the former, but now deceased, Pharaoh Utteric. This made me once more one of the richest men in Egypt. I was able to place my palaces and other suitable accommodations in the city at the disposal of King Hurotas and his wife, and also his minions the petty kings.

Pharaoh Rameses also elevated me to the rank of Lord High Chancellor and Chief Minister of his cabinet. His cabinet consisted almost entirely of the thirty-two officials selected by Utteric for execution who were waiting in the Garden of Joy, which had previously been known as the Gates of Torment and Sorrow. When Rameses sent for them, at my suggestion, they came trooping joyfully into the city of Luxor and went unerringly into their appointed offices in the palace of government to take up their duties under me.

Precisely six months after their triumphal return to Luxor, I, as Lord High Chancellor, uplifted Pharaoh Rameses and his wife, Pharaohin Serrena Cleopatra, to the throne of Egypt for their formal coronation. Almost four hundred invitees packed the great hall of the palace. These included fourteen other emperors and kings from the lands surrounding the great Middle Sea.

Egypt was restored to her former glory and I could not forbear to smile as I placed the golden crowns on the heads of my two most favorite persons in all the world.

HARPER LUXE

THE NEW LUXURY IN READING

We hope you enjoyed reading
our new, comfortable print size and found it
an experience you would like to repeat.

Well – you're in luck!

HarperLuxe offers the finest in fiction and
nonfiction books in this same larger print size and
paperback format. Light and easy to read, HarperLuxe
paperbacks are for book lovers who want to see
what they are reading without the strain.

For a full listing of titles and
new releases to come, please visit our website:

www.HarperLuxe.com